CARYDDWEN'S CAULDRON

Caryddwen's Cauldron

PAUL HILTON

BLACK ACE BOOKS

First published in 2000 by Black Ace Books
PO Box 6557, Forfar, DD8 2YS, Scotland

www.blackacebooks.com

Coda motif, fol. 447, by Boo Wood
Inspired by a Celtic tuppenny

Typeset in Scotland by Black Ace Editorial

Printed in Great Britain by Antony Rowe Ltd
Bumper's Farm, Chippenham, Wiltshire, SN14 6LH

A CIP catalogue record for this book
is available from the British Library

ISBN 1–872988–47–4

For my parents

Principal Fragments

I

The Misfortunes of Finbar Direach

1

‘This must be the place. Or if not, it can’t be too far away,’ Triona Greenwood, the new Heritage Commissioner, told her two companions.

Yet far from being relieved after their arduous journey, she felt ill at ease and vulnerable. Perhaps coming here had been a mistake, or would result in mistakes further down the line. Despite these misgivings, or because of them, Triona never questioned that the grant to the Centre for Alternative Healing must be handled personally, for the sake of everyone involved. It was the first major assignment since her promotion into the job. But she alone knew the true issues, and how much depended on the outcome of her trip.

They had a cold coming of it, and by no means at the best time of the year. All the same, with modern four-wheel drive vehicles and global positioning technology a trip to West Penwith, even in the most desolate days of December, holds no special terrors. Travelling swiftly in a specially designed Heritage Land Rover, they departed the city in high spirits, sped through Surrey’s opulent glades and at noon were cheered by the sight of the henge stones, where a few windswept Druids were going through the motions for winter solstice. None but Triona guessed that, if challenged, they would turn out to lack real insight into the old traditions and to be actuaries, librarians, and governors of minor public schools.

After the flat terrain they journeyed through brown bluffs, past towns and across heathlands before bridging the Tamar, and Triona explained how its name, like that of London's river, derived from the arcane word for time. But, she added, *that* torrent was not so easy to negotiate, however much a person might wish to run athwart it. If by this she meant herself, the implication was lost on her companions, whose minds were preoccupied by where they were going to have lunch. They mentioned this concern more than once, but Triona was reluctant to waste daylight and urged them onward into a landscape increasingly transformed by its wintry burden, where drifts lay across fields and sedges and icicles glittered on every sprig and spray. Once they thought they saw a woman in a black veil and white furs crouched beneath a blighted thorn, but when they looked again it was two ravens feasting on a dead ewe.

Still, they made progress. On the A30 and the B3280 the ploughs had been out and it was possible to maintain a steady 40 miles per hour, but near their destination visibility closed in and they were glad to gain the safety of a nearby village.

'We'll ask directions at this friendly inn,' Triona told her companions. 'No doubt the locals will put us right.' Sure enough, a welcoming fire greeted them and when it was perceived they were strangers, a space was cleared closest the hearth, the flowing glass was extended from every side, and it seemed nobody could do enough. But when Triona revealed her objective, a shadow seemed to fall across the room, and the cold wind rattled the casement stays. 'We must find our way to the Centre for Alternative Healing,' she explained, 'and preferably before sunset.' The words were scarcely out of her mouth than all conversation abruptly ceased, the barmaid shrieked in alarm and dropped a flagon of fine home-made cider, prepared to a secret recipe handed down through generations, and those nearest the newcomers shrank back, while those furthest away leaned forward, eager not to miss the slightest detail.

'You don't want to go up there,' warned the eldest villager at length, as the others nodded agreement. 'Not today. Not ever. Not if you'll take the advice of those that know most about it. Not if you value your peace of mind . . . '

When pressed as to why, the men drowned their beards in well-filled tankards and the women looked mutely away, each reluctant to be the bearer of bad news. It was clear that relations between the village and the clifftop were less than cordial, for it had been a place of unfortunate omen long before its present use. Earliest stories connected it with figures from remote legend, and through history and pre-history a watchtower had stood on the site, warning communities below of sea-raiders, storms and other pelagic incursions. But later it was used by the authorities to monitor shipping, and once sixteen longshoremen were gibbeted from the cliff edge for failure to comply with import duty regulations. From that point, bad reputation clung to the place, and rumours swarmed around it like flies around a cow's behind. Still, it exercised fascination on a certain kind of mind, and was rarely untenanted even before the present sect of healers made it their own.

'We can't argue with their medical achievements,' acknowledged the villagers, when they had recovered from the initial shock. 'But too many things have happened there that are not easy to account for, even in this scientific age.'

'I think you're trying to tell us something,' Triona said.

'Only this,' the villagers repeated. 'On no account climb the western headland at dusk on the shortest day of the year. Or if you do so, don't expect to come down the same person as you went up.'

But Triona thought to herself that change is the inevitable lot of human beings, and is often the only alternative to staying the same. Therefore she thanked the villagers, whom she understood meant well, but said she and her companions had come here to do what they must, and if necessary, they were prepared to take the consequences.

'Besides,' she added, 'it may only be ignorance and superstition that make you feel as you do.'

The villagers misunderstood this remark and said they would not go so far as to accuse the occupants of the Centre of ignorance and superstition, even though it was no stranger to unusual goings-on. But, they said, if they were Triona, Heritage Commissioner or no Heritage Commissioner, they would meet its leaders on neutral ground, and make it clear that they were not going to stand for any nonsense.

Triona thanked them for this advice, but then as she turned to leave one woman, bolder than the rest, clutched her sleeve and thrust something into her hand, and when Triona looked down she felt oddly unsurprised that it was a root of common hogweed skilfully woven into a fairy knot, which in those parts is supposed to guard against anything untoward. 'Do not stay up there tonight,' warned the woman, pulling her shawl closer as if against an unseen chill. 'But if you do – place this over the latch of your door before you sleep. For although under normal circumstances the reputation of the Heritage Commission is sufficient protection in itself, you are a long way from home, and I don't believe you've told us your entire purpose in coming here.'

'You seem to understand my reasons better than the others,' admitted Triona, 'and perhaps you've guessed why I'm drawn towards the very fate you wish to protect me from. I would say more – but the hour is getting late, and I've no wish to be caught in the open after dark.'

After this conversation they had left the inn, although they were aware that the muttering of voices continued long after its cosy world was barred behind them. There was a track leading upwards through the foothills, but before long they had to abandon the Land Rover and proceed by donkey, and near the summit even the donkey needed to be abandoned and the new Commissioner and her young assistants, both inexperienced in this kind of work, were obliged to haul their equipment by hand. Their ascent took them across vertiginous crags and through furze brakes, peat bogs, and fathomless crevasses, until they were overwhelmed with mud and mire, soiled with clammy ordures and stuck about with burrs, briars, and brambles, all under a fine dusting of winter snow.

Under such circumstances, even when they finally breasted the rise, Triona could not be certain of their position, but guessed, for better or worse, they were nearing the journey's end. 'This looks like it,' she repeated. 'But appearance isn't everything, and I've been wrong before . . . '

The structure loomed up from a fold in the high ground, its dark stones capped with snow, a ruined tower buttressing its seaward side. The granite pile extending inland lacked any sense of design, as if the stones had been allowed to find their own lie and level, and then topped off by such slates as came to hand. Perpendiculars slouched at drunken angles, sagging roof beams sagged further under a weight of snow. Bushes and shrubs round about were stunted by high winds. A single rowan tree rose aloof from the main building at a distance equivalent to the length of its own shadow in the ailing light. Closer by was a stand of elders and a snow covered bramble thicket. The herb gardens were spiked with frost and a fuel stack comprised old fence posts, window frames, and the chainsawed remains of a fishing boat deck. Woodlands suitable for logging are no longer known of west of the Fal estuary. 'Well,' she added, 'dusk is coming on, and it's too late to go back.'

Perhaps for Triona, it had always been too late. Had she not always known that she must make this journey, or a similar one? She was now a Heritage Commissioner, and such responsibility is not given to many. Yet in the deep, companionless reaches of the night, she sometimes questioned fundamental decisions regarding her past and future. In her earliest years, she had taken all her parents could give her, and the best schools that were to be had. But childhood in the charmed surroundings of Coldharbour Abbey seemed far away. Her favourite sister had been lost under circumstances which disturbingly recalled the legends of a lost people. She had a number of other sisters, but they were compromised and might be in danger, although it was still unclear why. The husband she thought she loved had turned out to be a person she hardly recognized. Dreams of Leatherwing came to her with greater frequency, although she did not yet know his true nature. More than once, she found herself envying the sister who had gone, and thought she would do anything to be with her. 'But life', reflected Triona, 'is not that simple – and death may be even less so.'

So she set her face towards the Centre for Alternative Healing, in which life and death were so inextricably intertwined. Although modern hospitals have sometimes been criticized for the insensitivity of their financial controls and the dereliction of their sanitary contractors, the Centre for Alternative Healing made the poorest of them look like a five star hotel. But in the modern hospitals people died, and in the Centre for Alternative Healing people lived. So it was said. Therefore there should be no contest. But, thought Triona, there is always a contest. All you can do is keep an open mind.

The door, when they reached it, was heavily constructed in iron and decorated with symbols from now forgotten history and inscriptions which might have meant anything, or nothing. The knocker was shaped like a lady with the head of a doe, and when swung, echoed hollowly into the edifice suggesting that however much of the building was visible above the hillside, its galleries reached deep within. They heard no footsteps when these echoes died, but the portal swung wide to reveal a young woman in the traditional attire of a public relations executive, which went oddly with her surroundings and was entirely in contrast to the appearance of Triona and her assistants, their assault on the slopes having left them drenched, dishevelled, and besmirched with every kind of organic residue.

'I'm Triona Greenwood, from the Heritage Commission, and these are my two assistants. We're sorry we look as if we've been dragged through a swamp,' Triona said rather accusingly, 'but what with the weather conditions, the climb, and the state of the paths – well – we could have fallen to our deaths, and no-one would have been the wiser.'

If the woman in the doorway had entertained this possibility, or was aware that certain interests would have been served by exactly such an accident, she gave no sign of it. 'I'm Linden Richmont. I've been doing promotion and liaison since the management changes,' she announced with the breeziness peculiar to her profession, although for a variety of reasons Triona knew this only too well. Linden Richmont did not look like a member of an alternative healing community, especially one which you couldn't get to without being nearly killed and covered in mud, but there had been many changes at the Centre. She quickly checked their credentials and let them know that, whatever the outcome of their visit, it would be the Centre's policy to make them as welcome as possible.

'And don't worry about the floor,' she added, looking at their encrusted footwear. 'One of the first things we intend to buy with the grant, is a doormat. You have to understand there are still people here who consider that any subsidy from the establishment would be selling out. It starts with a doormat, they say, and ends with a multi-million dollar entertainment complex and theme park. Look at Findhorn, they say. What can you do? They see themselves as a spiritual community dedicated to the ancient Celtic arts of health and healing. As they put it – we are not EuroDisney.'

'Still,' said Triona, 'in a clinical environment . . . '

'I know what you mean. But these traditionalists say, if people get dirt on them from the climb, let them wipe it off on the walls and chairs. They'd tell you that our menial, Finbar Direach, sponges everything down regularly enough. They think the old ways are best. They think that the occasional bit of muck getting into the medicines plays a part in our outstanding success rate with inoperable conditions. If it isn't broken, their view is, don't fix it.'

'Yet you yourself', ventured Triona, who had read the files in detail, 'are a modernizer.'

'If the world stands still', she replied, 'how can it ever go forward? But I'm still seen as an outsider, because I report to the new investment company. There are very few people here that I can rely on.' And she tapped the side of her nose significantly.

'I believe we understand each other,' answered Triona, who knew more than she wished to reveal about the recent investment by Myles Overton's controversial leisure group. 'And in this day and age, understanding is everything. We'll talk later. The truth is, no-one really knows who they can trust. Even my assistants sometimes seem to have their own agenda. I don't mind telling you there are people who'd just as soon see the Centre closed down as not. But for the moment, keep that under your hat, because it's early days.'

Linden Richmont nodded, as though this were no more than she had expected. As she led them through the passages and hallways, she explained how she had taken her present position after leaving a management post at EuroDisney, where she began to question the value of what she did, and even, on occasion, to doubt her own abilities. She worked mainly for the external investment company and the Centre was not her only nor even her main responsibility as a publicist. But she had been able to bring to the alternative healing industry the discipline, contacts, and interpersonal skills of a competitive commercial environment, and this had enabled her to rise rapidly in its hierarchy. 'Just because the goals of an organization are humane,' she said, 'there's no reason why its operation should be inefficient or woolly-headed.'

Her success had nevertheless made her enemies as well as allies; enemies who were jealous of her pay and position and said her high standing had nothing to do with interpersonal skills and she had never worked at EuroDisney. On the contrary, Linden's enemies muttered, she was drafted in to fend off press enquiries when the old Head of the Centre disappeared under suspicious circumstances and Myles Overton, the famous Australian leisure-industry mogul, acquired an undisclosed percentage. Myles Overton's connections, they believed, were the only reason they were being considered for a grant at all. Linden was there to safeguard his interests, for Linden was amongst those closest to him. Not to put too fine a point on it, there was talk that she was his niece, and she was being groomed for the very top.

Rumour, of course, is rumour, and truth is truth. But Triona had read the files, so she knew there was more than a little substance to what Linden's enemies asserted. Myles Overton's interests spanned the entertainment and leisure sectors, extending from cable TV and consumer products to clubs, travel, and as a logical extension of his hotel chain, privatized penal institutions. Triona was aware that Linden Richmont handled publicity for the whole group, because Triona's sister Nuala was in one of the privatized penal institutions and knew her well.

That, among other reasons, was why, when the assignment at the Centre came up, Triona knew she must take it herself. There had been too many coincidences. It was clear that someone was up to something, even if it was hard to see who, and what. But for the moment, if Linden Richmont chose not to say, 'Hi, I know your sister, I visit her all the time in my uncle's gaol!' then Triona chose not to say, 'Hi, my sister Nuala's told me all about you; thanks for bringing her all the copies of *Country Living*!' Better, thought Triona, to play one's cards close to one's chest. Even though she knew that Linden, like herself, secretly belonged to the Network of Successful Women, there was too much at stake to confide in her.

Out loud she said that she was not particularly concerned about truth, or even rumour, but must simply satisfy the Heritage Commission that its money was being wisely spent. For the figure of a million pounds had been mentioned – and everything should be done by the book.

'I'll give you a tour of the facility,' Linden Richmont agreed, 'and introduce you to everyone of importance. Feel free to ask any questions you wish – since, as our guest, no request you make can be refused. Having said that, though I'm a modernizer myself, there are some traditions all visitors are asked to respect.'

'My job', said Triona, 'is about respecting traditions. But what have you in mind?'

'Well, the first one is, you're asked never to open the sealed door at the western extremity of the building, nicknamed Rhiannon's Perch by some of our younger acolytes. Of course it's nothing but a superstition, but there are those who are convinced that opening it would prove our undoing, and a major disaster could not be averted.'

'People's beliefs are an important part of their culture,' replied Triona. 'Even when they seem difficult to understand.'

Linden Richmont looked a little happier at this, but hurried on to the next point.

'The second thing is – you're free to eat and drink from the various herbal preparations and potheens which have made the community famous. But while you may use any other receptacle, make sure you don't take even a sip from the Cup of Charms, which hangs in the pantry above the Aga. Obviously as educated people we can't take too much notice of old stories, but the consensus here is that to sip so would bring bad consequences not only to the drinker, but to all loyal members of our community.'

'I'd as soon drink out of one cup as another,' said Triona. 'So that won't be a problem. But the herbal preparations sound nice.'

'They're very nice,' Linden confirmed. 'And very good for you. But the third tradition is just as important as the other two, because you may speak to any member of our little group, but on no account must you exchange a single word or even a gesture with Finbar Direach, the caretaker here. For although he knows nothing of importance, he's a danger to himself and others. I have to tell you that it's only by isolating him in this remote spot and employing him in menial tasks that we can prevent a repetition of the kind of cataclysmic event in which he's previously been implicated.'

Although from these words Triona was sure Linden Richmont had her best interests at heart, she could not help feeling a stab of curiosity about what had been said. This was in no way diminished by the glimpse of a hooded figure of strange appearance and meagre stature, who, as they were talking, slipped past them into the shadows making some affectation of domestic duty. For it was clear this individual had been listening to everything they discussed.

'This is a strange place,' Triona observed to her assistants, although perhaps she had always known it would be. 'And this Finbar Direach character, unless I'm much mistaken, is by no means the least strange of its denizens.'

'Strange,' answered the assistants, 'but true.'

'Well,' Triona told them, 'there's no time to speculate. A recital of original music and poetry has been prepared in our honour tonight. We'll need to change our clothes and dry out our equipment. Whatever happens, it's important to act naturally, and not give the impression that anything untoward is afoot.'

But although Finbar Direach's cowl concealed the details of his face as he slipped past them, just before he disappeared his eyes peered from beneath it and directed a single, terrible glance in Triona's direction. The burden of that glance was neither of defiance nor threat, but only a deep enduring sadness and an overwhelming access of guilt. Whatever Finbar Direach had done, whether deliberately or not, it was clear that the consequences were as impossible to endure as they were to elude.

2

It is said that beyond the crags of West Penwith a forest once grew where now Atlantic waves crash grey and indefatigable against the Longships Reef. And it is true that, on the very lowest spring tides, one may find the petrified stumps of elms and oaks beneath the water, together with the remnants of flint axes, bronze shoe trees and charcoal burners' huts. Certainly a flourishing community sustained itself where now only fulmars, spider crabs, and oar-weed find an environment truly congenial to their needs. Yet the fact that a culture existed in those parts and was lost to the encroachments of the sea is no evidence for claims that it possessed any unusual qualities or value. Still less that it was synonymous with a Celtic mysticism linking the necromancer Leatherwing, the vanished race of the Tuatha de Dannaan who were once the ruling powers of the archipelago, and the magic cauldron that belonged to Caryddwen, Druid alchemist of the *Mabinogion*.

This last artefact does indeed figure frequently in the legends of the area, as does the Arthurian Grail with which it is often identified. Both vessels are associated in stories with the acquisition of wisdom or spiritual enlightenment, the indefinite prolongation of life, and cures for various ailments over which conventional medicine cannot prevail. Such stories may have their roots in historical events but have been vastly embellished over the centuries. Quite possibly embellishers included the spiritualists, homeopaths, and yogis whose loose association formed the basis of the Centre for Alternative Healing. Clearly they were glad to have a provenance for their procedures and claims. Historical background, however, weighed little with the Heritage Commission, which was mainly concerned with the Centre's amenity value. But it added colour to the place and was one reason for disproportionate press interest, and therefore the delicacy of issues concerning the involvement of the authorities in its activities.

3

'The delicate nature of such issues can't be overstated,' remarked the authorities in a secret conference they were holding on the subject with Strategic Marketing plc, their independent consultants. 'Remember Stonehenge. Remember Findhorn. This time it may be different – we have an operative on the ground. But the dangers are self-evident.'

'The Heritage Commissioner – Triona Greenwood – is a safe pair of hands,' replied the executives from Strategic Marketing. 'Even if she weren't, we can state that one of her assistants is already on our pay-roll. Look askance if you like, but when you hired us to assist in this affair, you demanded results, not pussy-footing around. Remember, if we all play our cards right, this could be what we strategic marketing experts (small s, small m!) call a win-win situation for all concerned.'

The executives were undoubtedly thinking of merchandising rights, split-revenue deals, video royalties and recording contracts. They could already see, in their minds' eyes, people walking around in tee-shirts saying:

My Sister Went to the Centre for Alternative Healing Who Cured Her Of Terminal Ovarian Cancer And All I Got Was This Lousy Tee-shirt.

They were confident that the creative boys would tidy up the slogan, and they knew a winning formula when they saw one. And that was before you even talked about the amazing herbal remedies for cellulite and baldness which, the marketing executives thought, had even more going for them than the cancer cures. The semiotic history of the British Isles and the links between Celtic mysticism and sea-level change could not have been further from their minds. Myles Overton's money was involved, because the authorities insisted that a project like this could only be carried through in partnership with a private sector investor. And everyone knew Myles Overton cared only about the bottom line. Strategic Marketing did not know that the Heritage Commissioner on whose dedication to duty they set such store had a more deeply rooted and personal reason for trekking out to the nethermost regions of Cornwall in the teeth of a blizzard. Had they had any inkling of this, it might have changed everything.

4

Although the welcome at the Centre was hospitable and the standard of entertainment high, Triona Greenwood's impression of underlying disquiet was not altered by the events of the next few hours. One of her assistants, for example, disappeared during the fish course. While the Head of Security at the Centre reassured her that foul play was unlikely and promised they would send out search parties at first light, she could not feel entirely relaxed about this occurrence.

Again, when she surveyed her companions at the top table, she felt persuaded that those not highly eccentric were clinically insane. The monastic garb and the complete disregard for conventions of grooming and personal hygiene scarcely figured in this assessment. It was their faces that gave such a perturbing impression of inner chaos, although each seemed to conceal more than it revealed. Triona felt some element of humanity was lacking – as if they were the remnants of an ancient and nightmarish race. Yet from time to time she thought she could see in them dark reflections of more familiar figures.

'I know you . . . ' Triona kept thinking. She did not know the Chief Healer, about whom so much had already been written in magazine articles and investigative reports. His hump back, withered hand and trembling jaw made it equally difficult to look at him and to refrain from looking at him. The knowledge that filled his dark, hooded eyes seemed corrupt and dangerous. Yet he suddenly made her think of her friend Neill Fife, the psychologist, whose back grew as straight and tall as a rowan tree.

The Librarian and the Pharmacologist had the look of men entrusted with secrets so urgent they might burn their way out of the very hearts that contained them. Yet the Librarian's owl-like eyes and mole-like hands suggested Oswald Hawthorne, who grew up near Triona and her sisters at Coldharbour and whom they all believed to be an oick. And the drunken Pharmacologist made her think of Rufus Stone, the alcoholic investigative journalist who first broke the strange story of her lost sister.

The Head of Security was younger than his colleagues and resembled no-one Triona knew, although members of the security community are practised at appearing anonymous. Like Linden and certain others, it seemed likely he was among the modernizers. But even he had an equivocal and furtive manner. He kept a tame raven on his wrist and constantly stroked its neck feathers the wrong way, as if preoccupied by an insoluble dilemma.

Of the more junior communicants and novices there were others who made Triona briefly think of people who figured elsewhere in her life, or even of her own sisters. But the feeling passed.

'I don't know you,' she thought. Perhaps certain tricks of the light project grotesque parodies of what might have been and what might yet be. Perhaps all of us throw distorted shadows upon the screen of history, or perhaps we ourselves are the distorted shadows history throws upon the screen of circumstance.

Certainly, all their dinner companions shared the air of intrigue that characterized the Centre, and were constantly passing coded notes back and forth and making remarks behind cupped hands in strange, forgotten tongues. 'One life is not all,' the notes and the coded remarks seemed to say. '*One life is not all . . .* '

'It's just their way,' explained Linden, though plainly embarrassed. 'Don't think they mean to be impolite. But now – let the entertainment commence!' Clapping her hands, she gave the signal for the first performers to mount the improvised platform at the end of the eating area. 'The tradition is that we take turns,' she whispered to her guests. 'And every participant at supper gives some form of recital or rendition.'

'No – really . . . !' exclaimed Triona seeing where this was going. 'I honestly have no talent at all for this sort of thing! I really have to pass on this one . . . '

'If only', replied the drunken Pharmacologist out of the corner of his mouth, 'it were always that simple.'

More than once during the evening, Triona wondered about the exact meaning of his words, and why the others had signalled him so fervently to be silent. But the lateness of the hour and the heaviness of the wine eventually drove the matter out of her head, perhaps because there was so much else that also required clarification. When Linden Richmont showed her up to the neat but sparse little room that had been prepared for her, the two women looked deeply into one another's eyes as if for a moment linked by some unspoken bond, but then drew apart as if the secret they shared was one that neither felt ready to acknowledge.

'We'll speak more fully in the morning,' Linden promised. 'Now you must sleep, and I still have work to do. But remember, bolt your door and windows tonight, and on no account open them before sunrise or I can't answer for what might happen. You might think I'm being dramatic. But perhaps we both know I'm only saying what needs to be said. Goodnight, and may your repose be untroubled by strange noises or muffled footsteps.'

5

Perhaps the authorities and the management experts with whom they enjoyed such an unhealthy relationship should have realized things had gone sour when they received an unsigned message indicating that a body had been found face down in a vat of herbal restorative. Only a disproportionate preoccupation with material gain or fear of punishment by Myles Overton could have prevented them from pulling the plug at that juncture. Or perhaps they felt matters had already passed the point of no return.

6

At the Centre for Alternative Healing, the west wind prowled around the eaves and rattled the casements, the sea boomed against the cliffs below and night-flying storm-petrels sought shelter among hollows and clefts in the building's lee. Triona could find little repose after Linden left, for she was troubled by an obscure sense of something important left undone. She dreamed fretful dreams about pieces of hogweed root, latches on doors, and the benefits of listening to advice from villagers in friendly inns. But although she could not sleep, she could not wake up either, and her little talisman lay ineffectually on the bedside table. The other reason for Triona's restlessness was that there seemed indeed to be an unusual prevalence of thumps and bangs and movings about outside her room. When she awoke at midnight to find a message from Finbar Direach, she knew these disturbances had not been imaginary. She could not ignore the warnings she had received, and recognized trouble when she saw it. For Finbar Direach did not mince words.

I know who you are, said his note, which was discreetly slipped under Triona's door, *and why you have come here. Meet me behind the sealed entrance at the western extremity of the building, where we can take a draft from the Cup of Charms and talk about the old days. For whoever loses the past can never gain the future, and it is truly said, that one life is not all . . .*

Clearly, thought Triona, any move to accept this invitation would be inconsistent with the undertakings she gave Linden Richmont. But the desire for more information was strong, and she would hardly be the first, through lack of training, to confuse information with knowledge, and knowledge with wisdom. She was certain that even if Finbar Direach did not have all the answers, at least he could help formulate the questions in a more cogent and perspicacious way. And she needed to know how anyone else could have an inkling she was drawn here by more than Heritage Commission business. 'I don't think it can do any harm,' she said to herself, 'if I only stay a little while.' The corridors leading to the meeting place were intricate, and more than once Triona was concerned that she might wander into the old mine workings which she knew extended beneath the structure. Finally, however, she arrived, dishevelled and out of breath.

7

Did Triona open the door, she wondered, or did the door somehow open her, and slip through her when she was not looking – leaving her standing, panting, on its further side? Finbar Direach, at any rate, was soon beside her on Rhiannon's Perch – not a room but a balcony or lookout post, a square yard of granite ledge overlooking the precipice, and beyond, the angry surf and the lighthouse that intermittently flung her companion's lined features into stark relief. She was struck as before by his small size, yet he had a powerful and disconcerting presence as if an immense body of history had been condensed into him. Yet when he greeted her he seemed unassuming enough, and even concerned about her feelings.

'Don't worry,' he reassured her, although he had to raise his voice because of the wind. 'And call me Finn! I mean you no harm. Although if the modernizers find us here – well, I leave that to your imagination . . . '

'Well, I came, anyway. And I want some answers. Who are you? How do you know so much about me? What do you mean when you say you know why I've come?'

His eyes rested on her, as grey and measureless as the sea. 'I know you are one of six sisters, and you have come here from Coldharbour.'

'Well, you're wrong. I've come here from the Heritage Commission.'

'I know you are looking for someone.'

'Perhaps everyone, in the end, is looking for someone,' she countered warily.

'Yet in your case the search has become your entire life. You would give much – perhaps too much, to acquire information as to her whereabouts.' Something in his demeanour suggested that for every word he said there was another word he did not say. Perhaps, she caught herself thinking, he might indeed hold the answers to the questions that had been haunting her for so long. On the other hand, she could not entirely forget Linden Richmont's remarks about Finn, and was also aware that he had no real status in the Centre but was only the cleaner and general dogsbody, indentured here, perhaps, as a punishment for some nameless crime.

'I need some answers,' she repeated. 'Where's my assistant? What's going on?'

'Drink this,' he replied, holding out a vessel of liquid. 'It'll make you feel better. It's only plant extracts and spring water, with a dash of herbal potheen. But the cup is the Cup of Charms, and perhaps no more need be said.'

Triona looked at his offering with a sense that if she did what she was asked to do, it would not be easily undone. The wind whipped her hair across her face, and she could taste spray even though they were far above the sea. She hesitated. She had always been brought up to believe it a bad idea to accept home-made intoxicants out of a blighted cup from a stranger haunted by some nameless atrocity, especially when balancing on a precipitous and gale-swept ledge. Yet, as the lighthouse beam swung past, she thought also of her own none-too-conventional family, of the loss she never truly accepted, and of the questions which had dogged her for half a lifetime. Just as the Centre had become the last hope for supplicants of whom ordinary medicine despaired, so it was, for Triona, the last chance to find an answer which no ordinary avenue of enquiry could supply.

'Well,' she said, 'here's to the future.'

After she sipped the preparation from what seemed an irregularly shaped and very poorly designed piece of pottery, he began to talk. Slowly at first, but then with increasing agitation. The wind, meanwhile, died down as the centre of the depression passed overhead, although the swell increased with the turn of the tide.

'Your assistant, at least, is safe – but only because I managed to reach his side in time. Rumours of an attempt on his life are no exaggeration, for there were those who perceived him as a threat, and when they realized he was on the brink of discovering their secret, they took the only action they felt was open to them. Had they not made the mistake of trying to drown him in industrial strength Rescue Remedy, even my intervention would have been futile. As things stand he is in good hands, for there are still people I can rely on, even though respect for the old ways is dwindling, and as you've guessed, your other assistant has already betrayed you. Transport to take them both off the hillside is being arranged, for it's too dangerous to wait.'

Exactly what secret the community would take such drastic action to protect, Finn did not immediately unveil. He talked to her about the Centre, and how it had grown up in this fateful region where sea and sky and human understanding blend in a mysterious indeterminate haze, how it was charged with an immemorial trust, but how this trust was being betrayed by cynical manipulation of age-old secrets. A manipulation of which he, Finbar Direach, had also become the victim.

'Inevitably the Centre has its modernizers,' he acknowledged. 'And they set little store by the proud antiquity that has made us what we are. Perhaps their hearts are in the right place. But they need to understand that there is more to the alternative-healing business than a glossy brochure and a catchy slogan.' Gradually it dawned on her that he was really telling his own story, but that this story was older and more convoluted than she would ever have guessed.

'The western headland', he observed, 'is of course no longer where it used to be, whether you take it that the sea has risen, or that the land has sunk. In any event the promontory is no more, where Caryddwen stirred the great cauldron she had from Bran, into which the dead could be thrown dismembered and decayed yet would rise in the fullness of their vigour the very next morning. Nor is anything left of the windswept eyrie where she prepared her remedies as gulls and ravens wheeled beneath the cliff edges. All is vanished under the hinge of the horizon. There is now no relief from the embrace of death, and once it has taken hold of a person, it drags them out of the sunlight as the sea-goddess Ran – surely another name for Rhiannon herself – dragged drowning sailors down in a net woven from mermaids' hair.'

The inference that Caryddwen too had been overwhelmed, and claimed by implacable forces, was not lost on Finn. The implication that he himself was to blame for this occurrence weighed heavily on his conscience. It had been no deliberate act of Finn's, he was at pains to point out to Triona, that resulted in the drowning of a quarter of the archipelago, the disappearance of the causeway out to the Western Isles, and the loss of valuable remedies that ensured immortality and resistance to disease. Yet that he had been instrumental in these events he was in no position to deny.

It began, perhaps, the day Mannannan Mac Llyr Mac Lugh, then a prisoner of Queen Maeve of Skye and therefore restricted in his movements, entrusted Finn with an unbreakable trust. 'They say every man's refuge is his prison,' asserted Mannannan Mac Llyr Mac Lugh. 'Although in my own case, the sooner I'm able to break loose from the insidious snares and entrapments of Queen Maeve of Skye, the better I'll be pleased. But take this poem to Caryddwen, in her cloudy bower at the last extremity of land on the south-western peninsula. When she sees it, she'll certainly know what to do, and the course of action which should most propitiously be pursued.'

Saying this, he gave Finn a poem called *The Lament of Mannannan Mac Llyr Mac Lugh upon his Incarceration by Queen Maeve of Skye*, which was the saddest poem ever composed in the entire history of the archipelago. So sad indeed it was, that it could not even be written down – because the very quill that inscribed it would burst into tears diluting the ink to such an extent the words turned to mist in front of the writer's eyes.

'But remember,' added Mannannan Mac Llyr Mac Lugh, 'you may never tell this poem to another living soul – or if you do, make sure you never tell it to a harp player. But if you do, on no account must you tell it to Martyn McMartyn of the Silver Fingers, who has in his repertoire the saddest tune ever written in the history of the whole archipelago, which no man or animal can hear without weeping, and which is called *The Lament of Martyn McMartyn on Having his Hand bitten off by a Banshee and being Obliged to get it Replaced by a Prosthesis*. For if that ever happens, it will go ill not only with you and me and the peoples that currently inhabit these peaceful islands, but also with countless generations as yet unborn, in lands and continents so far not even dreamed of.'

Now as Finn left the island of Skye these facts were fixed in his brain and it was only a series of bizarre coincidences that led him to compromise the trust that was placed in him. He travelled long and far within the mountains and the valleys of the north, and whenever he came to a river he fell on his face and swam, for bridges and other monuments to human dominance over nature meant nothing to him. But one evening at nightfall he came to a remote bothy from which drifted the sound of music and the jangle of many instruments, and it was in that direction that he tended his footsteps. And as he drew closer, it was clear that a *fleadh* and a singing contest were in full progress, and expert musicians and poets were vying with one another to produce the most virtuosic recital.

'You may join us if you wish,' the chief of these revellers told Finn once the latter had announced his identity and the nature of his journey. 'But I should reveal straight away the rules of our contest, which are that the winner shall receive a magic mandolin which always sounds the correct string no matter how inaccurate the player's right-hand technique, but that the loser shall have his head struck from his shoulders, as is only proper. But perhaps these terms are too exacting for you?'

'People have called me many things,' Finn retorted. 'Both directly to my face, and by rumour-mongering and innuendo. I have been upbraided for self-seeking, indolence, failing to keep up the proper observances towards spiritual authority, and other shortcomings a thousand times worse. I have no friends to speak of, and my enemies are more numerous than grains of sand on the beach, or grains of salt in the sea. But no one has ever accused me of turning down a challenge.'

In this way Finn was accepted into the proceedings, and in accordance with the rules a cup of mead was passed round the circle from right to left, and whoever had the cup took a sip from it, placed it in front of him or her, and commenced their recital, whether a poem, a song, an excerpt from a prose epic, or a philosophical theory. But as soon as the cup came to Finn for the first time, and he cleared his throat to sing one of his favourite ballads, he suddenly found that his mind was filled only with the words of Mannannan Mac Llyr Mac Lugh and the profound and far-reaching melancholy that had gripped him as a result of the oppression he received at the hands of Queen Maeve of Skye. And far from being able to sing or speak, Finn's eyes filled with tears and a lump filled his throat, and he waved the cup past, emitting no articulate sound from his lips.

'This will redound to your disadvantage in the competition, Finn,' the other bards noted. 'But whatever happens, perhaps it is only what was destined to happen, and this is only the first round.' And they passed the cup on.

As the cup made its way round the circle, some of the bards sang high, and some in a low bass voice which was gravelly to the ear. Some intoned moving stanzas of poetry, while others put across carefully marshalled facts in a rhetorical style. Suffice it to say, all entries were of a very high standard and it was a difficult and invidious task to judge between them. Only one person seemed to lead the rest in the sadness and the lugubriousness of his playing, but Finn could not clearly determine who he was, for he remained always in the shadow, furthest from the glow of the flames.

But as the competition went on it seemed only too soon that the cup once again came to Finn, and all eyes turned to him to see what he would do. He took a deep draught, and cleared his throat to recite a poem, but once again the only lines that his mind would engage were those of the poem Mannannan Mac Llyr Mac Lugh had given him to take to Caryddwen – and the words of Mannannan Mac Llyr Mac Lugh regarding the consequences of breaking his promise.

Finn opened his mouth and made a sound halfway between the first line of Mannannan Mac Llyr Mac Lugh's poem, and a grey seal choking on a herring, and then he closed his mouth again with a great effort of will. And not without considering the drawbacks of losing the competition, he waved the cup past.

'Your efforts so far', the other bards could not help remarking, 'have hardly stood you in good stead. Yet nothing is ended before it has finished, and, when all is said and done, this is only the second round.'

Again, the cup passed round the circle. Some of the participants recited obscure passages in ancient tongues, and others racy verses in a vernacular style. Some of them struck rippling glissandos and arpeggios from their instruments, whilst others favoured the curdling drone of the pipes or the fitful growl of the *bodhran*. Each offering seemed as good as the one that came before it, and twice as good as the one that came after it, until the discernment of the listener was defeated in a panoply of sounds, rhythms, and images. Yet if you had to choose one out of all of them, it was still the same shadowy figure who seemed to hold himself aloof from the rest, but from whose harp the notes ran out pure and bright like the lively water of a mountain burn from between the heather-fringed rocks. Even without knowing the person's name, Finn could see that he was the favourite in this matter – yet something about him made the hairs on the back of Finn's wrists stand on end.

At length, once more, it was Finn's turn. This time as he picked up the fateful cup, he noticed that the claymore that leaned symbolically in the corner of the bothy was a dangerous, sharp-looking object, and one you would not willingly involve in a violent encounter with your cervical region. But although Finn's mind was strangely focused by the idea that if he were to lose the competition the other bards would not rest until they had separated his head from his body, he still could not muster his thoughts around any line of poetry other than that which Mannannan Mac Llyr Mac Lugh had designated for the ears of Caryddwen only.

'But', prevaricated Finn, 'he did not unequivocally say I wasn't to tell the poem to anyone else, or even indeed forbid me to tell it to harp players in any absolute sense. To be honest, he seemed more worried about a fellow with an ersatz hand, and to judge by the way these people play their instruments, none of them is particularly disadvantaged as far as digital dexterity is concerned.'

The more Finn thought about this, and the more he looked at the sword in the corner, the more it seemed to him that Mannannan Mac Llyr Mac Lugh had indeed been fairly relaxed about whom Finn could tell the poem to, and indeed, on reflection, had more or less encouraged Finn to recite it to everyone he met. 'After all he's done for me,' Finn said to himself, 'I can do no less for him.' Blinking back the tears that poured into his eyes as soon as he uttered the first syllable, and swallowing down the lump that welled up in his throat as soon as he spoke the first word, he commenced to recite the saddest poem that ever was spoken in these islands.

The silence that gripped his audience, though it seemed to go on for an eternity, was in fact no longer than a few seconds. It was like that distressing hiatus when you know you have stubbed your toe, and you are waiting for it to start to hurt. For a moment everything was still. Then, as Finn continued his recitation, his words were punctuated by a terrible cacophony of stifled sobs and the steady susurrus of teardrops cascading on to the straw-covered floor. As he finished, there was indeed a hush, albeit broken by the occasional howl of grief as one of the company recalled a particularly poignant metaphor. Then, as one, they rounded on Finn with a terrific burst of clapping and acclaim, crowning him with ivy wreaths and drinking his health a thousand times over, for, they said, it was the saddest thing they had ever heard.

Only one of them was silent – but then, as that one stepped forward from the shadows with an unfathomable expression forming around his mouth, Finn's heart shrunk within him, for he noticed that slung over the man's back was a harp of ebony wood strung with the hair of mermaids, and that his left hand was made of pure silver.

'Know then, that I am Martyn McMartyn of the Silver Fingers,' declared this formerly reticent individual. 'I shall only say this. The magic mandolin is yours, Finn, and likewise the admiration and respect of all of us here, for I warrant that is the most evocative and heart-rending piece of verse these islands have ever known. But wait till I fit it to this little tune I wrote, for then we'll all hear a sad song which will make *Carrickfergus* seem like a bawdyhouse heeltap in comparison.'

And before anyone could stop him, he unslung his harp and ran his silver fingers across the golden strings. And before even the first notes had died away, the tears were streaming down the faces of all the assembled multitude. Nor, after the first few bars, were even the mice that nestled beneath the floorboards of the bothy immune, nor the owls that hunted after them through the moonless night. The tears flooded from them like an autumn dew, and not even the wood anemones and heather bells and rowan trees that hemmed the hilltop could forbear to join the watery chorus.

Before Finn could say anything, the seven bards from the little gathering sallied out into the countryside, pausing only to cut the head off the least successful entrant in accordance with the rules of the competition – who had noticeably been crying twice as hard as anyone else. As they dispersed through the misty islands, for every person they played the song to, that person played it to seven, and for each person those seven played it to, that person played it to forty-nine. Soon the saddest song had spread exponentially through the community and there was such a weeping and lachrymal outpouring among men, animals and other sentient beings that the tears turned into trickles, the trickles became streams, the streams became rivers, and the rivers became raging torrents hurling and plunging down to the unsuspecting sea.

And before anyone could take any useful action at all, the great heaving bosom of the ocean had been swelled by this unanticipated spate and had impartially overwhelmed both the outlying islands and the coastal plains, making of Caryddwen's original fastness a mere point of rock around which the boisterous Gulf Stream churned and reared.

8

Deep was Finn's anguish after the events just described. 'I brought death into the world, where it was unknown before,' he said to Triona. 'For previously when anyone perished or was destroyed by illness, in battle, or as a result of a capital penalty, their friends would simply take them up to Caryddwen's Promontory, where they would be thrown into the cauldron, to rise the following morning with all their faculties and prospects renewed. But now this is far from the case, and destruction is rife within our land. For this I am to blame, and as punishment I must accept the judgement of the Tuatha de Dannaan, however harsh their sentence might appear to be.'

But although Triona was not the most knowledgeable person about the mysteries of early Celtic legend, she was not the most ignorant either. Her mother, for her own reasons, ensured that Triona and all her sisters read the *Mabinogion*, the *Book of Lismore* and the *Yellow Book* of Lecan, and were in no way untutored in the pre-Christian heritage. Although Triona had learned something since she came to the Centre for Alternative Healing, it was what she knew already that prompted her to come at all.

'It may be that you overstepped the mark,' she replied, when she had taken Finn's narrative in. 'If what you say is true, there's no doubt you disobeyed the instructions given you by Mannannan Mac Llyr Mac Lugh. But modernizers would say you did only what you were bound to do, and the vanishing of the western lowlands was part of the geological destiny of the archipelago. They might also suggest that though Caryddwen was lost and her cauldron shattered, its fragments washed ashore in a thousand sequestered coves. And that where they lay in sands and salt-marshes or were carried inland by storm-winds, tidal incursions, or mud clinging to the feet of seagulls, a wonderful pharmacopoeia grew to perpetuate Caryddwen's legacy.'

He shook his head sadly, as though he had heard all this before but knew only too well it was an attempt to fudge the issue; that, in the end, any knowledge preserved was hardly a shadow of what was lost. But such was his desolation that she still tried to comfort him.

'You look downcast,' she pursued. 'But couldn't it be that certain people – and I'm sure the modernizers at the Centre would include themselves – learned to gather the herbs and exploit what remains of the old power? Which, while attenuated and no longer able to cure death as a whole, would work reasonably well on non-fatal conditions like warts, sore throats, and unsightly hair loss. Then again, if someone had a fragment of the cauldron itself, even inoperable cancers might—' she stopped, for she saw she wasn't too far off the mark. Yet still she realized this told him nothing he did not know, but merely exacerbated the far greater knowledge that was eating him away from within.

'That's all very fine and dandy,' he said at length. 'And I can't deny you've hit on one of the secrets behind the Centre for Alternative Healing. But you'll no doubt be telling me next that Caryddwen's unfinished remedy is still secretly preserved by her faithful assistant Little Gwion, until the day she returns in the form of a white doe to save us from ourselves.'

'I can't tell you anything,' Triona said, 'if you're so ready to take the blame for everything that's wrong with the world. Things just aren't that simple. I know, because I've been there myself. I've blamed myself time and again for the loss I suffered long ago, just as you blame yourself for the loss of the cauldron. Yet, in the end, self-recrimination is just a form of arrogance, because we must all take responsibility for our own destinies, even if it is not in our power to avert them.'

Finbar Direach, however, allowed a little of his bitterness to show. 'There are always people who take the romantic view,' he said. 'No doubt you've been listening to Linden Richmont. But I'm here to say that she's not what she seems, and the Tuatha de Dannaan did not make so light of things. For once it was clear that the waters had overwhelmed the cauldron and smashed it into a thousand pieces, and that each piece was washed deep into the landscape so that it would seemingly take a thousand years to find, they took a very serious view of the matter. Had it not been for the intervention of Mannannan Mac Llyr Mac Lugh himself, who finally escaped from Queen Maeve of Skye's lofty prison-place by sliding down his own beard, it would have gone hard with me. As it was, when they had discussed my case, the judgement was laid upon me to travel the world in human form, unable to resume my natural appearance until I had discovered every last one of those pieces, acquired possession of them without violence, extortion or duplicity, and made good what was destroyed through my negligence and lack of forethought.'

With that, Finbar Direach said, the Tuatha de Dannaan turned into eagles and winged their way back to the windswept and waveswept wastes that were their last domain. He described how he had afterwards wandered the restless islands for many lifetimes, and searched the minutest recesses and remotest reaches of the land. 'Perhaps', he said, 'I've found ten fragments of the cauldron, and perhaps I've found a hundred. But the truth is I've found and hidden away all the pieces except two. But for one of those two pieces, certain elements in the Centre for Alternative Healing have been holding me here against my will, compelling me to perform menial tasks and using its healing virtues for their own benefit and betterment.'

'You mean . . . ?' began Triona.

'Exactly,' confirmed Finbar Direach. 'As you've already guessed, that fragment is nothing less than the vessel from which you just drank, and there's no one better placed than yourself to appreciate its unique powers. For you'll find that if you happen to have any inoperable cancers it will clear them up a treat, but if you have not, it still carries the legacy of Caryddwen, so everything that was obscure to you will soon become clearer, although some things that were previously clear, may grow more obscure.'

'But why me?'

'Could I do any less for you, in return for my freedom? For I was permitted to leave this place only by Rhiannon's Perch from the western door, and through that door I could pass only if it were opened for me by a person of pure heart and profound understanding, who was a true spiritual follower of Caryddwen herself.'

'This is going too fast,' Triona told him, holding on to the side of her head.

'You're right,' he replied, his elation dropping away like a wave that rises against a harbour wall, and as quickly recedes and dissipates. 'For nobody is ever truly free, and myself least of all. There is still the last and smallest fragment to be found, the one I've never been able to discover, and time is no longer on my side.'

'If no-one's ever truly free, it's possible no-one's ever truly wise either. Perhaps we're two of a kind, because despite your famous potion I still know as little as ever I did about the object of my own search.'

'Your sister Karen, who vanished when you were still a girl,' he acknowledged, stroking his small beard with his crooked wrist and kicking one heel against the parapet.

'You know the story. Everyone knows the story. It was in all the papers, to say nothing of TV documentaries and a paperback book by Rufus Stone. But you don't know what happened to Karen. Nobody knows what happened to Karen.'

He looked at her oddly but let her talk, even though the wind was getting up again and time was running short. She gave her side of the story of Karen's disappearance, although it was impossible to gauge his reaction. She described the party in the grounds of Coldharbour Abbey where her sister was last seen alive, although there were still people who claimed otherwise. She mentioned Myles Overton's early interest in Coldharbour, and how she, Triona, became involved with one of the marketing executives sent to assess its potential as an exclusive rural health club and spa, or perhaps a secret headquarters for the Myles Overton Group. But when she finally married the marketing executive her friends thought she did it for the wrong reasons and the relationship was ill-starred from the first. It was then, said Triona, that the shadow of Myles Overton spread across her life, as it seemed to have done across the Centre for Alternative Healing, and across the lives of her sisters.

'My story's not as long as yours, nor as colourful. But like yours it has no ending. Like you and a thousand other people I'm no longer leading my life but following it, trying to find how the story turns out. But maybe you've got some kind of information that will help me in my search, since you obviously come to the whole thing from a different perspective?'

'Maybe I do, and maybe I don't. But I can tell you this. There's many of us spend our time hiding from what we claim to seek, and fleeing from what we pretend to pursue. Before you ask any more – be certain that you want an answer!'

The sea boomed its dour unending song as if a thousand miles away, and the stark landscape loomed up all around, but Triona could no longer see it. What if people found what they were looking for? If they were defining their very identity by their search, in the moment that they discovered the object of their quest, they would lose themselves. Finn, perhaps, had discovered exactly this in his pursuit of the fragments of Caryddwen's cauldron, diminishing a little with each one that was unearthed until in these last days he was tired, frail, and lacking in vigour. Yet, Triona thought, if that was the price of finding Karen, she was ready to pay it. She remembered their conversations together during those last turbulent days at Coldharbour. The two eldest of the six sisters, one growing bright as the noonday sun, the other immersed in secret dark. She stood with Finn on the little windswept eyrie, waiting to hear him say what she already knew, that Karen had not gone but had been taken, and that she was with Leatherwing, Finbar Direach's own ancient adversary.

'It appears', Finn repeated, 'we have both lost things, but your coming here was no accident. Let me put it this way – each time I found a little more of the cauldron, I lost a little more of myself. Let me put it another way – your sister Karen is with Leatherwing – for reasons which will become only too clear. But the only way to free her is to complete the reconstruction of the cauldron. I've broken the back of the task, but the last and smallest piece I cannot find, and I must hand the job over to someone more qualified to do it. Now you have drunk from the cup I offered you, you are under an obligation and an unbreakable trust not to refuse me . . . '

'I've got no obligation – except to myself, and my family.'

'That may be enough. You may think I've told you all this to reveal some conspiracy of Leatherwing or Myles Overton to destroy the world. But your own sisters are in the greatest danger. For the Tuatha de Dannaan let it be known that until the cauldron was recovered, the human community could never know peace again. But that would never happen until six sisters came from Coldharbour, to fulfil what has been foretold.'

'Well you can tell the Tuatha de Dannaan from me that half my sisters are in no position to come from anywhere or fulfil anything. And those of us still left don't wish to suffer the same fate.'

'I cannot tell the Tuatha de Dannaan anything, because they're sleeping and may not be disturbed. But do you think I'm the only one who knows what they foresaw? Your sister Karen has vanished, your sister Chantal is in exile, and your sister Nuala is in a prison of which Myles Overton, as if by accident, has acquired an undisclosed percentage. Take it from me, our adversary, whether you believe it's Myles Overton or Leatherwing himself, cannot yet act openly. But he knows that if the sisters can be eliminated or compromised, nothing will stand in his way.'

'My sisters' circumstances are the product of their own attitudes and actions. Besides, we weren't talking about my sister Chantal or my sister Nuala. We're talking about my sister Karen.'

'Well, if you ask me, all your sisters have been having a run of unusually bad luck, and believe me, bad luck's a subject on which I'm somewhat of an expert.'

But Triona was still suspicious of Finbar Direach. He seemed to know so much that she could not help wondering whether he himself had delivered Karen into captivity or worse. Or whether he was using her vanishing as a ruse to secure Triona's help on his own project. It even crossed her mind that he was in the pay of Leatherwing, or that he was Leatherwing in person. Then again, he might merely be a couple of bards short of an eisteddfod.

'I need more proof,' she told him. 'I need something tangible. Especially if I've got to convince the others.'

For answer he told her many things about herself and Coldharbour that no stranger could have known. Seeing she was still indecisive, he produced from his pouch a lock of hair, and pushed it into her hand. 'Sometimes I'm here, and sometimes I'm there,' he confided. 'But although I've been confined in this remote place for more than a little while, I don't miss much of what goes on. Nor am I entirely without assistance in the outside world, as I hope, indeed, you yourself will soon assist me. Yet what I show you now was not acquired without difficulty and hazard. For I must tell you that one of my agents crept into the very chamber where your sister lies, and stole this lock of hair at great personal risk – and you can see it's been freshly cut!'

'Here – at last – is hard evidence,' Triona said, her eyes filling with tears. 'But I can't allow my longing to cloud my judgement. Karen's hair was as dark as a moonless night, whereas this is blood-red. Karen's hair was like the finest gossamer, whereas this is as coarse as codline.'

'Well,' said Finbar Direach, 'your sister has suffered much over the years, and suffering can change a person.'

Yet his face was shrouded in shadow, and as she returned the lock of hair, both of them knew what neither of them could quite put into words. For according to legend it was Leatherwing who had blood-red hair as coarse as codline, and Triona and the other sisters had seen it a thousand times in their dreams. Nor, unless Karen was found, could they ever be free from those dreams. For this reason alone Triona saw it would prove difficult to avoid being caught up in the little fellow's bizarre enterprise of finding the last fragment of the lost cauldron of Caryddwen.

'Still, I don't see why, if you could find all those other bits, you can't ferret out the last one . . . '

But again, as if through a shift in the light, she could see how old he was, and weary. If he were not thrown into Caryddwen's cauldron, he would die. Everyone always dies if they are not thrown into Caryddwen's cauldron, and this has been a recurring theme in history, from the day of Finn's original error to the present. One can rail against him if one wishes, thought Triona, but that's the truth of it. Even so, she made one last protest:

'I can't do it. Why ask me? I owe you nothing! Your search is your search, and my search is my search.'

'I don't think you quite understand,' he said almost sadly. 'There is only one search, and you no longer have any choice.'

9

As he spoke, there came from the depths of the facility a harsh inhuman shriek as of someone who discovers that what they value most in the world has been stolen from them. As they listened, this was followed by the unmistakable noise of sleepers being roused out of their beds and security being alerted. Loud garrulous voices cried out to the thieves to come back so that they could subject them to unspeakable death and mutilation, and it was clear everyone was taking the disappearance of the Heritage Commissioner, Finbar Direach, and the oddly shaped drinking vessel very seriously indeed.

'They can't have got far!' the voices urged each other. 'Leave no stone unturned. Everything depends upon regaining what is ours!' The clatter of footsteps spread along the passageways towards them, and before long Finn and Triona looked at each other in consternation as they heard the sound of something heavy being swung at the bolted door.

'Let me talk to Linden Richmont,' Triona told Finn. 'This has all been a misunderstanding.'

'The only misunderstanding is yours if you think she can help us now, even supposing she wanted to. No – there's only one way out, and we must take it before that door goes.'

Triona looked at him, and at the dizzy drop and the jagged rocks at its foot. Intellectually she knew the jagged rocks were neither here nor there because from heights above eighty feet hitting water will kill you as certainly as hitting stone. But the jagged rocks, she couldn't help feeling, would add insult to fatal injury.

'I'm not going down there! Linden Richmont is a reasonable person. I'll take my chances, thank you. We haven't even got a rope.'

'That did not stop Mannannan Mac Llyr Mac Lugh, during his daring escape from Queen Maeve of Skye,' Finn replied with a resolute expression.

'Look,' she said, catching his drift, 'I don't know whether this is a dream, whether it's real, or some hybrid of the two brought on by the drink you gave me. But if you think I'm going to clamber down a hundred feet of cliff with the most accident-prone individual in the history of the British Isles, you've got another think coming. Besides, Mannannan Mac Llyr Mac Lugh was able to make use of his beard, which had grown prodigiously long during the time of his incarceration, whereas in your case we're talking designer stubble.'

'That may be true,' said Finn, as the first panel of the door splintered and cracked. 'But it's also true I have a small bottle of the new herbal remedy which the marketing people insisted was to be given absolute priority, and which, when mixed in a fragment of Caryddwen's cauldron, I have some hopes for.'

'What is it?' she asked unkindly. 'Liquid rope?'

'I believe', replied Finn equably, as another panel split open, 'there was some mention of hair-restorer.'

Mercifully, Triona did not afterwards recollect much of the journey down the cliff face. She remembered Finn stirring the mixture carefully and applying it to his chin, and she could not deny there was an immediate impression of follicular activity. But whether the descent was made mainly by this means, or by the sparse growth of fennels, horsetails and marram grasses from clefts between the rocks, she could never be sure. She was aware they were harassed by numerous ravens, gannets and choughs undoubtedly in the pay of the people above, and incontinently bombarded with solid objects thrown from a considerable height, and that they were lucky to survive the experience at all. But by the time she once again felt in full possession of her faculties they were three miles away, at the crossroads where she had left the Heritage Commission Land Rover, and it all seemed like a bizarre hallucination.

'It was a great escape!' Finn assured her as he discreetly wiped shaving foam off the corners of his jaw, having now dispensed with the appendage to which, perhaps, they owed their lives. 'It will one day become the stuff of legend itself, when the last lost fragment of Caryddwen's cauldron is recovered and our story can be narrated to an admiring audience.'

'As far as I'm concerned, I've had enough of legends for the time being, and unless I can give you a lift anywhere, our acquaintance is at an end. I've been having bad dreams recently, and nobody likes having bad dreams.'

'As I said before we were interrupted, you cannot so easily escape the part that's laid down for you in this affair. Especially if you want to see your sister again. Though you've helped me recover the penultimate piece, one more is missing, and the search falls to you, and to your sisters. If you had no wish to take on the obligation of finding them, you should never have drunk from the Cup of Charms.'

Seeing there was no point in reasoning with him, she sank down in the heather and put her face in her hands and remained in that position for half an hour, even though the sounds of pursuit could be heard across the hillsides. When she looked up he was gone, and she wondered whether he had ever even been there.

'Maybe', she muttered, not knowing whether she felt most sorry for herself, or for Karen, 'I can ask my sisters to help – or old friends who value our friendship enough not to care if they make fools of themselves. We may sometimes have parted on bad terms, but a sister is a sister, and the friendships of childhood never truly end, for the friends of our childhood make us who we are.'

She let her mind run back to Coldharbour and its many secrets, wondering not for the first time why you could hear the sea in the snail shells found beneath its great oaks, even though the snails themselves had never travelled beyond the flint wall on the southern slope. She let her mind run back to the heady days of adolescence, then Karen's disappearance, and the time after that. 'I may even contact my ex-husband, as he still works for Myles Overton,' she said to herself. 'More and more, I suspect he knows something. But every precaution must be taken. I'll need to conceal the Land Rover where it won't be easily found, for no doubt they're watching the roads. Perhaps it'll be necessary to apply for some leave from the Heritage Commission, while this affair is sorted out. But first I must send a letter warning of my return to Coldharbour. It's been a long time, and I can't be sure of my reception.'

But when she heard the news on the Land Rover's radio, she knew she could no longer be sure of anything.

II

The Mysteries of Coldharbour

10

When Triona's letter reached Coldharbour it was the morning after Peter Goodlunch died, the authorities were rattled because things were happening faster than they anticipated, and a wan moon stood in the chilly sky. Surprisingly it was Oswald Hawthorne who refused to entertain the idea of welcoming Triona back, while her sister Sophie and Neill Fife said it would, perhaps, be the answer they had all been waiting for.

'Life is a rungless ladder,' said Oswald. 'Leaning against a crumbling wall. She made her choices long ago, and there's an end to it.'

'Do we really make choices?' asked Neill, struck by a curious thought. 'Or do they make us? How difficult to tell whether the river drives the watermill, or the watermill drives the river! Yet until we know the answer, even the most blameless existence seems dogged by acts of apostasy and denial. Let's have some coffee and arrowroot biscuits, and talk the whole thing through.'

Oswald, however, thought the time for talking was already over, and even this offer could not lift the desolation that lay across his heart.

To understand why Oswald was so upset when Neill received the letter from Triona, it would be necessary to understand why, many years before, Triona told Oswald that their time together meant more to her than she could express in words, and that she hoped, whatever happened, he would not hold it against her, and they could still be friends.

'I don't understand,' Oswald said nervously.

To understand why Oswald did not understand, it would be necessary to know the significance of a past amongst the ruins of Coldharbour Abbey, oppressed by the nightmare of Leatherwing and the loss of Karen, who meant so much to all of them. For it was within the sound of the abbey's long-silenced bells that six sisters were born into the oldest family in Britain, the two eldest, Triona and Karen, being twins. And the link between Coldharbour and the sisters was as definitive as it was indefinable.

'Never forget, you belong to the oldest family in Britain,' Triona and Karen's mother told them as soon as they were able to speak. 'But don't look for us in Debretts. We have always been ex-directory. For all that, we have our destiny! It's indefinably linked to the destiny of Coldharbour and Coldharbour's ancient denizens, and you will know it when it comes . . . '

Their mother was a celebrated eccentric who drank an alcoholic preparation she made herself from woodland plants, but their father was a barrister so the family did not do badly. The sisters were very close, yet very different. There were Triona and Karen, Sophie, who became a schoolteacher, Dawn, who became a single mother, Chantal, who became a revolutionary and Nuala, who became imprisoned for a crime she did not commit, although Chantal may have. They played on the downs, blew dandelion clocks to count the passing hours, picked wood anemone petals to see who loved them, and poured out their dreams beside the dreamless river. They swore loyalty to the end, but they did not know the end would come so soon.

What they really wanted from life was a mystery, even to themselves. They all liked Neill even when Karen claimed him for her own. They knew Oswald was Neill's friend so they tried not to make fun of him for being, as they put it, a bit of an oick. But they remained aloof until the one night shortly after Karen's disappearance, when Triona stayed with him – perhaps needing, in her confusion, something familiar to cling to.

To understand Triona's need, and the sisters' feeling at the time that Coldharbour had somehow turned against them, would require an understanding of its turbulent history. For example, some said it was to Coldharbour that Dermot and Grania once fled from the rage of Finbar Direach's namesake Fionn Mac Cummail. And that their betrayal made Fionn wish betrayal upon the land which sheltered them, laying that region open to many incursions. Coldharbour was reputedly the billet for Henghist and Horsa, the first Gothic overlords of Britain. At different times it provided lodgings for St Brendan the Navigator, William of Occam, Cornelius Agrippa, Bishop Berkeley, Sir John Franklin, and several nineteenth-century poets and radicals. It was known that John Wilkes founded a notorious club there, although this relocated to the inner city and was ultimately acquired by Myles Overton as part of his expanding leisure empire.

'Coldharbour has its own agenda,' Triona once acknowledged. 'But so do we!'

With Karen gone, she nursed the legacy of Caryddwen and her kind, which had passed from mother to daughter down centuries of subjugation and surfaced in the ideas of the women's movement of the late twentieth century. The other sisters, Dawn in particular, also found in these insights a way of reinterpreting themselves. But it was partisan wisdom which left many non-women feeling deserted and often drove them into the ranks of the oppressor. For during the same period cupidity and self-serving became the rule among those in authority. Powerful individuals like Myles Overton were able to subvert the people's will, corrupt and intimidate officials, and by their control of the leisure and media industries appropriate for their own ends an immemorial heritage.

The truth is, to understand the issue between Oswald and Triona, one would need to understand human understanding itself, and all that conspires to pervert it. But most, one would need to understand that the Tuatha de Dannaan never perished after the fateful battle of Cattraeth in 610 A.D, but only sought rest and respite in a secret place. That Cattraeth itself and other great conflicts between Gothic and Celtic, linear and cyclic, theist and animist, modernizer and traditionalist, are still being fought. That the battlefield is the human heart, and the greatest heroes may not even be aware they are fighting. To understand anything, Neill was fond of remarking, it is necessary to understand everything. But let that pass.

'This is not about you, or Neill or the others. It's not about any so-called legacy – it's about *me!*' a much younger Triona told a much younger Oswald when he demanded an explanation for her sudden coldness toward him. 'I need some space, so that I can find out who I am. Whatever happens, the time we had together will always mean a great deal to me, and I know that on one level we will never truly be apart.'

'I think you're trying to tell me something,' Oswald muttered.

'Perhaps I am, and perhaps I'm not. I'm confused. I love you, as I love everyone, but love, on its own, is not enough. Perhaps I've known this all along but been unable to admit it, even to myself. Sometimes a person needs to be free, before they can even be a person.'

'If it's about the other night—'

'The other night was beautiful. I have no regrets. But this goes deeper. To tell the truth, there are things about myself that even I am completely unaware of. I'm a walking contradiction. Sometimes I want one thing, sometimes another.'

Oswald had a feeling Triona was holding something back, despite her protestations of ingenuousness. This was confirmed when their friend Damien Lewis, who was an expert on women and unfailingly a Jack-the-Lad, said helpfully:

'I think she's trying to say she only slept with you as a one-off and you shouldn't take it as meaning anything. She's got another boyfriend called Peter Goodlunch who has a sports car and works for Strategic Marketing. He's found her a job there and they're going to share a waterside flat on the artificial lake in Milton Keynes.'

Oswald turned the colour of celery and shook his head in disbelief. Yet he had known the truth all along but been unable to admit it, even to himself. For me, he thought, there was nobody before Triona, and there will be nobody after her, one-off or not. Whether Triona chose Peter Goodlunch to achieve independence or to escape from it scarcely mattered. Perhaps, as the eldest sister, she knew things the others could only guess at. Perhaps she already suspected that Myles Overton sought to acquire the deeds for Coldharbour itself, either to turn it into a privatized prison or for some other reason. And that Karen's discovery of this was linked to her disappearance. Unquestionably, someone on the inside, yet secretly belonging to the Network of Successful Women and working towards an appointment with the Heritage Commission, would be well placed to subvert any such plan.

Or again, perhaps Peter Goodlunch with his sculpted features and well polished roadster offered Triona what Oswald never could, and Neill, she knew, was out of bounds. However things stood, Triona could not share her thoughts with the others. One night in the Stepping Stones pub near Coldharbour she saw that her secret had been revealed. She looked defiantly from face to face, and knowing her sisters would never understand, she covered her eyes with her hands and rushed out to start a new life.

She was not the last. As if the loss of Karen broke some fundamental connection, the other sisters drifted away and became mothers, trainee teachers, or freedom fighters. Oswald stayed, perfecting the status of an injured party, although – as Peter Goodlunch said about him to acquaintances – it's easy not to sell out if you never get any offers. To Oswald, it was the loss of Karen and then Triona which truly destroyed Coldharbour, and the later fire, attributed to natural causes or possibly a mad woman in one of the attics, was incidental.

Neill made a success of his life, as everyone knew he would. As a leading psychologist whose name was known even at the highest levels, he appeared to forget Karen, his childhood sweetheart, and in due course married a famous supermodel. Yet when the time came to move to the country he surprised everyone by buying a house not half a mile from Coldharbour. During the same period the deeds of the main buildings passed to the Heritage Commission, because, the planning committee was told, a private sale would not be in the public interest. Triona's part in this was never revealed, although later her connection with the Heritage Commission was put on an official footing. Yet she visited Coldharbour seldom compared with the other sisters, for whom it continued to exert such a curious attraction that, even when they were far away, it was seldom far from their thoughts.

Perhaps they really did feel they were the oldest family, and Coldharbour was part of their covenant with history. Their mother, who had told them this so often, did not long survive the disappearance of her favourite daughter. She became gloomy and fretful, and would eat only tinned peaches and watercress. When she knew her last hours were approaching, she climbed into a rowan tree and summoned her daughters to her.

'Our family is old,' she repeated. 'Perhaps the oldest in Britain. It is so old it has lost its name, for we recognize only the female line. Now that line must pass from me to you. Do not forget me, and do not forget your sister Karen, nor abandon hope of her. Our family is old, so it has many friends, but also many enemies, although neither may appear in their true colours. Your father has never been short of a shilling, so I have no doubt you will all do well in life. I myself have nothing to give you but my blessing, and this recipe for hogweed ale, which, if anything, is the secret of a long and happy existence.'

With these words, she fell out of the rowan tree and died, and the recipe fell at her feet. They took and buried their mother, the tears flowing down like rain, but their father stood apart, and afterwards took up an offer of work overseas and was seldom heard from thereafter. At the funeral, Triona thought she had never known such a sense of her immemorial family since she last saw her maternal grandmother, who suffered much from pre-senile dementia and called them all by the names of Celtic enchantresses.

'You are gone,' Triona whispered as she dropped a garland of rue on to her mother's casket. 'But your family goes on, and, as the eldest, I will never allow it to be scattered or subjugated by its enemies. This I promise, by the name that is now lost, and the love of the six sisters, which will endure all things.'

11

By the time of Triona's letter from Cornwall, the sisters had gone through various changes, although their relationships with the male sex were volatile because they insisted on respect and equality and the male sex was not ready for this. And Coldharbour drew them. Sophie, after her marriage broke down, had obtained the post she always wanted as head of the local school, a screech-owl's flight from the broken stones of the abbey. Dawn lived in Stepney as many single mothers do, but took her two daughters out to see Sophie because of the country air. Only Chantal never came, because she was lying low in foreign parts, and Nuala, because she was laid low in one of Myles Overton's prisons.

Coldharbour was never rebuilt after the last fire and afforded little in the way of shelter. But they came there just to watch the ivy twining through the fallen masonry, the jackdaws and wrens nesting in ivy-covered masonry that had yet to fall. Perhaps three or four evenings a week they might find themselves walking on the downs. Then their untended steps would tend along those same well trodden tracks, down from the ridge of the escarpment to the valley and the stalactite bridge, up past laurel and holly brakes to the now desolate lawns out of which the ruin ranged and reared. Here the past met the present, and old friends, too, could feel comfortable meeting. Neill, as Karen's ex-boyfriend, had almost been part of the family in the old days, and began to become so again. He and Oswald Hawthorne were still friends. Perhaps their increasingly unlikely friendship reflected the strange confluence of lives which Coldharbour and Karen's disappearance underpinned. As for the sisters, they knew at least that they had each other, and they were tied together by something deeper and more dangerous than any of them understood.

Oswald, in contrast to the others, had gone from adolescence to mid-life crisis with nothing in between, so he clung to the sense of continuity that Coldharbour represented. To him, Karen vanished only yesterday. It was therefore surprising that he so forcefully resisted the reappearance of Triona.

'She needs our help. The other sisters have an obligation to her,' Sophie told Neill and Oswald when the three of them met at Neill's house to see what was to be done. 'Oswald – it's nothing to do with you.'

'I . . . we would have done anything for her – and she went away. She showed everyone else the way to leave.'

'That's all in the past.'

But Oswald was unable to leave the past behind. Rather he carried it with him like a snail carrying its shell, and retreated into it whenever the world grew too much for him.

'The past is all we have,' he said, between perplexity and conviction, 'and Triona abandoned it.'

'You're blaming her for things that would have happened anyway. You're blaming her for destroying a relationship which only existed in your mind. Why – you'll be blaming her next for Karen's disappearance . . . ' Neill stopped, aware for the first time that this was exactly what Oswald did blame her for. Perhaps he always had.

Although Neill respected Oswald as a friend he could not regard him as well adjusted. Oswald was the kind of person who would borrow your books and eat oranges while reading them, with the result that they came back covered in yellow acid fingerprints. Oswald was unwaveringly loyal and would die for you if necessary, but eating the oranges was something you came up against every day, whereas dying wasn't. It was not that Oswald failed to think of others, he just failed to think of details. If he stayed with you and brought you coffee in the morning, you needed a new stair carpet. Neill was not a stair-carpet-oriented person, but equally he couldn't very well leave it covered in coffee stains. So Oswald irritated him faintly both because of the stains, and because Neill didn't really want to think of himself as caring about stains, but he did. As for Oswald helping with the washing up, forget it. He put the plates in such unusual places that they were never found until years afterwards.

Oswald lived in a small house by himself and could not hold down a job. People like Oswald never come to terms with life. If they relate to people at all, they do so in a way that is too intense. They can't let go, thought Neill. It frightens people off, because people prefer to be casual. Oswald did not understand how other people thought. Neill, on the other hand, knew exactly what people were thinking at all times, and took care that what people thought he, Neill, was thinking, was what he wanted them to think he was thinking. Which is why they did not think he thought about Karen.

'Look,' said Neill, 'the letter was written on Tuesday, so she must already be on her way. She'll stay with Sophie at the schoolhouse because there are lots of spare rooms, and she doesn't have to be around more than a few days. But we ought to find out what she wants. She may be in trouble. We have a responsibility.'

'We need to stick together', added Sophie, 'like sisters.' She remembered Oswald. 'And old friends.'

Oswald clicked his knuckles with a sound like dead twigs. 'If you remember – we didn't stick together. Triona left. People said certain things before they went off to university or teacher-training college, or to take up offers of employment or voluntary service in emerging nations. But the things they said were not abided by. People allowed themselves to lose touch. They squandered their strength and creativity, and only when they were tired and bankrupt did they think of coming back.'

'As for strength,' Neill answered, 'we've always known we were not strong enough to change the world, yet too strong to be changed by it. But as for coming back – did any of us ever really leave? Didn't Coldharbour stay with us while everything else just flowed by, as an eddy maintains its position in a flowing stream? But it could be that we need Triona, as much as she needs us.'

Oswald muttered something about people making their beds and lying in them, and something about the various partners the various sisters had chosen over the years, none of whom had turned out to be Oswald. And, finally, something uncomplimentary about Peter Goodlunch.

'Oh!' said Neill. 'That's the other thing. Peter Goodlunch is dead.'

12

Peter Goodlunch, according to the authorities, had taken the easy way out. Foul play could safely be eliminated, and they gave short shrift to the rumours that his fate represented some unspeakable punishment meted out as a result of events at the Centre for Alternative Healing. And the other rumours that it represented the avoidance of some even more unspeakable punishment. There could be no connection, said the authorities, between this incident and the fact that Goodlunch's estranged wife was implicated in the theft of a valuable artefact and the release of a dangerous psychotic who was under a community-care order at the Centre. Still less with the disappearance of Triona's sister Karen Greenwood many years ago, on which the file was in any case closed. If Triona would like to contact them, said the authorities, they would be able to eliminate her from their enquiries, and the situation could be contained.

Peter Goodlunch used to say:

'When you do business with Myles Overton you always get the arse end of the deal. But even the arse end of a deal with Myles Overton can make you a millionaire twenty times over.' But although this was unquestionably true, it was not enough. Finally he had discovered what the arse end of a deal with Myles Overton really meant, and being a millionaire did not cover it.

'Perhaps', it was suggested after Peter Goodlunch's demise, 'his success was too much for him.'

And again, 'Do you think he knew something? Do you think he discovered something so nefarious that even a marketing executive could not live with it?'

Speculation was rife. 'If you ask me, Myles Overton was at the bottom of it. Someone needed to get Peter Goodlunch out of the way.'

'We'll never know.'

Whatever persuaded Peter Goodlunch to evict himself from a world in which he had until recently cut such a striking figure, it was not lack of material advantages. He had an island in Scotland, a mansion in Rickmansworth, and a yacht in Cannes. Following his strategic campaign for Myles Overton's Leisure Group, he was arguably the most respected marketing guru in the world. In the years since he was divorced from Triona his sex life was full and varied, he kept fit, and he had many friends. Investigation into his medical records failed to reveal any evidence of terminal cancer.

Why would someone in his position drive a top-end German sports car at 120 mph off the M25 and into a row of Wimpview homes? The incident attracted attention for many reasons. Peter Goodlunch's Porsche was a non-standard model souped up to his special requirements, which shot flames out of its exhausts and incinerated designer cyclists when you changed gear. Wimpview homes are not built for that kind of impact. The vehicle unfortunately ploughed through six sitting rooms one after another where families were watching the Johnny Toupée show, ironically now showing on Myles Overton's own Leisure Channel following the relaxation of ITC rules on joint ownership of media. The scale of the fatalities led to demands that sports cars should be taken off the road and three-piece suites should be equipped with steel space-frames and safety belts.

Of Peter's closest friends and mistresses only his secretary Tracey had any inkling of the underlying cause of the tragedy, and its far-reaching consequences for herself and ultimately for his ex-wife Triona and her friends. This was partly because she had a unique insight into his character and partly because he had left her a secret package explaining everything – although, he wrote, she had better keep it under her hat.

'He used to tell me sometimes that it's only when a man has achieved all he set out to achieve, that he is compelled to face himself. But until today I never understood,' Tracey told Dave Doom, Peter's original partner in Strategic Marketing Plc but now Myles Overton's right-hand man, when he came to her diplomatically two hours after the accident to explain that the firm would be sadly unable to keep her on.

'What are you getting at, darling?' said Dave Doom without a trace of endearment. 'You think when Pete faced himself he didn't like what he saw?'

'I think', said Tracey carefully, 'that Peter could be understood on many levels. People thought they understood the real Peter, but all the time it was just a front. He was a very lonely man.'

'He had his ex-wife, his mistresses. He was never hard up for a bit of totty, you can take it from me. Darling.'

'He used to say people sleep together as an alternative to getting to know each other. It's a way to relate, yet still stay strangers. Peter had no-one he could really talk to.'

'Did he talk to you?'

Tracey opened her mouth and then saw that Dave Doom was looking at her in the way he used to look at clients in the old days, when he charged them for consumer surveys which had never actually been done, since Dave Doom found it more cost-effective to make up the statistics himself. Suddenly she felt frightened. Strategic Marketing was no longer the friendly little company she joined before Myles Overton took a direct although undisclosed interest in it. The three original partners, the third being a rather ineffectual managing director, had become secretive and suspicious, most of all towards each other. Although there was more money than ever before, they were close-fisted and went through each other's expenses with pocket calculators. They tried to find out the access codes on each other's electronic organizers.

Each was sure the others were entering into secret arrangements with Myles Overton. Each was trying to do exactly that on his own account, and believed that he was the only one who really had a relationship with Myles Overton anyway. Myles Overton had that effect on people. Nobody liked him; everybody wanted to be his friend. Myles Overton encouraged this rivalry and back-biting and spread rumours confirming the worst fears of each of the partners in turn. But when Dave Doom moved off the board of Strategic Marketing altogether and was employed directly by Myles Overton's office, and an insider nominated by Myles Overton effectively supplanted the ineffectual managing director, it was clear which way the land lay. And suddenly Tracey guessed that, whatever she knew, it was too much for her own good.

'Peter didn't tell me anything,' she said finally. 'But I sensed his need, and his inner fear . . . '

'I hear what you're saying,' Dave Doom told her. 'But things have gone beyond all that. Myles Overton's got involved. He wants results. Like, yesterday. You've got no reason to be afraid of me, darling. I only want to help. Pete's death can't be easy for you.'

'I don't know what you mean. Besides, five minutes ago you said I was fired.'

'Did I say you were fired? But you and me understand each other better than that, darling. One hand washes the other. Tell me what you know, and I'll be able to protect you. Now – what do you say?' As Dave Doom spoke these words, however, he had edged round the desk and now his long arm clawed out and closed on the sleeve of Tracey's jumper.

'Get *lost!*'

She twisted and left the garment with him, grabbed her bag and the package from Peter Goodlunch and fled, using the stairs not the lift and hearing her former employer's footsteps behind her, punctuated by shouts of:

'Company property!'

If something was worth dying for, it was definitely worth not giving to Dave Doom. Tracey did not stop until she reached a McDonalds, and in the hard shadowless light she ordered a regular size Cola and fries, and unfolded the piece of paper she had first unfolded an hour ago in the ladies toilet at Strategic Marketing.

When Peter Goodlunch gave her the letter and told her to open it if anything happened to him, she assumed he meant no more than missing a diary appointment or having his cell-phone go down. Yet even then she experienced foreboding. With the long hours and frequent minor crises of working on the Myles Overton account he had been isolated from his family and his mistresses, who Tracey thought were grasping bitches anyway. So they had become close – although for a long time neither realized it.

Tracey knew all the secrets of the company, and how it paid Doom International (Zurich) SA for non-existent 'research services' a million dollars a year to foil the tax-man. She knew a considerable amount even about the Myles Overton account. For example she was aware of what the ineffectual managing director had to do in the old days to persuade one of Myles Overton's contracts managers even to give them the introduction, and how sore he had been afterwards. But none of this was different from normal marketing consultancy practice. There was something else, Tracey thought, and over the past months she had looked on helplessly as it gnawed at Peter Goodlunch's nerves and gave him spots on his chin. Something which was all too evidently connected with the message she now clutched.

> Dear Tracey *[it began]*, by the time you read this, the Porsche and I will be spread half-way across Sussex and my account with life will be closed. Some will say I have taken the easy way out, but had there been any alternative, believe me, I would have given it serious consideration. As things are, my only regret is in leaving you, without ever having told you what I hope you have always known.
>
> Tracey, I don't expect you to understand everything I say, much less what I have done, but bear with me, because your fate and that of countless others may depend on it. Perhaps it's only when a man has achieved all he set out to achieve that he is compelled to face himself. But when I faced myself I knew I could never again face you, since my love for you is all that sets me apart from the morass of sham, fraud, and counterfeit that my existence has become. All the same, I can't expose Myles Overton without putting you in danger, and that I could never do.
>
> I must tell you now that, although my career has been a succession of unspectacular crimes and trivial deceptions, in recent months I have run up against something so far-reaching, and so incalculable in its evil, that by comparison I am St Francis of Assisi. Time is running out, and even now I think I am being watched, so I must cut this letter short just as I must cut short my life itself, before I compound the immense damage I have already done.
>
> From now on, it's up to you. You must find the six sisters whose coming was foretold, and through them a research psychologist called

Neill Fife. Tell him I sent you, and give him the ring you once gave me as a token of our friendship, which I am returning with this letter. He will know what to do for the best, and will prove a good friend in the trials to come.

And now I can say, and do, no more. A man needs friends to overcome his enemies, but he needs enemies to overcome himself. But in this conflict I am the one who has been overcome, and now there is only one path for me to follow. Do not forget me, and whatever the future reveals about the past, try not to lose your belief in the present we shared together, for it was the happiest time of my life.

Your friend,
Peter.

So it was that Tracey, her puzzlement for the moment immersed in sorrow, first learned that Peter Goodlunch returned the affection she had for so long believed hopeless. Things like that were always happening to Tracey, although not usually in such a spectacular way.

'It's because people don't take me seriously,' she said to herself. Although stricken with grief and not a little frightened, she could not help feeling extremely annoyed that he could not have been more straightforward about the whole thing. But this is not the way of people who work in marketing. Their entire profession revolves around a panoply of terms and techniques designed to state the obvious in such a way as to make it wholly unintelligible.

Tracey sat in McDonalds so long that all the ice melted in her regular-size Cola. She looked at the letter, and the ring she had once given him, passing it off as a joke. It was not a joke, because set in the ring was a tiny pearl found in her navel when, as an infant, she had apparently been set adrift in a wicker basket, and was washed up on a lonely beach on the Isle of Orkney. Stories that this involved some Gaelic shaman were the result of confusion following reports of a baby brought ashore by the Old Man of Hoy, which were interpreted as referring to an individual rather than a landmark. Yet Tracey always suspected there was something out of the ordinary about her origins, and that the pearl was the key to some secret inheritance. Peter Goodlunch, however, did not know all this. She had given it to him on a sudden impulse during a business trip to Dublin because she was sure they were going to become lovers and she wanted him to have the most valuable thing she possessed. But somehow the phone rang and it was Myles Overton needing Peter to go back to London on the next flight, and the moment was lost.

Now, it was lost forever. Yet more might be lost, if Dave Doom caught up with her. Maybe loss was all part of growing up, because although Tracey had aged since the morning, she was still only nineteen. She did not know where to go, or who to turn to. Dave Doom would even now have his heavies out looking for her. The six sisters meant nothing to Tracey, for Peter Goodlunch had omitted to mention that one of them was his ex-wife, perhaps out of some misplaced delicacy of feeling. She herself had no sisters, she reflected, as a result of being adopted under such unusual circumstances. And Neill Fife was only a name.

13

When Triona fell asleep on the train she dreamed she was being towed across a frozen landscape by fourteen dragons, one for each of the fourteen cylinders of the diesel engine. Where she was going was obscure, until all at once she found herself back in one of the secret rooms at the Centre for Alternative Healing. Or perhaps a yet more secret room elsewhere. And Karen was there too, seemingly bound and helpless, and Triona asked her about Leatherwing, but could not be satisfied by the answer.

'He's everything and nothing to me. We're each other's destiny. I'll never be rid of him. Nowadays he is all I exist for, yet he's my destroyer.'

'You speak almost as if you love him.'

'Can you think of any reason I'd be here, if I didn't?'

'You let him take you?' Triona was lost for words.

'Things aren't that simple.'

Karen turned away, the gold manacles that held her wrists to the bedstead clanking as she shifted position. Triona could see that hung about the walls were numerous handcuffs, tawses, instruments of torment and PVC thigh-boots, as unlike the Wellingtons they had worn in the woods around Coldharbour as one piece of plastic footwear can be unlike another.

'Thank you for coming, Triona. You'll never know how much it means to me. But there's nothing you can do. You must leave now, because soon he'll come for me, and if he finds you here . . . '

Triona smiled. 'Neill and our four sisters are guarding the passage. They'll buy us a little time. We're going to get you out of here.'

'It's too late, Triona. Don't you understand? My life belongs to him, as his belongs to me.'

'I know you don't love us now, and you can't love us. But people think because love is only one word, it only describes one thing. We can't compete with Leatherwing, for he takes what he wants. I knew that right from the start, when I caught you looking out of the windows towards the open sea beyond the downs, just as if I wasn't there. But I told myself, "Don't give up. Just because love is one word, it doesn't mean it only applies to one thing." So you see, here I am. I'm going to help you whether you want me to or not. If I have to fight Leatherwing, I'll do that too, and the others will help me. But first of all, we're going to get you away from this place. Because there's one thing that we have in our possession that neither Leatherwing nor his shadowy clan have any conception of.'

'What's that, Triona?' For the first time a hopeful note entered Karen's voice. None knew better than herself about the smallest fragment of Caryddwen's cauldron, although she could not conceive how Triona and the others might have gained access to it.

'Bolt croppers,' answered Triona in her dream, succinctly, if disappointingly. 'Oswald?'

With dexterity surprising in someone who didn't have the reputation for it, Oswald Hawthorne emerged from the shadows and cut away Karen's bonds. She did not try to prevent him, but looked at him with a kind of sadness.

'We'll never get out. You'll all die for nothing.'

'If we did die, it wouldn't be for nothing. But we aren't planning on giving up the ghost just yet. Don't forget Neill has studied our situation, and knows a trick or two of his own. There are disused mine workings beneath this building, and if we can just reach the lower levels there'll be no stopping us. Or, as a last resort, we can always slide down Finbar

Direach's beard!'

'For the last time, both of you, please leave me here. You don't realize how things stand. I'll be tied to him wherever I am, and I'll bring terrible danger to all of you. If you try to save me, the attempt will betray you to him, despite all I can do.'

'As to that, we can sort it out in due course. But now – there is no time to lose!' Helped by Oswald, Triona dreamed she took her sister in her arms. Karen was almost as light as a dream itself – her whole body weighed not more than a few pounds. Her face was pale and her breath against Triona's neck was unnaturally hot. But there was no more argument left in her and she clung to them as they carried her down the steep passage to where the others were waiting. As they descended, they stepped over Peter Goodlunch's body, but Triona could not bring herself to feel any emotions she felt were appropriate.

At the end of the corridor there were others waiting. She recognized Chantal, Damien Lewis, Nuala, and Dawn. But the dream grew hazy, and they all seemed to have foxes' ears, and they told her that Karen could not leave at present, for she had been too long with Leatherwing, and it was not safe to be alone with her.

14

The night after they received Triona's letter and Oswald said that she couldn't come, there was snow on the ground and the wind was whisking dead leaves through the underbrush. Shadows ran across the downland like a fleet of dark ships, and nobody could rest easy in their mind.

'Life', said Oswald, 'is a flightless eagle, staring up at an airless sky.'

'People build their own prisons,' said Neill, 'with the labour of their hands.'

'You mean Coldharbour?' Oswald asked.

'I mean everywhere.'

They sat side by side and rubbed their chins in their hands and considered the human condition, and in particular the impact upon it of the passage of time.

'We're not growing any younger,' said Neill. 'And still we have not done what we were put on earth to do.'

'I haven't done anything,' said Oswald. 'I'm an accountant.'

'Most people would say the opposite about me. There was an article in *Psychology Tomorrow* saying I'd crammed into one lifetime the contents of four – and still found an hour to give them an exclusive interview. My work has been used in negotiations at the highest levels of the international community, I'm on a dozen committees and quangos and I've been consulted, in my time, even by Myles Overton, albeit indirectly, through his marketing department. My positive thinking book *Life Outside the Hourglass* has topped best-seller lists in thirty-six countries. But sycophants are one thing, and truth is another. I move in the most elevated circles, but deep inside I know they are still, in the end, circles. In the long empty reaches of the night even I experience a pervading sense of desolation, and more than once I've thought of taking the same road as Peter Goodlunch, although possibly in a less ostentatious vehicle.'

'I don't like to be maudlin, but since I was fired from my last job for adding up the figures wrong, the same thought sometimes occurs to me, especially when I'm standing in the queue at the social security office. Our paths have diverged, yet they're strangely parallel.'

'Still, I've got the feeling there's unfinished business for both of us, before we can put the final full stop to the terrible sentence of life.'

'I know what you mean. But let's walk down the overgrown pathway and past the cracked wishing well, so we can feel the breeze on our faces. It's on occasions like this that time means nothing, although under normal circumstances it seems to mean so much.'

The two friends, deep in thought, made their way through the brambly growth where once earls and abbots strolled in philosophical debate, or poets and courtesans gambolled in opiate-driven euphoria. The wishing well stood in what was once a rose garden, but briars now possessed it entirely, along with convolvulus, bindweed, and vetches.

'I wish . . . ' began Oswald, unwittingly laying his arm on the crumbling structure which, coincidentally, had a design not unlike Caryddwen's cauldron itself. 'I wish—'

But to the surprise of both, Oswald's wish was evidently so strong and profoundly felt that it broke the already cracked wishing well in two pieces, and a cloud of dust and debris momentarily filled the glade and blotted out the sun. When the air cleared a little, it revealed a fully grown woman standing where the wishing well had been. She wore a red Dior dress with a dark shawl, high boots and a goat-skin handbag, and was brushing the dust out of her flaxen curls, her eyes brim-full of strange understanding, yet weary with the sights they had looked upon.

'*Triona!*' said Oswald, as if the one word contained as much meaning as the hold of a full-rigged ship struggling to gain the pierheads of its native harbour after a wild and world-girdling voyage.

Nobody embraced.

'Now then,' said Neill, 'I think it would be a good thing if we made our way back to the little pub by the Stepping Stones. Sophie's there and Dawn's come up from London with the kids and Rufus Stone, her reporter friend. And I asked Damien Lewis to come, from the old days, even if he is a bit of a Jack-the-Lad. We could walk, but I have my Isuzu nearby, and perhaps the drive would do us good.'

15

Once they were all together, Triona carefully told the full story of the destruction of Caryddwen's cauldron, the Centre for Alternative Healing, the unusual events that befell her there, and the final escape by shinning down a miraculous outgrowth of beard produced by a homeopathic baldness remedy.

'You escaped death', Damien Lewis put in, 'by a whisker.' He never let slip the opportunity for a smart-arsed remark. It had got him into difficulties more than once, and currently he was in trouble with the authorities and Neill was helping him.

'I'll drink to that,' said Rufus Stone, which these days was about all he did.

They asked each other whether they had heard about Peter Goodlunch, being careful of Triona's feelings since she had after all been married to him. Then the conversation moved to more general topics. Who was shacked up together and who was in prison; who had just formed a band? The inevitable catching up needed between acquaintances who have not seen each other for so long a period. Only when these matters had been cleared up did they return to Triona's narrative.

Sophie, who as a teacher was the most forthright, said:

'The story about Finbar Direach is a good one, Triona. Only, you'll understand we can't quite take it at face value. If he escaped with you, where is he now? There's no doubt you've been under a great deal of stress recently, and—'

'You don't believe me.'

'We're not saying that – but remember, you've been away a long time,' said Dawn. 'You can't just turn up and say, "Trust me, I'm a Heritage Commissioner." We think you only got that through being in the Network of Successful Women anyway. Things move on. People change. Beliefs we may once have held – not that I'm saying we ever held them – but even beliefs are not for ever.'

'I can see, in the cold light of day, that it might seem strange to have met a former confidant of the Tuatha de Dannaan, drunk from a piece of Caryddwen's cauldron and promised to find the remaining piece in order to save Karen from Leatherwing and civilization from collapse. I was always the cynic and the modernizer, when the rest of you were swapping tales of Druids, banshees and gruaghres, to say nothing of Leatherwing himself . . . '

'That was then, and this is now,' said Sophie uneasily. 'I'm not denying we swapped a few tales, but you need to get it in perspective. There have always been stories about Leatherwing and Coldharbour. They go right back to Shelley's and Byron's time. The two of them were going to write an epic on the subject, if Jane Austen hadn't complained to the authorities so they had to escape to Italy and got killed. But these are only stories.'

'Some of us', added Dawn, with a pragmatism born of unrelenting motherhood, 'have to live in the real world.'

'So you don't believe I'm speaking the truth?'

'We believe you believe you're speaking the truth. Obviously something untoward happened to you, and this Finbar Direach was linked to it. But from the physical description, it sounds just as likely that the person you encountered was Seamus "Eight Pints" McGallon, front man of the celebrated Celtic punk band that will always be known as The Pits. You've been under a lot of stress lately, what with Peter Goodlunch, and . . . well, think about it.'

'If I hadn't been told by a contemporary of Tuatha de Dannaan, how would I know the full history of the abbey, and the reason it's always proved the downfall of those associated with it?'

'I beg your pardon, but no-one knows the origins of Coldharbour. It says so in all the guide books. The records were lost in the Dark Ages.'

But Finbar Direach had told Triona of events long before that, for he suspected she might have difficulty making them believe her, and he felt that if she were in a position to supply a credible and down-to-earth explanation for the strange paradoxes that surrounded Coldharbour Abbey, it would make her other claims seem less far-fetched. Unfortunately the explanation did involve some characters more usually associated with legend, but, as he pointed out, the greatest test of truth in a story is whether it has the quality of entertaining people.

16

Finbar Direach's account of the origin of Coldharbour referred to a time long past, when, he said, two young blades of the Tuatha de Dannaan set out in their boat to try their hands at a little fishing, and chance their arm against the finny denizens of the turbulent deep. As luck would have it they hung their nets on the port side, and little did they catch except for the white spindrift that lay on the waves, which vanished and ran through their fingers as soon as they brought the nets inboard. They hung their nets to starboard and scarcely fared any better, for they caught nothing but the west wind which cat's-pawed the sullen swell, and it escaped again the minute they hoisted the meshes aloft.

'The fish are not running today,' observed Oisin. 'Or they are not swimming. Do not ask me to explain the habits of such watery individuals as fish seem to be. Suffice it to say that today we shall haul home neither gurnard nor guppy, but must content ourselves with an insubstantial fare of wind and water until the sunset obliges us to pull for the harbour mouth.'

'You may be correct,' replied Angus. 'And if you are, it would be a fool who would contradict you. But what if we make towards that old lobster-pot marker hard on the lee bow, and try if we cannot profit from another's diligence?'

Thinking this would be a fine joke, they plied their oars with vigour and were quickly up with the solitary marker, to which, as rapidly, they made fast the bows of their little boat. Having accomplished this, they began to pull up the line without further ado, to determine whether they could indeed reap benefit from the labour of someone else's hand. Reluctantly at first the cable came home, and many were the weedgrown fathoms they heaved up from the deep, until they were beginning to wonder whether there was any end to it.

Then, just as their concentration was beginning to slip, the rope terminated in a running splice to a length of silver chain, which was shackled in turn to an intricately crafted lobster pot of burnished gold, embossed with strange runes and hieroglyphs the like of which the two brothers had never encountered in their waking lives. But stranger still, in the centre of the golden lobster pot sat a magnificent green spider crab with seventeen baleful red eyes and great jagged claws that could crush a man's wrist – or worse.

'I am getting a bad feeling about this,' said Angus. 'And I'm for throwing it back at once, for like as not, in doing what we've done, we have stirred up some kind of trouble which was better left alone.'

'Throwing it back would be an option,' agreed Oisin. 'But I'm for bashing its shell in with the back of an oar, and feasting on its marrow and entrails.'

So that is what they decided to do. But no sooner was their meal complete than a great rushing was heard from beneath the waves, and Mannannan Mac Llyr Mac Lugh himself appeared before them, fierce and furious, for this was in the days before Queen Maeve of Skye had him snared in her own lobster pot.

'What has been done today cannot easily be undone!' shouted Mannannan Mac Llyr Mac Lugh. 'For you must know that this was no ordinary spider crab you've just devoured, but my own son by the sea goddess Ran. What you took to be a golden lobster pot was her womb, in which the unborn child was slowly growing to maturity.'

As Mannannan Mac Llyr Mac Lugh made clear, what had occurred constituted an outrage, even though no malice had been involved. Indeed, the brothers considered themselves lucky that their punishment was not of the capital kind, for Mannannan Mac Llyr Mac Lugh was not known for his forbearance. As it was, Caryddwen interceded on their behalf and in the end they were instead sentenced to be indentured as labourers for a year and a day to the first ordinary man they met on the road, for no more than the pay and conditions two common journeymen might command.

It happened that as they walked inland to face this encounter, their paths crossed with a venerable monk dressed in a hood and a cowl, who had spent a long lifetime wandering the islands with no more goods and possessions than the gown upon his back and the book in his hand, relying on the charity and goodwill of others for the means to keep body and soul intact.

'I have wandered a thousand miles,' said the old monk. 'But in the twilight of my years, what would I not give for my own little stone chapel, that a couple of hulking lads like you could easily construct? A haven and shelter to make my religious observances without fear of human intrusion or the remorseless depredations of wind, rain, and bad weather.'

At first, the monk was most solicitous to his two artisans, plying them with the best that his meagre trade of begging and scrounging could afford, and never secreting away a gold or a copper coin for his own use, when he could pass it across to them as part of their conditions of hire. Gradually, however, as the little oratory rose from amongst the scrub and began to take shape as a robust and handsome construction, the monk, who had never possessed anything in his life, began to experience the anxiety and jealousy of ownership.

'I hope it's clear in your minds that although you are building this, it's mine, and mine alone,' he told them. 'And whilst I don't mind you sleeping in it while it's being constructed, don't think that when it's done you can sponge off me as unpaying guests or simply come and go as you please, taking advantage of my easy-going disposition.'

When work commenced on the roof and the three of them finally had some protection against the elements, he changed his mind about the sleeping arrangements and took to insisting the two labourers should make their beds outside in the rain. They were not from that time forward allowed into the sheltered part of the building unless the management of the site absolutely demanded it. Further, he began to conceal some of the funds he had been able to acquire through his begging activities, reasoning that, once complete, the chapel would require a certain amount of expenditure on upkeep. He now gave them only the minimum amount of food he felt was consistent with survival and a reasonable work output. He exchanged the surplus provisions for a large iron clock which he hung in the chantry in order to ensure they did not try to cheat him by starting work too late, or finishing too early.

When, finally, a year and a day had passed and the building was complete, the monk saw how beautiful and stately it was and became filled with a terrible malice against his two workers. For it is common that people feel resentment towards someone who has done them a good turn, and consider themselves compromised by those who have helped them. He began to tell himself that the building was created by his own efforts, and that he had his work cut out supervising the two lazy good-for-nothings it had been his misfortune to be saddled with. So he drove them off with most un-monklike curses and some fierce dogs which he procured from nearby farmers, and warned them that if they ever came within seven miles of his property again, he would not be so lenient.

The two young scions of the Tuatha de Dannaan, although of an easy, open character and not inclined to bear a grudge, could not help feeling they had been treated shabbily for the excellent job they had done. Certainly, there was no building like the little chapel, in the whole length and breadth of the archipelago. 'Upon the monk we can exact no retribution,' they said. 'What happened between him and us was perhaps only what we deserved as a result of our ill-advised actions in the matter of the spider crab. Besides, it would be improper to wish any baleful destiny on the place as long as it remains dedicated to ecclesiastical use.'

Yet for future generations it was a different story, because the two aggrieved workers put confusion on the building, upon those who occupied it, and upon all subsequent works on the same site. The structure frequently burnt down and had to be rebuilt, but because of its unusual reputation it went on to become the dwelling place of a succession of colourful individuals. Not least of them was the romantic poet Percy Bysshe Shelley, at one of whose wild parties Lord Byron claimed to have had Jane Austen in the arboretum, which was why she complained to the authorities. Also, on the more sinister side, a story grew up associating it with Leatherwing. According to this legend, he was empowered to steal away on her sixteenth birthday the darkest daughter of the house, as a grim retribution for the ignominy that the brothers had suffered in the building of it.

'But whether Leatherwing needs the permission of a half-forgotten story to unleash his shadowy power, I can't even guess,' finished Triona. 'I'm only saying to you what Finbar Direach said to me, and as you can see, it's not the sort of thing a person would make up.'

17

When they had heard this narrative, they could doubt no longer the words that Triona spoke, the reality of her encounter with Finbar Direach and, consequently, the obligation upon them all to detect and discover the remaining piece of the lost cauldron of Caryddwen, if they ever hoped to see Karen again or save the world from desolation and dissolution.

'As a psychologist,' said Neill, 'I consider the contents of the human mind are more real – in the most important sense of the word – than the contents of the world beyond it. In honour of the eponymous Bishop I call the mind a sort of Berkeleycard, which draws credit from our inner being to purchase experiences from a remote, external and ultimately unknowable reality.'

'The story', said Oswald, 'was a great deal more intelligible than your explanation of it.'

'You've obviously never studied literary criticism or you wouldn't find that surprising. In any case, explanations are a way of paying one person's debt with another person's IOU. Nothing in life is absolute. Let me put it this way. The old Druids were no fools, and after careful observation of human existence their conclusion was that the mind only exists in so much as it thinks. Therefore, said they, its existence is nothing more nor less than the existence of the thoughts that occupy it. So if two minds have the same thought, they are the same mind, however distant in space or time. But thoughts are like the dark rooks that fly home to the elm groves at evening, and they maintain their own communities and commonwealths, rather than occurring in isolation. What are these communities and commonwealths (demanded the Druids) but human souls? But, they added darkly, some may be inhuman souls as well, for is there not a rumour that the people of the earth were originally designed as prisons for miscreant spirits? It is all one, said the Druids, but follow our path with diligence – for its name is Peace.'

'I'll need some time to think about that,' said Oswald.

'It seems to me', Sophie said, 'that we're already in danger, and time may be short. There's one piece of the cauldron still to be found, and there were six sisters. But Karen's already vanished, Chantal's abroad and we don't know whether she's alive or dead, and Nuala's locked up. Mother used to say we were the oldest family in Britain, and we'd know our destiny when the time came. But if you ask me, someone's getting their destiny in first. We all need to make our own decisions, but as a teacher my entire life has been dedicated to uncovering the world's secrets, and I'll help Triona do whatever has to be done.'

'For the sake of my own little daughters, I'll do what I can,' Dawn said, stroking their small heads. 'Although, as a single mother, I don't even get time to draw breath.'

'And I'll do what I can too,' said Damien Lewis, although everyone knew he could not become actively involved at present due to the problems he had with the authorities.

'And me,' Oswald said finally.

'That'll help a lot,' Dawn said exchanging glances with Sophie, although the irony was unkind.

'Yet we need to know more about Finn Direach, and the cauldron itself. We need to read *The Golden Bough*, and *The White Goddess*,' Sophie said.

'And *The Lord of the Rings*,' said Damien.

'I think', said Sophie, 'that some things are best understood in a figurative sense.'

'Figurative or not, what confronts us is of great importance,' Neill told them, for he had an inveterate tendency to give instructions. 'I suggest we assemble at Coldharbour this very night and make whatever plans we can. If I'm right, this task is crucial in our relationship to each other, to Coldharbour, and to Karen in whatever strange region she now inhabits. There'll be those who try to stand in our way. The authorities may have guessed that Triona came here, and, as we all know, Myles Overton is hand in glove with the authorities. Be there at midnight, after the pubs close. Until then, keep your eyes open for anything unusual.'

18

If Neill thought the authorities or Myles Overton were concentrating on Triona Greenwood, he was making a grave miscalculation which would later return to haunt him. The authorities and Myles Overton had other fish to fry.

'I don't care how you flaming do it, find Tracey Dunn! And until you've flaming got her, don't flaming bother coming back!' Myles Overton roared down the phone at Dave Doom. Thankfully he was unaware Dave Doom had let her escape him when he was close enough to grip her sweater.

'You have to help me find Tracey Dunn,' Myles Overton urged Linden Richmont in gentler tones, for she meant more to him than he cared to admit. 'Be shrewd. Use contacts. Go undercover if the direct approach won't work, because I've got that flaming drongo Dave Doom doing the strong-arm stuff. Check out the angles. I'm relying on you, girl, because there's a side to this business that could really put my ding in a sling.'

'We must find Tracey Dunn,' agreed the authorities. 'It's in everyone's interest that nothing happens to Myles Overton's ding.'

Tracey hid as an unmarked car cruised ominously past, its occupants looking this way and that. She needed to get out of town. The London directories listed several hundred Fifes and even the N Fifes ran to dozens. Doubtless Peter Goodlunch meant to give better directions, but was interrupted by the need to commit suicide. She made her way down Shaftesbury Avenue and into Charing Cross Road, but then the lucky ring Peter Goodlunch had returned to her came into its own. She found herself looking into a bookshop where a large dump-bin displayed several hundred hardback copies of a well known self-help book called *Life Outside the Hourglass*, remaindered at a fraction of the publisher's recommended price. *This book will change your life!* boasted the promotional material. But there was enough biographical detail about the author for Tracey to know what she had to do. *Coldharbour*, she said to herself, repeating it over and over, so that, after she crossed the footbridge to Waterloo, she would not forget which station to ask for.

19

When the knock came at Neill's door he was not surprised. He was expecting something of the kind. Triona could easily have been followed, although he guessed they would not send the heavies in. At least not at first. They would use the subtle approach, a friend of a friend, a hard-luck story, anything to wheedle their way into his confidence, and learn the plans he had made.

'Hide behind the Chesterfield!' he told Triona. 'And Oswald – you hide in the woodshed. I'll deal with this.'

Sure enough, when he opened the door, a young girl was standing before him. As a trained psychologist he instantly knew that anyone who took such pains to look so completely unlike a spy for Myles Overton could only be one thing. She's a spy for Myles Overton, he thought, or I'm Sigmund Freud. Yet the situation must be handled carefully.

'Doctor Neill Fife?' the girl said. She wore a light coat and held a carrier bag containing a few essentials. That was all. She was trembling from the cold.

'Well, I'm not Sigmund Freud.'

'May I come in?'

'To be honest, I'm in rather a hurry.'

'I'm Tracey Dunn. I was Peter Goodlunch's secretary. Well, mmm, friend. It's taken me nearly four hours to get here from London. I think they're looking for me.'

Clever, thought Neill, very clever. Her body language told him she was cold and frightened; that she would like him just to take her into his arms like a lost nineteen-year-old, so she could cry into his tweed jacket. But of course that was exactly what she would want him to think.

'Peter who?' said Neill.

'Look – the letter he wrote me, and he asked me to give you this ring. Apparently it's very important. It's something you're about to start looking for. With some sisters. It's all here in black and white.'

'It's very nice,' Neill replied examining the ring closely, for he would not have been surprised if it concealed some form of listening device. 'But you can tell whoever sent you that this is not about rings, or pearls.

And you can tell them that next time they want to speak to me, they can come themselves instead of sending some bimbo, and they should try to get the story right.' And with a magnificent gesture, he stood back and slammed the door.

'That', he told Oswald and Triona, 'is how it's done.'

Triona breathed a long breath. 'Well, I'm glad one of us is a psychologist!'

But Oswald, who was only an accountant, watched the young girl turn away from Neill's opulent Virginia-creeper-covered porch and make her way down the gravel drive. He could see by the motion of her shoulders that she was crying. It made him feel a bit funny inside. Then he drew the curtain, which meant he missed seeing Linden Richmont drive by and miss seeing Tracey Dunn, who dodged into the bougainvillea just in time.

'I think we can congratulate ourselves on a good evening's work,' Neill said, feeling rather pleased with his actions.

But time would show the incorrectness of his conclusion.

20

Later that night, Neill cut a hazel wand from a nearby copse and drew a circle in the dark leafy loam while the others watched in curious anticipation. 'We have a year,' he told them, for he had learned from Triona that the last lost fragment needed to be recovered before the three thousandth anniversary of the Tuatha de Dannaan arriving in Britain. 'We have a year, and that may not be one minute too long. Even for six sisters and their friends, it won't be easy. To succeed at all, we must promise to be as faithful to each other as to the task itself, and to sacrifice everything, if that is the price demanded of us.'

'You can rely on a man to start drawing circles and taking charge,' put in Dawn, as a single mother and a figure not unknown amongst the radical post-feminist groups in which the spirit of Caryddwen is most palpable.

'I wouldn't worry about Neill – he loves making up rules,' Oswald consoled her. He might possibly have offered to search with her, if only to spite Triona – but she had brought Rufus Stone, who had said he would do so, and that he was prepared to drink to it.

Neill, however, was getting into his stride, for despite his scientific training he had an irrepressible sense of occasion. 'The main thing—' he pursued, before Triona could back Dawn up on the taking charge issue and start asking who'd found Finbar Direach in the first place. 'The main thing is to do all we can. But let's agree to gather here exactly twelve months from tonight, when the moon stands high in the constellation of Capricorn the goat, and winter again lies on the land like a vast frosty veil. By then it should be clear whether we've met with success, or whether through our own shortcomings or circumstances beyond our control, it's been our misfortune to fail. Yet failure mustn't enter our vocabulary, nor any euphemisms for it. When the time comes, the last fragment of the lost cauldron of Caryddwen must be placed inside this circle, and Finbar Direach will appear to collect it. If not, Karen will be lost forever, and the very purpose for which we were put into the world may be subverted and betrayed.'

When he put it that way, they all agreed the venture must be undertaken, and it must not be undertaken lightly. As if by a pre-arranged signal, each chose from the surrounding area a distinctive stone and placed it on the circumference of the circle, as a symbol of the commitment he or she was making. When these stones were set equidistant, the perimeter was further underscored by markings of sulphur and lime to ensure the wind did not erase what had been drawn, nor the rain wash it away.

'From this moment', Neill observed, 'there can be no turning back. But, at the risk of sounding like a psychologist, it's true a person ultimately becomes what they seek. So when we find what we're looking for, we should not be surprised if we find we've found – ourselves. In the meantime, we must at all costs keep our activities secret from the world at large, in case we're exposed to derision or open disbelief. That we ourselves believe in what we're doing is enough. That we believe in each other is more than enough. And now we must raise the parting glass, for already the grey fingers of dawn are reaching across the rim of the horizon, and it's time we were gone.'

A toast was quickly proposed and glasses of hogweed ale drained with a will, and seven shadowy figures, followed by their even more shadowy shadows, dispersed through the lightening dawn. Yet not before some had the impression that an eighth figure stood briefly silhouetted amongst the trees to the east of the clearing. As if the image of a beautiful but mysterious woman had momentarily formed in the unravelling twilight, and as quickly re-clothed itself in shade. Others thought, though neither they nor those who saw the woman mentioned it for fear of being laughed at, that amongst the trees to the west of the clearing there was another form. Something shaped from a billowing miasma that stained black even the darkness itself. And they thought that although its appearance was human, that was the only human thing about it.

III

The Clay Man

21

'I have purchased', announced Finbar Direach when he met Triona at a secret rendezvous, 'a bubble car. I need something inconspicuous and fuel-efficient. It is old, but the piston rings have been replaced. It will suit my purpose, and enable me to travel round the country incognito.'

'If I'm right,' said Triona, 'it'll take more than a bubble car to get me where I need to go.'

'That's no more than the plain truth. But from this moment, our paths must diverge. I cannot help directly in the trials that lie before you. I cannot say where you will next see me, nor when, except that it will be under the circumstances you least expect. What must be done is the task of the sisters themselves. If you need help, I know you have many offers.'

'Just so long as it isn't Oswald Hawthorne,' she laughed.

22

The *Mabinogion* as a complete cycle of Celtic poetry was first written down during the twelfth century. But, Sophie told Triona, it is so filled with inaccuracies and irrelevancies that the serious scholar might shout out loud with frustration. One wonders, she said, whether the original authors understood the human condition at all. In the *Mabinogion*, expropriation of people's sisters quickly resulted in them invading Ireland to put matters right, and even turning themselves into a magic bridge. The question of babysitters or supply teachers did not arise. Perhaps this was why Finbar Direach understood nothing of practicalities, and wanted the sisters to act immediately. He told Triona he knew little about the hazards they would encounter, and could reveal little of what he knew.

'But you may have to face the Clay Man,' he told her. 'And you'll need all your strength for the job.'

'Never mind strength,' Dawn and Sophie said when Triona reported this. 'We need notice. You can't expect—'

'Last night, at Coldharbour, you said I could count on you,' Triona reminded them. 'You told Neill that only the love of sisters and the loyalty of friends would enable us to prevail.'

'We still say that. We just need a bit of time. This isn't the *Mabinogion*. We can't just drop everything and—'

'Are we sisters, or aren't we? Don't we all still dream of Karen? And worse? Don't we all want to find out the truth?'

'We're not saying we won't go – we just have to make some arrangements,' repeated Dawn, who was apportioning sponge fingers, repairing an injured knee, and putting batteries in a toy banshee. 'I can't dump the kids off just like that.'

'You've got a sling, haven't you? All single mothers have a sling. Bring them along!'

'There might be danger. When you're in my position, you look at your kids and you think, I'm all they've got, and they're all I've got. This Clay Man. Sounds dodgy, I would say. And believe me, in the inner city, I've met my share of dodgy blokes.'

'Oh, you can't believe everything Finbar Direach says. I'm not even sure you can believe *anything* he says. He says he's just bought a bubble car. I don't know about any Clay Man. Maybe I'm just playing along with Finn to get to the truth about Karen. Clay men? Fragments of a magic cauldron? Come off it!'

'But *you* believe in them, for all that.'

'I can't help it, ever since I drank from a fragment of Caryddwen's cauldron, which made clear what had always been obscure, and obscure what was previously clear. That's why I'm the only person who can see

Finbar Direach as he really is. He thought he tricked me into taking the drink, but perhaps I tricked him into offering it. Perhaps I knew what I was doing from the moment I set out for West Penwith. Before she died and fell out of the rowan tree, our mother said our destiny would come for us. Why not meet it halfway? But it doesn't matter what we believe, it only matters what we do. I've told the Heritage Commission that after what happened at the Centre for Alternative Healing I need a break. They were very understanding.'

'You can't lie to me, I'm your sister,' replied Sophie, who had earwigged the phone call. 'You told them you were visiting Strategic Marketing at their head offices in Milton Keynes, about secret plans for a lasting monument which requires investment from the private sector. But really you want to go there because of Peter Goodlunch.'

'Well, there's some truth in that. Mark my words – that'll be where the clues are. Karen's disappearance. Peter's death. Tracey Dunn sent to spy on Neill Fife. They're all pieces of the same jigsaw.'

'Or the same magic cauldron.'

'Is there any other? Anyway, you promised you'd join me. Besides, you put a stone in the circle, so you've got no choice. With Nuala where she is, and Chantal where *she* is, I need you!'

'Well, I suppose if Neill Fife's coming . . . ' Dawn conceded. 'I mean, we've all got a soft spot for Neill, even from the old days . . . '

'He's got commitments. Oswald wants to come with us.'

'What, the little oick?'

'Shhh!'

'The little bogeynose?'

'Shhh!'

And they all laughed, as only sisters can.

23

Life is not about following white stags, exchanging spouses with enchanted kings, or invading Ireland over the honour of a princess. True, the authors of the *Mabinogion* maintained that honourable behaviour is the only way for people to succeed in being what they are. And even a modernizer like Neill Fife could not disagree with this. Yet it is easy to maintain integrity amid the grand sweep of epoch-making events and tests imposed by kings and shamans. More difficult is to be true to oneself and one's friends amid the banal minutiae of existence. For example, the humdrum business of searching a vast and untidy landscape for a small piece of a large cooking utensil.

'Yet if it's dull, boring, and humdrum you want, I'm afraid I'm your man,' Oswald told Neill the evening before he set out from Coldharbour, as they watched overhanging willow branches draw fitful eddies in the placid flow of the river, and reflected on the impermanence of human happiness, and the permanence of human unhappiness.

'Life is a rudderless ship, drawn up upon a tideless shore,' said Neill. 'But you shouldn't run yourself down. You have your own diffident charm, and your apparent tawdriness conceals a keen intelligence. Besides, where would the world be without accountants to tell us what everything's worth?'

'Perhaps you should have told that to Triona, before she ran off with Peter Goodlunch all those years ago. She fancied you, too, as all the sisters did, despite you being involved with Karen. But she thought I was an oick.'

'Isn't it time to put those days behind us? After all, Peter Goodlunch is dead, and anyway Triona dumped him a decade ago. In the end, you have to let go . . . '

This was hard for Oswald to do, because when Triona left, even though what was between them never existed in the first place, he felt his insides were wrung like a dishcloth, and his life would never be the same again. It was due to this internal wringing that he had not wanted her to return to Coldharbour, and when she addressed him directly, pretended to be looking out of the window and thinking of something else. 'Surely, as a psychologist, you must understand more about what goes on in women's minds than most?' he asked Neill.

But although Neill was married to a supermodel, even he was not conversant with every nuance of the female psyche, nor indeed the male, which is so uncannily similar to it. In particular he could never understand what they saw in Damien Lewis. 'Many modernizers believe the mind doesn't actually exist. They think it's a fiction we invent to explain the otherwise preposterous behaviour of those we meet,' he explained. 'Setting that aside, what can be said of Triona, Peter

Goodlunch, and yourself? Some say women fall in love with failure, but sleep with success. Perhaps Triona got it backwards. Some say women can never go easy, but look for meanings in every word and every gesture – for they're certain nothing happens by accident. Also, they can smell desperation a mile off. But in Triona's case the explanation might be simpler. I believe, in essence, she couldn't stay with you because you couldn't let her go, and she went to Peter Goodlunch because he didn't need her to come.'

'You think the Porsche had nothing to do with it, then?'

'Don't forget that she left Peter Goodlunch as well.'

'She used to say she was a walking contradiction, torn between her desire to be a woman and her determination to be a person. Also she said things would never have worked out with me because I put used socks back in the sock drawer and picked my nose. She said she needed some space to find out who she was.'

'Perhaps that's what we all need. On the other hand perhaps it's a piece of nonsense picked up from a self-help book. As for the nose picking, it's purely a question of values. In some circles the human bogey is considered acceptable; in others, not. Many believe the issue is whether one disposes of it discreetly into a handkerchief, or attempts to smear it on the underside of a chair. Yet we can no longer concern ourselves with trivia. We need each other now more than ever before, and I believe Triona needs you even more than she needs you not to need her.'

Oswald was silent, and the river flowed softly, murmuring as if with a thousand voices, and caressing as if with a thousand fingers the shallow weed-grown boulders of its immemorial bed. Overhead, the nightjar trilled and a single star stood beside the moon.

24

When he had thought about Neill's remarks, Oswald wanted to reach out to Triona, for she seemed suddenly vulnerable. But when he overheard her saying she wanted Neill and not himself to accompany her, he was seized by the need to behave in a sulky and resentful way. He told her he understood why she would have no use for a boring accountant who collected tin-openers and lived alone with beige curtains and a cat. He put on a teeshirt saying, 'Save Time – Die Young' and became abandoned to self-pity and listened to Leonard Cohen records, which Damien Lewis said was unhealthy, and that he should get a life. Oswald said Triona never respected him and once when they were children had attached a rope to his tree house and the other end to the saddle of a pony and pulled it down, with Oswald in it. Neill's tree house was bigger and better made than Oswald's, and Triona did not attempt to pull it down. She might, perhaps, have liked to climb up there with him, but at that time Neill had eyes only for Karen.

Oswald left Coldharbour, therefore, with an air of affront. He explained that having made a commitment to find the piece of cauldron he was honour-bound to pursue it. 'But', he said, 'you needn't think there's the slightest chance I'll succeed. I'm just going through the motions.'

As he walked towards the bus stop, Triona drew alongside him in her large car with Dawn and Sophie and Dawn's two little daughters. Perhaps Neill had told her how hurt Oswald was, or perhaps they thought they needed him after all. 'We seem to be heading in your direction. Can we give you a lift?'

'You can't give me anything to make up for what you took from me so long ago. Besides, where I'm going, I have to go alone. But if I don't return, think of me sometimes, and remind Neill to feed my cat.'

Oswald had in fact no idea where he was going, although he inwardly dreamed of success, since that would show Triona what was what. He asked everyone he met about giant cauldrons, but they shook their heads and looked at him as if he had said something odd. On the bus he talked with a beautiful young Norwegian called Solveig who happened to be looking for the last lost root of the mythical world tree Yggdrasil, but she was having no luck either. He did not know what form fragments of Caryddwen's cauldron took, or whether they could assume the appearance of other commonplace objects to deceive the senses. The original container was capacious enough to encompass an entire army. But the last fragment was the smallest, perhaps so much so that it could get stuck up someone's nose without their even noticing, and end up scraped on the underside of a piece of furniture. If one could get hold of Finbar Direach and have him reveal his secret store of already discovered fragments, one might, on the principle of the jigsaw puzzle, deduce the appearance of the absent component. But that individual, strangely, considering what he expected of Triona and her friends, seemed unprepared to put himself or his knowledge at their disposal.

Consequently Oswald's spirits were low and hope seemed merely to mock at him, but his accountant's brain never ceased to propagate ideas and hypotheses. Neill had said, 'The signs will be there – for those who know how to read them.' It occurred to Oswald that, at the Centre for Alternative Healing, people were very exercised with claims about mystical properties and unusual effects.

'I think', he reflected, 'wherever this fragment is, it will always betray itself. It can't help it. If you are a bit of Caryddwen's cauldron, in this humdrum world where education has been replaced by training and the scale and scope of human fantasy is comprehended within the price of a lottery ticket, you would want to shout out:

'Hey! Am I something else – or what?'

Where would one look for evidence of counter-intuitive activity and bizarre phenomena? Obviously in the share listings of the *Financial Times*. Clearly, one would target companies whose stock was trading at a level disproportionate to their PE (Price/Earnings) multiple. Or, for modernizers who favour a valuation better reflecting growth potential in more volatile markets, their DCF or Discounted Cash Flow analysis. If such a company could be found, there was more than a chance that the anomaly was linked to the last lost fragment of Caryddwen's cauldron.

'Or, of course, the directors could be bent,' Oswald thought, as he ran his fingers down the columns.

25

The scandal of Strategic Marketing Plc was ultimately reported as a matter of bent directors, although the truth was deeper, and more sinister, than the broadsheets unearthed. They never accused Myles Overton of direct involvement, although the company was a major supplier to his leisure operations. But word in the City was of tainting, and no more need be said.

Oswald's greatest advantage and his most secret sorrow was that people underestimated him. It created a tendency to underestimate himself, which made him oick-like and cost him the affections of Triona. 'I am', he used to say, 'a bogey beneath the chair of life – and perhaps I only get what I deserve.'

Because they underestimated him his companions expected little of his foray. He said no farewells, nor even turned his head to look at Coldharbour nestled beneath the wooded hillside, or his own little dwelling nearer the road, where for the last three years he had lived with his cat, his beige curtains, and his collection of rare tin-openers. By foot and then by public transport, he followed whatever clues he could, already beginning to suspect what lay beneath the erratic movements of Strategic Marketing shares on the OFEX market. But others also took an interest in the erratic movements of Oswald.

'Oswald Hawthorne is heading north,' whispered the first watcher. 'This could be a key move. Triona Greenwood and her sisters may intend to meet him there. They may have information that has so far escaped us. Word must be brought to Myles Overton as quickly as possible.'

'Don't show your hand too soon,' replied the second. 'For we're as likely to be punished for unwarranted alarmism, as for withholding vital facts. But keep track of him. If the last fragment is located, the shit is really going to hit the fan, and we must do whatever we have to.'

'You need say no more. But whatever happens, let's keep a low profile and from now on communicate only through secure channels. For this is the end game, and as such, it's a game no longer.'

'Oh, I forgot to mention,' added the second watcher, 'Tracey Dunn got to Neill Fife but he sent her off with a flea in her ear and we found tracks heading back towards the railway cutting. There's no reason to doubt we'll catch up with her soon, and whatever secrets Peter Goodlunch passed on to her will be ours for ever.'

Nor were these exchanges the only evidence that Oswald's progress was observed. When he reached the mainline terminus, something that resembled a bubble car was backing discreetly into the station car park. Further, as he prepared to board the northbound train, he encountered Linden Richmont, disguised as a ticket collector.

'Where are you going?'

'To Bletchley, and perhaps beyond.'

'Take my advice,' she told him softly, 'and don't go too far . . . '

But as he climbed into the carriage, he knew that this was one journey from which there could be no turning back, even if it meant carrying on to the end of the line.

26

Oswald's plan was simple but relentless. He consulted an old ordnance survey map he inherited from his father who, regrettably, never lived to see him qualify. His objective was a site at the edge of one of Britain's most prosperous industrial areas, well served by road, rail and fibre-optic cable. For although Strategic Marketing had offices in the West End, its main production facilities and call centre were out of town, and it was there, Oswald thought, that the answer must lie.

He could perhaps have masqueraded as a representative from an office equipment company, but, as an accountant, he abhorred the direct approach. Besides, everyone would be on their guard after the death of Peter Goodlunch. Therefore he made discreet enquiries and discovered that a party of auditors was just then visiting Strategic Marketing's operation, and these individuals were not known by sight either to the people at the facility, or to one another. It would be an easy matter, he thought, to cultivate the acquaintance of a member of the audit team during the journey northward, engage him in a seemingly innocuous discussion about corporate contracts and human relationships, drug his coffee, knock him unconscious with a large stone wrapped in a handkerchief, and impersonate him in order to deceive the authorities, Strategic Marketing themselves, and anyone who might be even now be on Oswald's tail.

As luck would have it, he experienced no difficulty identifying a member of the audit team when they changed trains at Bedford. The man was, like himself, of meagre build and nondescript appearance, although he also slightly resembled the front person of a leading thrash folk band. How easily, reflected Oswald, our roles could have been reversed, had he been brought up in the shadow of Coldharbour and known Neill and the rest. And, of course, Karen – for she and I had secrets none of the others knew about. Yet perhaps they kept secrets from me as well! He bit his lip. Often, even in the old days, Oswald felt an outsider. Unable to excel in martial arts like Chantal, compose plaintive ballads like Nuala, flirt like Damien, or display the broad-shouldered calm authoritativeness that made them all instinctively look to Neill for leadership.

When Karen vanished, Oswald was the last to see her alive, and so the police questioned him endlessly about the numberplate of the unmarked car he said had carried her off. They sometimes implied that there had been no unmarked car and Oswald had crushed her head with a large stone wrapped in a handkerchief, and hidden her body in concealed tunnels beneath the wishing well at Coldharbour. They had, they said, evidence connecting Oswald to a secret sect of voluptuaries who routinely killed young women in this way. But no body or concealed tunnels were found, and Oswald was left only with a terrible self-recrimination about being unable to recall the registration number. Neill said that choosing the profession of accountancy, which after all is nothing except recalling numbers, was Oswald's way of punishing himself. And that Oswald would be better off as an estate agent or a theatre critic.

'I sometimes think my only friend there was Karen,' Oswald told the member of the audit team. 'After she and Triona were gone none of the sisters wanted anything to do with me. They were derisive about 'selling out to the establishment', which is how they saw accountancy exams. But I promised my dying father I would take them, because he always wanted me to make something of myself.'

Oswald spoke awkwardly at first. Although his plan was to induce a false sense of security by pretending to engage the auditor in conversation, he was not used to talking about anything but amortizing capital expenditure or collecting unusual kitchen implements. But the stranger seemed strangely receptive and Oswald warmed to him, feeling he was somehow familiar.

'It is as though you're the friend I never had,' he said.

'We accountants need to stick together,' said the auditor. 'I can tell you, my own friends thought little enough of my decision to take up the profession. They called it humdrum. I suppose no accountant can ever explain to a non-accountant the heady thrill of a year-end reconciliation, the satisfaction of writing back an accrual, or the aesthetic gratification to be had from an aggregated cashflow report. But how does Triona fit into all this? For in your relationships with Karen's other friends I sense you were treated shabbily – a kind of emotional underdog.'

'There may have been an element of that, or they may even have secretly suspected I had a hand in whatever happened to her. That's why what took place between me and Triona meant so much. In staying with me that night, I felt, she forgave me for something I had never even done. Still, there's no point saying that in my despair over Triona I was just re-living the loss of Karen. That, in a sense, was true for each of us. The loss of Karen represented *all* loss. Just as there are foreign lands where the earth's crust is thin and the molten core boils close to the surface, so Karen seemed close to the core of all things, and in losing her we lost something at the core of ourselves.'

'Yet sometimes, one just has to let things go,' said the auditor, his eyes unfathomable. 'I myself have lost more than most people. But in becoming reconciled to loss there is much to be gained. Perhaps even freedom itself. To show what I mean I'll tell you, if you have time, the story of a young poet. I've updated it from obscure works attributed to Dyllan, the legendary Cymric bard. And although the plot is far-fetched, the motivations ring true.'

'I've got plenty of time,' said Oswald, although he thought it odd his companion had access to a text most people considered lost. 'The train doesn't come for an hour and three quarters. I'm intrigued to hear about this poet, and what happened to him.'

So the auditor began to relate how in his tender years the poet, whom for convenience he said he would call Caolte, was not well versed in manly pleasures, but was a great one for going down to the tidal river and trying his luck with the rod and reel, to see what sport was to be had among the scaly scions of the estuary.

'That's not unusual in adolescent boys,' replied Oswald. 'And no doubt a healthy and wholesome pastime. This isn't going to be about a spider crab, is it?'

The auditor ignored this remark but went on to assert that no sooner had Coalte embarked on this activity, than he felt a terrible weight and stress upon the line, as if it were snagged on some submerged obstacle. As he reeled it in, the water churned and boiled and at length he managed with superhuman effort to land an immense spiny fish of the kind usually called a John Dory.

When the fish saw there was no sense in further struggle, it miraculously found the power of speech and said, 'What you have done today is a feat of not inconsiderable strength, skill, and cunning, and I shan't deny you've got the better of me on this occasion. But in these cases I'm empowered as a child of Ran, goddess of the sea and wife to the Celtic patron of fishing and literature Mannannan Mac Llyr Mac Lugh, to grant any wish you choose to make, in return for setting me once more at liberty upon the bosom of the water.'

The auditor added that, not being experienced in matters of this kind, Caolte soon named a certain sum in silver which he felt was adequate recompense for his trouble, and would advance him in the opinion of his friends and his ability to acquire life's easements and comforts.

'It was a lucky day for him, then,' put in Oswald.

'His luck,' said the auditor wryly, 'was only just beginning.'

He said that when the arrangement was concluded to the satisfaction of both parties, Caolte lost no time in going into town with his new-found wealth. Yet he had the misfortune to fall among swindlers and chargers of extortionate prices, so that by the time the sun went down, there was nothing left of his little hoard, and precious little to show for what had gone.

'He needed a good accountant, the moral is,' Oswald observed.

The auditor agreed with this, but told Oswald how the young man returned to the spot where he had previously been so fortunate and cast his line once again. No sooner had it touched the water but there was a mighty swirling and clamour and once more, after no small contention, the great fish was hauled up upon the bank and again began to talk about terms.

'Where I went wrong before was obviously to opt for a reward of silver, rather than some more precious metal, and perhaps to settle for too small a quantity to make a fundamental difference to my life and my living,' Caolte said. Within a short space of time an agreement had been reached, and Caolte went on his way better off by a large quantity of gold coin and bullion, and the fish went on its way having regained its freedom, and, as the auditor put it, 'Who shall say which was the better off?'

For a while, he continued, Caolte lived well on what was gained by this day's work, but the sensation of accruing large quantities of wealth over a short period of time left a deep impression on him. Before long he began to yearn for a repetition of the experience, not for the money itself, but for the sense of heightened perception, of greater aliveness, in the process of gaining it. Accordingly, he took what was left of the gold to a notorious gambling house, and quickly secured a place at the richest and riskiest table. Many hands of cards and throws of dice were played that night. He saw sums change ownership that represented the entire lives and livelihoods not only of individuals but of whole communities, and credits and debits corresponding to the rise and fall of vast dynasties and empires. But as the sun rose to illuminate a grey and bitter dawn, he could not fail to notice that the pile of chips at his left hand had diminished greatly in quantity, and was, in fact, entirely gone.

'This indeed was bad luck,' commented Oswald. 'Only counterbalanced by the good luck of getting the money in the first place. In many ways life is like an accounting ledger, but the balance, at the end, is always even.'

'Even or odd,' said the auditor, 'it was with sadness not unakin to wisdom that Caolte retraced his steps to where he had previously encountered the remarkable fish.' He went on to tell Oswald how Caolte spun the lure across the surface of the water with a heavy heart and a heavier hand, thinking it unlikely that someone who has squandered two opportunities would be vouchsafed a third. But contrary to all expectation, no sooner had he cast the line than there was a commotion ten times greater than the previous occasions, and the prodigious fish leapt clear of the water, the hook firmly embedded in its lip. As before it was no easy task to land so formidable a catch, but at length the creature was dragged flapping up the foreshore and, benefiting from the same marvellous faculty of language as before, commenced to negotiate its release.

Caolte, however, was more circumspect than previously. 'Although I'm still young, I haven't been slow to learn the lessons of my last two requests. I now see that although material wealth is important and up to a point essential for happiness and popularity with the opposite sex, inner peace is even more fundamental, and can be enjoyed only in the certainty of another's affection. Therefore as my final wish I would ask neither for coin nor precious metal, but to be given a beautiful woman for my own, and experience the many benefits and blessings that flow from this.'

'Indeed, that is more valuable than money,' said the fish. 'Even so it lies in my power to do as you ask, if you'll just help me back into the water, for I doubt if we'll ever see each other again. But remember, even love means little without freedom, just as freedom means nothing without love. Human virtues are such that, to possess any one of them, one must possess all. They're like a pyramid, where the most elevated are closest together, until at the apex they converge into one. True freedom, therefore, is identical to true love, and one can never possess something, unless one can let it go, which you may take either as a piece of advice, or a warning.'

With these remarks the fish made its escape down to the depths of its watery fastness, and was never seen again. Caolte, meanwhile, walked pensively along the dike, watching the tide turn so that the waters of the ocean ran inwards through the land, and trying to make sense of what had been said. Then, where nobody had been before, he noticed a young girl hooded against the wind, who asked for his assistance in negotiating the slippery banks.

'I find I love you, and can no longer live without you,' he found himself saying before they even reached the weed-grown lock gates separating the tidal from the non-tidal reaches of the river.

'Since you say that,' the girl replied, 'I feel the same. Or even more so because I'm a woman, and women have perceptions and sensitivities even they themselves can't fathom. For rather than a simple urge to possess, they long for mutual fulfilment in a stable relationship.'

'It sounds as if this time your hero was in clover,' said Oswald. 'Good fortune literally fell into his lap!'

'Unfortunately', the auditor replied, 'things didn't go so smoothly, for the rest of Caolte's poem consists of a poignant lament for the numerous infidelities of his new love and what he saw as the perfidy of the spiny fish.' As time went on, Oswald learned, Caolte began to realize that everything he did to bring the girl closer had the effect of driving her further away. When they walked by the river, she called his attention to this and explained his possessive behaviour was preventing her feeling any love for him. Although, she said, love is a state of being, not a state of feeling, and one can easily love someone without feeling anything for them at all. It was then that he began to sense everything slipping away.

'It sounds, indeed, pretty slippery,' said Oswald.

The auditor said it was slippery enough, because she told him, 'Our love has grown too easy, like reeds upon the weir. What the fish said is true. To have one virtue, you must have them all, and to have love without freedom is as bad as to have freedom without love. Both, ultimately, must destroy us.'

By these remarks Caolte could see that her thoughts were already for rambling, and she would never rest until she escaped from both freedom and love, and surrendered to a clay man in whose indifference she could lose herself.

'That', she said to Caolte, 'is the way things have to be, until people's minds become elevated enough to see love and freedom as identical. But this will never happen until six sisters recover the last fragment of the lost cauldron of Caryddwen – if at all!'

Oswald looked at the auditor rather sharply when he reached this part of the story. He seemed to know more than he should, but this did nothing to change Oswald's plan of action. Nevertheless he did not make his move straight away, but thanked the auditor very much for the story, which he instinctively felt contained some moral lesson.

'Think nothing of it,' replied the auditor. 'I liked you the moment I set eyes on you. I saw at once the keen spirit beneath the tawdry exterior, and as we talked it occurred to me how easily our positions might have been reversed. I cannot help directly in the trials that lie before you, but I'll give you this advice. Find the Clay Man, wherever he may be, for he alone knows the whereabouts of what you seek. When you meet him, you'll need all your strength for the job, for you must strike your chest three times, and stand your ground. And now, I've said all I can. I only hope it's enough.'

But Oswald could only think of the promise he made at Coldharbour, and how he pledged no sacrifice would be too great. Not even, by implication, the sacrifice of his own integrity and good name.

'Your story was good, and your advice is better,' he replied. 'Although what use they'll be, only time can tell. None of this makes my next step any easier. At the time of my brief night with Triona I was young, and lacking in self-knowledge, and everything you say about love and freedom may be true. But now I must tell you that with the loss of Karen and then of Triona herself, the police investigation and the loneliness of a solitary existence, I've become everything I abhor. In the short time we've been speaking I've come to like and respect you. To think of you almost as a brother or a long-lost friend. Yet that hasn't stopped me drugging your coffee, and now I'm going to break your head with this stone, in order to procure a greater good, or unprocure a greater evil.'

After a few sharp blows it was over, and Oswald, well pleased with the success of his plan, carefully exchanged his grey Burton suit for the grey Burton suit worn by the member of the audit team, congratulating himself on his good fortune that they were exactly the same size.

27

As Oswald was bludgeoning consciousness out of the auditor in the waiting room, Tracey Dunn was lying low somewhere in the Midlands, waiting until the time was right to make a move. The three sisters were on the road, and it made them feel like girls again to open the windows and catch the breeze in their hair. Perhaps the lack of any rational order to their activity saved them for the moment. Myles Overton, then at least, could have crushed them like butterflies had he so wished, and made it seem an accident. On the other hand, Triona Greenwood was playing a clever double game, because there was talk of a lucrative contract with the Heritage Commission, and Triona was on the allocations committee.

'Better hold our horses,' decided Myles Overton.

'And tie our kangaroos down,' agreed Dave Doom ingratiatingly, for he was determined to master the Australian vernacular, and had purchased many Rolf Harris records to help him.

Myles Overton, in any case, had a lot on his mind. His interests in foreign parts were a drain on his energies, since being a multinational leisure-industry tycoon is a full-time job. Also there were industrial problems on the warehousing and distribution side of Strategic Marketing, since staff loyal to Peter Goodlunch had finally had enough.

The authorities assured Myles Overton he could rely on their support in the matter and promised to sort it out. But the trouble-makers refused to back down even in the face of police action.

'It's not the flaming money, it's the flaming principle, right?' Myles Overton explained to Linden Richmont.

'Funny, that's exactly what the troublemakers say. But in that case couldn't we just meet their demands, which are really quite modest, and gain a victory in the court of public opinion?'

'We can gain a victory in the court of the flaming Crimson King for all I care,' Myles Overton replied robustly. 'Except I don't give in to blackmail.' But in a secret message he told his operatives, 'I don't want Linden given the full dirt on this one. I don't want her bloody compromised, right?'

The operatives sent a secret message back that a nod was as good as a wink, but they didn't like the sound of this Oswald Hawthorne. What if he'd got wind of something? Accountants, they knew, could be tenacious bastards. Oswald Hawthorne was heading north, although no-one knew his exact destination. Triona Greenwood was connected through her ex-husband with the very malcontents who were a thorn in Myles Overton's side, although she claimed that she was only leaving Coldharbour to undertake an important negotiation. Others of the same irritating little coterie were making their presence felt. Even Triona's sister Chantal was heard of in a little-known frontier state, stirring up opposition against Western investors and armaments suppliers of whom Myles Overton could not deny being one.

Neill Fife was re-reading *The Golden Bough* and *The Lord of the Rings*, certain that some elusive pattern lay beneath recent events. He took phone calls and maintained a token presence on the lecture circuit. Yet increasingly it seemed to him he was acting out a life no longer his own. Even his wife and children seemed detached – filled with their own projects and preoccupations. One day she came to him and said, 'I need some space. I'm leaving, and taking the kids. When was the last time you bought me dinner, or took me to a wild party? You never talk to me as you did before we were married. You're using me as an excuse to grow old.'

Neill did not answer, because he had other excuses. Every day Coldharbour seemed to rear higher and more ominous, and Karen was seldom far from his thoughts. He could not help thinking too about Triona, who had seemed to keep meeting his eyes when they were reunited at Coldharbour. But at the end of the day she was Karen's sister. Also Oswald had a strange obsession with her as a result of a single night's indiscretion.

So that was all there was to it.

A hundred miles away on a railway platform two watchers, foiled by Oswald's trick, realized too late that the unconscious figure beneath the Burton suit in the waiting area was not their man. Nor, it turned out, was he as badly damaged as they surmised, for no sooner had they turned their backs than he mysteriously slipped away and took himself out of the situation, leaving them with nothing to show for their trouble at all. They slapped their forearms in frustration and cursed Oswald roundly, but it did no good.

'Lost the bastard at Bedford!'

28

Due to the need to deploy his victim convincingly, Oswald took longer than anticipated. Difficulties with connecting services meant that he missed the main party of accountants. He had to call them up and say he would join them the following morning at Strategic Marketing, since he would be unable to make the pick-up point by the time the courtesy bus was due to leave.

Few visit Milton Keynes if they can avoid it, since it is a desolate place where people have to do what they can. When Oswald arrived, no lodgings were available so late in the evening. As it was a fine night he decided he could do worse than walk across country to Strategic Marketing itself, where arrangements could quickly be made. This would give him the opportunity to scout the area for signs of cauldron fragments, and also collect his thoughts after the long journey. As he looked for a pathway through the featureless terrain, he recalled that it was hereabouts that Vortigern once wandered in search of Rowena when the fate of a nation turned on their love. But this thought saddened Oswald, since his own search was only for a piece of shattered crock. Triona was to the best of his knowledge far away, and he could hardly start searching for her even if she weren't, having rebuffed her when they last met.

Also there was no path, for pedestrianism is unknown in Milton Keynes. Instead, he found a series of broad roads, all entirely level, and with a roundabout every two or three miles. For an hour, for two, and then three hours, Oswald made his way down these roads, which had names like Saxon Street, Vortigern Way, Rowena Avenue. The adjacent fields contained models of extinct beasts, but neither the animals nor the names could conceal that the place had been abandoned by its own past. Having reflected on this for a while, Oswald began to reflect on how chilly the wind was getting, and after walking for a further hour and another hundred roundabouts, he became unsure of his bearings.

'I'll cross over the road and sit down under that sign saying Carydd-wen Corner, and breathe a little. It can't be long now . . . ' he decided. He seemed to have been walking in a kind of doze, around which nightmares involving auditors prowled incessantly but could never quite gain access. But as he crossed the broad highway, the sudden roar of an engine froze him in his steps, and headlights screeched across the night. In the last of his consciousness he became aware of an unmarked car bearing down upon him, and then something struck the side of his head like a rock wielded by a homicidal maniac, and everything was black.

29

'Sisters to the rescue!' shouted Triona, Sophie, and Dawn, with ill-concealed glee.

When they left Coldharbour, they felt as if they had been let out of school for summer. They felt they were going on an unsupervised camping holiday, and not to find a fragment and rescue a long-lost sister at all. For a while they could not take cauldrons seriously but were excited just to be off on a trip together. Deep down, each knew that what she believed she was escaping from awaited her at the journey's end. But they wound the audio up and the windows down, and managed for a moment to forget.

'Being together like this is true freedom,' said Triona, throwing an apple core out of the window. 'With men, there are always strings, even when there aren't chains. Peter Goodlunch or Oswald Hawthorne. Maybe even Neill Fife – they're all the same. Freedom's more frightening – but it's more real. Freedom isn't about escaping from your fears, it's about confronting them. Perhaps that's what Finbar Direach was trying to tell us, when he said we had no choice about going on this search.'

'He said *you* had no choice,' said Sophie. 'He didn't say *we* had no choice.'

'Freedom and love are the same – they make your heart boil over,' said Dawn. 'Still, where I've been living, there's too little of either. That's why the children mean so much. I just look at them, and my heart boils over.'

'My heart boils over when I read old poetry,' Sophie said. 'And when I teach it to my fourth form. Shelley and Byron – such hard acts to follow! That's why I divorced my ex-husband, because Shelley and Byron were such hard acts to follow.'

'You divorced your husband because he was a chancer, and drank your blood like wine,' Dawn said.

'Well you can talk, because you never had a husband.'

'I never felt the need.'

'You must've felt it at least twice,' her sisters said, pointing at the two young nieces who were falling asleep in the back, exhausted from bickering about the rules of I Spy.

'I have my dreams, like everyone. But who knows how they will end . . . ' she gave them a mysterious look, as if to say, even though you're my sisters, my private life is my own, and you shouldn't ask me about the fathers of my children, or my dreams. Perhaps indeed, the two are the same.

'Let's not talk about men,' said Triona. 'Since good ones are harder to find than a fragment of Caryddwen's cauldron, and bad ones are almost impossible to lose. Frankly there's no knowing what goes on inside their minds. Maybe Neill Fife ought to write a book about it.'

'It would be a very short book,' said Dawn.

'If you've ever read *Don Juan* . . . ' began Sophie, but Triona said the secrets of love and freedom could never really be found in books, except possibly the *Mabinogion*, and even that was deeply flawed.

'Let's drive forever,' she cried. 'Just three sisters from the oldest family in Britain and their two little nieces, in search of their own legend. Nothing can stop us! If there are roadworks on the M1, we'll take the A5.'

The sisters had a Volvo from the Heritage Commission, but filled with light-headedness they drove it all over the road like office equipment reps in a beat-up XR3i. Perhaps Triona was a little melancholy, because taking the roundabouts at speed made her think of Peter Goodlunch. Perhaps Sophie was sad, for she had made a bad choice of husband many years ago and since leaving him had loved only her work, her students, and long-dead poets. Or Dawn, because a single mother has little time to be herself, and rather than the fathers of her children, she had to live with her dreams.

'Well, we'll just have to stir our own cauldrons!' they laughed, hiding their troubled thoughts in fragile joy and revelling in the ride like teenagers, while Dawn's little girls remembered drugs education classes and wondered if their aunts had taken Prozac.

If any of them thought that, in a world where Caryddwen's cauldron was re-assembled, they would be able to find what was missing from their own lives, they said nothing. They did not think so far ahead. They were certainly not looking for men, or anything resembling men, and to say they were looking for fulfilment is just to say they were human. Everyone, Triona said, is looking for something. But, she added, it would be a good thing if they all started looking for somewhere to eat, because with all the excitement she was famished. Then, as they pulled in to park at the Jolly Snacker, her eyes were blinded by tears for the first time since she encountered Finbar Direach, heard about the death of her ex-husband and rejoined her family and friends.

'I'm sorry,' she sobbed. 'Sometimes I feel everything that's happened has left me at the mercy of my feelings. But I've got no way of knowing what my feelings are.'

Dawn had absorbent tissues, for like all young children, hers were subject to a constant leakage of fluids. 'Sounds simple to me,' she said. 'You feel somehow responsible for what happened to Peter Goodlunch, because you think it's linked to what happened to Karen, and what might happen to us.'

'How do you mean?' asked Triona.

'She means', explained Sophie, 'that we've always thought of what happened to Karen as something that just happened to Karen. But what if it's all of us? What if someone else has got hold of the same idea as Finbar Direach, about the last fragment being found by sisters from the oldest family? It makes you think. Especially as three of us have already been lost, locked up, or put beyond reach.'

'It's not that I actually think that,' Dawn told Triona hastily. 'It's just that I thought you thought it, and that might be why you were crying.'

'Even so,' said Sophie, 'it wouldn't hurt to be careful.'

But Dawn said that hunting for a magic heirloom on the say-so of a thousand year old oddball whom nobody but Triona had ever seen, and in the process going up against the world's most powerful and dangerous business empire, was not the kind of thing you could be careful about. Her levity was helpful in comforting Triona, although it was due mostly to feeling their search would come up empty, and therefore the risks were minimal. She felt this because they had nothing to go on but Triona's feelings. Triona's feelings, in Dawn's experience, were unreliable. They got Triona into a quite unnecessary marriage with Peter Goodlunch, although they had a joint income of six figures, sat on the top table at charity events, and she raked it in from the divorce. Triona's feelings could not differentiate love from freedom, and if you pressed her, she said, 'I'm a walking contradiction,' as if she were proud of it. To have feelings, Dawn thought, you need to have children. So she did not think Triona's feelings would take them to any sort of fragment of any sort of cauldron. She thought Triona's feelings would take them to Peter Goodlunch's funeral, which was to be held at the Atheist Centre at Milton Keynes the following day.

'We'll go to the funeral,' Triona said, drying her eyes. 'And to the offices at Strategic Marketing, because I've got some Heritage business. A lasting monument is needed, and private-sector money has been spoken of.'

'What, a monument to Peter Goodlunch?'

'No, to the dawn of the new age.'

In fact they had all heard talk of a lasting monument for the coming epoch. People believed it was three thousand years since the Tuatha de Dannaan first set foot on British soil, and that the Heritage Commission should mark the occasion in a fitting manner. Triona's name had been mentioned in connection with this task, although the Heritage Commission were sympathetic to the problems she had in her private life, and the fact that she needed space.

'My work is very important to me,' she told her sisters, as they ordered extra chips for the children.

'And mine,' Sophie agreed.

'Don't think work is any less important, just because you don't get paid for it,' Dawn warned.

Triona looked at her sisters critically. In her opinion Sophie was too wrapped up in her subject to be a really good teacher, and Dawn too immersed in post-feminist radicalism to be a really good mother. One lived in the past, and the other in her dreams. I was always older than the others, thought Triona, even in the old days, and I always had my feet on the ground. But then again, why have I never got over Karen's disappearance, and how have I come to get involved with a tenuous individual like Finbar Direach? What really happened that night at Coldharbour? Talk of unmarked cars gets one no-where. Whatever's at the bottom of the events at the Centre for Alternative Healing is also at the bottom of Karen's disappearance. Whatever's at the bottom of anything, is at the bottom of everything. If Finn has taught me nothing else, he's taught me that.'

So, between happiness and sadness, the three sisters finished their meal. There had been no sign of any unusual fragments of anything on the journey up. Dawn thought she found a fragment of Caryddwen's cauldron in her burger, but it turned out to be a fragment of the shield of the warrior bard Aneurin, which shattered into a thousand pieces when invading Goths broke the Celtic line during the battle of Cattraeth. This splinter struck a passing cow with such force that it entered its genetic structure and passed down the generations until ironically served up in a Flame-Grilled MegaBite to someone searching for the very cauldron whose loss, according to many authorities, made defeat at Cattraeth inevitable. But history is full of such ironies. Triona would have complained to a waitress, but Dawn knew employees were unlikely to influence management practices. For all she knew the woman could be a single mother like herself, struggling to make ends meet. So she left the fragment neatly on the side of her plate, and shortly afterwards they left, determined that nothing would stand in their way.

'I just need to call Neill on the mobile,' Triona said.

She let him know that they had already reached Dunstable, and things were looking good. She had learned that a small group of ex-employees, formerly loyal to Peter Goodlunch, had made a stand. She said she would lend them as much support as her duties with the Heritage Commission would permit, and meanwhile find out what she could. 'There's something going on,' she said. 'But I'll call you again when I know more. I think, at any rate, I'm where I can do the most good, and while the Heritage Commission deal is still on the table I know we're reasonably safe. But don't think I'm checking in. This is just a social call. And don't say anything to Oswald.'

'Oswald's gone his own way. I haven't heard from him. No other news, except my wife's taken the children away because she needs some space of her own.'

Triona did not know how to react to this information so instead she produced some equipment from her handbag, deciding to make her eye liner darker, and her lipstick lighter. She never got on with the supermodel anyway, thinking her shallow and self-obsessed. Then again, it was inevitable one would compare her with Karen, and under the circumstances, it was easy to idealize Karen, and see her loss as representing the loss of everything truly important.

Nevertheless, for now, it was essential to concentrate on the practical aspects of that loss. Unquestionably, Karen was in contact with Strategic Marketing if not Myles Overton himself at the time of her disappearance, because Strategic Marketing were involved in producing feasibility studies for the acquisition of Coldharbour. In those days Triona thought, or claimed to think, that butter would not melt in Peter Goodlunch's mouth, despite feeling it would melt rapidly in Myles Overton's. And although Coldharbour was saved by the timely intervention of the Heritage Commission, any part played by Triona in this was entirely covert. At the time, indeed, the other sisters saw her as betraying their cause to her lover, like the Celtic king Vortigern whose desire for Rowena forged the ill-fated alliance that brought Saxon warlords to Britain.

Yet nothing is as it seems. Vortigern was tricked into his action by Leatherwing and Queen Maeve of Skye. Triona, for her part, may have been playing a game as wily as anything Leatherwing could devise. The truth is, nobody knew why she took the position Peter Goodlunch secured for her. He thought he was using her, but perhaps she was using him. It was all a long time ago, and what happened may only have been what was meant to happen.

'It's hard', Triona said to Neill, 'to make people understand one's position. I know how that feels. I'm sorry about your wife, but she always had her own agenda. She never liked the house at Coldharbour, and perhaps it was only a matter of time.'

'In the old books', said Neill, who had read nearly all of them, 'it's said that when Caryddwen's cauldron is reassembled the kings and queens will call home their armies, and every man will come to his wedded woman. But that could be intended in a figurative sense.'

'I dare say it could,' said Triona.

Before very long the sisters were back in the car. They kept a look-out for fragments of Caryddwen's cauldron, but when it grew dark they sang snatches of old songs to keep their spirits up, so nobody quite noticed a lone figure shambling across the highway until it was too late.

30

When Oswald woke he found himself in a warm bed with the first sunlight streaming through the window. A figure was silhouetted against the pane and for a moment he thought it was the ill-fated auditor. Then he saw a man of around sixty, bearded, who looked at him with kind yet sorrowing eyes.

'We've been expecting you,' the bearded man said, after a gentle enquiry about Oswald's condition.

'I don't see how,' Oswald said, feeling for lumps and broken bones. 'Since I was travelling incognito, and I've obviously been brought here in the aftermath of some freak hit-and-run accident.'

'You were lucky to be found. We have fast roads in these parts, and few would stop for an accident victim. But drink this – it'll do you good.'

He held out a cup of herbal restorative and Oswald took it uneasily, since he couldn't help recalling what had happened when Triona drank one. 'Where am I?'

'Within a mile or so of your destination,' said his host. 'But in another sense – as far from it as could be. But I'm forgetting my manners. The other guests are assembled downstairs, and everything's prepared. The meeting is ready to begin. You'll want to freshen up and change your clothes. You won't be needed for the early stages so you have a little while to prepare yourself and make ready for what's to come. I'll return within the hour so we can go down together, but meanwhile, I think you'll find everything you need.'

It is, on the face of it, unlikely for any human being to find everything they need, but especially so for Oswald Hawthorne, who needed to find a fragment of a lost cauldron, or a clay man, or Karen Greenwood, or all three. Inspection of the room revealed none of these to be in evidence. He prowled a little, testing the panels and the window catches. But he saw nothing of importance, and heard only whispering voices beneath the window and behind the door, and of that whispering only one word was intelligible, and that was a name:

Tom Baleworker.

'Who', Oswald asked out loud, 'is Tom Baleworker?'

Perhaps the whisperers heard him, or perhaps they did not. He moved over to the panelled oak door, trying to catch more of what was said. When he laid his ear against the keyhole he thought he heard another ear listening at the keyhole from the opposite side, but when he opened the door there was no-one there. This gave Oswald a bad feeling. He could not help speculating that he was among people who did not have his best interests at heart, and that none of his friends knew his whereabouts. He realized it was not impossible he had fallen into the clutches of a secret sect of voluptuaries who routinely abducted and murdered accountants for their own perverse gratification. Again, his captors could have been hired by the family of the auditor whom Oswald did such a bad turn, and were perhaps planning some spectacular revenge.

Returning to the room, he looked in the drawers and inspected the bookshelves, but found nothing of interest but a slim volume entitled *Milton Keynes in History and Legend*. In this Oswald was surprised to see a version of the talking fish story and a fable about a magic chain owned by the celebrated Palestinian Druid Sullivan Mac Daffyd (known to the world as King Solomon), neither of which had obvious local relevance. A re-telling of the romance of Rowena and Vortigern merely skated over the complex issues involved, but then the book came open at a well-thumbed page, and Oswald was struck by the heading which said, in unambiguous words:

Chapter III – The Clay Man.

'Perhaps', he thought, 'I'm getting to the bottom of things.'

The book was written in a modest, almost apologetic style, as if acknowledging itself part of that desperate clutch at the past which gave the area plastic dinosaurs, Saxon Way, and Rowena Close. The idea of Solomon attending a convention of shamans there was as preposterous as Joseph of Arimathea visiting Glastonbury to plant shrubs, and clearly introduced to flatter the town's pretensions as a conference centre. But, the book maintained, the legend of the Clay Man had been prevalent locally, and was going to have to be put in the *Mabinogion* – only the authors found they had too much material already, and held it over for their next book, which, unfortunately, they never got round to writing.

The story was prefaced by an illustration of a young woman in peasant dress on the point of throwing herself from a high tower, her expression mingling terror and relief as if she had been tried almost beyond endurance, but finally settled for the easy way out. As Oswald read, he could see the story had been passed down from generation to generation and lost nothing in the process, although some of the racier parts were probably added at the behest of the marketing department at the publishing house.

31

The narrative began with a woman from a village not far off, whose husband, though manly in appearance and pre-eminent in home-making and providing, was for personal reasons unable to make their nights together as fulfilling as were their days. In those less complicated times people were content to accept what nature gave and not to resent what she withheld, and the woman made little complaint. But as she grew older the lack of a child to call her own became a preoccupation, and she sought assistance, sharing her thoughts with the local wise woman and herbalist. The wise woman agreed to do what she could. And, she said, she would charge nothing for her services, except that if the child's father offered any sort of love-token she would take that for her fee.

Who knows whether what happened next was merely coincidental? One morning as the wife went out to gather rushes for the floor of their humble dwelling she was accosted by a banshee, which claimed to be in the service of the Tuatha de Dannaan. When she remonstrated with the creature, it replied that it meant her no harm, but that in nine months she would bear a beautiful baby daughter. The child must in all respects be brought up normally, except that under no circumstances was she to be allowed to leave the village, and if strangers came, she must hide until they had gone. But, said the banshee, if a stranger did set eyes on her, it must not be anyone connected with the castle just across the valley, or it would be the worse not only for the girl and her family, but for countless generations yet to come. With that it bowed, and as a token of what had passed between them presented her with a small heart made of green onyx. This was passed to the wise woman as agreed, and nobody thought any more about it.

In those days such cases were less rare than now, so the situation was accepted at face value and the child, named Deirdre – which means Conceived In Unusual Circumstances – soon developed into a well adjusted young girl with all the aspirations and predilections one would expect, a wholesome curiosity being not the least of them.

'This business about hiding from strangers,' she said to her mother. 'Obviously it's of no great significance whether we know why I have to do it, or not. The important thing is we have our health, we have each other, we're popular in the village and untroubled by poverty, scandal, or any oppressiveness from the castle across the valley. All the same—'

'All the same,' retorted her mother firmly, 'the issue is closed, and on this subject a certain person's mouth would do well to be likewise. And don't mention the castle across the valley, for it's bad luck.'

But on Deirdre's sixteenth birthday, a horseman forded the river and clattered through their little village, claiming to be a steward of the estate and demanding that the cottagers present themselves in order to be assessed for revenue purposes. Deirdre hid as directed in a rowan tree, but in her curiosity she crept nearer and nearer the end of the branch to get a better view. Then, all at once, it broke, and she tumbled to the horseman's feet. As soon as his gaze fell on Deirdre, it was as though a cloud passed across the sun that illuminated her young life. His eyes glittering, he instructed her father that he wished to take her for his wife, and the alternative was that the entire family be hanged, their little cottage put to the fire, and their property sold at auction.

Deirdre's father and mother were ready to accept the gallows, for people were more fatalistic in those days. But Deirdre pleaded with them to let her sacrifice her happiness if it meant saving their lives, and accordingly the marriage arrangements were made for noon the following day.

Again they consulted the wise woman, but she told them things looked serious, since the castle across the valley was once one of the seven secret resting places of the Tuatha de Dannaan and no good ever came out of it. She could only think of one useful course of action, but even that, she said, would be difficult enough. 'The only thing that'll stop 'un marrying you,' she said, 'is if you're wed already.'

'Yet what man will dare take me, when it's certain what fate he'd suffer at the hands of the steward for pre-empting him in sharing my bed?'

But the wise woman knew what must be done. Fumbling in her pinafore, she took out the green onyx heart that was given her so long ago, gathered clay from the riverbank, and set to work. By evening she had completed her task. At her feet lay the lifelike figure of a clay man fresh from the oven, to whom Deirdre's mother could not help noticing the wise woman had given as much more of what is necessary for nocturnal fulfilment, as nature had given her husband less.

'Marriage', said the wise woman wisely, 'is marriage. By the time we've dressed 'un up, this'll make as pretty a groom as anyone ever saw. And quite sufficient to deal with Master Steward, when he comes tomorrow.'

As things turned out, she was not far off the mark. Early the following morning the village gathered for a simple but touching ceremony, and the stranger, as they thought the clay man to be, performed his public functions no more stiffly than many bridegrooms they had observed, and (because the wise woman insisted that for authenticity the whole matter was consummated in the usual manner without waiting for nightfall) his private functions a great deal more stiffly than most. What did

Deirdre think when she had to go to bed with a clay man? According to the legend, nobody can know what women think about such matters, as opposed to what men like to think they think, and what they think only because they like to think men like to think they think it.

It may have been because her natural father was a banshee, or just that she was exceptionally hot-blooded, but the effect of their encounter on the clay man was very marked. Whereas previously he had been cold and immobile it was soon clear that an interaction that would have left many normal men prone and exhausted had the reverse effect on the clay man. Before anyone could usefully add to the situation, he had roused himself up out of the marital bed and gone into the next room for a drink of water and an oatcake.

Unfortunately, at that exact moment the clock struck noon and the steward appeared at the door, realized he had been duped, and approached the clay man with many expressions of resentment and antagonism. The steward raised his mace, the former clay man countered with a shoetree, and a considerable battle ensued. After a long and calamitous exchange of blows, it was the clay man who finished off the steward by breaking his head with a rock wrapped in a kerchief, and taking the steward's clothes (for he had none of his own) he rode back to the castle with his bride in the saddle behind him.

As he looked very similar to the original steward and the occupants of the castle were scarcely likely to think that their overseer had been destroyed and his place usurped by an animated mud pie, the situation carried on as before. But if the previous incumbent was an apt student of cruelty, this one, lacking the benefits of a normal upbringing, quickly proved himself to be professor emeritus. The re-telling of the legend dwelt on the atrocities for which the clay steward was responsible, but in the oral tradition, distortion and exaggeration are the rule rather than the exception. Certainly, however, within seven days of her wedding night Deirdre decided rather than face her monstrous spouse again, she must take the easy way out. When her husband came clamouring on her chamber door with tumultuous fists, she threw herself from the highest turret, never to rise again.

'I can see', said Oswald to himself, 'why a person would be struck by the tragedy of that story. That's not to say it's entirely accurate. Probably the bit about the castle being one of the seven secret resting places of the Tuatha de Dannaan is a flight of fancy. Still, every region has its fated spots. Nobody brought up near Coldharbour needs convincing of that. But I wouldn't mind betting what's on the site of that castle now. It's not surprising Strategic Marketing shares are volatile. And I'd like to know what became of the clay man. For the unfortunate auditor was clear in one respect at least. Only a clay man can lead me where I have to go.'

But at that moment a bell rang in the distance and a voice cried:

'The meeting is about to begin!'

'What meeting?' Oswald wondered. He feared the worst. 'What are they going to do with me? Who's Tom Baleworker?'

At that moment the bearded man was framed in the doorway, and it was apparent these questions would soon be answered.

32

There were still people who could remember the day Tom Baleworker came to Strategic Marketing – but not many were prepared to speak about it. It was said he came out of nowhere and presented himself at the front gate in the blast of a northeasterly gale. More than that no-one knew. His collar was turned up against the wind and the brim of his hat turned down, and he kept his face shielded lest anyone should perceive that, compared to the chill of his eyes, the northeaster was like the balmy breeze that stirs palm fronds on a Caribbean beach.

Security at Strategic Marketing was by no means lax even in those days. Yet when the gatekeeper challenged him the newcomer leaned very close and said just one word, which made the man's veins stand out like lime twigs and his lymph glands contract in fear. There is no record of what was said, since the gatekeeper dared not repeat it to a living soul. But soon his hair fell out, his memory failed, he called in sick with an inoperable cancer, and took to his bed never to rise again.

Once within the compound, the newcomer affected an easy and outgoing demeanour. He reported at once to reception as the notices clearly required, and soon let it be understood that he was available for employment. He indicated that he was a good communicator at all levels, an excellent team player, and since he was a single man money was not an issue and he would, indeed, be prepared to give his services free of charge for a trial period. He gave his name as Baleworker and was initially set to work baling paper in the waste department. In this he was so willing and cheerful that he progressed to a supervisory grade and was moved into the upper offices. Then, when one of the marketing managers mysteriously died, the company was glad to have such a promising internal candidate.

During this period the managing director was a sycophantic character whose strategy was to placate the shareholders with toadying words, maintaining that Strategic Marketing was holding its own in a declining sector. Tom Baleworker, taking his new responsibilities seriously, compiled a report on the sector which showed that, far from declining, it was one of the most lucrative to be found, but that Strategic Marketing was losing out badly to competitors in terms of product quality, production deadlines, and after-sales service. By an administrative error this report was copied direct to the Board without the managing director having sight of it. Very soon Tom Baleworker was summoned to London for a meeting with the directors of the offshore trusts in whom the main shareholdings resided.

'It is not my policy to criticize other members of the team,' he told them. 'And the management at Strategic Marketing are undoubtedly nice people.'

'Perhaps too nice?' suggested the directors of the offshore trusts shrewdly.

'I didn't say that,' said Tom Baleworker. 'But I've made a short-list of things that have confused me about procedures there, although naturally these are areas in which I'm not an expert. I wouldn't go so far as to use words such as *mistakes*, or *incompetence*, or *complacency*, but perhaps if we all pull together, there are ways in which things can be tightened up . . . '

'He's trying to protect his colleagues,' the directors noted. 'Which is very laudable. However, what we're running here is a business, not a spiritual community based on love, mutual understanding, and the progressive self-realization of the absolute. The time has come for matters to be taken in hand.'

'We're lucky to have him,' they told one another after he had left.

If any of them knew that there was more to it than luck, they kept quiet.

'Give him whatever he asks for, and keep a low profile. If anything goes wrong, we can always say we were unaware of his methods.'

'His demands are still quite modest. All he wants is a free hand. He's asked for Linden Richmont as liaison, if her uncle agrees and her other responsibilities permit.'

'We'll have to work something out.'

'Also, of course, Peter Goodlunch can still look after the public-relations aspects.'

'I'll get on to it right away.'

The dismissals, the motivational mottos and the new disciplinary regime began soon afterwards. Sales meetings became legendary. Tom Baleworker believed in leading from the front, and took a great pride in his ability to incentivize people. 'You have missed your target two weeks in a row,' he would say to a representative. 'I could fire you, but I know you have a sick wife and two young children. Let's face it, you're unlikely to find another job, especially with the references I would give you. So I've decided to do you a favour. Instead of dismissing you for the incompetent lazy self-serving complacent flabby malodorous wanker you are, I'm going to have you held down while I drive this iron spike through your foot. Call me an old softy if you like, but on this occasion I'll let it go at that. But if you don't meet your targets next week, I'll have your wife and children brought in and do the same to them.'

Fortunately, this did not need to happen on the first such occasion because the salesman concerned, despite a day or so in hospital, did meet his targets and in due course became one of Tom Baleworker's most loyal supporters – leaner, fitter, and far more motivated. They often joked together about the incident of the rusty spike and the salesman thanked Tom Baleworker for what he had done, since, he said:

'It really sorted me out.'

Many other cases were dealt with similarly, and it was not uncommon to hear screams of pain emanating from sales meetings, and the cleaners had to deal with quantities of blood and viscera afterwards, although they did not dream of complaining and were grateful for their jobs. Nevertheless, it was rare that anyone actually died of injuries inflicted in this way, and perhaps that was why Tom Baleworker's regime was, in a curious way, more popular than the general sense of slackness that prevailed before his time.

In those parts of the company still under the direct influence of Peter Goodlunch, things were different, but little better. Tom Baleworker's personal, almost mesmeric style was absent there and management was by decree. People would come to work one morning and find a notice saying, 'To meet production targets, employees should now report in at 7.30 in the morning instead of 9 o'clock. We must all pull together and anyone arriving after that time will be summarily dismissed.' Or, 'It has come to the attention of the company that some employees asked for extra money for working longer hours. We must all pull together, and anyone who mentions this matter again will be summarily dismissed.' Peter Goodlunch was never informed of these decisions and was absent from the facility for longer and longer periods, confining himself to the London office which handled the creatives and the statistical analysis.

There was a suggestion box where people could denounce colleagues they felt were not pulling their weight, with a small bonus being paid for any information which led to a summary dismissal. More generalized notices said things like:

'If you're not part of the solution, you're part of the problem.'

'There are no problems, there are only opportunities.'

'All work and no play makes Jack a good bonus.'

'We must all pull together, and people who don't pull get the push.'

'The winner sees a glass that is half full, the loser sees a glass that is half empty, but we must all pull together, and anyone caught drinking on the premises will be summarily dismissed.'

Many of these notices drew on tenets that were originally well intentioned and not a few were borrowed from Neill Fife's self-help books. But in Tom Baleworker's hands they became a fearful rubric, with any perceived transgression resulting in instant dismissal or bodily injury. Extra security guards were recruited and gradually the security team took over most supervisory functions. Tom Baleworker believed that the key to a smooth-running business lay in discipline.

In an interview with *Management Tomorrow* magazine he explained:

'Let's say a worker is loading bales for his supervisor. If I want more bales loaded, I don't hire another worker. I buy the supervisor a stick. If I want even more bales loaded, I hire a further supervisor and provide him, too, with a stick. This method never fails.'

This was bound to cause a certain amount of insecurity and resentment, although Tom Baleworker regarded it as motivating. 'Keep the scum terrified for their lives,' was a management strategy seldom taught in the best American business schools, except perhaps in covert form. But it did no harm to the share price of Strategic Marketing and in financial circles the company began to be seen as 'going places' and analysts switched their prognosis from 'accumulate' to 'buy'. Linden Richmont inevitably heard some of what went on, since it was her job to stop everybody else hearing of it. She tried to reconcile herself to the worst excesses by repeating that, after all, no-one was obliged to work for Strategic Marketing if they didn't want to. Meanwhile, Tom Baleworker made a number of staffing and management changes based on best practice in certain overseas military dictatorships of which he was an admirer.

33

When his host materialized in the doorway, Oswald was ready for anything. But the old man seemed surprised at the sinister interpretation Oswald had put on events and spoke in a manner that was grave, but not unfriendly.

'They're all downstairs. They're waiting for you.'

'Who are?'

'All of them. They thought you might want to address them and let them know your plan.'

'Perhaps', said Oswald, wondering if either of them was entirely sane, 'we'd better start again at the beginning. Can you tell me exactly where I am?'

'But we were expecting you. Aren't you the negotiator from London?'

Oswald made a sound resembling '*Ah!*' And after a few more moments of discussion, the two understood each other much more clearly. From Oswald's point of view, things were both better and worse than he had expected. Better, because the house, its location, and the strange manner in which he had arrived there inevitably produced thoughts of werewolves, human sacrifice and orgiastic rites. Worse, because they wanted something from him that would unquestionably compromise his cover story.

'There's a number of us,' the bearded man said. 'All suspended employees of Strategic Marketing, loyal to the late Peter Goodlunch. We have a long-running dispute with the company. None of us is by nature militant. We're engineers, designers, computer operators and bought-ledger clerks as well as labourers, loaders and line workers. Now Peter Goodlunch is no longer here to state our case, we've offered every compromise to bring management to the table – but without success. We've appealed to the authorities, but they tell us they can't get involved. Our grievances are many, but we're ready to grasp at straws. Even industrial action itself was a last resort. We put up with wage cuts, fines for sneezing or going to the toilet, and far worse. But Tom Baleworker clearly set out to orchestrate a confrontation. And sooner or later the inevitable had to happen.'

'Can't you take the matter higher up?'

'We've tried to engage public sympathy and attract the attention of Strategic Marketing's shareholders, but to no effect. Our personal savings have been used up in the struggle. As a last resort we sold what few possessions we had left to raise money for a professional negotiator. Ideally we would have engaged Neill Fife, because of his influential work in the field of industrial disputes. But the fees involved were prohibitive. In the end we found an independent management consultant who agreed to help us, travelling here disguised as a member of the audit team to avoid detection. He was due on the five o'clock train, so naturally we thought—'

'It's all becoming clearer,' Oswald said, with a rather uncomfortable feeling in the pit of his stomach and a certain hotness in his cheeks, for he could not help feeling in part to blame for the absence of their intended visitor. 'But I don't see how I can help you.'

'At least address the guests,' urged the bearded man. 'For there are people here I think you already know. Who can say – perhaps we may find some common interest after all!'

Oswald did not think so, but he knew that without intending to do so he had undermined their efforts, and also was struck by the determination and quiet dignity of his host. One can push a person so far, Oswald thought, but in the end, everyone has the power to make himself like a clay man, and become immune to all normal fears, apprehensions, constraints and inhibitions. Without this ability there would be no war; but also no peace.

Oswald was not naive, however, and could see that the titles of Negotiator and Management Consultant were both euphemisms. If the talks broke down, the ex-employees would clearly require instruction in basic military tactics, weapons drill and hand-to-hand combat. Perhaps it would be necessary to mount a frontal assault. If only, he thought, Neill were here to advise – and Chantal, who had so often demonstrated her ability to turn simple peasants into freedom fighters. But only Oswald was there, and no-one knew better than himself how misplaced were their expectations of him. He wondered who had given his hosts these expectations and colluded in representing him as some kind of negotiator, while knowing he was not.

34

But Oswald did not wonder long. 'Triona!' he cried, the moment he entered the crowded room. 'Dawn?' he said, and then, uncomprehendingly, 'Sophie?' Then, slowly, things began to fall into place. Dawn's two daughters sat at their mother's feet. They were very pleased with themselves because they had listened at several keyholes and had been running about whispering 'Tom Baleworker!' all morning, as a result of having been forbidden to mention the name out loud.

'I can explain,' Triona told Oswald.

'You ran me over!' he said indignantly.

'It was dark – we thought you were a hedgehog,' said Dawn.

When Oswald discovered that Triona and her sisters had not only got there before him, but also done their best to mow him down on a public highway, his feelings were mixed, as if in some antiquated cauldron. 'You followed me! No – you knew I was coming here, and you've been waiting for me. What's going on? Why did you tell them I was a negotiator from London?'

'I think', said Triona looking at the other guests, who were beginning to be a little confused themselves, 'we'd better bring you up to speed.' She told him as briefly as she could that they, like himself, had set out in search of the piece of Caryddwen's cauldron, and their enquiries had led them in the same direction. Peter Goodlunch could have helped these enquiries by dropping a line to his ex-wife before popping off. But he had chosen instead to confide in a nineteen-year-old bimbo, which frankly, Triona said, not to speak ill of the dead, was about his level. So they had to find out what they could. They didn't follow Oswald, Triona said, they offered him a lift. But they had guessed he would end up here, because they knew how his mind worked.

'And the meeting, and this house?'

'He', she said, nodding at the bearded man, 'is a spokesperson for workers loyal to Peter, and invited us to stay. My cover is that I'm here for the Heritage Commission on a secret project, and also to pay my last respects to Peter because his funeral is at the Atheist Centre the day after tomorrow. My sympathy with the protesters must be concealed for fear of victimization. Anyway I can help them best by working from the inside. When I heard the negotiator had met with an accident I had to think on my feet, since that would have been the final straw. Running into you – though we didn't mean to do it so literally – was a godsend. Unless they have professional representation at today's talks, their position will be forfeit.'

'Well, I'm an accountant, not a negotiator, and I won't do it!'

'All you have to do is turn up wearing a Burton suit and look like a management type. You don't even have to speak. It's a small sacrifice to make—'

'It's always the most self-sacrificing people in this world that cause the most suffering,' said Oswald, somewhat forgetting the suffering he himself had visited upon the auditor.

'You say that – but you haven't yet met Tom Baleworker.'

'I won't meet Tom Baleworker,' said Oswald, 'because I won't do it.'

'Oswald . . . ' Sophie said, with an imploring look.

'All right, I'll do it on one condition.'

'What's that?'

'*She* has to apologize for pulling my treehouse down.'

'I'm sorry I pulled your treehouse down. And you're not an oick.'

'Then I don't seem to have any choice in the matter. But I'm still just a boring accountant, not an industrial relations expert. I've got to do it my own way. If there's a confrontation, I'll do what I can. But any negotiator needs an edge. If I'm right, everything we need will be in the books. Go in, hit the files, and get clear, will be my strategy. The regulatory authorities will do the rest.'

'For an accountant, you're a brave man,' said the employees loyal to the late Peter Goodlunch. 'We'd go with you if we dared, but we have fought our battles already, and defeat was the only outcome.'

Some of them also came to him secretly and suggested that perhaps he, too, should cry off. They said they would make him one of them, and share with him their meagre possessions. They told him they had no jobs, but managed to make out somehow. 'Whereas,' they warned, 'if your attempt backfires, we may *all* be destroyed, you and the sisters as well.'

Oswald shook their hands, and told them he would never forget their offer if he lived to be a hundred. 'Never in my life have I been made to feel so accepted – not even at Coldharbour. You're like the family I never really had. But I made a promise, and it can't be broken. Now – I must assemble the equipment I need, and familiarize myself with the layout.'

'And I', said Triona, 'will keep my appointment, as befits a Heritage Commissioner and her two assistants.'

'I suppose we have to be the two assistants,' said Dawn, looking at Sophie grumpily.

It seemed to them that all too often in their childhood Karen and Triona as the elders had played the roles of queens, enchantresses, and heritage commissioners, and Dawn and Sophie had had to be Triona's two assistants, while Nuala and Chantal had to be Karen's. Perhaps, if Nuala and Chantal had been allowed to be enchantresses more, they wouldn't have ended up respectively behind bars and beyond reach. But let it pass . . .

'All right,' said Sophie, although she was head of her own school and enjoyed considerable standing in the community. 'We'll be the assistants. But how this helps with Caryddwen's cauldron is beyond me.'

So it was settled, but none of them looked forward to it.

35

The afternoon followed the morning all too speedily, but soon everything was ready. Taking care to go by separate routes and present themselves at different gates, Oswald and the bearded man made their way to a scruffy room on the ground floor for talks on the industrial-relations problem, while Triona and her sisters were ushered up to a plush penthouse suite where a team had been assembled to discuss the Heritage project.

To anyone familiar with formal negotiating techniques or Neill Fife's self-help book *Negotiate To Win!* the set-up on the ground floor would be familiar. In keeping with the tradition of a smoke-filled room, technicians had ignited cigarettes in the air-conditioning ducts and ensured the ashtrays were well topped up. The heating was set too high, the chairs were uncomfortable, and the glasses of water had grey scum floating on the surface. Oswald and the bearded man were seated at one end of a long table, and the company's team, which consisted of experts from a top London negotiating firm, sat at the other.

The experts had certainly read Neill Fife's seminal book, because they opened by stating their most extreme position, hoping to shock their opponents into compromise. 'We have the full backing of the management,' they said. 'And if it comes to that, Myles Overton himself, although we're forbidden to mention him by name. Any agreements we enter into are binding on the company, and we trust this matter can be resolved to the satisfaction of all parties. But we mean to stand firm, and we won't be dictated to. As our opening position, therefore, we propose that everyone who has involved themselves in this dispute to the detriment of the company's reputation and business interests should be put to death by public hanging, their cottages burnt and their possessions sold at auction.'

Oswald, unused to industrial disputes, found this proposal unnerving. But the bearded man merely pointed out that it explicitly contravened the provisions of the Industrial Relations Act of 1991. While he shared their desire for a speedy solution, he suggested some compromise might be acceptable to both sides, along the lines of unconditional re-instatement for all suspended employees, compensation for lost wages, personal hardship and emotional stress, and Tom Baleworker being put on trial for crimes against humanity.

'Humanity is not on the table,' replied the London team. 'But now, perhaps, we can get down to business.' Although much was then made of a search for common ground, both sides concentrated mainly on restating the same positions in different words, and accusing one another of being naive, misinformed, or unreasonable.

'Your negotiator doesn't seem to be saying much,' the London experts sneered after a while.

'The most important thing in negotiation', Oswald said, for he too was familiar with Neill's book and indeed had done most of the proofreading; being good at semi-colons; 'is to be able to listen.'

'He's a good negotiator,' added the bearded man. 'He's reserving his position at the moment, but I can tell you he's some ideas up his sleeve.'

'To me,' said Oswald, 'what matters is the bottom line. It's all about the numbers.'

When he said that, the experts from London nodded approvingly, for they respected a man who went straight to the bottom line.

'If we could just have discovery of the relevant accounting documentation?' suggested Oswald.

'What? The secret files in the locked storeroom on the topmost storey?' said the London experts, resuming their hard-line position. 'Not a chance!'

'I think', said Oswald, 'I want to go to the toilet.'

36

When Triona and her sisters entered the office suite prepared for them, there were fresh flowers on the table and they were offered a choice of Volvic or Perrier in Bohemian crystal glasses.

'Although Myles Overton is nothing to do with this company for tax reasons, and Tom Baleworker can't be with us due to prior commitments, they both want you to know this project has their full commitment and backing, and they will be taking a personal interest at every stage,' their hosts assured them.

'The Heritage Commission', stated Triona, 'will be delighted to hear it. But let me introduce my two assistants, Sophie and Dawn, who serve me in a menial capacity.'

'They look rather like you.'

'To be honest, they look up to me so much they've taken to imitating details of my personal style, so people often say there's a similarity. I look on them as my little sisters—'

Dawn choked on her Volvic. But notwithstanding, there was serious business to be done. Apart from the well groomed executives of Strategic Marketing, many consultants had been brought in on the project from London, New York, and Los Angeles.

'I can't tell you too much at present,' said Triona. 'But the Heritage Commission has an historic occasion to commemorate, and we need ideas for a lasting monument.'

'Ideas', said a Strategic Marketing executive, 'are what we're best at!'

'Perhaps we could use the Internet!' said one of the consultants who had been flown in from New York. At such meetings there is always a consultant from New York who tells everyone that perhaps they could use the Internet.

'I'm not ruling anything out at this stage,' said Triona.

'Perhaps we could create an enormous theme park, along the lines of EuroDisney,' said another consultant. 'With games, and rides, and lots of corporate hospitality.'

'Or a world-wide sporting event in which athletes from all nations and all disciplines compete for the glory of their countries and themselves – and we could hold it at four-year intervals in a different city each time—'

'I think that's been done,' put in Sophie, who had never been to a high-powered marketing meeting before, and was surprised there was so little to it.

There was no shortage of other ideas from the consultants, although Triona observed the executives from Strategic Marketing began after a while to look uncomfortable and adjust their collars. The executives from Strategic Marketing had always noticed the number of ideas someone has varies inversely with their responsibility for following them through. As the offerings increased in ambition, scope, and assumptions that third parties would collaborate, the executives adjusted their collars more and more. They knew it was themselves, and not the consultants, who would have to carry the ideas out. With Peter Goodlunch gone, they were responsible to Tom Baleworker. 'We have all', they whispered to each other, 'heard the stories about the spike.'

'Well,' said Triona, after an hour or so, 'I think we can all congratulate ourselves on a good meeting. I shall need preliminary creatives and an outline business plan by the 24th, including details of financial backing and the sponsorship package. For the government is determined this project should be accomplished using only private-sector finance, and I've no doubt that Strategic Marketing has the right team for the job.'

'It's in the bag!' whispered the consultants, thinking of their fees.

'And now', added Triona, 'my sisters – that's to say my assistants – and I would like to use your toilets, after all the excitement and mineral water.'

37

'I hope you know what you're doing,' said Oswald when the sisters joined him in a remote corridor, beside a dusty storeroom.

'We were hoping you would,' said Dawn.

'Come on. We haven't got much time. And there may be surveillance cameras,' said Sophie, pointing upwards at a small swivelling apparatus which ominously followed their movements.

'The door's locked,' said Oswald. 'But I brought tin-openers from my collection, and a Swiss army knife. As we accountants say – be prepared!'

'Are you sure this is wise?' enquired Triona, who had learnt the hard way that prying open forbidden doorways in strange buildings sometimes leads to unforeseen consequences.

'I made a promise. Unless I can get to the ledgers, the truth will never come out, and the suspended employees will be abandoned to their fate.'

'But really, that's not what's on your mind at all,' said Sophie shrewdly. 'Because if my guess is correct, you're really after the confidential papers of Peter Goodlunch.'

'Well – there should be no shortage of those,' Triona said. 'I never knew anyone with so many secrets, even when I was married to him.'

'Especially when you were married to him,' said Dawn. 'Men are all the same.'

'What would you know about being married?' the other two demanded.

'I think', said Oswald, 'we'd better get on with it.'

When they entered the storeroom there were spiders crawling in the corners of the ceiling, and three filing cabinets stood against the far wall. A single long window with a Venetian blind filled the place with uncertain light, and beyond it, eight storeys down, the ground rolled away into an artificial lake landscaped to resemble the moat of a castle.

'I'm only an accountant, but I have to do what I have to do,' said Oswald. 'We must work fast, because, from what I've heard, Tom Baleworker is a bad person to cross.'

'One of the worst,' agreed Triona.

Outwardly Oswald did his best to appear confident, for he knew that Triona was watching him and throughout his life he had only wished to shine in Triona's eyes. I need to be able to let go, he thought to himself. I need not to want things so much. Love is the opposite of desire. It's a state of being rather than feeling, and implies freedom rather than possession, as the magic fish made clear. To want things brings fear of failure, and if one fears failure, failure is inevitable. But most of all, I have to find the confidential papers. Then Triona will respect me as a human being, and I can win her affection.

But when he opened the first filing cabinet, the runners squealed like a lorry-load of pigs on their way to market. Horrified, they became aware of footsteps ascending the stairs.

'Hide!' Oswald told the others. There was nowhere to hide except the ledge of the window, but they climbed up quickly, and Oswald pulled the blinds across.

'Who's there?' demanded a voice. 'For we must all pull together, and if anyone is found in an area for which they have no authorization, they will be summarily dismissed!' The footsteps grew louder, and all at once they heard Tom Baleworker himself pounding on the door with tumultuous fists.

Oswald assumed his most deferential air, and was not slow to let Tom Baleworker in. He filled the door frame as he entered, and his relentless eyes went to left and right, for he was certain something was afoot. But when he saw Oswald, he began immediately to underestimate him, and soon concluded he was dealing with an insignificant little pipsqueak. He knew they had the auditors in, and recognized Oswald as an accountant of the most tawdry kind. Still, he had given clear instructions that all auditors were to be confined to the administration area, and anyone allowing them to wander round unsupervised would be summarily dismissed. He made a mental note of the person's name who was primarily responsible for stopping auditors wandering around unsupervised. Then he weighed the rival merits of addressing the pip-squeak, and of removing his liver and wringing it out like a dishcloth. Curiosity briefly outweighing vindictiveness, he decided, in the best tradition of the *Mabinogion*, he would ask Oswald what news he had, and try to elicit from him what he knew.

'What news has the little bean-counter for the Chief Executive? And what is he up to in a restricted area?'

'No news,' replied Oswald, trying hard to stand his ground. 'Except I'm doing the best job I can, and I've been sent up here by my line manager to find extra beads for my abacus, since the revenues we need to count are so enormous.'

Now although Tom Baleworker was relentless, psychopathic and unremittingly bad, he was also full of conceit and self-satisfaction. There was nothing he liked better than to be reminded how high his revenues were, unless it was sticking spikes into people, so he was slightly mollified.

'Well,' he said, 'there may be extra beads here, or there may not. But you'll have little success looking for them if you keep the blinds drawn like that. I'll open them for you, and then we'll see what we shall see.'

'Oh, there's no need for that,' said Oswald hastily. 'I've already found everything I require. I just need to tidy up after myself, and then I'll come down.'

'Well,' said Tom Baleworker, 'make sure you do, because a tidy company is a productive company, and anyone who doesn't tidy up after themselves will be summarily dismissed!' And he turned and left.

'Phew! That was close,' said Dawn as the sisters emerged. 'Talk about dodgy blokes.'

'We'd better hurry,' said Triona. But when Oswald opened the second filing cabinet, the runners screeched like a flock of seagulls mobbing a raven, and they soon heard footsteps on the stairs for a second time.

'Hide!' Oswald told the others, and they again concealed themselves behind the blinds.

'Who's there!' came Tom Baleworker's unmistakable tones. 'We must all pull together, and if anyone is having a quiet fag in the stairwell they will be summarily dismissed!' When they heard him pounding on the door once again, they knew he had discovered no-one on the stairwell, and that it was all up to Oswald. He resumed his deferential air, and quickly opened the door.

'What news has the little bean-counter for the Chief Executive?' glowered Tom Baleworker, for he was starting to wonder if the pipsqueak knew more than he was letting on. 'And what is he still doing in a place he was told to stay out of?'

'No news,' replied Oswald. 'Except I'm still doing the best job I can, and I've been sent by my line manager for even more beads, since none of us even dreamed we would be dealing with such long numbers.'

Reassured that the revenues were larger than even the auditors had been able to anticipate, Tom Baleworker could scarcely conceal a smile of self-congratulation. For, he thought, though money can never buy a person happiness, it can purchase huge amounts of unhappiness for others, and it was in making others unhappy that Tom Baleworker's chief happiness lay. Malevolence, he felt, was a state of being rather than of feeling, and he perceived himself to exist only in proportion as he was able to inflict suffering.

'Well,' he said, 'there may be extra beads here, or there may not, but as I told you before, you'll need to open the blinds if you expect to find what you're looking for, and then we'll soon see how the land lies.'

Behind the blind, Triona shivered. From anxiety, without question. But also from something else, which she had experienced with Peter

Goodlunch when she first met him, before she realized that behind his ambition and his Porsche he was just like anyone else. It was not a feeling she would ever have admitted to Dawn, who was a post-feminist radical, or even to herself. But she thought, for the merest moment, that Tom Baleworker was everything Oswald Hawthorne wasn't. Then again, she recollected, Oswald Hawthorne was everything Tom Baleworker wasn't.

'I'm waiting!' said Tom Baleworker. 'Are you going to open the blinds, or carry on working in the dark, like a little bumbling mole?'

'Oh, there's no need of that,' said Oswald. 'I've got what I came for. I just need to enter it in the consumables book, and I'll come down directly.'

'Well,' said Tom Baleworker, 'make sure you do, because a company that enters things in the consumables book is an organized company, and anyone not found being organized will be summarily dismissed!' He turned and left, although not without a long backward glance beneath narrowing lids.

'Phew! That was close,' said Sophie. 'Talk about dysfunctional characters.'

'We'd better hurry,' said Triona. But when Oswald opened the third filing cabinet, the runners shrieked like a clan of banshees pillaging a luckless village, and once again, the sound of approaching footsteps filled their ears.

The sisters hid, and the now familiar voice resounded in the stairwell. 'Who's there? For we must all pull together. If anyone is caught sneaking around things that don't concern them, summary dismissal will be the least of their worries!' But when Tom Baleworker again pounded on the door, Oswald let him in, picking his nose in a humble and unassuming way.

'What news has the little bean-counter for the Chief Executive?' roared Tom Baleworker, for this time he was certain something was up. 'And what's he doing rummaging through our secret files?'

'No news,' replied Oswald. 'Except that I'm doing the best job I can, and my line manager—'

'If you think that story about beads is going to wash a third time,' shouted Tom Baleworker, 'you've got another think coming! Do you think I don't know you bean-counters have state-of-the-art laptops, with zip drives, and character-recognition software and built-in modems with mobile telephone links? You must think I'm stupid! You must think I have the brains of a clay man! But people who cross me soon find out they've made a big mistake. People who cross *me* find out they've made the biggest mistake of their careers. You may be certain that I know what you're looking for, and you won't find it in there!'

Seemingly, the security people had done their work well, and whether officially or by his own clandestine means, Tom Baleworker was not ignorant of the sisters, their friends, and the task they had set themselves. Oswald remembered the advice of the auditor, and although he did not think the time was right to start smiting his chest three times, he refused to give way.

'I don't know what you're talking about!' he said, although his voice wobbled like a drunk man on a bicycle.

'And I suppose, you little bean-counting bastard, you don't know about any auditor attacked on any station, and haven't heard of three sisters and a nasty little oick like yourself, stirring up trouble where it's not needed and trying to discover something that's none of their business.'

'I don't recall hearing about an oick of that description,' Oswald said, playing for time. 'But then, I'm only an accountant.'

'Don't talk back to me!' shouted Tom Baleworker in a sudden rage.

'I was only trying to say—'

Tom Baleworker turned red, and then pale, and with a visible effort, controlled himself. Oswald wondered if he had some agenda that precluded squashing the intruder like an irritating fly. Perhaps he was secretly saying to himself that although he worked for Myles Overton, under the right circumstances the position could be reversed. Perhaps he was thinking that, if he could just gain the ear of Leatherwing, things might be very different, and that, after all, he should play things carefully, for there could be a hidden benefit for him in this matter.

In any event, when he spoke to Oswald again, it was in low, cunning tones. 'I have a bad reputation,' he confided. 'Some say I killed a gatekeeper with a single word, and people who cross me do not prosper. Nevertheless you will find I can deal squarely when I wish, and we may have common interests. The truth is, I know you don't care about ledgers or employees loyal to Peter Goodlunch. The real reason you're here is something very different, and far deeper. But you won't find what you're looking for, because the instant Peter Goodlunch died, I had his confidential papers brought to me, and only I know the secret they concealed.'

'Secret? What secret?' asked Oswald, making his eyes as wide as he could although he sensed his negotiating position was slipping.

'I think we both know what I'm talking about,' said Tom Baleworker slyly. 'Now – do we have a bargain, or shall I just break all your limbs?'

Oswald hesitated, but he was not sure how long he could hold the line. Yet before he could open his mouth, there was a clatter behind the Venetian blind and he knew he was no longer alone. 'As to the bargain,' Triona said, as she stepped from her position of concealment with all the dignity jumping off a three-foot ledge would allow, 'you had better ask me!'

'What have we here?' said Tom Baleworker.

'You'd better ask us too!' put in Dawn and Sophie, making their own presence known.

'Well,' chuckled Tom Baleworker unpleasantly as he recognized the potential of the situation, 'first a little bean-counter, and now three sisters from the oldest family in Britain. It's very nice of you to drop in. It's very nice indeed, because even a powerful Chief Executive may have an eye towards bettering his position, and there are those who would be interested to know I have the three sisters from the oldest family in Britain in my hands.'

But Oswald interposed his small self between Tom Baleworker and the sisters. 'You said you wanted to make a bargain,' he said. 'And the sisters are under my protection.'

'*Your* protection, little bean-counter?' Tom Baleworker exclaimed, with a laugh like the cracking of bones. Even the sisters smiled, because each of them was skilled in T'ai Chi, the well known martial art originated by a lost tribe of ancient Chinese Celts and passed down from mother to daughter, growing more deadly with each successive generation. Oswald, on the other hand, was only skilled in double-entry bookkeeping, which is notoriously ineffective in a scrap.

'*Your* protection?' repeated Tom Baleworker. 'What can you do to protect them?'

'For one thing,' replied Oswald, standing as straight as he could because Triona was watching him, even though his feet felt as if they were a thousand miles from his head. 'For one thing, as the Chief Executive observed, what I've got in my hand is not an abacus at all but a laptop computer equipped with zip drives, internal modem and mobile telephone link. I'm only an accountant, but though I haven't found Peter Goodlunch's documents, I scanned enough others to interest the regulatory authorities. Even for a little bean-counter like me, it was a small job to press 'send' and transmit everything by data link to Neill Fife at Coldharbour. And if anything happens to Triona, or the rest of us, he'll certainly know what to do.'

But Oswald stopped, wondering if he had gone too far. Tom Baleworker had never come across such temerity in his waking life, and the experience made him turn such successively dramatic shades of colour that he could have hired himself out to a discotheque, were it not for the terrifying expression and the veins pulsing and heaving like pump hoses on the *Titanic*. Thinking they were facing a showdown, the sisters instinctively went into the Position of the Striking Crane, although perhaps even an entire striking construction site could not have stood against the full fury of Tom Baleworker's rage. Yet formidable as his anger was, Oswald may have been correct in guessing he had a secret agenda. For, with a visible effort, he managed to control the impulse to extinguish life from the four companions.

'I see', he said instead, 'that you like your little joke! Ha, ha! I like a little joke myself. I have often said that anyone who doesn't like a little joke should be summarily dismissed.'

'I think you were about to offer us a deal,' said Triona levelly.

Tom Baleworker leaned down and whispered a single phrase which only Triona and Oswald heard. For a moment when he spoke, they thought their lymph would freeze inside them, leading to inoperable cancers. Yet they quickly understood that only Tom Baleworker now knew the whereabouts of the last lost fragment of Caryddwen's cauldron, but that Tom Baleworker would tell them nothing unless they found him what he coveted most. This, he let them know, was nothing less than a legendary heirloom mentioned in the literature of the dark ages, and in a copy of *Milton Keynes in History and Legend*, which had fortuitously come into Tom Baleworker's possession. The heirloom was a chain, he said, whose wearer could not be disobeyed. With its help he could overthrow Myles Overton, win the confidence of Leatherwing, marry Linden Richmont, and ultimately hold the world in the palm of his hand.

'Get me the Chain of Command', he told them, 'which Solomon gave to the Kings of the Desert, and I will tell you the secret of the last lost fragment. This I swear by an oath no Chief Executive can break. But the task I'm giving you will not prove an easy one. You'll need the help of Triona's sister Nuala, who's scarcely in a position to be of assistance, and you may be sure that if you do not succeed, your lives will be forfeit.'

'That's as may be,' said Oswald. 'But in the meantime, what about the employees loyal to Peter Goodlunch, and the regime of spikes and other oppressive management policies?'

'And also', put in Triona opportunistically, 'the terms of the contract for the Heritage Project.'

'I'm certain', Tom Baleworker said, with a smile that made their hearts curl up like overcooked bacon, 'we can come to some arrangement.'

38

Therefore the situation was straightened out at Strategic Marketing Plc, and although in a negotiation nobody gets all of what they want, an uneasy balance of interests was achieved. It seemed, some said, as though Tom Baleworker was up to something, and had his own agenda. Others said: what did it matter? So long as not too many people got things stuck in them, and the workers formerly loyal to Peter Goodlunch were allowed to form an external company contracting their services to Strategic Marketing on a fixed-term basis with adequate financial and legal safeguards, 'Let us go forward,' they said, 'in a new spirit of co-operation and understanding.'

'Anyone who doesn't', added Tom Baleworker, 'will be summarily dismissed.'

But Oswald and the three sisters went south. Still he could not let go, and the mysterious link between feeling and being was beyond him.

He felt, moreover, that the business with the clay man was somehow unresolved, and the bad turn done to the auditor would count against him in the stand that he must one day make.

Triona, for her part, had glimpsed another Oswald beneath his unconvincing exterior, and reassured him over his part in events. 'Things will come right,' she told him. 'And as far as the mysterious auditor is concerned, a bang on the head is nothing to him, for if you haven't guessed, he was none other than Finbar Direach in an elaborate disguise. He intercepted the real auditor – or should I say the expert negotiator who unbeknown to Finn was masquerading as the real auditor – at King's Cross. There he felled him with a single blow and took his place for the rest of the journey, having hit upon the same idea of hoodwinking Strategic Marketing's security and finding out what he could.'

'To be honest,' put in Dawn, 'the entire rail network that day was littered with comatose auditors, as the expert negotiator originally dealt with the one whose place he took in a not dissimilar way. Whatever happened was only what was meant to happen, so you have no need to feel guilty.'

But Oswald's feelings were the one thing he could not control, even though he had, in Triona's eyes, increased in stature. For whatever the *Mabinogion* might imply, true love is based on something more complex than the admiration of high deeds. Oswald still thought that if he could win the Chain of Command, he would win Triona's love with it. But it was clear this task belonged not to him, but to Triona herself. And to her sister Nuala, whose current circumstances made her collaboration doubly difficult to secure.

IV

The Magic Fiddler

39

'Tell my sisters', said Nuala when she learned they needed her help, 'it may be too late. I hoped to walk again on the green downland turf, and drink the dewy air. But these walls have grown too high, and the guards have grown too cunning. I dreamed my sisters would come for me, but they were too busy. I dreamed someone else would come, and I still can't believe he's forgotten. Yet by the time the authorities decide to give me my life back, there'll be nothing left to give.'

'I'll tell your sisters,' said Linden Richmont, who in these last days was often by Nuala's side. 'Or I'll bring them here. But there are things you should know. The Centre for Alternative Healing has been compromised. Peter Goodlunch is dead, his secret lost. Triona and the others are on a course of action that can only bring them into conflict with the authorities – and with me. They may try to make you part of it. I want you to understand – I never meant things to turn out this way!'

'Bring them here soon,' said Nuala. 'Before the hour-glass is broken.'

But Linden could bring no-one anywhere without consulting Myles Overton first. For whether or not he was implicated in the abduction of Triona's sister Karen, he could hardly dissociate himself from the incarceration of Triona's sister Nuala. And this time the whole majesty of the law was behind him. Had he, as he claimed, acquired interests in penal institutions as a logical extension of his leisure industry activities? Were the terms of the sell-off to the private sector really too attractive to refuse? Or had he done so, as Finbar Direach implied, specifically to get to Nuala, and to have Linden Richmont forge a relationship with the sister who, with Chantal and Karen out of the way, was potentially the most troublesome?

Linden did not know the answer. She had not yet reached the point of asking the question. But she knew that if Triona wanted Nuala back she, Linden, would fight. Where had Triona been when Nuala needed her? Only she herself had been there for Nuala in her time of need, Linden thought. She forgot for a moment she had been there for Myles Overton.

40

Is there life outside the hourglass, Myles Overton wondered, or is there only madness? Sometimes he thought he lived on the edge of madness. What of it? Some of history's greatest achievers had kangaroos in their top paddock. He lived on the edge of madness, and he learnt to appreciate its qualities and colours. It was like living on the edge of a wood. You could stroll through it of an evening, listening to the rustlings in the hedgerows. You needn't venture far enough in to get lost.

Madness, to Myles Overton, was an amenity.

'I invented the myth of Leatherwing', he boasted to his niece, 'to scare the crap out of people, and play on their vulnerability to their own nightmares. I invented it for my own purposes and that's bloody that.'

But he sometimes seemed to have a quite different view of the Leatherwing business. Take the case of Karen Greenwood. Surely there was more to her disappearance than met the eye? The Myles Overton Leisure Group might be robust in its business practices, but, as Myles Overton said, it did not go around kidnapping tarts. If indeed that was what had happened – for while there were some questions Myles Overton refused to answer, there were others he refused to ask. 'Then again – I'm sometimes bloody mad. So who knows?'

When Linden returned to her office after visiting Nuala Greenwood and found the ineffectual managing director of Strategic Marketing waiting to ask advice, she knew Myles Overton would be mad. Word was already out that terms had been agreed with the malcontents. Tom Baleworker would claim the arrangements were made behind his back. His reputation would ensure this was believed, since no-one would ever suspect him of acting reasonably. Besides, Myles Overton looked on Tom Baleworker like a brother. The managing director on the other hand had been caught being lenient towards staff before. He was even briefly suspected of being in league with Peter Goodlunch. The Myles Overton Leisure Group used Strategic Marketing for branding and distribution in all its major activities; entertainment, clubs, cable television, sports and leisure supplies, football, hotels, and the recent diversification into alternative healing centres and privatized penal institutions. Any implication that it might turn into an enlightened and caring employer would cause its share prices to plummet. Linden felt sorry for the ineffectual managing director, but there was little she could do without going out on a limb herself.

'You'd better explain matters in person. You're better off if it comes from you rather than one of your enemies in the organization. That's the only advice I can offer.' For her own part she was covering things as best she could. She had to handle the press on Tracey Dunn, and issue denials all round about the Centre for Alternative Healing, since denouncing Triona Greenwood would be too dangerous. She arranged for a sympathetic interview with *Top People* magazine. She hoped that the way Myles Overton dealt with the managing director would not create another public-relations challenge. She touched his shoulder in a sad charade of solidarity. People think they can avoid selling their soul, she reflected, and merely rent a couple of rooms on the ground floor to make ends meet. But if they do, they'd better look carefully at the lease!

'If only', she said to herself, 'Myles Overton were not Myles Overton.' After Triona's fateful visit to Cornwall, Linden had felt as the managing director did now, even though in her uncle's eyes she could do no wrong. She was frustrated by what she saw as the theft of the unique selling proposition for a whole chain of franchised Centres, each with their little 'Cup of Charms' logo and a certificate in Celtic lettering explaining the significance of the legend. The dream that they could become the McDonalds of alternative health was very dear to her. She went to see

Myles Overton with a memorandum explaining matters from her own point of view, and listing those she felt primarily to blame for things going so badly awry. But, the note said, although it was not Linden's fault, as a senior executive she must take responsibility for the mistakes of others. Accordingly, while on a personal level he would always be everything to her, on a business level the only correct course was to ask to be released from her contract with the Myles Overton Group, so she could never let him down again.

'Don't be so bloody stupid,' exclaimed Myles Overton affectionately when he read the note. 'You and me don't need paper and writing. We belong to each other. That's the way it will always be. Now tear that flaming thing up and have a drink. And we'll talk about what we're going to do to those bastard drongos who let both of us down!'

There was no expressing Linden's relief at these words. Yet deep down she knew she would have felt greater relief had he let her go. She scarcely admitted this to herself, but she admitted it to Nuala Greenwood, with whom she had a curious intimacy even though the basis of their meetings was that Linden was in charge of public-relations for the prison, and Nuala was the biggest public relations liability any privatized prison could be stuck with.

'It's funny,' said Linden, 'sometimes I think you're the only one I trust.'

'Well, you know I'm not going anywhere.'

Nuala also thought that prison was relative, and Linden should watch out. 'Nobody can hold another captive without their complicity,' she quoted from Neill Fife's book on prison reform. 'I don't say you're Myles Overton's prisoner, as I am and my sister Karen may be. But I do say you may be your own, and his organization may be the prison you've built for yourself.'

That is why when Linden parted from the ineffectual managing director she felt a hot tear trying to creep out of the corner of her eye. She told him not to worry, since Myles Overton was not as bad as everyone thought, but although she tried to focus on the entrepreneur at his most charming, her mind kept getting the image of a dark fuliginous shadow with claw-like hands, which made her feel confused and insecure.

41

When Triona, Dawn and Sophie came to visit their sister Nuala in prison, the walls were made of steel and glass, and they knew they had not come as often as they might, and that Linden Richmont had come more often than she should. Among the reinforced screens they waited uneasily, opaque people in a transparent room. Dispassionate women in caps observed every movement of their faces. They spoke to each other as little as possible, avoiding each other's eyes as though they themselves had committed the crimes for which the glass walls provided retribution.

Although Finbar Direach said all the sisters must help in the affair of the cauldron, no-one thought it included Nuala, who was in jail, or Chantal, who might be anywhere. 'But Nuala must play her part,' insisted Finbar Direach when he met Triona at a secret rendezvous. 'For the Clay Man spoke the truth. I can tell you nothing further, for I'm going on a journey. But don't be surprised if it turns out I've been closer to Nuala than any of you, and for longer. Nor if it turns out that soon, I'll be closer still.'

'But how can that be true, with Nuala where she is?'

'I would like to say more on the matter,' he repeated. 'But I've a long way to go, and little time to get there.'

Nuala had always been slightly apart from the others, the father's favourite. She was always complaining of being ill although the other sisters thought she laid it on a bit thick. They saw her as flirtatious and attention-seeking before she was imprisoned and became a cause célèbre. They may even have thought that if she hadn't put on airs by claiming intimacy with individuals in illegal organizations, the problem with the authorities might never have arisen. It was just the same in her teens when she claimed a passionate affair with another notorious freedom fighter. Although if the Clay Man thought she might assist in recovering the chain whose wearer could not be disobeyed, maybe he knew something the sisters didn't. In their opinion, nevertheless, it was hard for Nuala to help them because Nuala was where she could help no-one, and no-one could help her.

'Tom Baleworker thought Nuala was indispensable. Clay Man or no clay man, he seemed to know what he was talking about,' Sophie reflected.

'Well, she's hardly likely to find the Chain of Command in here,' said Triona.

'Well, she's hardly likely to find it anywhere else,' said Dawn, who was already becoming disillusioned and had stated that if they were planning anything like the Strategic Marketing débâcle, they could count her out.

It is true that most prison governors would look askance if a notorious inmate requested several weeks parole to look for a chain with compelling powers to exchange with a clay man for information about part of the cauldron which once belonged to a mythical healer, so that their sister could be rescued from a shadowy figure allied to one of Europe's most prominent and successful leisure entrepreneurs who also happened to own the prison in question. And while the campaign for Nuala's freedom was gathering momentum, her health was poor and her options limited. There again, perhaps a prison is not a bad place to look for chains, after all.

'And that', Triona told Nuala through a device in a glass screen, 'is the bottom line.'

Nuala looked at her sister with tired wisdom. 'Well, I might've been able to help you once. But no-one came to see me, and many opportunities have been lost.'

'We're sorry,' said Triona. 'We're all sorry. But we helped with your campaign, and collected signatures.'

'Well, perhaps you did all you could. But this chain, now, can you describe it?'

Triona gave her the limited amount of information she had from Tom Baleworker, supplemented by some that Neill Fife got from the British Museum.

'It could be I've heard of a chain like that,' Nuala said. 'Or possibly not. In the end all chains are one chain. In the end, we forge our own chains in life, and in death too, for that matter.'

Triona fought an impulse to tell Nuala to pull herself together. She felt she'd been fighting an impulse to tell Nuala to pull herself together all her life. Nuala, she felt, was the most untogether of all the sisters, even including Dawn, who was so untogether she accidentally got pregnant twice. Nuala loved sad, melancholy things, wistful music, and ballads about people who dressed up as sailors to follow their sweethearts, and were discovered by the crew and thrown overboard.

'Think about it,' said Triona, knowing that Nuala's ambiguity was another of her affectations. 'If not for the rest of us, for Karen.'

'I was never close to Karen. The rest of you were closer to Karen. I had other intimates.'

This was true. Nuala was the only sister who was absent the night of Karen's disappearance. The police investigation made a big thing of it, but she had only been at a ceilidh somewhere, playing melancholy tunes. 'I'll think about it,' Nuala said. 'I might have a few tricks up my sleeve. Or if I don't, I might still have some influence with somebody who does!'

'Each of us has their own friendships and attachments,' Triona said soothingly. She did not want to debate what was real and what was not. She knew exactly what Nuala was talking about, but would have preferred her to focus on some more practical way of progressing the search. 'We all have our hopes and dreams. But the person you're thinking of has forgotten you and thrown himself into the politics of a foreign land. He can't help, and he won't come.'

'He promised,' said Nuala, smiling. 'And he still might be reminded of his promise. Although everything must follow its proper course, and I don't know how all this will help you with your missing chain.'

'Well,' said Triona, 'no-one knows everything, for sure. I promised I'd ask you to help, and I have.' She afterwards told Neill Fife she had not argued because she did not want to cause Nuala unnecessary distress. 'Nuala thinks she will be dramatically rescued by General Benyamin Al Jihad, the notorious Arab despot and ex-freedom fighter,' she explained sadly. 'Her misfortunes have finally affected her mind.'

Neill felt nearly as guilty as Triona because he too had visited Nuala only rarely, except while he was writing his influential book on the psychology of prison reform, which was in the same series as his influential book on industrial disputes. 'Her fantasies are all she has,' he said. 'Now is not the time to take those from her, when everything else has been taken. What we're seeing is attention-seeking behaviour, quite normal in these cases. We'll look elsewhere for Solomon's chain. In the British Museum, or the private collection of some potentate. There's no need to give up hope.'

When the tapes from the communication devices were sent up to the governor, and from the governor to certain interested parties, they too agreed that the matter would come to nothing. 'They've set up a futile dialogue with Nuala Greenwood,' said the interested parties. 'By doing so, they may be playing directly into our hands. Also they've given up looking for bits of cauldron, and are looking for bits of chain. Frankly, cauldron, shmauldron. The main thing is that your woman Nuala must be discredited, and swiftly. The campaign for her release poses a very real threat to the rule of law and to respect for authority in general. A wind of change is in the air, and that could be dangerous for all concerned. It's fortunate', they added knowingly, 'that Nuala's worst enemy is herself, and her second worst is her best friend.'

'That's true – but to understand how it came about, you'd have to go back to the old days at Coldharbour, and a schoolgirl who journeyed to a romantic destination. You'd have to understand what a strange alliance was forged there, and by what an unusual pledge it was sealed.'

42

The story of Nuala, Jihad, and the Magic Fiddler is obfuscated by the fact that by the time it excited general interest most of the people involved were either dead or insane, and some were dead or insane at the time it happened. Therefore inaccuracies of detail are only to be expected. Phelim Dalaigh's involvement and even Linden Richmont's were peripheral and as both were interested parties their accounts could hardly be objective. Besides Linden was afterwards entirely compromised. Triona had her own version, but she altered the facts considerably to compensate for what she saw as Nuala's penchant for self-aggrandizement. As for Phelim Dalaigh, some say he met his end even before the tale was told, perishing in an unspeakable manner from which foul play was never ruled out. But others say that far from having died, he never truly lived, and was identical with the Magic Fiddler himself, who in turn was identical with a certain gentleman implicated in a serious breach of trust and a catastrophic breach of sea defences.

What nobody will dispute is that Nuala Greenwood was wrongfully imprisoned for countless years because public opinion demanded a scapegoat and the authorities needed to be seen to take action. Nuala used to play mandolin with Neill Fife's friend Ewan McEuen who once supported the Battlefield Band at Fairfield Halls, but not even the severest critic of her musical abilities could regard that as a criminal offence. There was also considerable evidence that neither Nuala nor those apprehended with her had, on the alleged evening, been within a hundred miles of the alleged scene of the alleged outrage. Mistaken identity was a possibility. It was true that Nuala looked a lot like Chantal, and Chantal would cheerfully have done what Nuala was accused of doing, and blown up what Nuala was accused of helping blow up. But Chantal always maintained she had been blowing up something else at the time. She said the whole Nuala affair was a fit-up by the authorities, although she admitted the authorities might have been trying to fit her up, and fitted Nuala up by accident, so to that extent the mistaken-identity theory was accurate.

Whichever way it was looked at, Nuala's case turned on the question of whether she was at Phelim Dalaigh's Apocalyptic Ceilidh at the Railway Arms in Bolton. Yet a series of bizarre accidents prematurely evicted from the world all those who could testify to this. People wrote books on Nuala's trial and the books won awards. Television programmes were made which were universally agreed to be a credit to the independence and integrity of the media. But even when other people who did what Nuala was accused of doing began to be released due to changing politics, her own case ground wearily on.

Jihad, of course, would have heard about Nuala's battle for justice through Reuters and the BBC World Service. If he chose not to intervene, perhaps it was because he had sufficient problems of his own. Perhaps the time was not right to reveal his hand to the world at large, and risk disclosure of the story which had begun with a chance encounter in a tourist town, and even now was unfolding in a ruined city besieged by the dunes of the inexorable Sahara.

43

'He has things on his mind. He hasn't forgotten you,' Linden Richmont told Nuala the next time she came, not knowing whether she said it purely because it lay in her interests to play along.

'I knew that he wouldn't,' she replied. 'But there's no time. If he doesn't act, it'll be too late.'

Nuala's remark was no more than the truth, and the tears on her face shone sharp as diamonds. She did not tell Linden she had been visited by Triona and the others, nor that she had been asked to search within the prison walls for a certain item of interest to them. But by that time Linden already knew.

If Nuala expected much from Jihad, it was no more than he owed her. It seemed like a thousand years since two children had sworn unbreakable faith by the sea wall in the picturesque dockside of Tangier, a mile from the tenement where the young Jihad lived with his brother and his ageing father. The future general, at fourteen, was working as a waiter in a seafood bar. His father had fled from his native country to escape the oppression which was then commonplace. The two sons, one of whom later became a celebrated rock musician in the West, had to deal with life as best they could. Nuala, contrastingly, knew only privilege and security. She had travelled to Tangier on a school trip funded by the Drugs Education Trust on the grounds that if children observed the narcotics trade at first hand, they would be able to make clearer decisions on drug-related issues. When the handsome young waiter asked Nuala to go with him and watch the sun set over the ocean, she had never met anyone like him before, nor he her.

What was between Jihad and Nuala was only what is between any young couple who exchange tokens on the evening of the summer solstice, at the moment when the sun flashes green as it sinks below the Western horizon. The only difference was, destiny refused to let them forget it. While his brother Salman practised scales and scorned the constraints of a rigid ideology, Ben, always the sensitive one, made up his mind to set the world to rights. Hearing from his father about the injustices that had obliged the old man to flee the country of his birth, the youthful Jihad decided to return there, exact vengeance from his father's oppressors, and restore the honour of his family. He told Nuala of this resolve at their final parting beneath the harbour light, and it was there that they exchanged their keepsakes.

'If ever you need me,' Jihad told her, handing her a silver ring that had once belonged to the Queen of Lebanon, 'neither shout nor call, but think only the single thought of me, and my armies will cross the water and come to your aid.'

But all Nuala had to give was a piece of blarneystone presented to her the previous year during a school trip to Ireland, when she became infatuated with an apprentice on a cockle stall in Dublin. 'I'll never have any armies,' she told Jihad. 'Nor do I think my greatness in life will lie anywhere other than in the greatness of my love for you, and even that may be swallowed up in the twists and changes of unfeeling fate. But take this stone that was given me by the person I once thought closest to me in all the world. It's worth little, but remember that you were given it by Nuala Greenwood, one of six sisters from the oldest family in Britain, and in the time of your greatest need she will not fail you, but send the Magic Fiddler to be by your side.'

'The Magic Fiddler?' For a moment he thought she was joking, but a look into her eyes at once assured him of the seriousness with which these words were intended, and forbade him to enquire any further as to their meaning.

'I must be going,' he said instead. 'And by the time the dawn stretches her grey loom into the eastern sky, we will be in different worlds. Perhaps we will never be together again, but I know now that we will never be apart.'

Often afterwards he thought of the Magic Fiddler, but could discover nothing about him except a brief reference in some manuscripts his ancestors had on loan from the Library of Alexandria when it was destroyed by fire. For Jihad, although he never boasted about it, belonged to one of the oldest families in the region. These manuscripts referred to a legendary musician sent by the enchantress Caryddwen to play beneath the walls of Mannannan Mac Llyr Mac Lugh's prison, when that chieftain was incarcerated by Queen Maeve of Skye. He was sent, Jihad discovered, to fetch a certain message, but as things turned out, he did not carry out this task correctly – which led to many bad consequences.

Life went on, people lost touch with one another, and changed. Jihad's brother travelled to Ireland where he changed his name to Fast Jerry Sullivan and met, ironically, with the very cockle apprentice who first broke Nuala's heart, with whom he formed the seminal folk punk band widely known as the Pits. Ironically their front man, Seamus 'Eight Pints' McGallon, later based his style and appearance on what little was known of Finbar Direach. Meanwhile Nuala's own name became known in *fleadhs*, or exhibitions of traditional music. Her mother taught her about the Celtic heritage, and her father encouraged her to take mandolin lessons and express her creative side. In the Middle East immemorial hatreds were fuelled by new-found petroleum wealth and governments rose and fell in the fickle loyalty of the masses. For many years Jihad struggled in obscurity, but one day he was given a gold chain by a mad archaeologist who mistook him for the rightful heir of Solomon. His fortunes changed, and he finally achieved the power for which he had striven. He promised to rule according to the truth of Allah and the truth of his heart, and although he caused much suffering, the people loved him.

44

Although Myles Overton caused much suffering, it was not his principle motive. He had started with nothing, and he wanted everything. That was all. Every action he took, he saw as inevitable. In a rare interview with *Top People* magazine he outlined his philosophy; although it was agreed there would be no questions about the Centre for Alternative Healing, why the managing director of Strategic Marketing was on sick leave, or whether Myles Overton's security people were searching for Peter Goodlunch's ex-secretary, Tracey Dunn.

'Ask about how he built the business up from nothing,' said Linden Richmont, the publicist. 'And how he feels about the ordinary working bloke.' The interviewer from *Top People* magazine agreed to do this, and even said they could have copy approval if Linden would join him for dinner. But Dave Doom, who stood beside Myles Overton throughout the interview, said if the interviewer printed anything they didn't like he would get his legs broken, copy approval or no copy approval. And, Dave Doom said, if he propositioned Linden again, the consequences would make having his legs broken seem like a sensuous massage by a Swedish model. Clearly, the interviewer thought, Dave Doom had his own ideas about Linden Richmont.

'The ordinary working bloke is the salt of the bloody earth,' Myles Overton said when the tape was running. 'But the ponces and pissheads that head up the big corporations? Do me a favour! I make more money in an hour than they see in a lifetime. I can buy and sell them a hundred times over. I can buy and sell their flaming bankers. That's why I own the future. And that's what I call bloody progress.'

The world, said Myles Overton, was full of ponces and pissheads, and that was why the ordinary working blokes would prefer that it was all owned by Myles Overton. 'I built up my business', he said, 'because I know what the ordinary working bloke wants. He wants the right bloody product, at the right bloody price. That's all there is to it.'

Myles Overton made much of the fact that he had the common touch, and had started out with nothing. He was prone to suggest he had begun life as a humble sheep-shearer and wombat-hunter in the Australian outback, although everybody knew he was of central European origin and emigrated in his early twenties to Australia, where an advantageous marriage and a shadowy mentor enabled him to found a worldwide leisure network. Furthermore, although his essential genius was to provide the right product at the right price, he was careful to cultivate top officials and heads of state, and many of his enterprises were based on lucrative government contracts and privatizations.

'When your business empire was established and you came to the UK, you intended to buy a rural estate and adopt the lifestyle of an English country gentleman,' said the interviewer. 'Yet your bid to purchase Coldharbour Abbey was blocked by the Heritage Commission, who did not want it falling into private hands. Was that a major disappointment to you?'

'You can take it from me I don't get disappointed. I get *even*, right? When I want something, I bloody get it. As for Coldharbour, you can believe what you choose. You might think there was something there I wanted – but if there was, you can bet the dipshit Heritage Commission will never find it. And no worries – because I could buy and sell the Heritage Commission ten times over anyway, and still have enough change to pay off the bloody national debt!' He did not, however, mention his involvement in negotiations with the Heritage Commission itself about the contract for a lasting monument: perhaps even as a trade-off for the Coldharbour affair many years before. In business it is never wise to show all your cards, particularly when an interviewer from *Top People* magazine might infer you are up to something.

'Well,' continued the interviewer, unaware that Myles Overton had his own agenda, 'you eventually built your own headquarters to an award-winning design. As well as developing the Myles Overton Leisure Group into a leading export-revenue earner you've worked closely with the authorities in sport, education, entertainment and the media. Yet what do you say to those who believe de-regulation and the private ownership of national institutions undermines individual freedom?'

'Frankly, individual freedom is so much liberal bloody hot air. The ordinary working bloke doesn't give a dingo's spit about individual freedom. In my book, individuals only succeed by undermining institutions, and institutions only succeed by undermining individuals. I haven't paid good money for bloody national institutions just to see them undermined, right?'

'Yet you are the greatest individualist of all!'

Myles Overton pinched the bridge of his nose and rubbed the corner of his ordinary working jaw. 'Believe me, I'm a bloody institution.'

'And is it in this spirit that you have pioneered private-sector involvement in penal facilities?'

'The right bloody product, at the right bloody price,' said Myles Overton. Prisons, as he saw it, were a major part of the leisure industry and top of his list of national institutions ripe for commercial exploitation. He had tried but so far failed to buy up a few law courts in order to streamline the through-put to the facilities he owned. He saw no mismatch between the jails and his other leisure interests, and the interviewer, who had stayed in one of Myles Overton's hotels, realized there was indeed common ground. 'I cater for all the needs of the ordinary working bloke,' Myles Overton concluded. 'And if the ordinary working bloke needs banging up, he can rely on me to bloody do it.'

'Yet your most controversial inmate at the moment is neither ordinary, nor a bloke,' said the interviewer cleverly. 'How do you feel about the Nuala Greenwood case, and the fact that after all the embarrassment her behaviour has caused prison officials, it looks as if her appeal will finally be successful?'

'Straight up,' said Myles Overton, 'you can take it from me that anyone who ends up in one of my bloody prisons is as guilty as a turd in a bidet, and don't be surprised if some new facts come out to prove it. The ordinary working bloke knows that when someone's put in jail for something, it means they did it. And no shithead lawyer's going to prove otherwise.'

The interviewer from *Top People* magazine nodded, although secretly he read the left-wing press and believed that in the Nuala Greenwood case something had gone badly awry. 'And finally', he said, 'can you tell our readers the name of your favourite restaurant, and which three fashion accessories you consider you could not live without?'

45

Triona, Sophie and Dawn talked late into the night, and listened to Nuala's old tapes, although the songs were difficult to understand and the music was composed in Celtic modes, and washed over the listener like the sea over a half-tide rock.

'Have you seen *Top People* magazine?' Triona asked.

'What, the one with Neill Fife in it?'

'No, the one with Myles Overton in it. He says Strategic Marketing and the Healing Centre were nothing to do with him, and the authorities have information that will result in Nuala's appeal being quashed.

'It's always crap, that magazine, and they fake the "at home" pictures.'

'Still, I don't like this stuff with Linden Richmont . . . '

They were quiet, listening to Nuala's tapes and letting the harmonies wash over them like the salty waves. They had never listened much in the old days. When Nuala played to them at home, they had often started talking to her about some irrelevant topic right in the middle of a song. Sisters often find it hard to appreciate one another's talents. They found Nuala's lyrics obscure, self-indulgent, and very long. Many of them were about young girls dying at the hands of their enemies, rather than betraying a long-lost lover. There was one about a girl trapped in an enchanted prison-tower and finally rescued by a brigand prince who put her on a white horse and himself on a dapple grey, and made her the lady of as much land as she could ride on a long summer's day. At the time it was taped they thought it referred to Karen and were irritated that Nuala should now start identifying with the lost sister, which they saw as another affectation. Later, they didn't think anything much, but although they had nothing against traditional music, they preferred it done by the Pits or Van Morrison.

Now, the tunes brought a lump to the sisters' throats. Perhaps they had underestimated Nuala. Perhaps others had seen her true worth, and now it was too late. They did not go so far as to admit that they had driven her into the escapist dream of a distant yet powerful lover, or even driven her into the arms of Linden Richmont. But they made a mental note that if they ever had another sister, they would properly support her singing career, value her romantic notions about the human condition, and visit her more often in prison.

46

If Triona and the others visited Nuala in the prison they were searched in a humiliating way and made to talk through electronic devices. Linden, on the contrary, had unrestricted access, although Myles Overton had secretly ensured she was provided with a means to protect herself if anything untoward occurred. This meant Linden was the only face-to-face, non-eavesdropped-on human contact Nuala had, unless one counts lawyers. That, Triona thought, might be why she was so smug when they met on the stairs, Linden on the way in, Triona on the way out.

'Don't forget she's my sister – and if any harm comes to her . . . ' Triona warned.

'A bit late to start worrying about that,' said Linden. Their eyes met, as they had the night of their first encounter at the Centre for Alternative Healing, when Triona thought Linden had her best interests at heart. Now, as then, each seemed to know more than she was saying. In Linden, there was a kind of longing, for she herself had no sisters. In Triona, the feeling that Linden could help them so much – but had made her choices.

'Well,' said Linden finally, 'how's Finbar Direach?'

'Well,' said Triona, 'as I recall, the Centre for Alternative Healing had no record of anyone of that name or description.'

'Well,' said Linden, 'that would seem to be that, then.' And still, there were a hundred things they did not say. They passed one another uneasily on the stairs, knowing they would meet again. But when Linden went to Nuala, she found her much changed.

Under normal circumstances, Nuala and Linden would have had little time for each other. Linden was worldly, ambitious, and tone-deaf. Nuala was a musician and an idealist. The only thing they had in common was that neither of them had committed a serious crime against the state. Certain topics of conversation inevitably divided them. Nuala saw straight through Linden's attempts to reconcile her to the little schemes and inducements that form part of the regime of any privatized prison. It was she who pointed out the flaws in a scheme dreamed up by Strategic Marketing whereby long-term inmates could buy their own cells, working extra hours to earn the necessary money. But she seemed not to resent Linden for trying. Equally, subjects like Leftie Legg's upcoming book on Nuala's case, and her desire to communicate with him, were a sore point with Linden. So were Nuala's views on the internal affairs of the island of Ireland, which, like her circle of acquaintances, developed from her love of its music and had often been at odds with the rule of law. Nevertheless they were frequently able to skirt round the sensitive areas and found themselves enjoying one another's company.

Perhaps they were drawn together by guilt. Linden knew Nuala's conviction was secured by evidence largely improvized on the witness stand by the arresting officers, and was uneasy about her part in enforcing the resulting judgement. Nuala did not know Linden's relationship with Myles Overton and the authorities, but understood Linden was somehow charged with keeping the lid on things. Nuala, in contrast, was prone to attention-seeking behaviour like rooftop protests and making hostages of prison guards. This meant that despite her other work commitments Linden constantly had to be brought in to talk her down or negotiate a release.

The difference was that Linden allowed herself the luxury of self-pity, but Nuala never lost hope, even in the very darkest moments. The authorities had taken away her mandolin so that she could not play subversive tunes on it, but they were unable to destroy her spirit. Nor could they obliterate the belief that her childhood sweetheart would one day turn his attention to the wrongs she herself had received, as he had so successfully addressed the wrongs suffered by the poor and oppressed of his native land.

'He may have forgotten, or he may even now be exerting his influence in ways neither of us can understand. I can never give up hope.' Nuala shook her auburn hair back from a pale, shining face. 'Before I die', she added, 'I want only to know he remembers, and to hear once again the summer rain tumbling a storm across the downland meadows while Murdo Mulligan plays *The Boys of Blue Hill* on the Uillean pipes.'

Linden could not tell her that Murdo had been caught by a stray bullet in an unfortunate border incident. Nuala's reference to her own death was not rhetorical. By the time this conversation took place Nuala and her companions had been exonerated and the paperwork for her pardon was being put through as quickly as possible. But Nuala's health was far from ideal. She had a problem with her insides and specialists had given her only months to live. The Centre for Alternative Healing, which had the only documented success with such cases, was temporarily closed for business. So Linden found it easier to tell her that Murdo – together with Nuala's old bass player Connell, who was in fact a victim of the internal disciplinary procedures of an illegal organization – was fund-raising in America and could not be contacted.

Because of the health problem, Linden was obliged to visit Nuala in the prison hospital, and as she sat by her bedside they yarned like old friends about times gone by. And both of them cried, not for the sadness that is in the world but for the happiness that is only a hair's breadth out of it. They spoke, too, of Jihad himself, for although his politics were controversial and he had, perhaps for Nuala's sake, maintained a secret traffic with shadowy organizations within the British archipelago, it was clear he did only what he believed was right.

'I never met him, your Ben,' Linden said, drawn into Nuala's world despite herself. 'But one doesn't need to meet a true hero to know him for what he is. The heart of a true hero is like a lighthouse and his will can't be concealed or distorted. He'll come for you if he promised he would.'

'He needn't send an army. He needn't even come himself. Even if he thought of me, I believe it would make a difference . . . '

'I'm sure he thinks of you. I bet he thinks about you all the time,'

Linden said. They both knew she was prevaricating. A friend to whom one can tell the truth is good, but a friend who knows it already is even better.

'If you couldn't have your wish to see him, what other wish would you have?' Linden asked, her eyes brimming like weir-gates.

'To send the Magic Fiddler to him, as a reminder of our pledge. But sometimes I think that's just another adolescent fantasy, and I know that my time's running short.'

That night, as so many nights, Jihad dreamed again of seven fighters that streaked in under the radar and stormed the desert skies with orange, crimson, sulphur-gold and flame-brown.

47

The Magic Fiddler only comes to people when all else has failed them.

Jihad, lying beside the dry canal with the side of his face in the sand, his deep eyes staring at nothing, refusing food and water, was going through a period of self-doubt. He grew weaker every day. He was not necessarily a bad man, but a victim of the times he lived in. If he killed a thousand people, he only meant it for the best. Once, by an action which Jihad's enemies said he brought on himself, a city was struck by terrible weapons, and women and small children were among those who died. With their loss, Jihad's own self-confidence was also shattered. Although his faith as a Moslem was in no way compromised, it now seemed to him that God was merely making up the rules as he went along, like a policeman improvising on the witness stand. All Jihad had striven for now seemed meaningless, because although many crimes must be laid at his door, his only motive had been to make the world a safer place to grow up in for innocent children of all sects and nations.

The dry canal ran through a ruined township founded by an itinerant community of Irish monks who unknowingly sheltered the prophet Mohammed, and whose settlement as a result was protected for all eternity. This was a favourite resort of Jihad in times of stress and melancholy. With the surcease of the waterway during recent years, the place had gone into a long and irreversible decline. Tokens of the intrusive materialism of Western culture now lay half mud-submerged in the canal bed; hi-fi equipment, shopping trolleys and dish washers. Beyond, bleached masonry reared against an implacable sky. No light could break the gathering dusk. From the canal bank to the foothills in the north where the Sahara meets the sea, the buildings were deserted. No edict had been passed, no signal given, but family by family the people had departed. During ten years the rusty vans, handcarts and overloaded donkeys trekked outwards through the desert. Now only Jihad came here, sending away his guards and dervishes and refusing to accept messages.

'Perhaps I should have stayed in Tangier.' His voice sounded flat against the silent dunes, like someone who does not expect to be answered. He turned his face westwards away from all-seeing Mecca, and hooded his eyes with impenetrable shadow. When the Magic Fiddler approached, Jihad had been in this condition for forty days and forty nights and his destiny was upon him.

'Perhaps', he muttered to himself, 'I can serve my country better by dying. Revenge for the actions against us is out of the question. I can't lay my people open to such cruel reprisals as would undoubtedly be elicited by any move against the Western powers – or the International Community as we must now call them. Perhaps indeed I am a mad dog, as their leaders once alleged. But a dog is the most honourable of creatures for he is loyal to the end and one guarded the prophet Mohammed, peace be upon him, while he slept, as a result of which none of the Faithful should kill a dog. And as for madness, is it not esteemed a holy state in Islamic culture? Yet there comes a time when one has nowhere to turn. Perhaps it is better to end things now, and let history come, like a scene shifter in a provincial theatre, and create new patterns and perspectives.'

As he muttered these words in the confusion of his mind, he remembered someone whom he had never quite managed to forget, through all the twists and changes of unfeeling fate. Someone who was not part of the desolation around him, but of something which could never be destroyed. Whose memory, perhaps, had once given him the strength to carry on through the long watches of the night. He reached inside his robes and touched a keepsake that still hung from the great gold chain which once belonged to King Solomon. As he did this, his hearing was arrested by a thin cadence of sound which crept into his ears and wound itself round his sullen heart like ivy round a stone.

Looking up he noticed a small bubble car parked in the middle distance, and perched on a rock like a large unkempt crow, a curious fellow who appeared to be playing the Lebanese three-string violin. Jihad opened his mouth to be angry that anyone should have the temerity to creep up and start scratching and scraping their way into his time of grief. But the music snatched the anger away as the wind snatches a dried leaf. Surely all-powerful Allah, than whom there is no other God, must himself have inspired the little musician, so engagingly did he play!

The newcomer was little more than a metre and a half in height, and he had a wrinkled brown face filled with teeth so jagged they resembled a row of broken bottles on a fence. But the face was smiling for all that, and hazel eyes danced like fool's fire. The smile was a queer mixture of mockery, merriment and kindness. He was like no other individual Jihad had ever seen and equally his fiddle was like no other fiddle. Although it was made of carved wood in the conventional manner, the ardour of the music was too much for the timber laminates, with the result that they kept coming back to life and sending out impudent sprays of twig and foliage in all directions. This did not trouble the fiddler at all and nor did the fact that his music had a similar effect on the immediate surroundings. Desert stones jumped around like toads, cacti shook themselves and burst into flower, the sand hissed and whispered to create a soft percussion line in time to the music. Certain fossils which had shown little animation or vigour since the Pleistocene era rapidly jumped up, rubbed their eyes, and fluttered their leathery wings in appreciation. A few yards away a damp patch appeared on the ground and then a blue fountain chuckled and splashed into the air.

'You play very well,' Jihad said hesitantly, because after the music his voice sounded as coarse as sackcloth. 'But tell me, do you know *Desert Homeland, Country of the Free*? I am planning to make it our new national anthem, and I myself had a hand in composing it, coming as I do from a musical family.'

'Well, I know what I know,' grinned the fiddler. 'But I don't do requests, your worship.'

'What about numbers by The Pits? The bass player, Fast Jerry

Sullivan, was my brother. Jerry Sullivan, you know, is an anagram of Salman Ibn Jihad.'

'I would venture that anagrams are not your strong point. For one thing, there isn't an H in it.'

'In English, perhaps, but Arabic is another language, based in a different culture. But again, perhaps the lack of an H and various other letters may not be so easily got round. I must ask you to bear with me. I carry the burden of a great sorrow. I sometimes feel I have failed my people, my family, and myself.'

'You failed someone else too,' said the visitor gently, so as not to rub it in. 'Or had you forgotten?'

'I'm wondering', ventured Jihad, 'whether you came here of your own accord, or whether someone sent you.'

'Let's not talk about me,' said the Magic Fiddler. 'But let's talk about you.'

'You are trying to suggest I'm wallowing in self-pity at a time when I should be working to make the world a better place for others.'

'I didn't say that. You said that. Myself, I'm nothing but a fiddle player, as you must understand. The altercations of politics are all beyond me, and I concern myself only in matters of the heart.'

'Once before someone told me that, and said she would lead no armies, and that it would be love and not war that guided her existence. But it is impossible you should know who I speak of.'

'Well, I know what I know. Yet here's me thinking you yourself would have forgotten! But come with me down the *wadi,* and back into the ruined mosque with the dust-brown dunes lying heavily upon the windward side of its dome. For time is of only finite duration, and it occurs to me that the two of us should have a little talk.' General Jihad followed him. All of a sudden, he felt that someone needed him again. It meant a lot to Jihad that someone needed him.

48

The night the strike force invaded Hornsey there was rain in the air and the policemen were damp and inert on the street corners. In the prison hospital Nuala lay dying, for although everyone said she was within reach of her freedom and a substantial amount in compensation from the state, she was too ill to be moved from the feverish bed on which she lay.

'I don't want to die in prison. But if I must, then let the old musicians from the band be brought here, to play me to sleep,' she asked Linden.

'There's no need,' Linden said carefully. 'In a couple of days, you'll be as right as rain.'

'As right as rain?' Nuala's mind seemed to wander, as if recalling the abundant showers of wet childhood summers at Coldharbour, when the drops fell so big you'd think God were slinging them down from whiskey glasses. 'As right as rain? No, not quite. Even the doctors could not conceal from me the true lie of the land in that respect. They did their best to be cheerful, but someone came to me and said that the truth of it is, I'll be lucky to see another sunrise. Even if you could see the sun rise in this place.'

'Now you're romancing. Who could have told you such a thing, when nobody has been with you but me?'

'Pr'aps I just dozed off. At first I thought I heard it from my sisters, but they don't come here much. Then I thought I had the information from a very odd little character, who seems to hang around the edges of one's sleep. He warned me I shouldn't tell you everything I knew, either, for he said you didn't have my best interests at heart. He said you were, in short, here to do a job of work. I said I'd be the judge of who my friends were, thank you very much. I said I'd known about you for ages but we were no less pals if we happened to differ in the matter of politics.'

'That's a thing to say, when we've grown so close! You must be confused because of the medicine you've had,' Linden said with a flush.

Nuala needed to think before answering, and call reserves of energy from an ailing supply. When she did speak, Linden saw it was the truth, and tears pricked her eyes, for although she had betrayed Nuala from the first moment she looked in her face, she realized their friendship was in all likelihood the only real friendship she had ever experienced.

'Ah, don't take on so,' Nuala told her. 'We're friends, and we don't have any secrets from each other, even if we pretend we do. You think I don't know why you can't call the musicians? You think I don't know how they've died, one by one? You think I didn't hear how Fast Jerry

Sullivan died from excessive living, and Paddy Malone, who always loved being on the road, fell into an asphalt spreading machine and is now part of four hundred yards of the M25? You think I didn't connect the authorities with that, when everyone who was at the Railway Arms with Phelim Dalaigh that night started popping off like gorse pods in a July heat wave?' Nuala coughed a number of times, the first few for theatrical effect, because she was always prone to dramatize her situation, and the rest because she really did have a life-threatening illness, and everything she said about her health was true, whether she herself believed it or not.

'Do you think', she continued, 'I failed to guess that when Phelim Dalaigh allegedly caught his private parts in the bellows of his own accordion and died of shock, the Special Section was somehow behind it? Wasn't he after all warned that something of the kind might happen by a fortune-teller in his youth, and didn't he always wear a cricketing box for the fast tunes? No, there have been too many coincidences. Perhaps the authorities were even instrumental in bringing my sisters to see me after so long. Perhaps they thought my involvement would be playing into their hands, and compromise whatever plans have been laid. But there's one friend nobody can compromise, and he's the truest friend of all.'

49

The night General Jihad's elite corps moored their submarine in Greenwich Reach and swam in full commando kit up the eastern trunk sewer and out into the Crouch End drainage cut where it breaks surface beneath Alexandra Palace Hill, the people were at home watching Panorama and the authorities complacent and unprepared.

'Our opponents can make no move,' the authorities told each other. 'In twenty-four hours Nuala will be dead and in no position to refute the new evidence we'll then produce. Her guilt will be proved, seemingly out of her own mouth, and the other related appeals will be quashed automatically as a consequence. The government will be vindicated, Phelim Dalaigh's Apocalyptic Ceilidh will become what it has always been, a fiction, and the people will once again sleep easy in their beds.'

'It's a masterly plan,' the Special Section agreed. 'Nothing can go wrong. Although Linden Richmont can have no official rank and indeed no official existence as a government operative – for she acts purely as liaison with Myles Overton, we'll increase the rank she'd have if she had one to Colonel. Why, if things go on like this, she will soon be equal to Jihad himself!' They congratulated themselves on their astuteness and perhaps sent word to Myles Overton that the danger had been averted. But as they did so twelve shadowy figures smelling horribly of excrement swarmed over the parapet of the Hornsey Lane road bridge and hailed taxis down to Holloway, explaining that they were lager louts returning from a fancy-dress party. 'Funny,' remarked one of the taxi drivers 'I had Fast Jerry Sullivan in the back of my cab once. He had exactly the same nose as you.'

The operation was swift and devastatingly effective. As Linden was about to argue with Nuala once again and then stopped, at last accepting that Nuala really had known all along, sudden disturbances were heard at six points round the perimeter wall and brief silhouettes stood out against the lights of the tower blocks beyond. Then they heard the truncated cry of a guard being neutralized, and muffled footsteps were racing towards them through the east wing of the prison hospital.

'I now see', Linden began, 'I can conceal nothing. But I want you to understand that though I may have betrayed you in every practical way, and there might have been hope even for your health were it not for my meddling and subsequent failures, yet I never betrayed you in my heart. I had a job to do and perhaps the desire to get on in life or please others distorted my integrity, but I want you to know now that our friendship means more to me than anything else.'

At the time she said it, this was true, although her relationship with Myles Overton was complex and seldom far from her thoughts. When Linden was young and walked in the woods of the southern Australian state of Victoria, she thought the wind was caused by the movement of trees, and Myles Overton was nothing but a name. But as she grew older and discovered the movement of trees was caused by the wind, everything took on a new meaning. Then, in a notorious case, her parents were carried off by marauding dingos during a camping holiday, leaving the infant Linden, as sole witness, to face ever more tendentious questions from authorities determined to attribute blame. Only the influence of her charismatic uncle prevented a miscarriage of justice on the scale of that which later befell Nuala, which was perhaps why Linden had a unique insight into Nuala's situation. After his intervention in the matter of her parents, the bond between Linden and Myles Overton was established. At the time the entrepreneur's first wife, from whose fortune he derived the original capital for his corporate ventures in the leisure industry, had died under mysterious circumstances. Linden was his only family; she admired and looked up to him, and he gave her everything she could desire.

But at that time, as she told Nuala, she believed that human circumstances are caused by love, and never dreamed that love is caused by human circumstances, so there was always something missing from their relationship. This made her feel guilty because she owed him everything, and she resolved that she would never let him down, nor give him any reason to think her ungrateful or disloyal. After he put her through business school, therefore, she naturally graduated to his organization, and her loyalty, communication skills and ability to relate to people on all levels proved more valuable than he could ever have guessed.

'People don't understand him,' she told Nuala. 'They see him as amoral, relentless, devoid of human compassion, and possibly in league with a legendary monster called Leatherwing. They don't realize how much he gives to charity.'

'Everyone should refrain from making a judgement until they know the full circumstances,' Nuala said carefully.

'Yet although I've deceived you, I've deceived myself more, because I always convinced myself my actions were ultimately in both our interests.'

'You're still telling me nothing I didn't know, although I'm glad you've finally been able to say it.'

'You knew all this, yet you don't think less of me as a person?'

'I think very little of you as a person,' Nuala said, reaching out a desperately weak hand to touch that of Linden. 'But you're the only friend I have.' With these words, she pulled from her finger the silver ring that once belonged to the Queen of Lebanon and was given to her beneath the harbour light so many years before. 'Take this ring,' she urged, 'for the sake of what we've meant to each other. And now kiss me, because there's not much time.'

And that was how Jihad found them when with two of his most trusted commandos he smashed through the unguarded door of the ward. The two women were hand in hand, Nuala weak yet splendid with a strange inner power, Linden protective yet somehow confused. Linden's left hand held Nuala's right, but Linden's right hand held the means of protecting herself which Myles Overton had provided for her. Although this was only an industrial-strength pepper spray, Jihad was familiar with the Western Powers' achievements in chemical warfare, and could readily believe it to be a weapon of mass destruction. He paused, and took stock of the situation with the military precision which, together with the Chain of Command, had made him undisputed leader of the proudest and most turbulent province on the Mediterranean seaboard.

'I think', he told Linden, spreading his hands well away from his battle-scarred Kalashnikov. 'I think you have, how do you say it? An existential decision to make. Perhaps at this moment no-one but Allah, than whom there is no other God, and his guide Kdhir who in the literature of our faith signifies Truth, can assist you in doing what you believe is right.'

'Unless', cried another voice, as an unexpected figure stepped into the increasingly crowded room, 'Triona Greenwood can!'

50

'How . . . ' began Linden.

'The details aren't important. I met Jihad and the others on the road, arguing with a taxi driver over the fare, for they are a proud people, and don't like being ripped off,' said Triona. 'When I understood where they were going I said I would show them the way, since it was possible we might have a common purpose.'

She did not say whether any Magic Fiddler had led her to Jihad, nor whether the same Magic Fiddler was familiar to her under another name. But that was not important either. Slowly, Linden made her existential decision and lowered the weapon of mass destruction. By now everyone was ignoring it anyway, and she had a feeling events must be allowed to run their course. Meanwhile all that mattered to Jihad was Nuala, and all that mattered to Nuala was Jihad. Even the Chain of Command, for the moment, was forgotten.

'I came,' said Jihad, although his voice shook.

'You took your time.'

'There was much to do. But now – you must come with me. The taxi is waiting. It is of the new type with the snub nose, although the driver is grasping and opportunistic.'

'I thought it would be a milk-white horse, and you'd be on a dapple grey.'

'In the stables of my palace there are a thousand horses, each more beautiful than the last.'

'Can I ride for the length of a long summer's day, and still be the lady of the land beneath my horse's hoofs?'

'For seven days, or more.'

'I thought so,' she said, and closed her eyes contentedly, sinking back among the pillows.

'There's just one thing,' said Triona, as he gathered her sister's sleeping body into his arms. 'The Magic Fiddler, he didn't mention any sort of chain, did he?'

'He did not.'

'He always leaves the hard bits to us. The thing is, that chain. The one you're wearing the Blarney Stone at the end of . . . '

'It belonged to King Solomon himself.'

'These old relics. Funny how they always belonged to King Solomon, or the Queen of Sheba—'

'You speak as one who tries to bring down the price,' said Jihad, who came from a nation of horse-traders.

'It's only this, Nuala wanted . . . we wondered . . . well, if you want the truth, your chain – which you had from the mad archaeologist, and might have belonged to Solomon – is the legendary Chain of Command, said to be one of the lost wonders of the ancient world. We need it to give to the clay man, in return for information about the last lost fragment of the cauldron of Caryddwen, which will enable what is missing to be restored, and what is broken to be re-assembled. This, in turn, will become the means by which my sister Karen can be released from Leatherwing, who is in league with the international business tycoon Myles Overton and wishes to enslave the future.'

'I have heard of this tycoon. He is said to supply weapons of mass destruction to our enemies – although he calls them leisure goods.'

'Everyone's definition of leisure is different, and nothing has ever been proved. But you must ask Linden Richmont about Myles Overton's business arrangements, not me. On the other hand you, of all people, know the meaning of loss. And although Nuala is being set free, I don't think I will see her again after today. We need your help!'

But Jihad needed to be needed, and she had found his weakness. That, above all, had been the attraction of the pale girl beneath the harbour wall, who had played so charmingly on a tin whistle and told him he was everything in the world to her, and given him a Blarney Stone from Dublin market. Perhaps, too, he'd had his fill of authoritarianism.

'You ask much,' he said. 'It is fortunate I am a generous man. Yet it is in my mind there has been too much violence and dogma. The time has come when leadership must be by example, through open-handedness and forbearance. Still, there is much poverty in my land, and the people cry out in their need. I will give you the Chain of Command. But in return, you must find another lost wonder of the ancient world, the Bottomless Pitcher, which is never full and never empty, so the demands of my people can be satisfied forever, and my name will become a byword for munificence. But this will not be easy to do, for the treasure I speak of is hidden deep beneath the inner city. You will need the assistance of your sister Dawn – and perhaps much more.'

'That's all very well, but after what happened at Strategic Marketing, Dawn said she wasn't going on any more expeditions, because she had two children to think about, and a radical post-feminist lifestyle.'

'It is all one,' said Jihad. 'Then I will keep the chain.'

51

It was morning, and the rain had left the city clean and reawakened. A page of newsprint from the garish and terminally inaccurate *Sunday Scoop* had caught the updraft from the heating outlet at street level and whirled a hundred feet into the air where it hung and swayed uncertainly, as if wondering which way it should go.

On a purple island grey-green turtles tumbled in the breakers. Along the beach walked a glittering girl, and beyond were the mosques and ramparts of the country which the Irish call *Tir N'An Og* although other faiths have different names for it. There, indeed, the sound of fiddles is never long lacking from the atmosphere, and whiskey and sherbet are drunk into the balmy reaches of the night.

Linden felt at a low ebb: she had slept badly and things were not going well at work. She had failed to assert her authority in a moment of weakness and lost both the respect of her superiors and her own self-esteem. She could not be fired. Her relationship with Myles Overton guaranteed that. Dismissal from her ancillary role with the authorities would necessitate their admitting it existed in the first place, which of course they could not do. But a spot had appeared on Linden's chin as a result of stress, and she did not feel good about herself.

The newsprint lost its updraft and slid sideways and downwards until it rested on the dormer roof immediately below Linden's window. She did not need to read the splash about the terrorist attack because it had been all over the radio anyway.

Five guards neutralized, one prisoner abducted, the whole sinister force vanished within twenty minutes of the strike, accompanied by their helpless captive. A day of shame for national security! A day of ignominy for the principle of prison privatization, and of embarrassment for the minister responsible. The papers demanded that those whose lack of vigilance had enabled the evil men to achieve their goal should be sought out and punished. They demanded it with as much vehemence as they had demanded a victim so many years ago, when the day after a nationalist incident Nuala Greenwood had been arrested with four comrades for singing *Follow Me Up To Carlow* in Kilburn High Street when drunk.

To Linden, it was meaningless. Except that she dreamed someone would come for her too, and that her own imprisonment would be ended. Imprisonment which entailed no locks or security devices, yet from which she could no more escape than understand what it was that held her. She sighed and looked downwards again at the grey street where lines of vehicles were parked, so small they resembled bubble cars. If she fell it would not end at the street. It would go on for ever. She sighed again and thought how Nuala had called the person she desired most. A cry for help through which Linden had now lost her friend, her reputation, and her self-regard. But Linden had no-one to call. Dave Doom was known to have lascivious fantasies about her, and Tom Baleworker wanted to marry her – but he had his own agenda. There was no-one she could call, and no-one would call her. Had she secretly chosen Nuala as a friend simply because she thought Nuala could never be taken away?

Linden thought about love, and need, and loyalty, and truth, but her reverie soon turned to the way all these had been linked in Nuala's release, and to the curious musician who had interceded with her rescuer. Linden touched the silver ring that had once belonged to the Queen of Lebanon, and turned it round and round on her finger. As she reflected, she seemed to hear a skein of music twisting into her head and carrying with it the sounds of green cliffs, seagulls, ocean winds far off and friendly voices close to. The irresistible cadences, Linden thought, of ancient hills and woodlands, which normally would have had no part of this urban fastness.

Notes flew out of a little fiddle like birds out of a cherry tree. Their harmonies twisted time and place, and as the Magic Fiddler played, the city and the countryside were one, and the prisons were one with the free open spaces. All nations were one, their flags woven together in a chaotic tapestry, and Nuala and Jihad, hand in hand, reigned over regions liberated from pettiness and pragmatism.

Looking sideways, Linden was strangely unsurprised to see the impish fiddle player had materialized on the ledge next to her, and for a moment she saw more than she had ever seen before, and understood more than she had ever understood. She understood that if you have a true friend, even if she is gone, she will always be within reach. She understood that even treachery and misrepresentation are not strong enough to block the instinctive affection which links heart to heart. And she understood that because when it mattered most she had kept faith, she could still be forgiven, and might never have to do anything that would need forgiving again.

'At last,' Linden told her unlikely companion, 'I'm beginning to realize who I am. But don't think I haven't realized who you are, too.'

'I'm sure I don't know what you'd be getting at,' said the Magic Fiddler with a bright truculent chord. But at the same time his face, which she had never before seen without its cowl, seemed ready to dissolve into mirth.

'I saw you at the Centre,' she told him, 'and perhaps I've seen you in my dreams even before that. Admit it – you're not the Magic Fiddler at all! You're Finbar Direach, aka Phelim Dalaigh. We were together on Caryddwen's promontory, although you didn't reveal yourself to me then, nor to any of the modernizers.'

'Perhaps I was the Magic Fiddler before I was Direach, or Dalaigh, or any of a hundred other names I may have travelled under. It's of no importance, for the faculty of vision projects the mind on to the screen of the world, not the world on to the screen of the mind. The important matter is what's in your own mind, right now. For although you do not know it, you've been close to Leatherwing, and his power over a person is not lightly relinquished. If you do not decide to take the easy way out, you have two choices. But the consequences of your decision may be more far-reaching than you can imagine. Take it from me, I know about these things.'

'I don't understand . . . '

But they both knew that she did understand. Phelim Dalaigh's Apocalyptic Ceilidh had long been maintained by the authorities to be a fiction concocted to screen the activities of perhaps the most evil people ever found on Britain's shores. But Linden now understood that it had taken place exactly as stated in the evidence given by its many participants. Not only that, but it was taking place even now, and would be for the foreseeable future. And that she, Linden, was invited to go.

She understood, too, that if she took that path, she would have to give up on everything she had ever worked for, and say goodbye to man who had been like a father to her for so many years. A man who, though he might have destroyed a thousand lives, had been there when Linden needed him, and given her a life when she felt there was no hope for her.

This time a tear did manage to creep out of Linden's eye, like a prisoner out of a maximum-security cell. What the Magic Fiddler was offering is given to few, but for Linden, now was not the time, and perhaps the time would never come. She turned away. When she turned back again, the ledge beside her was empty, almost as though no-one had been there at all. Below, the city seemed to brood its secrets even closer than before, and among them the secret which alone could secure General Jihad's co-operation with Triona and her sisters. A secret which, now her choice was made, Linden must at all costs prevent them from unravelling.

V

The Well of Dreams

52

'Sometimes', Dawn Greenwood told her sister Triona, 'I think I'm losing touch with unreality.'

She had shorter hair than her sisters and many outrageous piercings. She was practical, but clung defiantly to her beliefs and to the lifestyle she had chosen.

'You're missing the city, that's all,' Triona said. 'You're different from the rest of us. Your dreams took you to the city, and now you've become part of it. Coldharbour can no longer offer you all you need.'

But Dawn sensed the conversation was becoming tendentious, and that it was Triona who needed her to re-establish contact with the city, for Triona's own reasons. The issue, as Dawn well knew, was that Triona wanted her to find a pitcher which was never full and never empty, to exchange for a chain whose wearer could not be disobeyed, to give to the clay man for information about the last lost fragment of Caryddwen's cauldron, the restoration of which would release their eldest sister from the power of Myles Overton and his shadowy coadjutor, thereby setting the world to rights in time for the three thousandth anniversary of the coming of the Tuatha de Dannaan.

'But why me?' said Dawn. 'And why the city?'

Perhaps once she would not have asked the question. Perhaps she would not have asked it even a month ago, before the risks they took at Strategic Marketing had made her look at her life anew, and question what she once thought self-evident. Dawn was always beguiled by the dreamlike convolutions of the city, and would once have believed anything could be found there and that magic jugs were two a penny. Now, she found herself asking whether Finbar Direach and Caryddwen's cauldron were mere figures of speech. Whether the Tuatha de Dannaan, Mannannan Mac Llyr Mac Lugh, even Leatherwing and the task of the six sisters were products of over-active imagination. Whether, in the end, the universe was a one-way street, Druid belief in transmigration of souls a poetic conceit, and escapism and wishful thinking sown with the seeds of their own destruction.

'And why now?' she added. When Dawn was first drawn to the city, perhaps with the idea that she was following the trail of Karen, it filled her with wonder. She looked down on it from the ridge of the Weald and it resembled nothing so much as a great cauldron, filled with a broth of moving lights. When she arrived there she met women like herself, who taught her how she could fully become what she had in reality always been, although the years rushed by like a mill-race and twice she became pregnant in unexplained circumstances. But at Coldharbour the support of her city friends seemed remote, their urban mysteries implausible. She found she did not want to go back, and for the sake of the children she *should* not go back. And if Triona and Neill Fife thought she would, then Triona and Neill Fife could dream on.

'When you're a woman and a single mother raising children on income support,' she told them, 'you can't live on dreams. I've tried it myself. I've tried for too long. Now I'm losing touch with unreality – and I'm glad!'

'Yet you can't escape your dreams either. Perhaps, in the end, all we have are our dreams,' Triona said.

'Well, I've run out of them. I can't afford them. I've got two little girls to feed and clothe and teach about life. It's all right for you and Sophie. You're your own people. You don't have kids. With me, it's different. There isn't a minute of the day when I can think of anything else.' She stroked the heads of her little girls, one hand on each. The first, Angharad, had dark hair like a jackdaw's wing and was thoughtful and ill-at-ease in social situations. The second, Berengharad, had yellow hair like a dandelion and was as open as a book, as free as the wind.

Dawn never got tired of talking about their endearing qualities and the interesting things they said. 'I love them equally, even though they're a handful. But the authorities don't make things easy. If single mothers were men, it would be a different story.'

53

'We must clamp down on single mothers,' declared the authorities, 'since most of them are women. Income support, rent-free accommodation, subsidized child care – we wouldn't be surprised if that was the reason they became pregnant in the first place.'

'No, the reason they became pregnant in the first place', explained the civil servants and marketing consultants, 'is that some bloke brought them home from a wild party, invited himself in for a coffee and started to—'

'That's as may well be,' interrupted the authorities hurriedly, 'But there's been enough of that sort of thing going on – or too much. The dream is over, and this is the reality. We're going to tighten up on the issue of single mothers. The gravy train must be de-railed. Our first responsibility is to the taxpayer, and that's the end of it!'

These sentiments were re-echoed by the minister responsible in his keynote speech, although he was clever enough to link them with the law-and-order debate and in particular with the Night Caller, whose attentions to urban women had lately enjoyed more than their share of column inches. 'The taxpayer has had enough,' declared the minister responsible. 'He does not want his hard-earned money spent on flats for single mothers. He wants it spent on policemen and prisons. If we could put single mothers in prison – different thing. But with the social climate as it is, we must put our priorities first. Take failing schools! Take social security fraud! Take stalking! As modernizers, how can we tolerate a menace like the Night Caller, and yet maintain a million floozies in a life of idle luxury?'

No-one could argue with this point even though the Night Caller himself, alleged to prey on women throughout the inner city, was said by some to be an invention of the tabloid newspapers in general and Rufus Stone from Myles Overton's disreputable *Sunday Scoop* in particular. The jury was out on the Night Caller, people said. The police had been unable to establish a clear modus operandi or to absolutely connect this shadowy individual to any specific case or victim. We may be talking urban myth, was a common view. The existence of an individual whose chief aim in life was to send women bad dreams seemed implausible. Yet the women themselves said these dreams were very bad indeed, and they sometimes culminated in a sensation that glittering strings of pearls, jewels and diamonds were deposited in their insides, which by morning condensed into strings of genes and chromosomes and left them unaccountably pregnant. This, the scientific community said, was unlikely, and cynics added that it was probably a skilful way of confusing the Child Support Agency. But myth or not, the idea of the Night Caller worked darkly on the imaginings of women. Many formed self-help groups with names like the Network of Unsuccessful Women and the Depressed Women of Stepney, and some moved out of the city altogether.

54

'To be honest,' Dawn told Neill and Triona eventually, 'I returned to Coldharbour to be safe. Times have changed, and the city's changed too. Women's groups can only do so much, and the laws are divisive. We've got "welfare to work" and the authorities won't rest until everyone is on someone else's payroll, or in someone else's jail, which comes to the same thing. They won't rest until everyone becomes a man. That's the bottom line. If you argue, they let you understand – but not openly – they may take your children away.'

'You can trust us. We'll never let you down,' Neill promised, while Triona rolled her eyes upwards. 'They're converting the old mill cottages into maisonettes under an affordable-housing scheme, and I can have a word with the site manager. We'll help look after your children too – even if their own fathers wouldn't.'

'The fathers of my children are my business. That's exactly the kind of stereotyping remark I'm leaving the city to escape.'

'You're not leaving to escape the Night Caller, then?' he said, half-jokingly.

'More like the Child Support Agency,' she told him, half-seriously.

Even to Neill, Dawn would not vouchsafe the secret of the fathers of her two children, nor whether it was one father, or two. Did she suspect Neill of being in league with the Child Support Agency? Did she suspect the Child Support Agency was being privatized and sold off to Myles Overton, who was somehow implicated in a fearful trade in tiny lives, perhaps even in partnership with the Night Caller himself? For someone who could not afford dreams, she did not stint herself on nightmares. Neill massaged her neck muscles, and Sophie, Oswald and Damien Lewis read her two daughters interesting stories derived from ancient Celtic literature and fed them hogweed broth until their eyes closed in innocent slumber.

But Dawn returned to her original point, for she suspected that Neill was going to say that before she came to live amongst them he wanted her to return to the inner city just one more time. 'And you still needn't think', she said, 'you can get me on another wild-goose chase after some old relic. Especially not with Rufus Stone, if you had the idea I could use the contacts he's made as a reporter. There's no use looking at me like that. I'm not going back. My first responsibility is to my children – and that's the end of it.'

'I never even mentioned Rufus Stone,' Neill said, his eyes as round and clear as dew ponds.

'Well, so long as it's understood . . . '

But what, when it comes down to it, is understanding? It is a kind of intellectual comfort – a feeling of familiarity, as when one is among old friends. Not an answer to questions, but an absence of the inclination to ask them. Neill, Triona, and Dawn talked long into the night while the boisterous wind rolled off the downs like a drunk man off a hay wagon, and ragged clouds blew past a sickle-shaped moon. They told each other their secret hopes and fears, and for a while things were as they had been a thousand years ago, when every day they rode the bus back from school on the upstairs rear seat in uniforms of wood green and sea blue, and felt behind the cushion to see if anyone had dropped fifty pence. But as Neill said, that was then, and this was now. The route had been privatized, and over-priced Transit van conversions twice a day were all that now remained where majestic green Routemasters had once reigned supreme, arriving every ten minutes and taking people wherever they wished to go.

'Your first responsibility', Neill told Dawn gently, 'is to your children, and all the children of the world.'

She said she would sleep on it, but she had lied about the dreams.

55

London, with its deep unchartered streets, has been the wellspring of England's dreams since salmon first ran in the Thames, and wild swans shook dew off their wings in the misty sedges. Yet confusion over its origins is endemic. To say that it guards a strategic river crossing and represents a link between European trade routes and the agricultural heartlands is to confuse cause with effect. In other words, the position and establishment of London probably dictated the position and establishment of other centres.

When the first settlements were made in the area, the land was dank and marshy and the river idled among many low islands. Yet modernizers who attribute the name to the concatenation of the Celtic words *lyn* and *dyn*, signifying a fort on a lake, take too secular a view. Nor is it entirely true, except as a kind of plagiarism, that the city was named Lud's Town for the Celtic King Lud who was crowned at Coldharbour Abbey in the year 62BC.

Lud, it appears, was a petty warlord with prodigious conceit and a genius for propaganda. The key to his temerity lies in the name itself. Reading its original form as Ludh and taking the d as silent (as in the Irish *Ceilidh* or *Fleadh*), it is obvious he was appropriating the title and attributes of Lugh, father of Llyr, grandfather of Mannannan, and forefather of all the Tuatha de Dannaan. Thus stories of Lud's kingship have been interpreted as symbolizing national unification in the cult of Lugh, but more likely represent the cynical assumption of divine virtue by a self-serving chieftain.

London, therefore, was Lugh's town. The fact that Nora Chadwick in her influential book cites Carlisle and Lyon as derivatives of Lugh, but ignores London's far more obvious claim, suggests she may lean towards the Druid confession herself and be loath to reveal their mysteries. Yet Dawn Greenwood and her sisters were never allowed to believe this was the whole story, for their mother, before her terrible valediction in the rowan tree, taught them well.

'Do not forget', she warned, 'the pivotal position of Lugh's ancient city in the history of this land, nor the link between its origins and the cosmological models of the new physics!' With that, she would never fail to tell them the story of how the universe came into being, and the legacy left by the peculiar way this happened.

For, she would say, according to the oldest traditions, Lugh created all things. The manner of it was as follows. At the start, nothing was real except the Dagda, who had a club and a large cauldron completely filled with unreality, which he stirred idly and without any firm purpose. Lugh, it is said, was bored with this state of affairs, so he went to the Dagda and asked permission to create the universe. The Dagda grew angry at such presumption, and secretly decided he himself would create the universe, for he could not bear to admit he had not thought of it first. Before anything more could be done, he upended his cauldron using the club as a lever (but of the subsequent history of the cauldron, Dawn's mother said, you shall hear more by and by) and sent the contents flowing forth in a great river, so broad that an eagle soaring to its greatest altitude could not see both sides.

When Lugh saw what had been done, he sent a magic beaver to dam the stream, and create many islands, banks, pools and eddies around which the flow could settle and condense. For although the Dagda's cauldron was full of unreality, largely in the form of dreams, modern physicists confirm that unreality is not as unreal as it seems, but is simply reality in a form which has not yet been fully realized. Such physicists of course refer not to dreams but probability curves, and the theory that they are the origin of everything has been conclusively proved by shutting cats in boxes.

Yet whatever the scholarly debate, Lugh's beaver did its work well, and soon the universe of dreams was dammed up sufficiently to establish the universe of reality, and the two have coexisted ever since. 'But,' said Lugh, 'all things must contain their own origins.' So although after a time everything appeared real and the Dagda's original universe of dreams lay beneath it as the water table lies beneath a fertile land, Lugh left a small wellspring through which the two could communicate. In due course a thriving community of monks, scholars and tradesmen grew up around the place where this was done, and it became known as Lugh's Town, and eventually Luton. But its inhabitants, perceiving Luton to be a dismal and lack-lustre name more fitting for a dismal and lack-lustre place, found a tribe to northward who lived in just such a spot, not far from London Colney, and who were prepared to exchange names for a good price.

'So you see,' Dawn's mother told her little daughters – seemingly a thousand years before Karen disappeared and their world fell apart, 'when people tell you that London was named after King Lud, just smile at them, and wink with one eye.' For, she told them, according to some accounts, the historical king's impudence angered Lugh himself, and as punishment he was imprisoned in the nether regions of his own capital, condemned for all eternity to guard the now buried wellspring that joined the worlds of the real and the unreal. 'But don't assume he is in any way associated with the Night Caller,' she added. 'For London's inner city is a many-layered region filled with odd inhabitants, where things are rarely as simple as they seem.'

Dawn's mother intended this information as a caveat, and indeed told Dawn she must never set foot within the boundaries of the city, or strange things would inevitably happen to her. But although this produced trepidation in Dawn, she inwardly thrilled with a kind of excitement. She was certain that, whatever lay within those confines, her own future lay with it. She knew her mother's advice was well-intentioned but even then she could not accept some of the details. She was sure, as many women are, that the Dagda was not male but female, and was in fact identical with the Great Queen in the *Yellow Book of Lecan*. But truth, she knew, can only be tried in the court of experience. Therefore at the first opportunity she cut her hair short and grew her fingernails long, resolving to leave the past behind. Scorning the green Routemasters of the countryside she boarded the only red Routemaster to go out that far, and soon found herself bound for Lugh's ancient fastness. She knew she would do this from the first, just as she knew, even when all those years later she told Neill Fife she would never go back, that the ticket was already in the pocket of her dungarees.

56

When the last edition had been put to bed and the subs had gone home, Rufus Stone walked through the rain-wet streets towards a little place he knew, his mind filled with restless thoughts, and his mouth with FreshBreath chewing gum. At forty, the hair around his temples was still the colour of a good Chablis, but his eyes were cloudy and dark like hogweed ale. He drank too much and had come to see his vocation in life as a receptacle for alcohol. The sight of alcohol still in a glass or bottle caused palpable discomfort until it could be decanted into his capacious craw. But when he reached his destination and saw his dinner companion had already arrived, he knew tonight would be different, and he would need to keep a sober head.

'You came,' he said self-evidently. 'Let's have a drink.'

'I need your help,' Dawn told him. 'At least, my sisters need it. I didn't want to leave Coldharbour, but there's something I have to do. For them – and for myself.'

'Take your time,' said Rufus Stone, for he had dreamed a hundred times she would say those words, 'and tell me what's on your mind.'

Yet as an investigative reporter he knew even more than she did, since she invited him to Coldharbour the night Neill drew the circle with the hazel wand, and he had thought even then they might have trouble finding the last lost fragment of Caryddwen's cauldron, and that in order to get information from the Clay Man they would have to procure the Chain of Command, which could only be done if they gained access to the Bottomless Pitcher. He had, indeed, intended to mention this, but with the lateness of the hour and the quantity of the hogweed ale, it slipped out of his head.

'You can rely on me,' he said, even though appearances were against him. 'You've always known that.'

She knew he would never intentionally hurt her, even though neither her women friends nor her sisters approved of trusting a tabloid journalist. She had met Rufus in the early days when they were both looking for Karen. She had maintained an uneasy relationship with him ever since – sometimes not speaking for a year, yet always knowing she could pick up the phone.

'I didn't want to come back,' she repeated. 'I've left Angharad and

Berengharad with my sisters – who are arguably the most weird people in Britain, and know nothing about child care. Perhaps what I need from you is an excuse to give up on this ridiculous business for ever.'

'I can't believe you mean that. I believe you think there's some connection between my stories on the Night Caller and the task of the six sisters.'

'I know. It's ridiculous. Just tell me I'm on a hiding to nothing, and I can go back to Coldharbour and start a new life.'

'Have a drink,' said Rufus, with the self-dramatization inseparable from his profession, 'because this needs careful thought. We may have to contact my Source. It will not be easy, but we need to know the word on the street. In the city, talk is cheap, and even silence can be had for a price. But before we make our move, we must be sure of our ground.'

'I don't know if I want to make a move. I came to see if you knew anything, because in the old days when Karen disappeared, everyone said you got further than anyone else, and dug deeper despite all the authorities could do to stop you. But that was then, and this is now. Tell me you think there's nothing to go on, and we'll leave it at that.'

'It doesn't matter what I think. My training is in facts, not opinions. And my reputation speaks for itself. If I get a good lead, I follow it up. *Have a drink!*'

She could not bring herself to say that his reputation was for inventing most of his best stories, and the *Sunday Scoop* kept him on not for the accuracy of his reporting, but because the outrageousness of his imagination amused its proprietor. Even his recent pieces about the Night Caller, which caused initial consternation and an early day motion in Parliament, were considered in some circles to be the work of a mind not wholly out of touch with unreality. Nobody at the *Sunday Scoop* cared about factual accuracy provided the libel lawyers were prepared to sign off the copy. As Rufus Stone always said – not everyone can be Leftie Legg. The dole queues were full of Leftie Legg, whereas the establishment would only tolerate one. You had to consider the practicalities of life. Rufus thought it easy for a rich man to stay true to himself and a poor man too, but if you had a job and twenty grand in the Abbey National, forget it. The world had you by the short-and-curlies, he would say, and that's it. Have a drink!

'If you think your life is tough, you should try being a single mother,'

Dawn said unsympathetically.

'I've tried most things – and at least single mothers get free accommodation.'

'That's an urban myth.'

'I'll drink to it, urban myth or not. But just one more, because it's getting late. If you're serious about this business, there's somewhere we need to go.'

'I'm not serious about it. I've lost touch with unreality, and I'm just going through the motions.'

Rufus ignored this remark, knowing she secretly wanted him to ignore it.

'We need', he repeated, 'to see my Source.'

57

They walked through the rain, following ever-narrowing streets with garrulous neon signs that clung around the eaves of buildings filling the night with lewd and lurid invitations. To Dawn some of it was new, but Rufus had come this way too often, and travelled down it too far. He was overweight and a garland of sweat stood on his forehead. Long years of only being as good as his last story had taken their toll, for at the *Sunday Scoop* only one person was better than their last story, and that was Myles Overton, who visited them every two months when his other business interests and football clubs would permit. During the last visit he threw a telephone at Rufus's head and told him he was a piece of shit and he didn't know why they employed him.

'You've been working there too long,' Dawn said.

But Rufus reassured her that despite the enlightened employment laws of the day, the incident was far from unique and indeed very few of Myles Overton's senior employees escaped having telephones thrown at their heads at some point, and Dave Doom had a switchboard. 'He's always singled out for preferential treatment,' said Rufus. 'Anyway, it turned out all right because Myles Overton liked my stuff on the Night Caller. I got a note from him saying: Now I bloody well know why we employ you!'

'I'm sure you framed it and put it on your office wall,' said Dawn sarcastically.

'The thing about Myles Overton is he hi-jacks your self-esteem and then serves it back to you in small, carefully measured portions.'

'Well – Leftie Legg would never have put up with it.'

They passed the Three Bishops Tavern north of Ludgate, and made their way through an underpass inhabited by many people who wanted fifty pence. But Dawn thought they really wanted to pull her down amongst them and suck the marrow out of her bones, like Jenny Greenteeth who catches little children when they tread on cracks in the pavement. She shuddered, for she had not told Rufus quite everything. But there was no time to speculate on urban myths. For, after several more twists and turns, they found themselves opposite a fissure or gap in the wall of the subway where brickwork had apparently collapsed. Within this fissure a small individual sat on a pile of fallen masonry. Clearly subject to delusions of a Delphic past, he wore loose-fitting robes from the bottom of which old Nike trainers protruded incongruously. A laurel wreath from which most of the leaves had long disappeared adorned his baseball cap, and below it the words *Know Yourself* were crudely stencilled.

Rufus said he had fallen on hard times but that once generals, heads of state and shamans had come to him for advice. But Rufus was famous for hyperbole. 'This', he said, 'is my Source – although for obvious reasons, I cannot reveal his identity.'

'Ach,' said Rufus Stone's Source, 'Bogger off, why don't you!'

'It's good to see you too,' Rufus said. 'This is—'

'Dawn Greenwood,' said Rufus's Source, 'one of the six sisters. I know.'

'He knows everything,' Rufus explained. 'Tell Dawn what you know!' He spoke with some authority. In the upper world he might have telephones thrown at his head and get ridiculed at Press Association parties for inventing facts. But down here, where a twenty pound note would buy the world and mindless acts of violence were a fact of life, Rufus himself was Myles Overton, the big boss, the emperor. Yet to someone who knows everything, hierarchies mean nothing.

'I know', the robed one asserted vacantly, 'that the man treads on the mouse, and the elephant treads on the man. But that in the end, the sky will fall on the elephant.'

Rufus said he would drink to that. 'But first, tell Dawn some more. Tell her the word on the street.'

'With due respect, go and stuff yourself, for I know no more than I've said,' said the informant. Despite Rufus's aggressive attitude he seemed to have a mind of his own.

'Perhaps this will refresh your memory,' replied Rufus. Crouching down beside the small informant he held up a crisp twenty pound note which he twitched suggestively between his fingers.

'I don't know anything,' the informant repeated, although there was a gleam in his eye.

'Everybody knows something.'

'Then why don't you ask someone else?'

'I did, but they told me to ask you. They said, "Don't let him fool you – he's not what he seems. He knows more than anyone, he's holding out on you." And when people hold out on me – it makes me mad. I am not Leftie Legg, and when I get mad, I tweak people's noses. Now – what do you say?' To show he was not bluffing, Rufus laid hold of his Source's nose in the unmistakable attitude of someone about to tweak it.

'It will go hard with me if I let on,' said the informant, although he, like Rufus, seemed somehow to be playing a part.

'It'll go harder if you don't. And sooner!'

Rufus's Source, either perceiving his options were limited, or for some secret reason of his own, suddenly seemed to change his mind. He leaned very close to Rufus, and spoke out of the corner of his mouth in the traditional manner of press informants, and tapped the side of his recently abused nose. 'Well, perhaps I do know what you're after, and I may even know who can help you find it,' he said rapidly. 'Although it would be dangerous to take the direct route. You must take care, or you may come up against forces sympathetic to Leatherwing himself, and the odds are stacked against you. For the Night Caller, whom some say is an urban myth, has his own form of reality. Remember what happened to the three bishops!'

When he said this, Dawn realized he did indeed know something, and very likely he knew more than he should. He knew, for example, that they were not the first to come looking for the Night Caller, for there had been problems from this quarter in the past. At that time people believed the source of the trouble was the unfortunate King Lud, brewing mischief in his subterranean prison, and three bishops had been sent to sort things out. But, as Rufus's informant made clear, nothing is as simple as it seems.

Initially, he reminded them, everything went according to plan. The first bishop was a large, robust man, to whom the very concept of fear was unknown. Setting out with a determined stride, he soon made his way into the lower reaches of the inner city. There, he took a winding way, making good speed and undeterred by any of the obstacles he met with. But before he reached his goal, he came to a broken-down gate guarding a secret passage, through which he knew he had to pass. On this gate sat a stranger whose identity was a mystery to him, for the face was covered by a dark cowl so that only the eyes could be seen.

'Let me pass!' demanded the bishop. 'For I have business with the Night Caller!'

'That's as may be,' said the figure. 'But I know you, even though you don't know me. I've been sent to guard this passage, and anyone who wishes to pass must choose some activity in which to compete against me, and only if they defeat me can they be permitted to continue.'

The first bishop was not fazed by this idea, since before becoming a bishop he had been a champion athlete, and his prowess was well known. 'I accept your challenge, and I choose a running race. But if you think you can catch me, you may be in for a surprise!'

In the event, it was the bishop who had the surprise. The more he quickened his pace, the faster his opponent ran also. For many hours they matched each other stride for stride, both on the level ground and up cruel slopes and inclines, until they sank down together exhausted, and the bishop was compelled to return the way he had come, his heart heavy within him.

'I failed,' he declared when asked how he got on. 'Yet there may be a lesson even in that. Perhaps each of us knows deep inside that one day they will compete against someone faster, stronger, or cleverer. And when that day comes, they learn that the only true measure of success in life is how successfully you come to terms with failure.'

Although these remarks had more than a grain of truth in them, the second bishop was not only unfamiliar with the concept of fear, but equally that of failure was entirely unknown to him. Like his predecessor he followed the deep and plunging way, and came at length to the broken gate and the cowled stranger, who accosted him in a similar manner and challenged him to a contest. This caused the second bishop no concern, for he was a champion thinker and a sophist of international renown. 'I accept your challenge,' he said, 'and I choose a philosophical debate, of which the winner will be the first to ratiocinate the other into silence.'

When this was agreed, they fell to arguing vigorously over many abstract issues, but although they harangued each other for fully two hours or three, neither seemed able to gain the slightest ascendancy, and in the end they both sank down exhausted, unable to muster another syllogism. Seeing that defeat stared him in the face, the second bishop, like the first, returned a sadder but a wiser man, and acknowledged he had little to add to his colleague's reflections.

The third bishop was smaller than the others, and well knew the meaning of fear and failure, and many other words besides. Reaching his exalted position had been a struggle for him, and his parents had sacrificed everything to send him to bishop school. He knew what it is to be only as good as your last synod, and he knew that in putting himself forward where others had failed, he risked ridicule and derision. Yet he was determined to try his luck, and like the others his attempt prospered until he came to the broken-down gate and the hooded stranger, who denied him passage until he should prevail in some contest of wit or limb.

'My limbs are short,' said the third bishop, 'and my wit is shorter. But although not everyone regards it as a virtue, I must reveal I am a champion drinker, and will be glad to vie with you in emptying cups of strong liquor, to see who can remain longest on his feet.' Nevertheless, he was suspicious of the other's eagerness for a contest, and furthermore the shape beneath the dark robes seemed strangely familiar. Indeed, when he examined it more closely, the third bishop was amazed to see it resembled his own liver, whose likeness had evidently been contrived by the Night Caller in an attempt to trick him. Quick as a flash, he seized it by its loose covering and shook it until it grovelled at his feet and promised to reveal everything it knew.

'Please! Don't kick my head in! I'll talk!'

'Well,' said the third bishop, 'it better be good . . . '

'Well,' explained the shape resembling the third bishop's liver, 'you have already guessed I was sent by the Night Caller, who's determined his secret must never be known. Therefore, when the first bishop challenged me to a running race, I took on the properties of his shadow, for no-one can run faster than their own shadow. Similarly, with the second bishop, I transformed myself into the echo of his voice, since nobody can out-talk their own echo. And, in your case, I took the form in which I now appear, for it's obvious that nobody can out-drink their own liver, or if they do, bad health is the inevitable result.'

The third bishop was satisfied with this explanation, for, he said, at least he understood why all their efforts had been in vain, and perhaps the secret of success is to know the secrets of failure. But, he told those who greeted his return, it is clear nobody can reach the Night Caller, unless they are able to out-run their own shadow, out-talk their own echo, and out-drink their own liver. And such a person is not commonly met with.

When Rufus Stone's Source reminded Dawn of this story, which until then she had always regarded as an urban myth, she was certain there was some deeper meaning concealed in his remarks, and that he himself knew exactly who could perform those feats, although he was for some reason forbidden to speak their name.

'I can see you're well informed,' she told him. 'But there's a difference between information and knowledge. There was a time when I thought that even I was party to certain secrets. But lately I've been out of touch. Well – let's not play games with each other. I'm certain that when you spoke about the person who could lead us to the Night Caller, you had someone particular in mind.'

'That may be false,' the little person replied in his most ambiguous voice, 'or it may be true. But what if I reply that you know who the person is as well as I do?'

When Dawn heard him say this she felt as though her worst fears had been realized, but she kept her composure, and passed a hand through her short hair.

'I see we understand each other,' he added, fumbling in his unsavoury garments and producing a moth-eaten mitten, 'but take this glove as a token of our meeting. For it will identify you as my friend, and the time may come when that is very valuable.'

Although Dawn sensed that this was a generous act she could not help feeling frustrated by all the innuendo, and appealed to Rufus to shed some light on it. 'Just get him to please tell us what he knows,' she demanded. 'You're the investigative reporter.'

'What do you know?' Rufus repeated in authoritative tones.

But the informant looked vacant again, as he had at first. 'I know that the universe is full of dreams, and its walls are made of green onyx.'

'I don't think he knows anything of importance,' Rufus said.

But as they made their way back to the surface and boarded the night bus home, she suddenly knew where she had seen those elf-like features before. 'I've just thought! He's the spitting image of Seamus "Eight Pints" McGallon!'

58

'People are losing touch with unreality,' Myles Overton told his trusted lieutenant and hatchet man Dave Doom. 'That's bad for them, and good for us. It's bad for them, because reality means money and power, which they haven't got, and so long as they don't see any alternative, they're buggered. It's good for us, because no bastard will believe what Dawn Greenwood is looking for, which in my view doesn't bloody exist anyway. So the future will be ours, and no dipshit can stop us.'

'I'd like to see any dipshit try,' agreed Dave Doom.

'They won't try, because they're dipshits. Besides, they're all in my bloody pocket anyway, the bankers, and politicians, and other pieces of shit. Or is someone going to tell me that I haven't compromised them all to buggery? Is somebody going to tell me we don't have all those wankers eating out of the palm of our hands?'

'I don't think anyone is going to tell you that,' replied Dave Doom. 'Unless they're a complete wanker.'

Myles Overton nodded, for he had expected as much. 'Mistakes were made at the Centre for Alternative Healing, and those responsible will be made to pay,' he said. 'Mistakes were made at Strategic Marketing and over Nuala Greenwood, and somebody's bollocks are going to be on the line. But before we make our move, we must find out more about Nuala's sister Dawn and that piss-poor bloody writer Rufus Stone, because they are up to some kind of mischief, mark my words. Take one of your security people if you can find one who isn't a total bloody drongo, and fill Rufus Stone's face with booze, and find out what's on his dipshit little mind.'

'You can rely on me.'

'I can't, because you are a bloody arsewipe, but unfortunately I can't fire you because everyone else is even bloody worse.'

'Thank you.' Flushed with pride, Dave Doom soon arranged for an unmarked car and a companion, for he knew that when you worked for Myles Overton, you were only as good as your last piece of unreflecting skullduggery.

59

When Dawn said goodbye to Rufus after their encounter with his informant, she was agitated and uneasy in her mind. 'Your Source told me everything – and nothing,' she said. 'But I never guessed things had gone so far. I must speak with my friends in the city, and let my sisters and Neill Fife know the way the land lies. If your Source is right, what we have to do next is as difficult as anything attempted until now. But from Coldharbour to London is only forty miles, and there's a meeting of the Depressed Women of Stepney in the upper room of the Three Bishops Tavern on the night of the fourth, for the rumour is they're taking matters into their own hands. On that night, we can share our dreams, and gather our courage for the task that confronts us. But not a word to anyone – or our entire enterprise may be put in jeopardy.'

No matter how hard Rufus pressed her, she would reveal no more. Perhaps deep inside she knew how difficult it would be convincing others that they should help in the quarter implied by Rufus' informant. She also knew that Rufus' own involvement would be seen as counter-productive, and let him know as gently as possible that she would need to handle things without him from here on in. After that she returned to Coldharbour to prepare herself for what she had to do, and he repaired to a little place he knew, where Closing Time was like a word in a foreign language. When a suitably disguised Dave Doom arrived with his security man, Rufus was well on the way, at his own expense, to achieving the very condition Myles Overton had hoped for.

'He's as pissed as a possum!' the security man said, not from any direct experience of these marsupials, but because everyone who hung around Myles Overton was prone to pick up such expressions, and indeed sooner or later they all developed slight Australian accents.

But Rufus was thinking about being out of touch with unreality, and why Dawn Greenwood seemed to have got more out of his informant than he could himself. When the newcomers approached he wondered hazily if they were two banshees sent by Lugh, the legendary forefather of the Tuatha de Dannaan, to teach him not to meddle in things that did not concern him.

'I wonder', he said as an opening gambit, 'whether you are two banshees?'

According to Dawn, who had it from Neill Fife, banshees are nothing but thoughts looking for someone to think them, which is the same as dreams looking for someone to dream them – so it was also possible that they were sent by the Night Caller. No doubt it was one such that had impersonated the bishop's liver. On the other hand Rufus was half inclined to believe he himself had invented much of the material about the Night Caller and therefore, in a very real sense, the Night Caller had been sent by Rufus. Either way, the newcomers had some explaining to do.

'I think', Rufus repeated truculently, because they did not immediately answer, 'you're two banshees, looking for trouble.'

'We want to buy you a drink,' said the elder banshee, stiffly but not impolitely.

'I see you don't deny you're banshees, then. Well, to be honest I don't think much of you.'

'Everyone sees the banshees they're capable of seeing,' said the younger banshee. 'But we've been asked – that is to say we want – to buy you a drink, and have a little chinwag.'

Rufus had to admit this was civilized of the banshees, even though their body language suggested a desire to butt him in the Adam's apple. Sometimes when a person has had a few drinks, the desire to confide in someone is overwhelming, banshee or not. So despite his promise of discretion, Rufus quickly found himself telling all he knew. He told them about his career as an investigative reporter, and how his first big break was to be assigned to the Karen Greenwood story. He had distrusted the official version of events and eventually traced her to the inner city, where several people swore they saw her working in one of Myles Overton's topless clubs soon after her disappearance. Further enquiries, however, met with a wall of silence. He told them what he knew about the Night Caller, and how the Night Caller's activities had intensified at exactly the time Karen disappeared. He said that now there was further information from an unimpeachable source, although Rufus was unable to make sense of it. Yet the Night Caller, if he existed, might also be connected with the six sisters and Caryddwen's cauldron.

Meanwhile he told the banshees that although he dreamed for many years Dawn Greenwood would one day need his help and that together they would save the world, she had told him he wasn't needed any more. She had said, in fact, it would be better if from now on the whole thing was handled as a women's issue.

'But this Night Caller, what does he do to women?' the banshees asked.

'He gives them bad dreams,' said Rufus.

'That doesn't sound too bad,' said one banshee.

'But these dreams,' said Rufus, 'are very bad indeed.'

'So why don't you just find him, and sort him out?'

Rufus told them how the Night Caller operated from deep in the inner city, where few cared to venture. You could not simply look him up in the Yellow Pages. Some said the Night Caller's dwelling was not a location at all, but a state of mind. If there were Yellow Pages for the human mind, no doubt the Night Caller would be listed in them. No doubt he would have a quarter page advertisement with a line drawing depicting Karen Greenwood as a topless dancer standing over a bound figure, its face hidden by a leather mask. Without question, such an advertisement would contain full directions for contacting him. For, it would say, his dwelling lies at the heart of that inner city that lurks deep inside each of us, and the dreams he sends, though bad, are fatally compelling.

Perhaps this was why Dawn thought it would need women to handle things from here on in, and Neill Fife, who was in touch with his female side. Since the Night Caller came mostly to women, his domain was accessible only through the mysteries of the pre-Celtic matriarchies associated with Queen Maeve of Skye, Caryddwen's shadowy predecessor. To such pre-Celtic matriarchies, only the most serious post-feminist single mothers' consciousness raising groups were true successors.

'They are meeting on the night of the fourth, in the upper room at the Three Bishops Tavern,' said Rufus, 'although this must be kept strictly confidential. But now – I've told you what I know – and in return you must tell me what you know – for that was our bargain.'

'We don't know what you mean.'

'Where's Karen Greenwood? For I never believed the official accounts, and unless I'm much mistaken, or still too sober to think straight, your presence here is no accident, and your involvement in these matters is far from casual.'

'We might know something, or we might not, but it'd be more than our job's worth to share it with you. Even if nobody believes your pieces any more. Besides, Karen Greenwood's whereabouts might also be a state of mind rather than a location. People who think they see her in a topless bar, an unmarked vehicle and a dungeon with Leatherwing might be equally right. Frankly, it's not our concern. We just work here. We leave kidnapped girls and bottomless pitchers to the experts.'

'How do you know about a bottomless pitcher?' Rufus said sharply, realizing he might have let slip more than he intended.

'You said you thought it's what the Night Caller uses to carry bad dreams to women.'

'I might think that – or I might think it's what Myles Overton uses to carry two banshees to spy on his employees. Or perhaps you are not banshees at all. Because one of you looks suspiciously like that sycophant Dave Doom.'

'Who knows? Perhaps the Night Caller sent us, too! But how can either of us be Dave Doom, if we don't eff and blind all the time? Enough questions, and enough answers! The way you can truly tell we're banshees is that we're permitted to speak to people only when they are too drunk to stand but not yet drunk enough to fall over. And though every word we say is true, no-one can ever remember a single thing about our conversation afterwards.'

'Well, up yours, Mac, because I'm a trained journalist and I just wrote the whole thing down in my personal organizer . . . '

'I can't understand it,' mused Rufus in the morning, 'someone's been writing a whole load of shit in my personal organizer. Then they've been sick into it.'

'You should leave that job,' Dawn said over the phone. 'Myles Overton's getting to you.'

60

'The Night Caller's getting to us,' said the Depressed Women of Stepney. 'But the authorities are unwilling to intervene, and the time has come for us to take matters into our own hands.' It seemed to them they needed a champion who would rid them of the Night Caller for ever, although, they conceded, such a person would not be easy to find. The word on the street was that it would have to be someone who could out-run their own shadow, out-talk their own echo and out-drink their own liver. But to the Depressed Women of Stepney, failure was a fact of life, so they had nothing to lose by making the attempt.

'Come to The Three Bishops on the night of the 24th, when the moon is full and the tide rises high against the city's wharves,' they told each other. 'We've organized a crèche. Dawn Greenwood's posh sisters might be there, and Neill Fife, who's been on the telly, but don't worry, he's in touch with his female side. The time for talking is over, and the time for action is about to begin.'

When the Depressed Women of Stepney met in the Three Bishops Tavern, there was rain in the air and the street lights were bearded with gold. They may have been morose and ratty, but they did not lack a sense of occasion. Agendas were distributed and the insignia of the organization hung in every corner of the little hall; the awards and trophies they had won were prominently displayed. As a mark of their commitment, they pledged their most valuable possessions as a reward for whoever would rid them of the Night Caller and to help defray any expenses incurred in the attempt. These were painstakingly laid out on trestles; hair driers, curling tongs, nearly-new children's clothes lovingly laundered and ironed, stereo radio-cassettes, fold-up buggies, candlestick holders, an antique fireguard and other household oddments. The Depressed Women of Stepney had little to offer, for life on income support allows few luxuries, but they gave what they had, and no-one can do more. When they had finished, the little display looked like the stall at a car boot sale which one passes with a sigh, making for richer pickings among the second-hand Van Morrison CDs, hand tools made in China for £1 each, or second-hand book specialists with their provocative editions of Rousseau and Sophocles and perhaps a rare and well-thumbed imprint of the *Mabinogion* or the controversial bardic cycles of Iolo Morganwg.

By the time Dawn arrived with her sisters Triona and Sophie, everything was ready. Unwilling to draw attention to themselves, they slipped in through a side door to join Neill Fife, whose Isuzu was already parked outside. Rufus Stone had been told he was unwelcome since the *Sunday Scoop*, although it broke the story of the Night Caller in the first place, unfortunately contained many pictures of supermodels without their upper garments. Nevertheless by cutting his hair short and dressing in baggy overalls and hobnailed boots he was able to pass himself off as a woman, and mingle unnoticed in the throng. Thus the companions installed themselves at the back of the room furthest from the glow of the fire, for they were eager to know what would be said.

'We've suffered enough at the hands of the Night Caller,' the Depressed Women of Stepney announced, when the meeting began. 'People say the dreams aren't too bad, but they don't know the half of it. They're very bad dreams indeed. But soon we'll know whether our appeal has been answered by genuine champions and people of substance, or just chancers, timewasters, and tabloid journalists with no real intention of proving their worth.'

'But first,' said the Chair, who although large and overstated had her own indefinable dignity, 'in accordance with the mysteries which are our heritage, there must be a sharing of dreams.'

When this had been agreed, they quickly prepared arrowroot biscuits and herbal tea, and in a simple but touching ceremony, passed the teapot anti-clockwise round the room so that each participant could fill her cup and, if she chose, reveal any thoughts she had which might shed light on their situation. 'For without dreams', said the Chair dreamily, as if the statement formed part of an immemorial rite, 'there could be no reality.'

61

'The reality', said Linden Richmont when the security reports came back, 'is we need to know more. Whether Rufus Stone's writing is piss-poor, or not piss-poor, is hardly the issue. This Night Caller business spells trouble. We all know Myles Overton has his own interests in the inner city, and we need to be careful what comes to light. Get me aerials, decoding equipment, and an unmarked van. I need to get involved personally, whether I like it or not, because Myles Overton wants nothing left to chance. We're going to the Three Bishops.'

'I agree with you, because Myles Overton has put me personally in charge, and we don't want anything to go wrong,' Dave Doom replied.

'Oh – perhaps he's personally made you his niece as well?'

Dave Doom was silent. Although he could have easily found a suitable riposte, such as that it hadn't been him who totally buggered things up at the Centre for Alternative Healing and Nuala Greenwood's prison, he knew Linden didn't have a boy-friend, and he fancied his chances.

Opposite the Three Bishops Tavern a defective street lamp spluttered and flicked in chaotic rhythm. Not fifty yards away, on the dark side of the street, an unmarked van drew up, and the slush squeaked under its wheels. On the side of the unmarked van it said 'Television Licence Detection Vehicle' and out of its top protruded numerous dishes, coils, periscopes and other listening devices, even the smallest of which was trained unerringly on the little red-brick building inside which the meeting was taking place.

The lookouts on the door were under no illusion about the significance of the black van. 'Either the Three Bishops Tavern hasn't paid its TV licence, or I don't know what,' said the first.

'I've heard that nowadays you can record an entire conversation by using a laser beam to pick up tiny vibrations in the window glass of the room where it takes place,' said the second. 'Do you think we ought to tell the others?'

'What, and interrupt the meeting right when the first person is telling her dream? Rather you than me! Forget it.'

'You're right. We were told to stay here and watch the road, and that is what we have to do. But wait till I tell you about a terrible bout of depression I had last week.'

The two lookouts resumed their conversation, deploring the hollowness of the existence they were obliged to lead, and discussing in detail the personal circumstances of their friends, all of whom seemed to have some sort of fiddle going, whether it was cheating on their TV licence or claiming income support when their boyfriend was living in. But inside the black van, state of the art computers were processing a billion pieces of information every second, and Linden Richmont was telling Dave Doom to get his hand off her leg, or she would tell Myles Overton.

62

Hardly had the first words of the Chair turned into a billion pieces of information in a nearby Transit van than all the women began to tell each other about their dreams as if they would never stop. Several of the dreams seemed very bad, but whether the Night Caller was implicated was a difficult question. A dream is not like a phone call, and one cannot simply dial 1471 to see where it came from. Many seemed merely brought on by the difficulties of a male-dominated world. One woman dreamed she was the moon, and was constantly bothered by Americans with huge rockets. One dreamed she was the Exchequer, chased through a bleak wilderness by terrifying contractors from the private sector who longed to possess her for themselves. One dreamed she was the future, put on the block and cynically auctioned off to pay for the present.

Nor were the visitors from Coldharbour immune from dreams, despite the benefits of country air. In Sophie's dream she was much younger, and ready for any adventure life would throw at her, like the great poets she admired. But her dream, too, was bad, for she thought she became somehow turned into a beautiful book, in which first Lord Byron and then Percy Bysshe Shelley had taken out huge pens and written torrid poems which left her flushed and trembling, yet strangely fulfilled.

Triona's dream had nothing to do with celebrated poets or purple passages. Instead, she thought she was a great isolated house, somewhat like Coldharbour itself, set into an isolated hillside. But in the dream there was a tall rowan tree a little way off, and Triona dreamed that one evening a storm came down, more violent than anyone could remember, and the rowan tree swayed and fell, crashing through her French windows and leaving her, in her dream, trembling and shaken. When she recalled this dream she thought it had all the hallmarks of one maliciously sent by the Night Caller, perhaps intended to stir up troublesome feelings between old friends. This was especially true since Neill dreamed he was a great rowan tree which was blown down in a storm and crashed through the French windows of a beautiful home, in a manner that gave him curious satisfaction. But, he felt, that was his affair and his alone. As Karen's ex-boyfriend and the husband of a leading supermodel it was proper for him to keep his dreams to himself, despite the tea and the arrowroot biscuits. Besides, unlike Triona, he did not think his dream or hers were the work of any Night Caller or bottomless pitcher, but that they were attributable to something closer to home.

But before Dawn could tell them that she herself had dreamed of a champion, and that Rufus Stone's informant had merely confirmed she was on the right track, the Chair gave her own opinion, for she did not think it right that Dawn's posh sisters should come down from the country and hog the limelight, with their waxed jackets and Queen's English.

'These dreams are all very well,' she acknowledged, 'but when you're stuck in the city on income support, even your dreams have to be practical. What if I said that despite all this talk of rockets and French windows, the truth is most of us dream of winning the National Lottery, or unexpectedly coming into a large sum through the death of an unknown relative or compensation for an industrial injury?'

'It's a point of view,' said Triona placatingly, 'and every point of view is valid, especially when you're talking about dreams. But even winning the National Lottery wouldn't bring us any closer to the Night Caller. That's why we have to explore all the angles.'

'You've certainly got a way with words,' said the Chair. 'But words can't take you beyond words. In the city what matters is action, and action always has a price attached.'

'Well, lottery or no lottery, it's hard for money to take you beyond money, or wealth to take you out of a system perpetuated by wealth,' said Triona, whose considerable income from the Heritage Commission was entirely paid for by the lottery itself. 'One can't be financially independent until one is spiritually independent.'

To show what she meant, she reminded everyone of a story her mother passed on before she died.

Mannannan Mac Llyr Mac Lugh, their mother said, was taken by Queen Maeve of Skye into the remote north far beyond the pole, and there marooned on an iceberg until he would tell her his secrets. It was not many years or centuries before this incarceration began to weigh heavily on Mannannan Mac Llyr Mac Lugh's spirits, and he started to cast around for some means of emancipating himself from his pitiable condition. Using only the labour of his hands, he constructed a beautiful vessel made of ice and snow, and set off to sail back to the warm and temperate reaches of his homeland. But the further south the boat steered, the heavier it lay in the water, and it is obvious that spars made of icicles and sails of woven frost cannot prosper beneath the full glare of the sun. When Queen Maeve of Skye caught up with him, the ice boat was almost gone, and while he could not be grateful for being taken back to his prison, the alternative was even less palatable.

'So you see—' began Triona, with the idealism of someone for whom material well-being is not a problem.

'I don't see,' said the Chair, with the materialism of someone who knows that high ideals fill no Asda trolleys. But, sensing her bitterness, Neill said gently that he realized life in the inner city, without a regular partner, must have many different stresses, and it is hardly surprising if the mind and body deal with these in many different ways, and he fully accepted the value of the National Lottery as a dream, since it had precious little as a reality. But, he said, this and most of the other dreams they had heard, probably derived from the Night Caller only in the generalized sense that the Night Caller had come to symbolize the sexual imperialism of the Invasive Gothic Male, although Neill emphasized that gender and ethnic categories were used only in a psycho-symbolic sense. This imperialism, Neill said, began when patriarchal modernizers overwhelmed an at-least-residually-matriarchal Celtic tradition in the battle of Cattraeth in AD 610, which was fought to determine whether the universe was linear or cyclic in character, and therefore what ethical and philosophical systems were most appropriate. Since then, he said, the positive, active and creative side of the female or Celtic identity had been marginalized, and its passive, receptive side colonized as a paradigm of desirability. In time, those colonized in this way lost control of their dreams, and came to desire only to be desirable.

'Neill thinks', Triona explained hurriedly, for she could see several of them getting ready to point out that Neill had started trying to dominate the meeting like the typical man he so eloquently denied being, 'that until the true female identity as symbolized by Caryddwen's cauldron can be reconstructed and the islands of Britain are once again governed by the queens of Skye, we will never fully regain control of our dreams, and our condition is inevitable. Personally, I can take the theory or leave it. But we need to be in touch with unreality if we're ever going to get to the bottom of this Night Caller affair.'

Dawn said she could hardly disagree with this, as she found it completely unintelligible from start to finish. If they would let her get a word in edgeways, she said, she would like to get back to the business in hand, for there was a way forward if they had the courage to take it. 'But first, I need to introduce a friend of mine, who was told to stay away tonight, but risked derision and humiliation by turning up anyway. For what I have to say is far-fetched in the extreme, and any sort of verification is better than none.'

The Depressed Women of Stepney nodded their heads, for they had loved and trusted her from the first, but when Rufus Stone emerged from the shadows only their long-standing regard prevented precipitate and possibly violent action. 'You appear', they told Rufus distastefully, 'not to be female.'

Whilst in theory they agreed that all genders were equal and gender distinctions psycho-symbolic rather than physical, and put up with Neill because he was a celebrity, Dawn's friends could not conceal old prejudices. Some even regarded the eating of meat from female animals as cannibalism, and bought only from specialist suppliers who certified their products as deriving from non-female sources. It was hard for them to be forbearing, since they had suffered much, and many of them recognized a reporter whose stories pandered to the basest proclivities of the Invasive Gothic Male. They even thought that the reason the original three bishops let the side down so badly was that they were all blokes, and one of them was a drunk. There was little anyone could tell the Depressed Women of Stepney about being let down by drunken blokes.

'I'll drink to that,' said Rufus Stone, for despite his large boots, he realized further deception was useless. He told them he was as much in touch with his female side as Neill was, and in his experience men who went on about empowering women were often trying to get inside their undergarments, but, he said, that was not important. 'The main thing', he told them, 'is we're all on the same side, and I'm here to tell you that Dawn is here to tell you nothing less than the truth, although we investigative reporters have always been too blinkered to see it.'

'Having said that,' Dawn added charitably, 'you don't need to be a reporter for the *Sunday Scoop* to be blind to a truth that's been staring you in the face for half a lifetime. I myself only put two and two together when Rufus's informant told me we needed someone who could out-run their own shadow, out-talk their own echo, and out-drink their own liver.'

'But surely, no-one alive can do those things,' said the Depressed Women of Stepney.

'Alive is a relative term,' said Dawn. 'In the old days of Caryddwen's cauldron, the distinction between life and death was only trivial. I'm just a single mother and a burden on the state, and I don't get much time to think about these things, so shoot me down in flames if you like. But I'm also one of the six sisters, and I've had dreams myself. Only one individual can do all the things mentioned. She knows the labyrinthine ways beneath the city better than anyone, although her name has become a symbol for terror and foreboding.'

'Surely you're not suggesting . . . '

'You can't possibly be referring to . . . '

'You don't mean . . . '

'But I do mean. And I am suggesting. Because just as you have to fight fire with fire, you can only fight dreams with nightmares.'

63

When Dawn fully shared her thoughts, told everyone about the informant who resembled Seamus 'Eight Pints' McGallon, and showed the superannuated mitten, those not inwardly sceptical were openly derisive. A modern woman has many demands made on her credulity by advertisements for soap powders, wrinkle-removing cream, and things that come through the door saying they have already won an amazing mystery prize. So it is hardly surprising there was no credulity left over for Dawn's suggestion that Jenny Greenteeth, of all people, should be their champion in the confrontation with the Night Caller. Those who had heard of Jenny Greenteeth at all considered her to be an urban myth. They knew her only as a childhood bogey-person who lives in drains and sucks the marrow out of young girls who fail to reach home in time for tea or who step on the cracks in the pavement. Naturally, the Depressed Women of Stepney had long ceased to entertain any fears on this score. If they were still careful about the cracks in the pavement, it is common sense to avoid unnecessary risks.

Perhaps their greatest emotion was a sense of disappointment that in the difficult business of tackling the Night Caller, Dawn's sisters had proved ineffectual and even Neill Fife, whose book *Mannannan Mac Llyr Mac Lugh and the Redundancy of the Invasive Gothic Male* they had all read, proved only to have a prurient interest in their nightmares and offered little practical help. Now Dawn herself, having held the window of hope open a little longer, had turned out to be a total screwball.

'Well,' said Rufus, 'you can call us screwballs, or worse, and in my case it may be all I deserve. But Dawn's right. I can't reveal the identity of my Source, since I don't know it, but he's got me all my best stories since I was a cub reporter and determined to be the Leftie Legg of my generation. In all that time, he's never been wrong. If we can reach Jenny Greenteeth and lay our case before her, we may have a chance.'

'Even supposing that were possible, why would she listen?'

'Because', put in Triona excitedly, for she knew more than a little about the old days, 'she hasn't always been known as Jenny Greenteeth and lived in drains. In times gone by she was the sister of Finbar Direach and high in the counsels of the Tuatha de Dannaan. Unfortunately she earned their enmity through no fault of her own. Once condemned to dwell in sewerage systems and subsist on a diet of human marrow, it was inevitable that her reputation would suffer and that she would become a figure of fear and opprobrium.'

'As a reporter for the *Sunday Scoop*, I know how she feels,' put in Rufus. 'Yet what's a little marrow, when in today's world there are respected and highly placed individuals who will suck out your very soul? Scoff if you like, but if you haven't got a better offer to help you destroy the Night Caller, Jenny Greenteeth is your woman.'

He had sceptical looks from many, but for people who didn't believe in Jenny Greenteeth, they were surprisingly reluctant to take any course of action that might lead to meeting her. But Neill said in the end it was up to the sisters and reminded them that Dawn had a special part to play.

'Typical of a man, to start working out who should do what,' Dawn said. 'Well, I'll do it – but only because *I* decide to. All I really want is to return to the country, and live with my two little daughters, and see them breathe fresh air that doesn't give them asthma and walk the woodland glades safe from social workers and members of the Child Support Agency. But I'm not having anyone say I did any less than my sisters, even though I refuse to be bossed around by Neill and Triona. As for Jenny Greenteeth, when I first heard her name in a dream, I woke in fright. But we all know what it is to be marginalized. We must learn to take people as we find them.'

But the other sisters could not bear Dawn to steal a march on them.

'Where you're going, you're going to need a bossy Heritage Commissioner!' cried Triona.

'And a sensitive schoolteacher!' cried Sophie.

When everything was agreed, they all hugged each other, which often occurs in meetings of this type, and the Depressed Women of Stepney agreed that through their mysteries they would do what they could to facilitate getting in touch with Jenny Greenteeth. If that were possible, everyone felt, Rufus Stone's informant's glove would come into its own, as it was now clear he was no less than Finbar Direach himself, who had, for his own reasons, been engaged in an elaborate pretence. To seal the arrangement, Dawn was invited to take whatever she thought Jenny Greenteeth might like from the trestles, as a gift from the Depressed Women of Stepney. There did not seem to be any fragments of cauldrons or bottomless pitchers, and Dawn was sure Jenny Greenteeth did not need a pram or a radio cassette recorder, but she settled at last for a simple bronze fireguard, which one of the women found some years ago at a boot fair and had no further use for.

'It's an odd shape for its purpose,' the sisters agreed, 'but it may bring us luck.'

'And now,' Rufus concluded, 'let's all have a little drink, and then go back and get some sleep, because tomorrow is going to be a long day. But try not to dream!'

64

In the van across the street, these exchanges were duly received by state-of-the art computer equipment, which failed to make any sense of them at all. To Dave Doom this was not surprising, because he had long believed they were dealing with wankers, not least because Myles Overton told him they were. To Linden, things had taken a sinister turn which she did not altogether like.

'This is changing from a simple surveillance job into something bigger,' she said.

'If you ask me, they're just a load of wankers. We've heard enough crap for one day, and we need to report back to Myles Overton as soon as possible. He doesn't tolerate slackness.'

'We'll report back when I say so. I want to know more about what's going on. We haven't got the full story. If it's about the inner city, Myles Overton has interests there, and their security is paramount. If it's about the Night Caller, frankly, it may be more than we can handle. One thing's certain – wherever they go, we'll have to follow them.'

'Better still we'll stop them going there in the first place. I wouldn't let it worry you. They're amateurs.'

'Nevertheless, I don't like this talk of Jenny Greenteeth. Believe me – I've met the brother. If she's as good at getting into places as he is at getting out, we've got problems. We need to have more information.'

But although there were many dishes and aerials on top of Linden's van, they didn't have one that could pick up dreams. Without it, they were left in the dark.

65

Inside every city there is an inner city. Or perhaps it is inside the people who are inside it. Beneath each city is a distorted mirror of itself. A murky and miasmal reflection rejoicing in all that the city above disowns, expropriates, and turns its back on. Yet this inner city is more real (or perhaps more unreal) than the outer and more visible city, as the roots of a tree are more fundamental to it than its leaves and branches. London was no exception, and to the forbidden region which lay amongst its immemorial foundations, Jenny Greenteeth's dwelling was the gatehouse.

'That's all very well,' commented Rufus, as they stood in the desolate street, 'but how will we find it?'

For answer, Dawn carefully tied blindfolds around everybody's face and asked them to link hands. It was not for nothing, she said, that they had been admitted to the mysteries of the pre-Celtic matriarchs, to whom this type of enterprise was a mere bagatelle. Sure enough, deprived of sight as they were, it was a matter of moments before the inevitable happened and one of them stepped on a crack between two paving stones. Before they could recover their bearings, they found themselves making their way down a dank and oppressive tunnel. From the barely discernible architecture and the characteristic odour of the fluid in which they found themselves walking, they soon identified this as part of the city's sewerage system. But they travelled no more than fifty paces before the tunnel opened out and their senses were assailed by a fetid catacomb.

As gatehouses go, Jenny Greenteeth's was one of the most uninviting. Rats, moles, leatherjackets and many even less savoury creatures made their way freely through its crannies, crevices and crawlways. But its principal inhabitants were fungal. Jenny Greenteeth lived in a fortress of fungus. Great columns and balconies of stinkhorn and bracket fungus reared out of the dank ooze. Agarics and puffballs jutted from every corner and cove in a grotesque parody of festive decorations.

Garish little toadstools filled every niche and giant stalagmites stood wrapped in a rich fur of mould and mildew, like aristocrats strutting in ermine. Walls once laid by the hands of men were now the substrate for a crawling mycelium of sapless life in myriad shades of wan luminescence. The bracket fungi made a curving flight of steps up to the heart of this edifice. At its summit, in a glowering chamber as broad as a man is tall, sat Jenny Greenteeth. Upside down in her hands was a young girl who had been late for tea *and* trodden on the cracks between the paving stones. The girl was struggling vigorously, for it was clear that Jenny Greenteeth did not have her best interests at heart.

'I'll tell my Daddy! And you better watch out coz he's a Policeman,' the little girl shouted. She had often been warned not to allow herself to be abducted by strangers in case they turned her upside down and sucked out her marrow.

Jenny Greenteeth laughed a dismal laugh. Her teeth were broken and her tongue split by nutrient deficiency. The skin of her face bore the same pallor as the fungus all around, while each of her thin fingers terminated in a long curved talon.

'Finn's sister', Dawn said, aware this was not creating a good impression, 'isn't quite herself. But wait until we show the glove to her, and offer her the useful fireguard.'

Sure enough, the reaction of an affectionate sister to news of her long-lost and much-loved brother, even under such circumstances, touched the sentiments of all present. Jenny Greenteeth snatched the moth-eaten keepsake and smothered it with a thousand kisses. In doing so she relinquished her hold on the little girl, who took to her heels and hurtled off through the labyrinth of passageways as fast as her expensive trainers would carry her. And never trod on the cracks between paving stones for the rest of her walking life.

'I wasn't really going to suck her marrow out,' Jenny Greenteeth said, aware that her behaviour had created in her new companions a degree of uneasiness. They did not wish to be impolite but they had seen what they had seen. It took a little while before they could look at her directly, and for the rest of their acquaintance with her they kept off the subject of marrow whenever they could.

'But I'm forgetting my manners,' she added. 'Why don't you all have some mushroom soup?'

66

Long ago, Jenny Greenteeth had been a beautiful girl, and in love. She had exquisite limbs, golden hair, and a voice like the dripping of honey from a well-filled comb at the end of a balmy summer's day. Nor were these the only attributes she possessed. She could out-run her shadow, out-talk her echo, and drink mead and potheen the whole night long without intoxication or ill health. She radiated such goodwill and gentleness of spirit that the birds of the air and the animals of the forest would settle upon her wrists or rub themselves against her legs, and the fish and bloodless things that live in the sea would crowd along the shoreline just to be near her. She passed her days in joy and her nights in peace and innocence, and it seemed that nothing harmful dared come within seven miles of her.

Her lover, in the careless arrogant euphoria that springs from youth and lack of experience, exclaimed, 'I vow you are more lovely than Naimhe, the Queen of the Night – if I do not speak the truth, may the Tuatha de Dannaan cast a blight of misfortune upon the both of us, and bring us down as low in life as we are currently lifted high!'

This was not a very sensible thing for him to have said. Naimhe, surpassed in beauty among the Tuatha de Dannaan only by Caryddwen, would perhaps have let it go by. But Oisin, the hero of the Fianna whom she had chosen above all mortals to share her bed, was outraged by what had been said and demanded justice. 'Your request, once made, cannot be refused,' the Tuatha de Dannaan told him, 'although in our experience these matters are always delicate and there is more than a chance of the cure being worse than the disease. However, if you insist, we will hold a beauty contest, and determine the matter once and for all.'

Jenny Greenteeth's lover, in his arrogance, acceded to this arrangement. Yet in those more high-minded days no-one would have contemplated anything like the wet-teeshirt competitions whose sponsorship was so successful in building circulation for the *Sunday Scoop*. Instead, it was decided that the judgement should be reached with as much dignity and taste as possible, and that not only physical attractiveness and a good figure but also personality and moral values would be taken into account. To decide the winner, three monks were selected from an abbey well known for its piety and spiritual standing, and the contestants were given seven days to present themselves at a grove in a sacred wood, which was often used for deciding important matters.

The rest, as they say, is history.

Whether or not Naimhe cheated by sending a magic bumble bee to sting her rival's eyelids until her face grew raw and puffy, and an adder to bite her ankles so that her legs swelled up like those of a gouty matron, the sentence of the Tuatha de Dannaan was absolute, and could not be reversed. Perhaps the moral is that even monks, despite years of spiritual training, cannot look beyond superficial appearances, and are as apt to make errors of judgement as anyone else.

As a lesson to others who might be tempted to challenge the leaders of the Tuatha de Dannaan, Jenny Greenteeth was therefore banished from any place where the sun shone by day, and from any place where the moon shone by night, and constrained to make her home in caverns and old mine workings where conditions were as unlike her former lot as it was possible to be. She might perhaps have clung on to some vestige of happiness even with this twilit destiny, but her lover, annoyed at having been made a fool of and declaring himself unwilling to settle for second best, was quick to abandon her to her fate. 'Because', he said, 'it will be better for both of us.' Clearly he had valued her beauty not for itself but only for the prestige he thought it could bring him, and in many ways it was a relief to her when, after some time, she heard he had been devoured by a banshee.

Gradually, as the years went by, she found that not only was she unable to venture anywhere where sun and moonlight touched, but she could no longer bear to eat food that had been exposed to either. Instead, she could sustain herself only by sucking the living marrow out of human bones, which did little to ingratiate her with those who dwelt above. In those dark days only her little brother remained faithful to her, bringing her small gifts and mementos from the upper world whose warmth she was forever denied, kind words and little verses of love and affection, when others spat at the very mention of her name. But in the course of time the curse even extended to him, when he fell foul of the Tuatha de Dannaan as a result of an error of judgement in a remote bothy.

'But there's no time to go into all this now,' concluded Jenny

Greenteeth after she had given them as short as possible an account of her circumstances and thanked them for the fireguard. 'Clearly, you've come here to ask for my help. Because you are of the six sisters, and for the sake of my own little brother whom I love more than anything in the world, I don't believe I can refuse.'

67

Dave Doom was high in the counsels of Myles Overton, but even he felt his legs grow weak when he thought of the news he was bringing, and his body felt out of line with his head. He was only too aware that Linden Richmont had got to her uncle first and made it clear that Dave Doom had insisted on being personally in charge of things, so that when those they were following trod on a crack between two paving stones and were unaccountably lost to sight, Dave Doom had to take full responsibility.

'Also he put his hand on my leg,' said Linden Richmont.

In the circumstances the best policy was to gloss over the negative aspects of the affair as quickly as possible. Although Linden could not resist the remark about the hand on the leg, neither she nor Dave Doom mentioned Jenny Greenteeth, because they felt they would not be taken seriously. Perhaps this was their greatest mistake. 'It is probably not important,' Dave Doom began, 'but our information is they're making for the inner city. But obviously there's no connection with any of our operations there, and definitely no reason to expect a breach in security.'

'Well then, you'd better make sure there isn't one, unless you want a breach in your flaming arsehole,' Myles Overton said. Even if his string of clubs was a minor component of his leisure empire, it still had its part to play in his plan to dominate this world and all others. Besides, there were good reasons why events past and present in Myles Overton's clubs should not come to light, for there were secrets that would not stand up to scrutiny.

'We know they're planning to take things into their own hands, but the good news is there are only five of them and they're mostly women,' said Dave Doom nervously, for no-one wants a breach in their arsehole. 'But there's the question of Rufus Stone. How far do you want me to go?'

'If necessary, all the way. With this Night Caller crap, they may stumble on something.'

But Myles Overton could not convey even to Dave Doom the full implications of anyone reaching the Night Caller's refuge. He may not have understood them himself. Increasingly, he was acting as if something impelled him to act, and departing from sound business practice. The Night Caller was the invention of his own newspaper. Yet it was conceivable Rufus Stone was such a bad reporter he couldn't even invent something properly, and that the Night Caller was therefore real. Certain information available to Myles Overton suggested this was so. Certain information suggested that if the Night Caller was real, and if certain people reached him, in certain circumstances, things could go down the gurgler in a big way. Myles Overton did not think this was just about exposing irregularities in his night-clubs, or their use in obtaining footage to compromise key officials. He thought it went deep. He thought it went right into the abyss.

'Do whatever you bloody well have to do,' he told Dave Doom when Linden was out of earshot. 'But don't let the bastards reach the Night Caller. Here's a map of the area. Don't ask where it came from. You need to have your people here, and here, and here. Use the best. And remember, this goes deep.'

When Dave Doom had his instructions, he quickly prepared a plan, and did not neglect to tell the authorities what was going on so that there would be no unpleasant surprises from that direction. Routes into and out of sensitive spots were carefully watched, although the real danger lay in a twilight world whose routes were not described in any A–to–Z, just as its business was not listed in any directory. 'I want the best there is,' Dave Doom emphasized, when he consulted his security experts, 'because this goes deep.'

Best Security, the firm to whom the job was eventually given, prided themselves in being exactly that. Their operatives were drawn exclusively from a famous airborne regiment, celebrated for anti-terrorism and bullying, into which recruits were never accepted unless they passed through a gruelling six-week training course which included being strapped to the underside of an iceberg for fourteen hours, thrown naked into a nest of ravening cobras, and repeatedly stabbed in the vitals with an eight-inch commando knife. 'Unless someone has been brutally and painfully put to death, we do not even consider them for inclusion in our regiment,' one recruiting officer explained, although for obvious reasons this was an exaggeration. Due to connections within the military, the security firm was in a position to be offered the services of anyone thrown out of this regiment for being too violent and psychopathic.

Therefore, once the arrangements were complete, Dave Doom was soon experiencing the feelings of complete security which only being surrounded by a large number of violent psychopaths can confer. 'I think you'll find', he told Myles Overton on the mobile, 'that everything is in hand.'

'Think about your arsehole, and make sure it stays that way.'

68

When Dawn and her companions penetrated the underground labyrinth that was the true inner city, to seek the Night Caller, who now seemed somehow connected with the wellspring between reality and unreality, the odds appeared against them. Yet in Jenny Greenteeth, they found they had a formidable ally. The truth is that few years went by in the earliest history of the British Isles without its peoples being torn by internecine strife. Slaughter, rapine and human rights violations were the rule rather than the exception. In those days the Tuatha de Dannaan were celebrated for the brilliance of their tactics and the remorselessness of their victories. In a community where women and men were equal, Jenny Greenteeth was as celebrated as any.

Many were the seemingly impregnable fortresses, guarded by magic mists lethal to the human lung, which the Tuatha de Dannaan overran by feats of skill, strength and sheer cunning, enslaving or disembowelling survivors with resistless zeal. Many a dew-bright dawn rose to the sight of four or five faithful comrades working their way up a fissure in some heathery escarpment, their faces darkened with ash and their bodies daubed with whortleberry juice to mask their scent from guard dogs. And Jenny Greenteeth brought this same bold spirit to the little group of friends who crept through London's secret underworld to confront the sender of bad dreams.

'If anyone wants any whortleberry juice . . . ' Jenny Greenteeth offered, but they thanked her no, they would stick to Sure Extra Dry.

'What we need', Neill said, 'is a plan.'

'Only a man would have said that,' Dawn commented.

They knew by now that their coming would be opposed. But Jenny Greenteeth was confident. 'At least', she said, 'we have the element of surprise.'

'They know we're coming,' said Rufus. 'They've got the toughest security firm in the country looking out for us. They're hardly going to be surprised when we turn up.'

'No,' she replied, 'but they'll be surprised when we win.' For a moment she smiled, and they saw her former brave and beautiful self again through features ravaged by years of hard living and a diet devoid of fresh fruit and vegetables.

'Well,' said Dawn, 'we'll see what we will see. But hurry – because it's nearly dark!'

'It's always nearly dark down here.'

With Jenny's guidance they were quickly able to reach the narrow passage where the three bishops had encountered the hooded figure. She agreed three contests with him and trounced him soundly in all of them – his tricks and dissemblances could not stand against her. Once bested he rapidly imploded and vanished like a puffball thrown against a tree. They continued onward, though the route grew strange and forbidding. Jenny led them by hidden ways to the nethermost reaches of the city, eastwards and south of the river beneath blighted land and subsiding venues notorious for violence and vice. And if there was dereliction above, what lay beneath was a thousand times worse – a ruinous and chaotic pattern of roots from long-dead trees and foundations of collapsing buildings. A maze of tunnels and runnels which sometimes opened out into great vaults and galleries fringed with curious unidentifiable vegetation, its foliage pure white because there was no light.

In one such gallery they followed a kind of a causeway threading a subterranean marsh past pools fringed with insect-eating leaves, spaghnum moss and standing stones long-fallen. Once the companions thought they glimpsed the entrance to a vast chamber where the Tuatha de Dannaan themselves lay dreaming of the day the lost cauldron of Caryddwen would be re-assembled and they could re-assert their existence and fulfil the people's need. But Jenny Greenteeth put her finger on her lips and led them onwards without a sound. Once they seemed to look down a corridor a hundred miles long, at the end of which was Karen Greenwood and a sinister leather-clad figure. But Jenny Greenteeth said that the ratruns of the netherworld connected locations far distant in time and space; things that happened long ago, or that might never happen. They passed a wounded king who reached out to them in mute appeal, and a lady pleading for protection against a large reptile. But Jenny Greenteeth indicated these were illusions and they must on no account stray from the pathway.

Finally there was only one gateway and one passage left. From the increasingly lurid atmosphere and the sounds coming from the basements above their heads, they guessed they were beneath one of the disreputable clubs that abounded in that part of town. Probably, it was one of those belonging to Myles Overton, where he freely entertained bankers, bishops, and ministers of state, and compromised them in the small hours of the morning. But down here no bishop ever penetrated, and only the urgent beat of the music betrayed the world above. Down here was the realm of Jenny Greenteeth, and the Night Caller. Although, unfortunately, someone had also found a way of positioning a number of professional psychopaths between the companions and their goal.

'Well,' said Rufus, taking a drink from his flask, 'this is it.'

69

The force blocking the way was small, but perfectly trained. 'We're expecting some visitors,' Dave Doom had told the security contractors, 'and they're not to pass this point. I don't expect any slip-ups, or Myles Overton will know about it. I don't need to tell you what he does to people who have slip-ups. He breaches their arseholes.'

The seasoned veterans and psychopaths may have had some reservations about what was expected of them, but they knew better than to ask questions. To men accustomed to arriving by parachute or abseiling down buildings and crashing through plate glass, holding hands and jumping on cracks in the pavement may have seemed pansy. Perhaps Myles Overton, or his shadowy mentor, knew some other way in. In any case, they arrived on schedule, and by the time the companions reached the last gate, it was well guarded. The security company knew that Myles Overton had said they should do whatever it took. Descriptions of the interlopers had been circulated, together with brief biographical details, and the men were prepared for anything.

For anything, that is, except Jenny Greenteeth, whom Linden and Dave Doom had neglected to mention for fear of being laughed at. Trained for the ruling elite of a warrior people, she deployed to advantage her select force of three sisters, a psychologist and an alcoholic journalist. Her tactics were simple. Dressed as streetwalkers, the sisters approached the security guards and asked for matches, while Jenny Greenteeth and the men circled round behind. When they struck, they struck in silence, but they did not need to strike a second time, for they did what had to be done. Nobody likes to see grown men having their marrow sucked out by a sewer bogey, their vitals trampled into pâté by three sisters practised in a deadly form of T'ai Chi, and their very belief structures annihilated by a highly trained philosopher. But there was no time for niceties. Even Rufus Stone played his part, for he had drunk so much to reinforce his courage that he was able to render adversaries unconscious merely by breathing on them. In a matter of seconds it was over, and except for one guard on the door of the Night Caller's crypt, the path lay clear before them.

Thus was the Battle of the Last Passage Leading to the Night Caller fought. It will never be recorded in any history book, nor debated in a seminar at Oxford. Yet as a battle for a Celtic as against a Gothic future and a cyclic as against a linear universe, it may have been the third greatest engagement ever fought on British soil, after Cattraeth where these issues were first tried, and another, as yet unfought action, where they would finally be resolved. Yet history was far from the companions' thoughts as, pausing only to slap each other's palms in the traditional Celtic gesture of triumph, they stepped over Dave Doom's elite security force and prepared to meet a far greater force, still concealed in the crypt at the end of the now unguarded passage.

70

As they approached the lair of the Night Caller, far above them the tempo of the music changed, for the Live Show was about to start. Before a distinguished audience of prime ministers, bishops and sheikhs a lurid pageant was unveiled. Who is to say whether the activities of the Night Caller himself did not in some way orchestrate it? As the curtain rose, the audience had time to notice that around the walls were pictures of members past and present, famous voluptuaries like Karl Marx, St Brendan the Navigator, Francis Bacon, Fyodor Dostoyevsky, Catherine the Great and D.H. Lawrence.

If only the constraints of space and current censorship laws would permit a full description of the Live Show at the club that probably belonged to Myles Overton, above the Night Caller's dwelling! It took as its theme the eternal conflict between good and evil, the orgiastic rituals of the pre-Celtic matriarchies and in particular what Queen Maeve of Skye did to Mannannan Mac Llyr Mac Lugh. It dwelt on the oppression of those loyal to the Tuatha de Dannaan at the hands of the Gothic invaders of the sixth and seventh centuries. It reproduced the cruel punishments meted out to the remnants of pagan belief in medieval and renaissance times, and more recently the bizarre abduction of a young girl by a nameless captor, her ordeal at his hands, and the role of their relationship in the corruption of a world.

Yet this was really an excuse for explicit scenes with young models and Page Three girls highly paid to explore the most perverse and unusual dimensions of human sexuality. They did so by means of a bizarre variety of chains, handcuffs, artificial sex organs and other equipment, together with participation from members of the audience who for greater effect had girded their bulging paunches in the leather and steel equipage of Gothic champions.

Even if they had witnessed this display, the companions all believed sex should take place in the context of a loving relationship and therefore the activities on stage would have held no interest for them. But they might have remarked that the powerfully built man in tails who introduced the show was surprisingly similar to Myles Overton. And that a captive girl looked reminiscent of Karen Greenwood, which was odd, because only a few minutes ago they seemed to have seen her at the end of a long tunnel. As Neill Fife might have said, much of human perception takes place in psycho-symbolic rather than actual space, and identities are simply the crystallization in time of more universal and eternal existences. But in fact Neill Fife said nothing of the kind, because they had a job to do, and the Live Show could have been a thousand miles away.

The last security man stood at the door of the chamber, but he wanted no trouble.

'Have you seen the Night Caller?' they asked.

'Who are you?'

'Those who sow the dream', said Jenny Greenteeth, 'must reap the nightmare. And I'm it!'

Quick as a flash, it was all over with the last security man. Looking neither to left nor right, they made their way into a little crypt where a single candle burnt. Over the candle, as Jenny Greenteeth had predicted, a figure sat on a melancholy throne carved from the living root of a tree – perhaps indeed the world tree, Yggdrasil. Beside him was a shallow well or font made of green onyx and wrought round with a cornice of ornate design.

'Welcome to my domain,' said the Night Caller. 'I have been expecting you.'

71

But instead of menace, there was in his voice an unfathomable sadness, for his story was the story of aeons, and the depth of his misfortune was beyond measurement. After they had been offered seats and refreshments and explained how they had got here and what had happened to the security guards, the Night Caller indicated that he would tell them as briefly as he could about his case, although he begged them not to judge him too harshly, for no-one can predict what will befall them in life, nor how they will react when it does.

'Once', began the Night Caller, 'I was high in the counsels of the Tuatha de Dannaan. My name was never spoken except with praise for my exploits on the battlefield, my skills at the chase and in contests of wit and limb. Chiefly, however, I was admired for my abilities as a bard and a harp player, which were considered without parallel amongst my contemporaries. Even after an accident with a banshee cost me the fingers of my right hand, my playing remained the subject of universal acclaim. The notes I formed could draw water out of a stone, fish out of the salt sea, or milk out of—but I digress . . .

'Suffice it to say I was called Martyn McMartyn of the Silver Fingers, and everything went well with me until the day Finbar Direach tricked me into putting to music a poem he was carrying to Caryddwen from Mannannan Mac Llyr Mac Lugh. I hardly need to remind you that things went badly awry as a result of that evening's work at the bothy. As a punishment, the Tuatha de Dannaan decreed that my silver fingers should be removed with a hacksaw, and those of my other hand cut off in the normal manner. Further, I was condemned to ramble no more through the green and verdant hills of my native country, but instead must offer to change places with the first person I met on the road, and whatever his burden was, I must carry it for the rest of my waking life.'

'That is certainly a severe sentence,' replied Jenny Greenteeth who had known Martyn McMartyn by reputation in the halcyon days before Finn's tragic error, although both of them were now changed out of all recognition. 'But what sort of burden did it turn out to be?'

'I will tell you,' replied Martyn McMartyn. 'After the Tuatha de Dannaan cut my fingers off and turned into eagles to fly back to their mountain fastness, I saw an old man standing beside the road, yet it was obvious that the cares weighing upon him were beyond what years could count. I quickly made myself and my situation known to him, and put myself at his disposal.'

'After all,' whispered Rufus to Dawn, 'it couldn't be worse than working for Myles Overton.'

'Shhh!' she said.

Martin McMartyn, who had turned out to be the Night Caller, inclined his head gratefully. 'You may well say *Shhh*, because what I have to tell you will repay close attention. My interlocutor, when he understood who I was and what plight I was in, fell to capering about and clicking his heels. For, he said, his name had once been King Lud, but really it was not his name at all, for in his youth and arrogance he had stolen it from Lugh, the creator of the universe. As punishment for stealing the name he had been condemned to guard a terrible secret left over from the time when the world of reality was condensed out of the world of dreams. He must guard that secret, Lugh told him, until such time as a fingerless harper should meet him on the road and relieve him of his burden. "But that time is as unlikely to come," added Lugh, "as a harper to prosper in his trade without fingers."'

When his new acquaintance calmed down, Martin McMartyn continued, he led him to a cromlech or burial mound hard by, under which was the chamber they now occupied. 'In this little crypt,' the nameless king explained to the fingerless harper, 'is a secret well. But don't think it is any ordinary well, for though it's neither deep nor wide, at its base is the spring from which eternity flows into time, and the world of dreams flows into the world of reality. But such a confluence is a vulnerable spot, open to all kinds of abuse, and therefore it has been my task, and must now be yours, to guard it without either rest or sleep, until the flesh drops off your bones.'

In this way, Martyn McMartyn said, the responsibility was passed to himself, but he did not have an easy time of it. In earlier years when the relationship between dreams and reality was close, the spring was a sacred place, and people came from far and wide to drink at it. In those days people were able to control their dreams, and the archipelago was ruled by women presided over by the Queens of Skye. But when the male line began to prevail and the Tuatha de Dannaan were at length threatened by Gothic tribes from the east, all this had to end. There was concern that by tracing dreams back to their source, the wellspring would be discovered by invaders and exploited for their own ends. Consequently Mannannan Mac Llyr Mac Lugh took his shield, which formerly belonged to his grandfather Lugh and which nothing could penetrate, and capped the well, separating dreams from reality forever, and eliminating any interaction between the two. Then he put confusion on the spot where the spring was, so nobody could ever find it. But just to make sure, Martyn McMartyn said, he himself was still left to guard the wellspring, since it was easy to imagine what difficulties would arise if the covering were tampered with or removed for any period of time.

'I can see why yours might be an important job,' Dawn said, for she was familiar with the male propensity for self-aggrandizement through their work. 'But about the dreams – and the pitcher that is never full and never empty . . . ?'

Martyn McMartyn sighed, for his load was heavy, and his story had hardly even begun. 'Few things are concealed from me,' he replied. 'Don't think me ignorant of the reason you have come here, nor that you're one of the six sisters. But I've guarded my charge faithfully for a thousand years, or even two, so you must let me go at my own pace. These words are painful for me to speak. For imagine my consternation when, many years ago, I received a visit from what appeared to be an itinerant craftsman who offered to replace the seat on my water closet for a good price, and when I then discovered a terrible mistake had been made! Imagine my despair when I realized that I had broken the trust imposed on me by the Tuatha de Dannaan, and perhaps compromised the very structure of the universe!'

'But if you lost the covering – that must have changed everything,' began Neill, who could appreciate the implications better than most, and unlike Dawn did not waste time asking why he left the stranger unattended in the first place.

'Exactly,' replied Martyn McMartyn. 'And great was the danger in which the world stood, because the dreams started gushing out into reality and there was little I could do to prevent them. You will easily believe I searched high and low for a replacement, but none could be found. Eventually I was lucky enough to come across the pitcher that is never full and never empty, which I have used ever since to catch the overflow. Needless to say this method is not perfect. Every so often there is some spillage, which has the inevitable effect of putting dreams and reality out of balance. If this results in cultural upheavals and unwanted pregnancies there is no-one more regretful than myself. If, as I fear, it played a part in the unleashing of Leatherwing and the untimely fate of Karen Greenwood, I can only apologize and say that if ever I'm placed in a similar position, I will try not to lose the Impenetrable Shield of Mannannan Mac Llyr Mac Lugh again.'

When they heard this explanation they were happy that the mystery of the dreams had been cleared up, but it left them in a quandary. As Martyn McMartyn pointed out, he would willingly give them the Bottomless Pitcher in a moment, but, as they could easily see, this would result in an incontinent leakage of dreams into reality, and quite possibly entail the destruction of the entire universe, a state of affairs that would benefit no-one.

But Neill had been considering things carefully, as befits a true savant. He had read the latest theories of Stephen Hawking and well knew his conclusion that we travel this way only once, for calculations on available matter, even allowing for the possibility of mass-bearing neutrinos, do not support the Druid notion of a cyclic cosmos. 'Let me put it this way,' he explained to the others, 'as the universe ages, it is thought to be steadily expanding and losing energy, and will one day become so vast and inert it will effectively cease to exist.'

'I know how it feels,' said Rufus. 'The same thing's been happening to me. But what's that got to do with the price of eggs?'

'There is not enough matter in the universe, either eggs or anything else, for gravity to take over and reverse this effect, eventually contracting the universe into a singularity from which the whole process can start again, thereby guaranteeing us an infinite number of lives, as the Druids believed, albeit half of them would have to be lived backwards.'

'I can see what you're getting at – but I still don't see what it's got to do with dreams, or pitchers—'

'Suffice to say that if, as some theorists maintain, a dream has a small but detectable mass, there may be enough of them in the universe to make up the deficit of material that is the difference between a recurring cosmos, and a linear one. This is why it is important to keep having dreams, thereby building up sufficient mass to stop the universe expanding and thus secure infinite life. And why it is so important not to let them spill over into reality, where they may be destroyed by unscrupulous individuals determined to secure their own objectives.'

'Come to the point.'

Like all his kind, Neill Fife was incapable of using one word when six would suffice, or coming straight to the point when it was possible to go round and round like a jumbo jet stacking above Heathrow. But he presently revealed to them that according to some strands of current scientific thought the universe is full of dreams and its walls are made of green onyx, although the associated mathematics are very hard to follow. 'The point is, if we take the Bottomless Pitcher, all the dreams will leak away, and unreality will cease to exist, throwing the universe out of balance and creating a linear rather than a cyclic future. This, I believe, is Myles Overton's plan, or the plan of his shadowy cohorts, who are determined that the universe should become linear in character, so that the evil they do can never be undone. To that end, in the distant past Leatherwing had once betrayed his own people to an invading enemy, and to that end Myles Overton seems determined to betray himself, for he believes one life is all.'

'I am afraid you're right,' said Jenny Greenteeth. 'For I remember it was exactly this line of reasoning that made Mannannan Mac Llyr Mac Lugh act as he did and sacrifice a valuable shield. It turned out, indeed, that he could ill afford to lose it, for shortly afterwards he was defeated by his old adversary Queen Maeve of Skye, who, determined to restore the old matriarchy, had allied herself with the forces from the east. The price was a heavy one, but he knew unless it was paid, the universe would sooner or later end, and that he could not allow.'

'On the other hand if we don't take the pitcher,' Dawn put in, 'we'll have nothing to exchange with Jihad for the Chain of Command, which we therefore won't be able to give to the clay man in return for information about the last lost piece of Caryddwen's cauldron, so the three thousandth anniversary of the coming of the Tuatha de Dannaan will arrive without it, and the world will likewise end, or fall beneath the hegemony of Leatherwing, which amounts to the same thing.'

'The only chance', declared Martyn McMartyn gloomily, 'would be to find the Impenetrable Shield once again, but that will be very hard to do. For legend has it the itinerant craftsman into whose hands it fell was set upon and killed by Christian knights on their way to the crusades to atone for their sins. "What a beautiful toilet seat!" said one. "I shall make it into a shield." Sadly, he was unaware it was impenetrable, so when danger threatened he ran away and was struck in the kidneys by a spear. As the fortunes of war reeled back and forth, the Impenetrable Shield was heard of first on one side and then on another, but passes from the record after the fall of the Eastern Empire and the Mongol raids on the cities of Asia Minor in the early 13th Century.'

'If I stand here a moment longer,' said Dawn, 'I'm going to get a GCSE in world history, and still be none the wiser.'

'I'm only trying to say that it may be beyond your reach,' he replied.

'But if it's ever to be recovered, you will need the co-operation of your sister Chantal, and perhaps others besides.'

'My sister Chantal', said Triona, 'is in exile, and in no position to help anybody.'

'Well,' said Martyn McMartyn, 'that is all one. I'll keep the pitcher that is never full and never empty.'

72

But as he said it, the sadness in his eyes deepened until they looked to Dawn like the eyes of Angharad and Berengharad when they had just fallen over and hurt their knees. 'I wish,' he said, as if speaking solely to her, 'it could have been otherwise.'

She looked into the eyes that were so like her daughters' eyes, and a thought formed in her mind, but it was so bizarre that she quickly dismissed it. 'Well, perhaps we'll find the Impenetrable Shield after all,' she said. 'In the meantime – try not to let too many dreams escape.'

'I'll do the best I can, for I've done enough damage already.'

Their eyes never left each other, but already they could hear footsteps above them, and they knew that Dave Doom's security men were re-grouping.

With an effort, Dawn looked away. 'I'll come back when we have the shield, and as a token of good faith, I'm giving you this picture of myself and my two little daughters. But—'

'Come on!' said Triona. 'We have to leave.'

When they were out of earshot she added, 'You certainly hit it off with him!'

'There was something about him.'

'There's something about Dave Doom's security men too, but I don't think we should stick around to find out what it is.'

'What about the Night Caller, Martyn McMartyn?'

'That, I think, you may safely leave to me,' said Jenny Greenteeth. 'For I intend to put confusion on the place, so that nobody can find it. If I don't, now our visit has warned our enemies about the pitcher, and they won't hesitate to steal it, with the consequences we already know.'

'You mean our actions may have created the very disaster they were meant to forestall?'

But Jenny Greenteeth repeated that she would put confusion on the place, and when Jenny Greenteeth put confusion on somewhere, confusion stayed on it. However, to make doubly sure, she used her long years of experience in this fetid world to great advantage. Borrowing one of the matches they took from the guards while pretending to be streetwalkers, she held it to an opening in the seeping wall. If the resulting tongue of flame had twisted itself to form the word 'methane' before their very eyes, her intention could not have been more clear. 'I think we'd better be going,' Jenny Greenteeth said, with the imperturbability of a person who knows they are more or less immortal.

Later, as they fled back down secret passages and sewers familiar only to Jenny Greenteeth, certain members of Jihad's special forces, and a few little girls who trod on the cracks between paving stones, they heard a distant crash and rumble. And thus they knew that the passages leading to the Night Caller's crypt, which was a state of mind and not a location, were now in a state where they could not be accessed, and the Night Caller, deep in the hollow earth, must wait until they came for him, and brought the means of his release.

73

It was Tuesday morning, but to Jenny Greenteeth, morning never came, for the light of the sun was denied her, as was even the pale luminescence of the moon.

'Farewell,' she told the companions. 'And remember me with kindness in your hearts, not for the sake of what I am, but for the sake of what I once was, the journey we made together, and the quest we fulfilled.'

'Come with us! We'll buy you dark glasses and give you protein extracts and supplements based on calcium and iodine, so you need never suck out anyone's marrow ever again.'

'I will never forget you asked me. But even if it were possible, I couldn't venture into the world of light. My loathsome appearance is a more effective prison than any the Tuatha de Dannaan could have devised for me. No – I will dwell here for ever, and subsist as I can, until the lost cauldron of Caryddwen which heals all things shall be made whole again. But that day may never come.'

74

It was Tuesday morning and Rufus Stone had uncovered the story of his life only to find it could never be printed, and been close to the woman he had set his heart on, only to find she was unaware of his feelings and had secretly set her cap for a three-thousand-year-old night watchman, even though she might not know it yet, and the night watchman was where he could do himself little good. 'Well, I'll drink to her anyway – and for that matter, to them both. For when you drink to two people, you must necessarily have two drinks,' he decided, locating a bottle of hogweed ale.

For Rufus's dream was that the Tuatha de Dannaan built a universe only for themselves, and the rubbish produced in the process had been dumped in a skip outside, and this skip was the universe now inhabited by human beings. But although cruel and capricious, they were not wholly without compassion, and they made a hole between the two universes, and screwed a top on it to prevent leakage. But, thought Rufus Stone in his dream, the hole between the two realities was nothing less than the neck of a bottle of hogweed ale. Gratefully, he removed the lid, and felt his lips communicate with a deeper and more powerful dimension, where loneliness was nothing but a word, and whatever is felt by one person for another was always reciprocated.

75

It was Tuesday evening and Dawn had already thought often of Martyn McMartyn and his strange employment. She dreamed she met him again and said, 'If the earth's too damp for you, I can put you up for a few nights. I've rented a place near Coldharbour – though it's only small.'

A night bus made its way out of the city and then out of the suburbs, and was soon negotiating the leafy lanes of the North Downs where the tips of beech branches slapped at the windows of the upper deck. Three women, no longer young, leaned wordlessly against each other in the hindmost seat. Later in her cosy flat Dawn fell asleep with her arms round her two little girls, Angharad and Berengharad, as they played with some atlases and maps of Asia Minor their aunts had purchased in Dillons when they were up in London, for they'd been discussing how they would find yet another sister, and ask her to help redeem something from the depths of the past, which would help purchase a new and more beautiful future.

When Dawn fell asleep, she dreamed again that a maimed musician leaned back on the settee opposite them, the wrinkles weaving themselves round his eyes like a raven's nest around two bright blue eggs. 'That's a pair of fine children and no mistake – but tell me who is the father of them, for I'd like to give my respects to him.'

'I think you know who – as well as myself.' It is best to cast a veil over what was meant by this remark, since the Child Support Agency would not scruple to purchase a copy of this narrative on expenses, and by careful analysis of the text, use its message to further their own ends. Yet a kind of understanding passed between Dawn and Martyn McMartyn formerly of the Silver Fingers but now of none at all, and despite the age difference it was clear that they had much in common, and her children would dote on him for his fund of strange and colourful stories.

'You're like the father they never had,' Dawn said in her dream, as across the night beyond the windows of her room, the lights of the city spread out upon the Northern horizon like the campfires of an invading host.

'Yet who knows the truth of it, after all?' Martyn McMartyn seemed to reply.

'Just tell me one thing – did all the dreams come from you? The ones that made all those other women pregnant – as well as me?'

'I had been alone so long, my hands destroyed, and all prospect of freedom denied me. Perhaps I was just reaching out for someone. I didn't realize it would result in so much distress and unwanted pregnancy.'

'But how can I be sure it won't happen again?'

'If I can find love – I'll need dreams no longer.'

Reassured by this, Dawn dreamed she agreed to settle down with him, and to forget the Pitcher, the Shield and his promise to the Tuatha de Dannaan. He told her that everything would be all right, for one day his fingers would grow again, and everyone would be happy – even Jenny Greenteeth. For, he said, what they had taken for an oddly shaped fireguard was nothing less than the Harp of Rhiannon, which in his hands could charm back her ravaged beauty, and undo the effect of her terrible existence. Everything, he said in the dream, would be well.

When Dawn woke she knew this could not happen. She must stay in Coldharbour, sleep, look after her children, and recover her strength. But before anyone's dreams could come true, somebody must contact her sister Chantal, the most fiery of all the sisters, for only she could win back the Impenetrable Shield, which they could exchange for the Bottomless Pitcher, which they could exchange for the Chain of Command, which they could give to the Clay Man in return for information about the last fragment of the Lost Cauldron of Caryddwen, so that what was missing could be found, what was broken could be restored, their sister Karen could be emancipated from the tyranny of Leatherwing and the world set to rights before the anniversary of the Tuatha de Dannaan setting foot on British soil.

But, Dawn knew, this would not be easy.

VI

The Aral Sea

76

'I worry about Damien,' Triona said to Neill. 'So much depends on him, and he has so little to offer.'

'He has Chantal,' Neill said obscurely.

'Who knows where Chantal is now? Who knows *who* Chantal is now? Things aren't as they were in the old days. I worry about him.'

She had some reason to be concerned. It was Neill's idea that Damien would be the best means of contacting Chantal, who would be the best means of finding the Impenetrable Shield, without which, it was now clear, their enterprise could proceed no further. But there were a number of reasons for doubting whether this was one of Neill's best ideas.

'It sounds fine in principle,' said Triona. 'But in practice you're talking about two people who will find it very difficult to work together.'

'Overcoming the difficulties we have with each other', Neill replied, 'is an essential part of overcoming the difficulties we have with the task that confronts us.'

But, as Oswald pointed out, the trouble was that Damien and Chantal hated each other, and always had done. Damien ridiculed Chantal's causes, Chantal railed at Damien's hedonism. Chantal wanted to save the world. 'The only misgiving I have', she used to say, 'is that I can't work out a way to do it without saving Damien Lewis.' She never missed an opportunity to point out that he was a person without a conscience. Damien said she was a conscience without a person. She devoted her life to helping others, he devoted his to helping himself. Oswald was confused when Neill told him they were both equally egocentric, but realized that this was why Neill was a psychologist and he, Oswald, was only an accountant.

'If you ask me,' Oswald's opinion was, 'they're the last people we should ask. They didn't get on even in the old days. And times move on, and people change. The only thing they have in common is that Damien's been in trouble with the law, and Chantal's completely beyond it. But even in that they manage to be on opposite sides.'

What he said was no more than the truth. They all knew that Chantal thought only about world peace, and had a bee in her bonnet about emerging nations promoting cash crops to fund arms purchases from multinational conglomerates. They all knew that Damien had an earring and a ponytail and never thought seriously about anything. But also that he had, perhaps deliberately, become involved with the very trade Chantal dedicated her life to stamping out.

'Although, having said that,' Neill acknowledged, 'he claims he was only trying to make a buck, and it was Myles Overton's activities that led to the whole thing getting out of hand and becoming a notorious scandal.'

But Triona, still the only one in any kind of contact with Finbar Direach, could obtain little information about the true facts behind Damien's case, let alone the whereabouts of the Impenetrable Shield, assuming indeed such a thing still existed. If Finn knew its location, he said, he would have found it long ago. He was irritated by remarks like *Where was it when you last saw it?* which he saw as unhelpful to any serious search. But he did confirm it might be in foreign parts, and let slip that, as a significant item of the Celtic reliquary, it conceivably could once have been offered by the Pasha of Kurdistan as a gift to the Eastern Emperor, whose dominions were unfortunately pillaged by the Mongol armies of Genghis Khan and their treasures dissipated through the steppes of Central Asia.

'It gives me pain', added Finbar Direach, 'that I'm unable to be more specific. For that, you will need the help of your sister Chantal, as Martyn McMartyn clearly told you.'

'If anyone can find the Impenetrable Shield,' said Neill, 'Chantal can. And if anyone can find Chantal, Damien can, although he himself may not yet suspect it. I know he's had his share of troubles – not least with the law. He needs to make a fresh start. But don't worry! I myself am going to give him counselling.'

77

Damien Lewis told the others he signed up with Neill Fife for counselling because he had become estranged from his essential self, and needed to find out who he was. In fact Damien was too much of a Jack-the-Lad to worry about who he was. The counselling comprised part of a package worked out by his defence lawyers to avoid the custodial sentence that Damien deserved so much more than the greatly wronged and strangely redeemed Nuala Greenwood. Damien had, the defence lawyers argued, suffered enough. By the time he returned to Coldharbour, his business activities had bankrupted him and his wife had left him, taking their three children, house, and Mercedes 500SL with electric roof.

'You see before you', the defence lawyers told the jury, 'a man who has become estranged from his essential self, with all that this entails. It's true he has the reputation of a Jack-the-Lad and drives a car with an electric roof. But we will argue that although some of his actions have been ill conceived, he always worked within guidelines laid down by the regulatory authorities, and besides, he was a very small fish in a very big pond.'

The defence lawyers were experts in their field, but with Damien they had their work cut out. His ear-ring and ponytail did him no favours with the jury. Nor did his open admission that he had been party to an international trade in leisure products that could potentially be converted into weapons of mass destruction.

Actually Damien's connection with the international arms business was peripheral, and to its major players he was little more than a joke. He was a familiar figure at trade shows, and had managed to get on the committee of the International Arms Dealers Benevolent Society. But for the most part his only involvement was as what his business card called a Parliamentary Lobbyist – a much misunderstood position which led to many difficult questions.

Lobbying, or facilitating informal contacts between members of the government and various vested interests, is an essential part of the democratic process. It could be argued that for his pre-eminence in this aspect of democracy Damien Lewis should have been given a knighthood rather than a criminal record. Unquestionably, the international arms trade has as much right to put its case as any other commercial activity. And Damien often boasted about his ability to gain access to the seventeen most powerful figures in the land, and took a great pride in the little enterprise he had created. 'You know,' he chortled when he first phoned back to Coldharbour to let them know what he was up to, 'this has got to be the business Chantal would have hated most of anything in the world! I tell you – she really was a conscience without a person.'

Unfortunately, while Chantal would have hated it, the jury were not over-impressed either.

The defence lawyers did their best. 'Damien Lewis is no angel,' they said, 'and we've all heard that when Myles Overton's business empire extended its interests into the international arena, some of the regulations may have been stretched. Although cargo manifests referred to the supply of ride-on lawnmowers, we now know these lawnmowers were equipped with caterpillar tracks and laser-guided grenade launchers. Official explanations speak of an infestation by unusually large and virulent moles, but the potential for military use cannot be disregarded.'

'Too true,' agreed the jury, 'because the moles may have been genetically altered to deliver explosives – or worse. The Americans did it with dolphins, but in a landlocked theatre, one would have to use whatever was available.'

'Yet who is really on trial here?' continued the defence lawyers. 'Is it Damien Lewis, or the Law itself? Myles Overton's Leisure Group infringed no explicit guidelines by equipping garden machinery with the legitimate means of self-defence. Export licenses were signed by high-ranking officials and ministers well versed in the public interest. True, Damien Lewis escorted the high-ranking officials to a Live Show at which compromising photographs were taken. But there's no evidence that this influenced the decision to sign, or in any way undermined the objectivity of the officials concerned. Corporate lobbying is a fact of modern business life. And Live Shows based on the orgiastic mysteries of the pre-Celtic matriarchy, with their traditional element of audience participation, are as much a part of this country's heritage as Morris Dancing or the Glastonbury Festival. The fact that some of the girls turned out to be in the pay of unfriendly powers was merely an unfortunate coincidence.'

'Though by all accounts the girls were friendly enough, even if the powers weren't,' whispered the jury, nudging each other significantly.

'In today's economic climate with its emphasis on market forces and the dominance of the private sector, there will always be a danger of transactions being misinterpreted. But this case has already been tried in the court of public opinion. Did not our client suffer enough when the *Sunday Scoop* exposed him in a full-colour special edition? Clearly, Damien Lewis was in the grip of forces he could not hope to understand, and never knew the full implications of his actions.'

'Still, it wouldn't have taken a rocket scientist to work them out,' the jury muttered to each other. 'Also, it's funny he was involved with the very armour-plated ride-on lawnmowers that were used against Chantal Greenwood. Or would have been, if she hadn't managed to intercept the consignment and turn them on their owners. Frankly, there's more to this than meets the eye, and talk about essential selves is a bit of a red herring.'

'You, who retain contact with your essential selves,' continued the defence lawyers, regardless, 'can hardly conceive what it is to lose one's moral identity. This is a man more to be pitied than penalized. His jaunty air, his ear-ring, and his ponytail are merely affected to conceal a terrible emptiness. And if he was implicated in exporting military hardware that might some day be used against Chantal Greenwood, perhaps that was just his way of trying to maintain some connection with her.'

'Sounds like the sort of thing Neill Fife would say,' the jury muttered, 'because, by all accounts, Damien Lewis never had a moral identity in the first place.'

The truth was that members of the jury had their work cut out to maintain contact with their own essential selves, which slumbered beneath an oppressive mulch of constraints and obligations like dry wrinkled tubers awaiting a spring that might never come. Unless, of course, a certain cauldron could be re-assembled. Nevertheless, under the spell of this eloquence they eventually acquitted Damien of the more serious charges. And the judge, perhaps influenced by Damien's connection with Neill, Triona, and ironically Chantal too, stopped short of sending him to Brixton or one of Myles Overton's own facilities.

'Being estranged from oneself cannot entirely exonerate bad behaviour,' he explained, 'because there is a prima facie obligation upon the individual not to become estranged from himself. Nor can vice, for the same reason, be regarded as a victimless crime, for it's a crime in which the criminal himself (or herself) is the victim, and the law has no less obligation to protect us from ourselves than from others.'

'Let's hear it', whispered the more libertarian jurors, 'for the nanny state!'

'Nonetheless, from the witnesses we have heard, not least Dr Neill Fife, whose reflections on our client's state of mind have proved so valuable, and Triona Greenwood, whose work with the Heritage Commission has shed so much light on the significance of the pre-Celtic tradition in modern society, we may conclude that the defendant could once have been an exceptional individual. Someone capable of commanding loyalty and friendship, and even on occasion of returning it. We must also take into account Chantal Greenwood and her part in the moral disintegration of the accused. It cannot be easy when a member of one's immediate circle is exposed as a notorious international terrorist, even if one never liked them much.'

'Well,' said the jury, 'he may have a point.'

'To sum up,' the judge summed up, 'a man needs friends to prevail over his enemies, and he needs enemies to prevail over himself. Nevertheless, justice must prevail over everything. The real facts behind this case may never come to light, but an example must be made, even if nobody is sure what it is an example of. I therefore sentence Damien Lewis to twelve months imprisonment suspended for three years, and require him to undergo fifty hours of psychological counselling. This I do with the object of rehabilitating him, as it were, from the inside outwards, and rendering him a more balanced and productive member of society.'

The newspapers were outraged by this leniency and showed all the pictures of the Live Show again. Accusations of a cover-up were widespread, and many imaginative alternative punishments were proposed by the tabloids, while some broadsheets felt the public had a right to know more about the involvement of top industrialists, politicians, chairmen of blue chip companies, bishops, city accountants and others whose names were withheld at the trial for fear of de-stabilizing the economy.

In written parliamentary answers, however, it was decided that it would be against the public interest for further inquiries to be made. 'When there's a rotten apple in a barrel,' said the minister responsible, 'we don't go out into the orchard and chainsaw down the tree from which it came.'

'We might, however, be tempted to cut out some of the dead wood,' responded his opposite number, to laughter and cheers.

'Someone as notoriously incapable of seeing the wood for the trees as the honourable member is', said the minister responsible with the wit for which he was famous, 'would do well to *bough* to superior judgement.'

Two days later pictures were released of a famous supermodel with suspected anorexia nervosa, and Damien Lewis, the much-headlined 'Pornmowers' scandal, and the committee set up to investigate standards in public life, were all forgotten. The post-trial publicity therefore only produced one consequence of any world-changing potential. Chantal Greenwood, at the time camped with two comrades on the edge of the horrifyingly polluted Aral Sea as special forces from three newly formed nation states closed in on her, heard a report about it in 'What the Papers Say' over the BBC World Service at half past four in the morning.

Something stirred at the bottom of Chantal's profound intellect, like a sleepy monster at the bottom of a clear lake. She had more immediate problems to address as a result of the security forces, the creaking of whose equipment was even now audible across the sunless and salt-encrusted plain, but to Chantal *akrasia* was just a Greek word, and her resolve knew no bounds.

78

'Our task', said Neill, 'is to unlock the future using the past as a key.'

'We might as well try to jemmy a safe with a stick of celery,' Damien Lewis told him cynically.

'The key', said Neill quickly, 'is to try. If a person will not attempt to try, then they will never attempt to succeed. Perhaps you're afraid of success?'

'How much do you get paid for this crap? Don't forget it's me, Damien, who saved you from a bizarre yet certain death the night Karen left Coldharbour, when friendship seemed the only important thing and psychology was just a Greek word. We both know we're just going through the motions to satisfy the court order. There's no need for method acting.'

'The money's not important. I only take on a limited number of private clients, and one of them's a supermodel with an eating disorder. You could have had a hundred court-appointed psycho-therapists. I took the job because I believe I can help you. And talking of money, in the old days with your free and easy attitude you were more contemptuous of the materialist lifestyle than any of us.'

'That was then, and this is now. Besides, I never abandoned my beliefs. They abandoned me.'

'So, as a kind of revenge, you set out to annihilate everything they were based on, and formed a parliamentary lobbying company.'

'It didn't happen like that. Frankly, I think that by counselling me you're really trying to counsel yourself.'

'Then how did it happen? At what stage did you forget who you really are - since that's what all this is about? For we psychologists believe that one can only regain the pathway by backtracking to the point at which one left it. Trying to cut through diagonally and join it further up will inevitably get you stuck in blackberry bushes and stinging nettles. But metaphors are one thing, and reality is another. Talk to me about Chantal.'

At the mention of her name Damien Lewis started violently – but as quickly regained his composure. In fact, he was so composed that he stared indifferently out of the window, lit a cigarette and started kicking the front of his chair leg with the back of his boot heel. 'There's nothing to say. Or nothing new. You know everything that happened. For all I can tell, you even orchestrated it, because idealism always fascinated you. Everyone knows Chantal took a stand in a little-known frontier state, and the international community decided to make an example of her. Personally, I think she had it coming – she was always arrogant. The story of her capture and escape became notorious. And after that she was beyond me, as she was beyond all of us. She became a political icon, which was what she always wanted to be. A conscience without a person. I hope she's very happy. And there's no point saying Chantal represents my expropriated moral self, as Karen represented your expropriated moral self – and for all I know Chantal's as well. This expropriated-self business, in my opinion, can be overdone. And you can rely on any of the Greenwood sisters to overdo it. The truth is that Chantal betrayed those of us who knew her as a human being, and in doing that she betrayed her own humanity as well as ours.'

'So you lost contact with her, and then lost contact with yourself?'

'You can't lose something you never had. We argued all the time. Where she is now, and what she is, doesn't matter to me. As a person, she was in any case a disaster. That's the best you can say about her – that she was like some natural disaster that overwhelms a landscape and then passes on, leaving people to try to piece their lives together again.'

'If I'm allowed to make a comment, the way you pieced your life together would make Doctor Frankenstein look like a Beverley Hills cosmetic surgeon.'

'I thought counsellors were supposed to listen, not make snide remarks.'

'The object, as anyone who has read my books knows only too well, is to liberate the truth. But like an animal that's been in a cage too long, the truth doesn't always realize someone's opened the door and it's free to go. Sometimes it has to be provoked into action. But one thing's clear. The time to talk about words will soon be over, and it will be time to talk about action. When the tide is at its lowest ebb, you can find the biggest starfish, and when a person is most despondent, their richest resources may be revealed. But whether those resources can prevail in the conflict that awaits us, only time will tell.'

Damien Lewis thought this was an odd thing for Neill to say, and fleetingly it occurred to him that it would not be out of character if Neill was up to something. If he was, it would not be out of character if he was up to it with Triona. Especially since Triona herself approached Damien later the same day and insinuated that although she was deeply shocked by the direction his lobbying activities had taken, he could redeem himself in her eyes if he could help contact Chantal. For, Triona said, she hardly needed to remind him that he too had made a promise when they put stones in Neill Fife's circle, and undertook to do whatever needed to be done.

'Why would I want to redeem myself in your eyes?' said Damien with forced jauntiness.

'For Karen's sake and Chantal's, if not for mine,' Triona told him.

'Have you ever thought that Karen might not want to be found? She came to Chantal and me when we were arguing that last night, and told us that although we could never get on together, one day we would need one another more than anything in the world. Then she said that if she stayed any longer, she would be in danger of forgetting who she was, and that in the end it's up to everyone to claim their own destiny. True, she'd had a few glasses of hogweed ale and a punch-up with Neill Fife, but if you ask me, Karen abducted herself, end of story.'

'And the unmarked car that Oswald saw, and the mysterious cloaked figure?'

'You've got a soft spot for Oswald. But we both know he's forever trying to attract attention as a result of being a boring prat. No, Chantal and I were the last to see Karen alive, although we never admitted it to the law. Chantal was the last person to speak to her, because I was called away to stop a fight due to Oswald throwing up into Rufus Stone's bodhran in order to attract attention.'

But then Damien stopped, because he recollected something else. Whatever Karen said to Chantal when they were alone together, Chantal would never repeat, but when Damien came back to her Chantal was the colour of houmous. Not many days later she said she needed to leave for foreign parts, for it might be necessary to make a stand.

'Karen knew what she was doing,' said Damien. 'You had to get up pretty early in the morning to put one over on Karen, let alone bundle her into an unmarked car without her consent. But you may be right that there's more to recent events than meets the eye. And if I wasn't estranged from my true identity, I might be prepared to help you find out what's going on.'

Triona said that was all she needed to hear from him, and put her fingertips against his forehead as a sign of forgiveness, and said she would give him full details of what needed to be done, and a list of some essentials, when she had more information. When she left, Damien felt a little closer to his old self again, for the first time in years. But back in his bare apartment dining on Mother's Pride and a tin of sardines, he succumbed to sentimentality and watched a nature documentary on the Environment Channel.

79

The Aral Sea has been strangled by a noose of cotton. Conventionally, the blame is laid at Brezhnev's door for the attempt to establish in Kazakhstan and Turkmenia a cotton-producing economy to rival that of India or the southern United States. The key to cotton production was seen as irrigation, and the irrigation project resulted in the damming and diverting of all the main feeder waterways to the world's largest inland sea.

In 20 years the area of the sea diminished by 45% from 47 million to 22.5 million hectares, and the number of species it supported diminished from 12,000 to 700. Its salinity changed from freshwater levels to nearly 40%, and its waters were poisoned by run-off due to the fertilizer necessary to produce a cotton crop out of the region's poor soil. Cargo and fishing vessels were stranded 90 kilometres from the nearest water, communities dependent on fishing were ruined, and even cash-crop exports never reached anticipated quotas.

Nowhere were these effects more noticeable than in the tiny autonomous republic of Kara-Kalpak which abuts on to the southern shores of the Aral Sea – or did until the Aral Sea receded northward revealing 27,000 square kilometres of seabed toxic with salt, agricultural and industrial waste.

Chantal's activities were never seriously intended to rectify matters. Petra Kelly, when the two had been intimate, told her, 'However desperate things become, we must never sink to the level of anarchy or mindless destruction. Our movement is founded in creativity and nurturance. And if we ever forget that, we diminish ourselves in the eyes of history.'

Chantal, already bitter, replied that sometimes mindless destruction was the only way forward. 'The eyes of history', she said, 'are blinded by dogma. People say you can't make an omelette without breaking eggs. But sometimes you have to pour a jerry can of petrol over the kitchen range and set light to it.'

The strain between the two women can clearly be seen in photographs released three weeks before Petra Kelly's suicide in the aftermath of the acrimonious rift in the German Green party between *fundis* and *realos*. After that, there was nothing left to tie Chantal to Germany or indeed to anywhere in Western Europe, and she drifted East, caught up in the brief idealism and then disillusionment following the restructuring of formerly communist economies.

By firing the cotton plantations of Kara-Kalpak she had no hopes of reversing the environmental disaster or even of mobilizing world opinion and bringing economic pressure to bear. She knew such pressure would not be forthcoming. Whether Central Asia had a few more or less thousands of square miles of unique marine habitat was of no consequence to the Western financial institutions and their political toadies. She would not have claimed even a symbolic value for her actions. If anything, they were a denial of value itself. An abnegation of moral identity and an abdication of political responsibility. As the momentum of a de-railed train may send it ploughing on through houses and allotments, so, during this period, Chantal's momentum outstripped her reason, her loyalties, even her own political agenda. She was running on empty, feeding only on an awareness that the fight must be continued, but without even a residual conception of who the sides were, and what would constitute victory or defeat.

Her plans, when she made them, were purely tactical. Holed up with a small hand-picked group in a blockhouse at the water's edge, she could see the approaching patrols, and their fate was sealed. Laying the tracks they were following had been difficult because what appeared to be firm ground was quicksand fifteen feet deep. More difficult still had been spreading a screed of rushes and water-iris fronds and covering them with a few inches of silt to make a crude causeway which, before it disintegrated into the quagmire, carried Chantal's pursuers just far enough to make it impossible for them to retrace their steps.

A line of incendiary devices sending the ill-fated troopers diving for cover in treacherous reedbeds completed the rout, and cleaning up the survivors with small-arms fire was hardly even necessary. Once it would have given Chantal satisfaction, but now it only increased the sense of emptiness which seemed to pervade her entire being.

80

'Your craving seems to be for emptiness,' Neill Fife told the celebrated supermodel and beauty Vanilla Kohn, who was on his counselling schedule after Damien Lewis. 'It is this that we must address together.'

'Do as you wish,' she replied in her exotic accent, 'but do not hope for too much.'

The truth was, she herself now hoped for nothing. The newspapers said she had taken to refusing food, and the pictures told their own story. Yet to Vanilla Kohn, far from her native country and remote from anyone for whom she could feel love or loyalty, it was as if she had come to refuse life itself.

'People call it a feeding disorder,' Neill told her, 'but we counsellors call it a *feeling* disorder. A feeling that nothing matters, and that only in emptiness can a person be fulfilled.'

'Actually most people use the term *eating* disorder,' Vanilla Kohn started to say.

Neill waved his hand impatiently. 'It's about what you feel yourself to be. About repudiating physical needs as if by doing so your essential self could be laid bare, the way receding waters reveal the bed of a dwindling sea. But avoiding bodily nourishment is a mere distraction from the real issues. Some would say it's ideological gormandizing one needs to avoid, and that problems arise from surfeiting on the egocentric values of Western materialism. Try not to watch environmental documentaries, for example, because they give a vicarious feeling of self-righteousness without requiring any genuine commitment. But whatever I tell you now is too late. The damage was done long ago, and to repair it we have to go back together into the past, and face whatever you never faced at the time.'

'Actually,' said Vanilla Kohn, 'I don't know what you get paid for this crap, because I can read it in any book by Edward de Bono. This morning I was opening the Milan Fashion Week with Bianca Cinzano and Tara Masalata. I know famous people and have affairs with film actors. When people ask me, "Where will hem lines be next spring?", I say, "At the bottom of dresses, actually!" I'm not stupid – whatever people think! For instance – I know you took my case because you suspect I have knowledge of a relic stolen from the Eastern Emperor and last spoken of near my native village in Kara-Kalpak, beneath the shadow of the Caucasus. But my time is short, and old loyalties cannot lightly be set aside. I will tell you nothing unless you can find someone to vouch for you whom I trust – but that will not be an easy task!'

Neill was not fazed by this negative attitude, for it is only what psychotherapists learn to expect, right from their first day at psychotherapy school. Besides, he believed, partly through positive thinking, that his books were better than Edward de Bono's, although he knew that Edward de Bono, being himself a positive thinker, believed the contrary. As a trained professional, Neill could detach himself from the therapist-client relationship. All the same he felt gratified that through his wife, who though increasingly alienated was also a supermodel, he had been recommended to Vanilla Kohn. Even if he had somewhat manipulated the situation due to a theory he had about the whereabouts of the shield that nothing could penetrate. The truth is that everyone loves a celebrity. But Neill knew that a counsellor must suppress his own ego and even his own opinions. The focus must be exclusively on the client herself, and on the secrets beneath the seemingly impenetrable shield of her mind.

'Tell me about the past,' Neill said. And then, as a shot in the dark, 'Tell me about the time you first met Chantal Greenwood.'

Although the supermodel still had the initials C.G. and a rowan leaf tattooed on her instep, Vanilla Kohn, unlike Damien Lewis, betrayed no violent emotion at the mention of the name. Her eyes remained remote and storm-grey. 'I was fifteen, at a political meeting in Ngorno Karabash. It was before I was discovered in the West, actually. But I was already well known as a local beauty and several of us had been invited to perform for the senior committee of the North Turkmen Radical Party, later to form part of the first coalition government, by putting on a wet teeshirt competition. It was Chantal who first taught me not to see myself as others saw me, and made me realize I was a woman, and a person, whether in that order, or not. We travelled together through the Balkans in the beautiful summer of '91 when all the borders were open and there was no word but revolution on anybody's lips. Then I was spotted by the buyer for Chimique, the celebrated fragrance house, and catapulted into stardom. But the person I was with Chantal is the only person I really know how to be. And that person is now as lost to me as Chantal herself.'

'But what's all this got to do with not eating?'

'I didn't say it had anything to do with not eating. You were the one taking that line, actually. I don't eat because I don't feel like eating. I don't eat because I want to be pure. I want to be myself, yet at every turn I feel contaminated and betrayed. I don't know what I want. What should I want?'

'Your case is unusual. But not, I think, insoluble. Yet it may be too much for me to tackle without outside help. I want to introduce you to a specialist, who's the leading authority in his field. Perhaps the only way forward is through acupuncture, reflexology, and deep hypnosis. I need to bring in Damien Lewis, whose case seems strangely linked to your own, and Triona Greenwood, because she's Chantal's eldest surviving sister, and will certainly know what to do for the best. It may seem to you as if you're being asked to help us rather than the other way round, but the counselling process is essentially double-sided. If you can be saved, this is the only way forward, however bizarre the outcome of our procedures.'

81

When Damien Lewis's flat was turned over, he knew immediately that it was a professional job carried out by experts, even though it had the hallmarks of a simple burglary with the purloining of his video, his gold cuff links, and his record collection.

'This was done by trained professionals partial to Van Morrison,' he muttered to himself. 'And there's more to it than meets the eye. Perhaps someone was looking for undisclosed material from my business activities implicating bishops, heads of state and other top people – or perhaps the whole affair goes even deeper.' To test this theory he glanced quickly into the hidden compartment where (for he had not been entirely frank with Neill) he kept the little file of contact numbers, ciphers, press clippings and map references that were his only connection with the person Neill thought was his only connection with himself. And what he saw suggested the accuracy of his worst suspicions.

It was at that moment he knew he had to find Chantal, and warn her. 'The authorities are undoubtedly at the bottom of this,' he mused. 'They think I know something, and that's why they shopped me over the Live Show affair. They want me out of the way. But why? No doubt the Special Section is somehow involved, and they believe I'm in touch with Chantal. Presumably they think the consignment of customized lawnmowers was actually intended to fall into Chantal's hands, and my hating her was just a front. Frankly, there's no end to the weirdness of their beliefs. But things are getting a bit serious. Perhaps they want Chantal out of the way, as they did Nuala. The six sisters evidently have enemies. A step has been taken from which there is no turning back, and what follows is only a matter of time.'

82

'At this time of year the passes in the Caucasus are still filled with snowdrifts,' Chantal told her companions, 'and what we have to do is not to be entered into lightly. But the sounds of pursuit are closer each evening, and if we can't make it south, we'll be surrounded and trapped. I will draw a line in the snow, and those who wish to tackle the mountains must cross over it, but as for those who are left, they're discharged from their obligations towards me.'

'There's no need to bother drawing the line in the snow', replied the companions, 'as there are only two of us, and we've already decided to come with you. Apart from anything else, the alternative would be torture and then violent death at the hands of our pursuers, so whether or not our obligations towards you are discharged would be the least of our worries. But let's camp beneath this overhang and try to get some sleep, for we will need an early start if we're to reach the tree line by sunset.'

'You are good companions,' said Chantal, 'and some would say that a person could not wish for better.' But her eyes seemed misty even as she spoke, as if she thought of other comrades, far away both in years and in kilometres, for whom *adieu* had only been a French word meaning goodbye.

83

'You are sinking back,' intoned the deep hypnotist to Vanilla Kohn, his arms weaving in curious rhythms as if playing an imaginary violin. 'Back to your inner self, where past and future are one – a state the Druids call *Awen*, but I will not tire you with references. But the truth is, you are in a deep sleep, and you know at last that one life is not all.'

But only Triona knew that whether one life was all or not, the deep hypnotist was really Finbar Direach in disguise, and he had put the real deep hypnotist into a profound slumber and secretly taken his place. 'It's better', said Finbar Direach, 'that the others are kept in the dark for the time being. Since the incident with the Night Caller our adversaries have been watching every step. For the moment Dave Doom and Linden Richmont are under a cloud as a result of their errors, and Tom Baleworker will make no move while he thinks you can bring the Chain of Command to him. Yet if anyone believes you're close to contacting your sister Chantal and unravelling the mystery of her friend Vanilla Kohn, the consequences could be far-reaching.'

'Well, you'd certainly know about far-reaching consequences,' Triona replied. But in the presence of the others, she avoided his eyes, and instead listened intently to the details of the session. She thought: Linden Richmont knew my sister Nuala better than I did, and this esoteric beauty may have known my sister Chantal better. How strange she does not seem to know herself, and needs Finbar Direach to tell her. Then again, do any of us know ourselves? Or do we all need Finbar Direach and his kind to reveal the truth?

Damien Lewis, whom everyone thought had no self worth knowing anyway, crouched on the edge of his seat biting his lip and watching the proceedings with every sign of animation. He had received the telephone call only last night and had little time to put his affairs in order, but when Neill told him that the progress of his sessions was linked to that of the famous supermodel Vanilla Kohn, he knew he could not stay away. 'Neill Fife is up to something,' he said to himself. 'But perhaps it is only the same thing that we're all up to.'

He watched the deep hypnotist narrowly. The deep hypnotist appeared to be a dishevelled stubbly person who would not look out of place among the derelict humanity at the heart of the inner city, living by busking and giving information to the tabloid press. He appeared to be a meagre individual with a glittering eye and a lyrical voice, but he kept his face always in the shadow. His appearance was strongly reminiscent of Seamus 'Eight Pints' McGallon the well-known folksinger, but Neill Fife said he was the flower of his profession and that in all Europe there was no-one with a more supple wrist.

'Now, who are you, and what are your surroundings?' continued the deep hypnotist, when the preliminaries were complete.

'I am Vanilla Kohn, the famous supermodel. But I have lost my way. It's actually a complete drag and so boring! I am wandering on the side of a mountain, and there is nothing to eat but snow, and nothing to drink but dew.'

'Go down the mountain, and cross the stream into the forest. Who are you now, and what can you see?'

The girl's voice seemed to change. 'I am actually Ivana Kropotko aged fifteen from Lenin Garden Flats in Muynak, which seems now a prosperous fishing community but later will become a landlocked ghost town. I am on the edge of a forest, near a small sparkling brook, at a time of symbolic change.'

'Go through the forest to its eastern border, following the course of the little stream. Who are you now?'

'I am Ivana Kropotko as a tiny child. I can tell warmth and cold, pain and pleasure, but I cannot tell self from other, other from self. I can give my name, but have no true notion of who I am. Yet I know that although I'm cared for by a poor fisherman and his wife, they are not my real parents. For after their baby daughter was drowned in a waterspout, they found me lying in a disused lobster pot on the edge of a tideless sea. Because I appeared to be the same age as the child they had lost, they took me home and brought me up as their own.'

'Follow the brook through the snow fields to the east of the forest,' the deep hypnotist instructed, the undulations of his wrist becoming more agitated every moment.

'I cannot go through the snow fields. It's dark there. I'm afraid.'

'Go through the snow fields, Ivana. You're safe, because I'm with you, and perhaps the pair of us are linked more closely than you might believe. Go onwards – it's the only way to find out who you really are.'

'I am crossing the snow fields, and I'm moving towards the mouth of the stream. But the fields are made not of snow but of snowflowers, which in the West are called cotton, whose white fibrous tops wave in a cool autumn breeze. Yet all this is nothing, because I now know who I really am.'

'Who are you?'

'I cannot tell you. You would not, in any case, believe it.'

'You must tell me. Don't you remember you promised to answer everything I asked? And for the likes of us, a promise cannot be rescinded.'

'It was the promise of someone who did not know who she was, and therefore not binding. But you may ask questions, if you wish, and I will answer as I can. For suddenly I find I know a thousand things, each one stranger than the last. For instance, ask me what runs faster than the deer, and what bites deeper than the snake!'

The deep hypnotist's eyes glittered as if with his own timeless knowledge, but he said, 'What does?'

'Time runs faster than the deer, and malice bites deeper than the snake. There are six sisters coming to save their inheritance, but they must race time, and overcome malice. But ask me what rises higher than the sky, and what sinks deeper than the sea!'

'What does?'

'The heart in love rises higher than the sky, but the heart forsaken sinks deeper than the sea. If Caryddwen's cauldron is reassembled, all hearts will rise, but if it is lost, the finest hearts will be lost with it. But ask me what flies darker than the night, and what blooms brighter than a flower!'

'What does?'

'We both know what flies darker than the night, and it is not to be dwelt on. But truth blooms brighter than a flower, and I will tell you the truth now, because you will never guess! I am a hundred miles broad, but my breadth diminishes each day. For a million years I have given and taken life, but given more than taken. I cannot eat, because I'm being choked and poisoned. Few have come to my aid, and those who do cannot always understand my true needs. But the truth is I am the Aral Sea, the Mirror of the Steppes, the liquid heart of an ancient and glorious landscape. Yet I am dying, and there's no hope for me unless through the intercession of the Mongol Emperors' direct spiritual successors I can undergo a symbolic re-birth to become once more what I have always been. But many things have to happen before that will be possible.'

84

When they saw that Vanilla Kohn was born Ivana Kropotko and believed herself to be the Aral Sea it made some things clearer, and other things less clear. The chances of a leading supermodel being a large inland sea beneath the Russian Steppes would seem extremely remote – perhaps even more remote than winning the National Lottery. But someone wins the National Lottery every week, so, looked at another way, the chances are good. Be that as it may, it was clear they were dealing with a bizarre phenomenon, and one that would stretch credulity to its limits. Neill had expected many things, but this was not one of them. However, he could see that various possibilities arose from the situation, and the reference to the Mongol Emperors was not lost on him, since it was they who had stolen the Impenetrable Shield.

'That people can be in former lives a famous historical person or animal is well documented,' he pointed out. 'That a person can be in the present life a distant, huge, but rapidly diminishing body of water is a conjecture new to science. But it's a fact that everything is connected, even if some things are more connected than others, and we cannot disbelieve the evidence of our own ears. What is clear is that unless some method can be found for persuading Vanilla Kohn to eat, the Aral Sea will inevitably collapse into a muddy cesspool and perish. And unless some means can be found to re-establish the Aral Sea, the most beautiful woman in the world is doomed to an untimely grave. Also, at the risk of sounding self-interested, our own final hope of discovering what we seek will perish with her.'

He looked for the deep hypnotist to confirm these remarks, but in the confusion the deep hypnotist appeared to have vanished leaving nothing but a silver pendulum, although he had been there only seconds before. Triona said he had gone to the toilet, but when he did not return they agreed his reputation for eccentricity was well founded, and his procedures raised as many questions as they answered.

'Well,' said Neill, looking at the still sleeping supermodel, and then at Triona, whom he felt was holding something back, 'from now on, it's up to us.'

'You'll be telling us next that to re-unite her with her essential self', put in Damien Lewis, 'we need to get her back to the Aral Sea.'

'I didn't say that,' Neill said, since it was one thing asking Damien to participate in their plans, and quite another revealing to him what they were.

'You had no need to,' said Damien, and flicked his earring with his finger. 'I didn't come down with the last shower, remember. But if I'm right, only one person in the world can help us. And for that person, it may already be too late.'

'You mean my sister Chantal,' said Triona. 'Tell us something we didn't know.'

'I will,' said Damien, rising to the challenge. 'Because I know where she is – or at least, how she can be contacted. But it won't be easy. The region is a political powder keg. Patrols are everywhere. Take it from someone who does lobbying for the international arms trade.'

'You have no morals,' Triona frowned.

'I never felt the need,' he said, with a little of his old jauntiness.

'Nonetheless', said Neill, 'you have your connections. If anyone is in a position to work out how the tactical difficulties could be overcome, you are.'

'I might be able to. But it would need an elite force, deployed rapidly and with split-second timing. In other words, as we armaments lobbyists say, serious shit.'

'It's a pity there's no way of exerting pressure on the authorities.'

'I'm not saying anything,' replied Damien, again seeming to take the bait. 'But if I could get to the minister responsible – you never know. There are certain considerations that might weigh with him, if you know what I mean.'

'It's better we don't know what you mean,' Neill said.

'We would still need to contact Chantal first, for ground support,' Triona repeated, watching Damien out of the corner of her eye.

'If she wants to be contacted.'

'I think', said Neill, 'she needs our help, as much as we need hers. I think you, Damien, are pretending to let us recruit you, but really you're trying to recruit us. I think that's why you came to Coldharbour the day Triona returned there.'

'I came to Coldharbour because you asked me. What makes you think I'd do anything to help Chantal?'

'As a trained counsellor, I can often see what is not obvious to other people. But things still won't be easy. There's no point pretending any longer. According to the World Service, the situation in Kazakhstan and the frontier states of the Aral Sea is volatile in the extreme. A hundred local warlords control communications on the ground, while the governments of the area exert only a token authority. The UN is powerless, and human rights are like words in a foreign language.'

'Chantal', said Triona, 'has always had an unnatural enjoyment of getting shot at. It's the romantic in her. Only it doesn't run in the family.'

'As a counsellor, and also in my research work', Neill said, 'I've had considerable contact with people pulled from burning aircraft or sunk in collisions under bridges. People find it hard to grasp the terrible finality of death – and yet it happens all the time.'

'Personally,' said Damien, 'I've always believed life is for living, and it's up to each of us to look after Number One. People call me a Jack-the-Lad, but Karen used to say every action has an infinite number of consequences and so produces an infinite amount of good and an infinite amount of bad. Therefore we can do whatever we like, because no action is worse than another. Still, my flat has been broken into and my Van Morrison collection nicked, and somebody must be made to pay.'

'We will need a plan,' said Neill. 'One that would be worthy of Chantal herself.'

There was a silence because, deep down, each of them knew he was right. Local knowledge would be required to take them in, and get them out. They would need signed authorizations, and permission to fly in restricted air space. Failure could not even be contemplated. They had the feeling they were getting out of their depth, and that the deep hypnotist might have intended to lure them into a trap. Perhaps Triona or Neill paid lip service to Chantal's idealism back in the old days. But if so, they vastly exaggerated the scale of their participation. Privately they had felt that if Chantal wanted to involve herself in other people's wars, it was her funeral. They themselves, they said, had their own lives to live. Perhaps the difference between them and Damien, was that they were sufficiently indifferent to feign concern whereas he was sufficiently concerned to make his indifference an act of defiance. Yet now they were faced with the death of a leading supermodel, the destruction of an important natural resource, the non-recovery of a significant item of the Celtic reliquary, and the forfeiture of Karen's release and perhaps of Caryddwen's cauldron itself. Under the circumstances, even the most cultivated indifference was bound to be affected.

'When you know you can't succeed, at least you know failure won't be a disappointment,' Damien said finally, giving his earring an emphatic tug. 'But let's put our cards on the table. Even if I can get to the minister responsible and persuade him to do what he can – we won't see much change out of a million pounds. And who has that kind of money?'

'Who indeed?' said Triona, feeling she was taking a step from which there would be no going back. 'Then again – who else? Luckily I still have the million pounds the Heritage Commission was going to give the Centre for Alternative Healing if Linden Richmont hadn't attempted to capture me and obliged me to escape down Finbar Direach's beard. We'll need to represent our expedition as primarily archaeological in character, and give out that we're seeking the Lost Treasure of Genghis Khan, known to legend as the Mongol Hoard. I can arrange for the money to be released immediately, so we can start without delay. It's likely that some of us won't come back, and indeed, that all of us won't. But Vanilla Kohn needs our help, and Chantal, and Karen – why are we even taking time to talk about it? It's time Damien Lewis contacted the minister responsible, and the rest of us made whatever preparations we can.'

So when the famous supermodel woke and said, 'Where am I?' Neill and Triona replied, 'You're going home.'

85

'Guns,' Damien Lewis explained to the minister responsible. 'Bombs, limpet mines, four pounds of Semtex and two lightweight air-portable Land Rovers with Salisbury axles and 2.5 Tdi diesels with raised air-intakes for wading purposes.'

'I have no idea what you're talking about,' said the minister, although both of them knew he was bluffing.

'Put it this way,' Damien said, 'I now know that it was your men who broke into my house. At first I thought that someone was after my most carefully guarded secret. I thought they were trying to discover the whereabouts of Chantal Greenwood, which even under the most rigorous interrogation I've never revealed since the day she left Coldharbour. But then I remembered even I don't really know where Chantal is, for she moves swiftly, under cover of darkness, and only a highly trained special operations unit with the latest satellite surveillance equipment could keep track of her. It dawned on me that the peculiar significance of Chantal, the Impenetrable Shield and the last fragment of Caryddwen's cauldron would be lost on you, and that the truth behind the raid on my apartment lay much nearer to home. Of the Van Morrison CD's we will not even speak. But perhaps *these* are what your people were after?'

The minister did not have to look at the papers Damien held in his hand. He knew at once he must co-operate, or face the consequences.

86

'The logistical resources for an operation like that', explained the technical advisers later the same day, 'would stretch us to breaking point.'

The minister fidgeted in his chair and tried to clean under his fingernails with the corner of his jotter pad. He had developed a feeling that there was dirt underneath his nails, but did not want to look down at them for fear of attracting other people's attention. He could not understand why his fingernails were always getting dirty, and everyone else's seemed to be so clean. 'War', he said, 'is a dirty word, for a dirty business.' He looked down at his fingernails accusingly. 'But sometimes it's necessary to let the world know where one stands.'

'Surely,' said the technical advisers, 'if the object is to let the world know where we stand, the Department of Covert Operations is an inappropriate choice for the task?'

'When I want your opinion, I will ask for it.'

'You did ask for it. That's why we're here. But there's no use fidgeting in that chair and looking at your fingernails. Clearly you're in some kind of a jam and need the military to bail you out. It may well be that we're your men. But we can't help you unless we're in full possession of the facts.'

But the facts were the one thing the minister was unable to share, since his primary reason for mounting the campaign was to ensure the facts remained suppressed. The publicity surrounding the Damien Lewis case had cost the minister many sleepless nights and although in the event he had never been linked to the scandal, he knew only too well how fragile a politician's reputation can be. The fact that Damien Lewis had photographs, dates, and cheque stubs was hardly lost on him. So when Damien asked for military intervention and implied that the consequences of not intervening would not only be catastrophic for the economies and ecological balance of key Central Asian democracies, but could also impact directly on the careers of highly placed individuals in government and industry, the minister could not deceive himself as to what was meant.

'I'll do what I can,' the minister had said, 'but you must understand you may be asking more than I'm capable of.'

But Damien Lewis only tugged his earring in a grim and meaningful manner. 'According to my notes that's exactly what you said to one of the Live Show hostesses just before—'

'You have no need to go on,' replied the minister. 'I clearly catch your drift.'

87

Later that day two shadowy figures met in a shadowy quadrangle, and a list of certain essentials was passed between them. 'A Hercules Transport plane, air-portable Land Rovers of the most up-to-date design, and stun grenades together with a dozen hand-picked men, is what the minister has in mind,' said the first, tapping the side of his nose in a significant way.

The second looked from his colleague to a small portfolio of cheque stubs, genetic-fingerprinting read-outs and similar material, and then back at the speaker again. Slowly, he inclined his head. 'Well,' he replied, 'it won't be easy. But there might be a way. Even the special forces have their special forces. There's one man who may be prepared to help in this matter, and can measure up to the formidable challenge it represents.'

88

Perhaps it was some half-recollected intuition that made Chantal turn back from the mountains, or perhaps it was an SOS message broadcast on the BBC World Service three nights in succession. 'Let the hunter return from the hills,' the SOS message said, 'and the fisherman go home to the sea. We'll meet you by the old abandoned oil derrick on the night of the fourth. But take care, for they are watching the roads.'

The mountain passes, in any case, were blocked. After a day of chopping through ice, even Chantal had to acknowledge that to go south would be suicide. Eastwards towards Bukhara and Samarkand the hills were infested with brigands and Chantal's description, accompanied by details of reward money, had already been circulated. 'It's the end of the line,' she said to her companions. 'But we'll sell our lives dearly. Also, if I'm not mistaken, there is someone back there who needs help even more than we do. Who knows the location of the abandoned oil derrick beside the Aral Sea, if it's not Ivana Kropotko, who was raised by a poor fisherman and his wife close to that very spot? Some people lead their lives, others follow them. But sooner or later, everything comes full circle, and we realize that the past is something we carry inside us, and from which there is no escape.'

'That's all very fine and dandy,' said the companions, who were becoming rather resentful. 'But there's half a regiment looking for us with the latest Kalashnikov rifles, and no ground cover between here and the coast. We thought you were supposed to be a great military leader.'

'There's an underground stream, tributary to the Amu Darya River, running through a tectonic fault beneath the cotton plantations,' said Chantal. 'For this whole area is prone to seismic disturbances. We must follow that stream past the margins of the forest and back to the coast. My friends will meet us, if only we can hold on long enough. But if you don't want to go . . . '

'Don't start drawing lines again, for goodness' sake,' said the companions. 'We had nothing particular planned for the rest of our lives anyway.'

'You are good companions,' said Chantal, 'and I will never forget you.'

89

'All we want is to go in, do a job of work, and get out,' said the captain.

'That's exactly right,' replied the lieutenant. 'We're professional soldiers, and people expect no less from us. By the way, do you know if there's any offensive nicknames we can call people who live in Kara-Kalpak, like Paddies or Argies or something?'

'I don't think', hazarded the captain, 'we can call them Argies.'

At that moment an unmarked car drew up at the main gates of the compound, its windscreen wipers slamming from side to side. The ranking officer gave his name to the NCO in charge of the gatehouse, spelling it out carefully for the avoidance of doubt. 'Colonel Sir Colquhardie Colquhardie-Custard,' he stated firmly, 'which though it's pronounced *Cowardy*, is spelt C-O-L-Q . . . '

'I know,' said the soldier on the gate. 'We was told to expect you.'

Colonel Colquhardie-Custard, not for the first time, found himself reflecting on the misfortune of his name, which had in no way facilitated a military career. Changing it by deed poll was always an option, but the name was a very ancient and honourable one, having been passed down from father to son for generations. Even the tradition that the eldest son took the surname as a given name was not to be overturned on a whim. The first Colquhardie-Custards had come over with William of Normandy, like many people with funny names, hoping perhaps that the legendary politeness of the English would help make life more bearable. Colquhardie-Custards had fought at Crécy, Agincourt, in the Wars of the Roses (on both sides) and at Trafalgar, where the Colonel's ancestor held the dying Nelson in his arms although that seafarer's final words, 'Kiss me, Colquhardie,' are widely misquoted.

'But there's no time to discuss genealogy,' the Colonel said, having given the lieutenant and the captain as short as possible an account of the situation regarding his name. 'We've a job of work to do, and time is running short.'

'There are four civilians, sir, who say they'll be flying out with us.'

'There's no time to discuss civilians,' said Colonel Colquhardie-Custard.

'They don't want to be discussed,' said the soldier, 'they want to be put on the plane. But unless I'm very much mistaken, sir, one of them's Vanilla Kohn, the famous supermodel.'

'That changes things,' said the Colonel softly. 'That changes things very much.'

Perhaps even then he knew this was his last mission. At the age of fifty, he had been obliged to pull many strings to be allowed to go on it personally. But he had an inkling, if Vanilla Kohn was involved, who might be waiting for them at their secret rendezvous.

90

Beneath a burned-out oil derrick in front of a dried-up lake, Chantal knew she could not hold out much longer. She fumbled in the pockets of her Parka for spare cartridge clips; four, five, only six. She strained her ears for the drone of a transport plane, but knew they were cutting it fine. The opposition was even more formidable than expected. And well equipped, since it was largely underwritten by the international arms manufacturers whose diverse interests now included the Kara-Kalpak cash crops, and of whom Myles Overton may secretly have been one. Chantal's companions had fought bravely but had finally fallen, with bullets in parts of their bodies they did not even know they possessed. Her enemies were pinned down, but it was only a matter of time before they brought the heavy guns into play.

Chantal's marksmanship was legendary, right from the time when as a young girl, she practised shooting the insulation cups off electricity pylons with air guns, accompanied by her favourite sisters Karen and Nuala, who always accepted her at face value. 'Oh, Karen, if you were only beside me now,' Chantal murmured to herself. 'Or to be honest, I'd even settle for Nuala or Neill Fife. But the news about Nuala is confused and paradoxical, and Neill may no longer be the person I once knew. Only Damien never changed – because he was always a person without a conscience. Still, when people have shared what we shared in those far-off days at Coldharbour, each becomes, in some important sense, the custodian of the others' essential selves. The situation here is clearly untenable, but sometimes it's better to be together in death, than apart in life.' This melancholy reflection was interrupted by a Kara-Kalpak soldier, braver than the rest, who raised his weapon from amongst the withered bulrushes not a hundred metres away. 'Pardon me,' Chantal added bitterly, 'while I blow your head off.'

The first string of cluster bombs that fell through the cloud cover took both sides by surprise. They were aimed by the latest laser technology so that one of them landed directly on the Kara-Kalpaki colonel-in-chief, although this was not critical since cluster bombs generally kill everything within three hundred yards of where they fall. Suffice it to say that the new arrivals had surprise on their side, to say nothing of cluster bombs, and the personnel and equipment were parachuted down with an accuracy unmatched by any fighting force in the world.

'The British Special Forces operative', Colonel Sir Colquhardie-Custard was fond of saying, 'is sexist, bullies recruits and lacks tolerance towards people of minority races and cultures. But the British Special Forces operative is the best damned fighting man in the world – bar none!'

'That's as may be,' said the Defence Secretary. 'But we still have to disband your regiment and offer you early retirement, as it's part of the peace dividend.'

'Let me show you what we can do,' argued the Colonel. 'Put it this way – what if my men can sort out this little policing business in Kara-Kalpak and win some Brownie points with the UN?'

'Leave the UN out of this – it would have to be a covert operation. But I can't resist a challenge.'

'Well—' began the Colonel.

'Well, Colonel, remember that if they fail they will be disbanded, for sure.'

'If they fail, being disbanded will be the least of their problems.'

The pride of British soldiery drifted serenely away from a Hercules transport aircraft, their white parachutes like seeds from a dandelion clock, but the time they told to their enemies was the trackless and ineluctable time of eternity. Far otherwise was the implication for Chantal as they landed on the mud flats behind her, stumbling forward to cover her position with a storm of high velocity ammunition.

91

Is it the truth, or is it another legend?

Perhaps no-one will ever know.

That there was a major skirmish on the shores of the Aral Sea at a certain time, on a certain date, is a matter of record. It was described only as a humanitarian intervention, and full details were released on a need-to-know basis. Reports were carried by Reuters, and the BBC World Service was quick to pick up on it. Vanilla Kohn, according to her press office, was out of the country during this period at a leading Swiss sanatorium, along with the counselling psychologist who was already helping her, and several of his assistants. Yet no-one ever came forward from the sanatorium to verify this information, and it could easily have been a red herring. It was certain that before the event, the sequence of pictures carried regularly by the tabloids told their own story of the famous model's rapid physical deterioration. Afterwards, different people said different things.

'You took your time!' Chantal exclaimed with practised military understatement when she saw who was emerging through the dust and mêlée of battle, half-crouching to avoid the bullets that sailed past their ears in an aggressive and belligerent manner. Yet her eyes brimmed with ill-concealed emotion, for she had been afraid they would arrive too late, and that she would fall into the hands of her enemies.

'Chantal! Where are you?'

'Over here! Stay down and keep behind the line of rocks. The main incoming fire is from the southeast. They drew back when the parachutes showed, but it's only a matter of time before they re-group and come at us again. Can't anyone lay down some smoke? Over here, and behind this wall.'

A number of the blurred figures beneath the ordnance were familiar, but nothing could equal Chantal's surprise when the first person she saw clearly was the last person she expected to see ever again.

'Damien!'

'There's no time for an explanation,' he gasped as he sprinted across the final yards of open ground and skidded down beside her.

'If there was time, I wouldn't listen to it.' She bit her lip and turned her face away. She knew that had she not received secret information enabling her to intercept a vital consignment, his actions would have been her downfall. Besides, even in the old days he was always undermining her. Once she had asked him to join her in the fight for freedom, and he had joked:

'The freedom of which side?'

Later, it was hardly surprising when he slipped into the ranks of the oppressor.

'We need to talk.' he said.

'The time for talking is over,' she told him distantly. And then, glad of the distraction, 'Triona! Neill!'

As each of them reached her, Chantal took them by both hands and then wrapped their heads in an arm-lock as a rough greeting. Neill, whom she had always admired, yet whom she felt had squandered his birthright for palaces of paper. Triona, whose guilt and frustration over Karen's disappearance made it impossible for her to share Chantal's uncomplicated worldview.

Then again, she was amazed. 'Colonel!' she exclaimed when the veteran soldier emerged, her voice filled with the bluff camaraderie only old enemies understand. If the air had not been full of incoming shells, bullets, shrapnel and rocket-propelled grenades, there is no doubt that greetings would have been more tender and protracted. Undoubtedly there would have been gossip about who had got divorced, killed by anti-terrorist police or mutilated by giant genetically modified moles. But, as Chantal again pointed out, there was little time for formalities.

Besides, one more person, who until now had held back, came forward to be welcomed.

'Ivana?' Chantal said softly, the name like a ripple on a calm sea. She helped support her former comrade's thin body and assessed the situation instantly. For, Chantal assumed, the supermodel's condition meant she had suffered the consequences of taking some stand against the authorities, necessitating a flight to seek concealment in her former homeland. Like most of Chantal's analyses, this was fundamentally wrong, but it lent itself to an immediate and clear-cut plan of action.

'We need to get you across the water,' she decided. 'We must make for the north-eastern shore. If we can just reach Khanay, I have friends. The whole area is like a powder keg, and there are a hundred warlords waiting for my signal. We need hard-weather gear, rigid-hull inflatables, and powerful outboard motors.'

'We've got them,' Triona said.

'Time is short,' Chantal repeated, pulling the starting cord of the most powerful outboard motor of all, 'and we have very little of it. This, as I see it, is the plan. Triona, me and Neill – and of course Ivana – into the boat. And you, too, Damien, because I want you where I can keep an eye on you. The rest of you hold the drop zone. Colonel, you and I were old adversaries in the Sudan, in Beirut, and in East Timor, but all that is over now. When I realized it was you, I knew they'd sent the best. I can only guess what strings you had to pull to make this mission possible. But now its success is in your hands.'

The Colonel gave a kind of ironic salute, for he had very little experience of being ordered about by known terrorists.

'We need one hour. If at the end of that time we do not return, pull out when the helicopters come, since we'll already be dead. The detonators are set, and the minutes are already ticking by. Neill, don't tread on that – it's an anti-personnel mine!'

'This is just like the old days,' the Colonel said.

'Good luck, Colonel – for what is done today will not quickly be forgotten.'

'Good luck, Chantal! We've had our differences and each has tried to kill the other a hundred times. But there's always been respect between us. Although my name may belie the fact – we will do our part, and nobody can do more than that.'

92

While the sun lowered towards the Caucasus, a military specification rigid-hull inflatable boat cleft the polluted waters out from the southern shores of the Aral Sea. As it breasted the short choppy swells, those aboard could hear ragged gunfire from the detachment defending the vehicles and equipment on shore. They knew their options were limited. Not for the first time, as they wiped the brackish spray from their faces, they reflected on the curious confluence of events underlying the plan hastily agreed by Chantal and Ivana.

Seven centuries ago, legend had it, Genghis Khan arrived – weakened and battle-weary, with only a few hand picked companions – at the edge of the Aral Sea. The Sultan's forces were closing in from the south, and wild Cossacks, intent upon vengeance for the pillaging of their villages and the rape of their women, were converging from the west. Three times, boats were launched to carry the Mongols and their booty to the safety of the north-eastern shore. But each time, as they reached open water, the sky darkened and a storm rose up against them, so that wind and waves forced them back to their starting point. Soon they could hear the Sultan's janissaries clashing their cymbals fiercely as they marched, and the distant hooves of Cossack ponies.

In desperation, the great commander prayed to the Aral Sea, which soon appeared to him in the form of a beautiful woman confessing she herself had caused the storms which prevented them from making any progress. For, she said, she had been stricken by his physical attractiveness and his reputation as a military leader, and would only let him pass if he agreed to consort with her for the space of a single night. Nothing loath, he did as she requested, and when the two spent the night together it did not seem one minute too long for either of them.

The following morning he and his faithful companions were carried securely across the sparkling waves, leaving his enemies gnashing their teeth at the water's edge.

'I bid you farewell,' the woman who was the Aral Sea told him as they reached the opposite shore. 'But you should understand our embraces were purchased at no trivial price. When I succumbed to my feelings for you, I became separated from the broad and watery domain that is my true nature, for I had chosen to leave the realm of being, and enter the realm of feeling. Therefore, I must wander the earth in human form until our fractured history is healed, so that feeling and being become one. But I do not think this will happen very soon.'

'I'm sorry to hear it,' said Genghis Khan. 'Although to some extent you've brought this misfortune on yourself. Yet there are other consequences you did not mention, because I prophesy that before the year is out you'll give birth to a hundred sons, each destined to become a fierce warlord. For their maintenance you shall receive the treasures I gained on this the most westerly of my campaigns, which the world will know as the Great Treasure of Genghis Khan, or the Mongol Hoard. You'll find gold and jewels for your welfare, and for your protection a hundred swords, one for each of your sons. While they remain united and their blades are kept sharp, the shores of the Aral cannot be threatened by apostasy at home nor cupidity abroad. But if they allow dissent to fall between them, or the swords to lose their edge, the land will become contaminated, the waters recede from the shore, and your enemies grow as numerous as sandflies on the beach. Against that day, I give you the Impenetrable Shield, which will hold back all danger and resist the depredations of time itself, until six sisters from a distant archipelago bring new hope, and the means of reconciliation with your ancient self.'

Thus, the account was passed down among the indigenous tribes of the area, although modern science can set little store by the campfire tales of nomads. But whatever the truth of the matter, the efforts of leading historians and adventurers to recover the Mongol Hoard came to nothing. Genghis Khan, by then ageing and close to the fateful riding accident which cost him his life, is reputed to have revisited the area in 1232 or 1233 with the intention of seeing his sons, but returned empty-handed and bitter. Perhaps, people said, his hundred sons had already broken their trust, and allowed dissent to break out amongst them and their blades to grow dull. The treasure, meanwhile, became enshrined in local legend, but every region has its lost treasures, its chimeras, and its sleeping kings. Some said a beautiful woman was sometimes seen walking along the shore beneath the full moon, decked in costly emeralds and carrying a bronze escutum. But others held that the Mongol emperor's booty was hidden beneath the salty waves and effaced by shifting sandbanks, sediment deposits and sub-surface currents as the centuries passed.

Whether the waters delivered up something of what was lost when the shoreline receded eighty miles, was never clear. Suffice it to say that Triona and her companions realized through a combination of deep hypnosis and positive thinking, that success in the task Finbar Direach had set them was almost within their grasp. Yet they knew also that one false move would precipitate their entire party into the pitiless grasp of failure, and that was a possibility they refused even to contemplate.

93

As they reached the centre of the sea, a clammy fret closed in until they could no longer see the details of each other's faces. Beneath this damp and fuliginous veil, what occurred took on a dreamlike character. Ivana, whose pallor had increased as the journey went on, told Chantal she wanted them to cut the engines.

'We must talk,' she said.

The boat slowed, pitching and yawing in the overfalls.

'You think you're taking me to a place of safety on the other side of the water, but I can go no further. For it's here, and nowhere else, my journey has to end.'

None of them liked the sound of this, for she looked shadowy and unwell, and the wind blew chill across the waves. 'Let's continue to Khanay and get help. It can't be anything serious,' they urged. But they avoided Ivana's eyes as they spoke, for whatever was wrong with her seemed to be worsening. Deep in their hearts they knew it could not be much fun to have as one's estranged inner being a large and fatally contaminated sea, round which factions strove in an armed and unending struggle. Especially since that struggle was for the favours of a few cynical foreign corporations whose sole interest was to de-stabilize the region and further increase demand for weapons of mass destruction.

'I'm sorry you have tried so hard, and that you've come so far,' Ivana said. 'But now I know who I truly am, I know our ways must part.'

Sure enough, as the mist cleared slightly, they discerned a low island looming on the port bow, and as the engines idled, they found the boat was drifting up a narrow inlet. On the island grew a single rowan tree, adjacent to a low building. Local legend had it that the tree was planted by St Brendan the Navigator when he passed that way in search of the continent of America many centuries before Genghis Khan's own visit. But the companions instinctively knew that the building was where the Mongol emperor and his seductress lay together that one fateful night. And that Ivana had returned to be close to a past from which she was tragically exiled.

'The Aral Sea is polluted,' said Ivana, 'and its vast interplay of lives is drawing to a close. But now, with the last of my strength, I have called together my hundred sons, whose fractiousness has brought things to such a pass. My blessing I cannot give, but perhaps there's something more valuable to be gained, if they only reach here in time.'

94

Back on shore, Colonel Colquhardie-Custard looked at his watch. It was sufficiently shockproof to withstand a direct hit from a cluster bomb, and waterproof to three times the depth of the Aral Sea at its deepest point. The reinforced glass face would survive an inferno, while the mechanism was unaffected by magnetism, gamma rays and laser weapons.

'This is a damned fine watch,' said Colonel Colquhardie-Custard to himself. 'It has served me well in many operations, both overt and – for there's no point concealing it any longer – covert. But if those bloody hotshots don't get that damned rubber boat back here before many more minutes have passed, this watch will be the only thing left of me.'

95

When the hundred sons of Genghis Khan came to the island, it seemed surrounded by a ring of strange water, unruffled by breeze yet with little wavelets leaping up vertically and falling back like mackerel before a thunder storm. But as the sons approached, still arguing among themselves with their blunt swords trailing shamefully in their hands, Ivana seemed to recover from her malaise and grow in stature and substance. When she spoke at last, her voice was as rich and fluid as the waters of the Aral itself. And as her words streamed into the consciousness of each of the comrades, their minds and personalities seemed to float in hers.

'You may think', she said, addressing her western friends and the hundred warlords without distinction, 'I have come here to leave you. But the truth is, only at this moment do we meet for first time. From the child on Aral's stark and shattered shoreline, through revolutionary years and then as a fashion icon, Ivana Kropotko and then Vanilla Kohn were really nothing but a focus for identities which others craved, yet could not live for themselves.'

At this, Chantal looked at Neill, and Neill looked at Chantal, for both, in their way, had been guilty of inventing their own Ivanas, to suit their distinct agendas. And as in their relationship with Ivana, so, perhaps, in all their relationships.

But how, wondered Neill, were we to know who she truly was?

'That I am the Aral Sea can no longer be concealed,' she continued. 'But the Aral Sea is all seas, the sea and the land are one, and all things within them are separate only in the separateness of their own perceptions. We search for our true selves like the philosophic fish who swims along the bottom of the ocean looking for water. We abandon our birthright for illusory gratification, as I did in the arms of Genghis Khan, but our birthright never abandons us, and sooner or later, comes to reclaim us. The time has come for me to leave you, but from this it follows I shall never leave you, and the self-sacrifice and courage you have shown will bring us together again when all things are brought together. When, as Genghis Khan foretold, six sisters will come from a distant archipelago to reunite what is disjoined, and make whole what is fragmented.'

The hundred warlords looked uncomfortable when she said this, for they felt in part to blame for the fragmentary way their region had developed. But Damien, who was least affected by the dramatic quality of events, said that reminded him of something.

'At the risk of interrupting – about these six sisters,' he began, 'their names wouldn't happen to be—'

'Shhhh!' said Chantal. 'She knows. She knows everything now. But the warlords are very touchy. If they think we've come to steal the Impenetrable Shield . . . '

'Ah,' said Damien, 'now we're getting to the crux of the matter.'

'It's not as simple as you think,' said Chantal out of the corner of her mouth.

'How do you know how simple I think it is?' Damien began, with a sense of the old irritation.

'Be quiet!' Neill warned. 'We need to propose a bargain.'

Unfortunately, it was not as simple as Neill thought either. The reunion of the wan and way-worn mother with her hundred sons was a touching occasion. It was perhaps because of this, and their respect for Chantal, who had constantly tried to unify them against the oppressor, that the warlords did not kill Neill, Triona and Damien on sight. But it is one thing to refrain from killing someone on sight, and quite another to hand over to them the Impenetrable Shield that was given to your mother as a wedding gift by Genghis Khan. Especially if its presence may protect her from the depredations of unfriendly powers and even the ravages of time and space themselves, and is perhaps all that holds back the forces of chaos from your already increasingly chaotic patrimony.

'But nevertheless,' the hundred sons of Genghis Khan reflected, 'if the swords we were given by Genghis Khan could only be sharpened again, the Impenetrable Shield might not be so essential to us. But according to legend that can never happen, unless they are sharpened by the grindstone whose blades never fail. And this, the legend says, is highly unlikely.'

'The legend is right,' sighed Ivana, 'because any attempt to find the Infallible Grindstone would require more even than the help of the six sisters, although Triona's sister Sophie would have a special part to play. For its secret can only be revealed through the minds of children and poets, and no-one knows how that could come about. Also, while two of the sisters are here with us, Sophie Greenwood may already be in danger, because the authorities are taking advantage of the absence of those she relies on most, and planning to move against her.'

'Suddenly,' said Chantal, 'you seem to know a great deal.'

'Suddenly,' said Ivana, 'I know that malice bites deeper than a serpent, and your sisters face an enemy who flies darker than the night. I know who I am, and who you are, and I know where your sister Karen is, although I'm forbidden to tell. But I know also what Karen revealed when you and Damien Lewis put your case before her the evening she disappeared.'

She said no more, but as she spoke both Damien and Chantal thought that she looked fleetingly similar to Karen herself, who had sat beneath another rowan tree many years ago. 'Is it better', Chantal and Damien asked Karen on that occasion, 'to devote one's life to helping others, or to helping oneself?' But Karen seemed touched with momentary splendour, even though apparently no older than they. 'My time is short,' she said, 'so I must measure my words with care. But understand that although every action procures infinite consequences and thus may be considered equally good and bad, this only applies in a cyclic universe, which is itself infinite. Let me reveal there are those who wish to shut out the past from the future and make it linear and therefore finite, so that evil actions produce only evil, and good ones produce only good. To defeat such people, the two of you must one day set your faces toward a far-off land, and make a stand beside a far-off sea. But if dissent continues between you, all may be lost, for the six sisters must unite as one, and their closest friends no less than the sisters themselves.'

'She was always portentous when she'd had a few drinks,' said Damien, looking down at his feet. 'We were sure she meant nothing by it.'

But some of Ivana's preternatural wisdom seemed to flow through Chantal, and she understood that all along Damien's intention in associating with the armaments business must have been to procure for her the weapons she needed, just as Genghis Khan had procured a hundred swords for the sons of the Aral Sea. In secretly ensuring the consignment was misdirected, he had been true to the moral identity he so frequently disowned. For Damien Lewis concealed even from himself the lengths he would go to for the woman he claimed to scorn.

'We must talk later,' Chantal said, swallowing hard. 'Obviously there's been a breakdown of communication between us. Yet as Petra Kelly used to say, although nothing is ever truly gained in life, nothing is ever truly lost, and history is only the future written backwards. Putting it another way, while we haven't got what we came for, we know what we need to do to get it. And the first thing is to regain the drop zone before the others give up hope.'

But before she turned to go, she came close to Ivana and touched her brow in a token of affectionate farewell, and the others did so too, wondering how they could feel such tenderness toward a person who was, seemingly, an inland sea.

'Wait for us!' Chantal called, against the roar of the engine.

'Do not be too long,' the golden-haired woman called back.

'Do not be too long,' the hundred sons called.

But as the boat pulled away, the island began to look less real, and it was no surprise when they found it was not mentioned on the chart. She's bought herself a little time, they thought, by pulling the Impenetrable Shield over it – but who knows how long? They pulled themselves together with an effort. They had deadlines of their own to meet.

96

A bullet flew through the air, inspired by the latest explosives technology out of the factories at Brno in the Czech Republic, whose pre-eminence in arms manufacture prompted the invasion that plunged the entire world apart from Switzerland into war. The bullet was of unimpeachable design and provenance and it travelled vigorously along in the direction of Colonel Sir Colquhardie Colquhardie-Custard. Such a bullet is unlikely to turn aside or linger in its career for anything, and the Colonel's upright stance and fearless demeanour merely served to present a more compelling target. It was just sixty seconds before the detonators went; the returning RHIB struck the shoreline and its crew leapt out to join the defending force. Those still unhurt helped comrades to where helicopters already fanned the desiccated beach into a sandstorm which sometimes obscured the whole scene. But the bullet, which cared nothing about the nature of courage or self-sacrifice, crashed into the Colonel's bell-like rib-cage, in which his heart had for fifty years thumped and gambolled about like a spider crab in a lobster pot, with a terrible clatter of exploding bones and organs.

'Go!' shouted the Colonel. 'Save yourselves – I can hold them off until the charges blow!' And then, when they still hesitated, 'Go on! Most of my men are already dead. There's nothing for me back home anyway. My name has already been mentioned in connection with early retirement. Damn it – go!'

Chantal, as light as a leaf, waved the rest of them towards the choppers but darted back and in a moment was beside him. 'Put your arm round my shoulders! We can still make it!'

'You make it,' grunted the Colonel. 'I've already come as far as I'm going. They've performed open heart surgery on me with an AK-47, and my blood is squirting in all directions. In a few seconds I will be dead, but if I'd lived to be a hundred, I would never forget you came back for me in the face of such odds. But now – you've done all you can. The chopper is waiting. Your friends need you more than I do.'

'During the past few hours,' said Chantal, 'we've all learnt something about each other – and ourselves. But be assured I'll never forget you either. I'll have a huge dun-coloured stone erected in the spot where you fell, bearing the simple legend *Custard's Last Stand*. For I don't think anyone like you will be here again.'

Then Chantal did a curious thing, because she leaned even closer to the old soldier, despite the fact that his chest was nothing but a broken mass of ribs and entrails from which blood was billowing in copious amounts. Her blue eyes peered deep into his and she said softly, 'Kiss me, Colquhardie.'

And he did, and he fell back, smiling, dead.

97

The first time anyone said, 'Where's Vanilla Kohn?' may have been during the flight back to Akra, or in the boarding lounge as they waited for a civil airliner bound for Heathrow. Yet her absence seemed strangely unsurprising. Nor, later, were they surprised at a report carried by the World Service that a precarious cease-fire had been established between government troops and the warlords of Kara-Kalpak, and a United Nations resolution had initiated a massive aid programme directed at saving the Aral Sea. But everyone knew these were stopgap measures, and the longterm prospects of the area depended on the resolution of wider issues and deeper conflicts.

Whether a gradual recovery of the Aral Sea would have coincided with a leading supermodel regaining the curvaceous profile for which she had always been famous, could never be known. Vanilla Kohn vanished from the gossip columns from that day forward. Some said she married a billionaire arms dealer, and others that she joined a Buddhist monastery. The theory that she had returned to her native country and was waiting to be united with her essential self once the Impenetrable Shield could be exchanged for the Infallible Grindstone was not easy to prove or disprove.

Meanwhile, a group of friends met back at Coldharbour to talk about the old days over a glass of hogweed ale, and speculate about what was false in life, and what was true. If there had previously been problems between two of them, these seemed insignificant in the light of the experiences they had shared together. If one had slipped into the ranks of the oppressor and lobbied for the sale of arms to regimes with poor human rights records, it was understood this had been done for the best motives. Besides, they agreed, nobody is perfect, and imperfection should not stand in the way of the attraction that sometimes forms between one human being and another. However, one of them did wish to emphasize that, perhaps if the other hadn't had such pretensions about being perfect to begin with, various misunderstandings would never have arisen. Possibly, replied the other, but if the first hadn't cultivated imperfection in such a deliberately provocative way, the misunderstandings would not have arisen either.

'For God's sake, can't you shut up arguing, you two?'

In the end, they made a kind of ambiguous peace. 'You may be a person without a conscience,' said Chantal. 'But don't worry, because I'll be your conscience.'

'You may be a conscience without a person. But don't worry, because I'll be your person.'

In this way each promised to become the essential self the other lacked, and if ever discord raised its head between them, as discord inevitably will, they pledged themselves to remember the mud flats of Kara-Kalpak, which, they felt, would cement their comradeship forever.

'But now', Damien said to Chantal, 'we need to lie low. I've already fallen foul of the law, and you're still utterly beyond it. It would be good to help with the business of the Infallible Grindstone. But if Sophie's involved, it's an education issue.'

They thought, as Triona, Neill and the others did, of Ivana's strange words, spoken to Triona almost as an afterthought. 'The hardest thing to find, is the thing you never lost.' From this they guessed the grindstone was somewhere close to home. 'The thing is,' they both said, 'our expertise is more to do with international arms traffic, Central Asian warlords, and world environmental issues. Other people are probably better at more routine stuff. Frankly, we're going on a camping holiday in Wales.'

'Enjoy your holiday in Wales,' Neill said. 'But frankly, the task confronting Sophie may be the hardest of all. Everyone knows the Infallible Grindstone is shrouded in mystery. Its whereabouts are a matter for futile speculation, and the authorities have already made their move.'

VII

The Stepping Stones

98

Rather than dwell on the difficulties inseparable from Sophie's task, Neill Fife told Triona it was important to be positive about what had been achieved so far, even though all they had actually found were other things to look for. Oswald Hawthorne, despite being an accountant, had given a very adequate account of himself at Strategic Marketing, and persuaded Tom Baleworker to promise them information in return for the Chain of Command, with which he believed he could topple Myles Overton and take his place.

Nuala, incarcerated as she was, had overturned a lifelong injustice, and been freed literally and figuratively despite the machinations of Linden Richmont, who was made to question her own loyalties. Although Nuala's rescuer would give them the Chain of Command only in return for the Bottomless Pitcher, Dawn's contacts in the inner city speedily led them to the custodian of that artefact, and the only reason they were not given it was that doing so would destroy the universe by a catastrophic leakage of dreams.

In an important contribution to world peace and the stability of the Caucasian hinterlands, their bid with Chantal to capture the Impenetrable Shield had been an unqualified success except that they did not get it. But the hundred sons of Genghis Khan readily agreed to trade it for the Infallible Grindstone, and that, in turn, led back to Coldharbour and Sophie herself.

'We have much to congratulate ourselves on,' said Neill. He had not yet fully realized that Sophie, whom the authorities had suspected ever since the events at Strategic Marketing, was a marked woman. For word had come to Whitehall that her school was failing, and that was the one thing Downing Street could never tolerate. Even as the companions journeyed back from foreign parts congratulating each other on the success of their enterprise, Sophie prepared for the entire apparatus of the state to be turned on her, spearheaded by an old acquaintance grown bitter and twisted with the passing years.

99

Long ago, when Sophie Greenwood was going to marry a chancer, Neill Fife received a letter from their friend Evan Hall, then training in educational psychology, who said they should all meet and discuss with her the way things stood. 'She should not sacrifice her freedom!' said the letter. 'She owes herself at least that much. She owes us all that much.'

'Freedom is a restless ocean,' Neill Fife wrote back. 'But desire is a rushing tide.'

They had all left Coldharbour by then, for it was three years or more since Karen's disappearance. In an upper room a few of the friends convened, but they could not agree on what advice Sophie should be offered. If her impending marriage was a problem, it was her problem, and they had no right to try to solve it without being asked. A problem shared is a problem halved, but a confusion shared is a confusion doubled, and more problems arise from confusion than anything else. It was likely therefore that Sophie was confused, and things would sort themselves out in due course.

Oswald Hawthorne said, 'I'm sorry to hear what's happened but I wish her well. Her plans are no concern of mine. No-one knows better than me what goes through a woman's mind when she's tempted by success and glamour. I'm sure it'll work out in the end, for we're all beads on the same abacus, even if the sums are sometimes incomprehensible.'

But Evan could only remember his last conversation with Sophie in the crab orchard at the back of the little school, one day when the last long summer had almost gone. Then, she told him she planned never to marry, for to be a teacher was everything to her, and she hoped one day to follow in the footsteps of the old teacher who had been Head of the school during her own years there, and who, had she not already had a father, would have been like the father she never had. In the crab orchard she and Evan had talked interminably, shivering amid the dewy ferns as the evening swept across the downs and ran in shadows like a fleet of dark-sailed ships, filling the valley from west to east. They dreamed a new breed of teacher would come and abacuses would be rent asunder. That the little school, in whose gardens Byron and Shelley walked when the Stepping Stones lay within the boundaries of the Coldharbour estate, would teach that truth is the only arbiter of right and wrong between human beings, and right and wrong are the only arbiters of truth.

'We can't let her take this step,' Evan said again, about the chancer.

But the faces of the others looked back at him like unlit windows, unwilling to reveal their feelings about the matter. Dawn's face alone was like a lighted window, with figures moving about and making themselves a cup of coffee.

'It isn't really Sophie's freedom that interests you, though, is it? Or even her ideals?'

'You're trying to say I want her for myself. But that's a crude way of looking at things. To be honest, spiritual affection is more enduring anyway. Physical relationships don't kill love, but they bring mortality to it. At the risk of being metaphorical, they break Caryddwen's urn.'

'There's nothing wrong with being mortal,' Dawn said. 'It makes you love life. Let things grow and die! Women know that better than men. Have kids! That's part of education too. But so', she added with narrowing eyes, 'is being honest with yourself.'

'But she's giving up her dreams. Life ends when one accepts that one's dreams are unrealizable.'

'Some people say that's when it begins,' Neill pointed out.

Evan thought again of that last evening long ago, the school, and the crab orchard. After Sophie left him there, he watched the tussocks come slowly upright again where her feet had passed, and fell into a kind of doze. He dreamed he was walking through a very similar orchard when he came to a tree with seven thousand leaves, and each leaf was curled into a little ear. 'What are you listening for?' he asked the tree. 'For the voice of Caryddwen,' it replied, the sound of its words like wind stirring the branches. Walking a little further, he came to another tree with seven thousand blossoms, and in the centre of each blossom a little gleaming eye. 'What are you looking for?' he asked. 'For the face of Caryddwen,' was the only reply. Further still, there was a tree straining under the weight of seven thousand crab-apples, but when Evan saw that each apple contained a little grieving heart he asked, 'What are you sighing for?' 'For nothing', replied the tree, 'except the tribute of Leatherwing – and the children already lost!'

Seeing that the trees were so single-minded he suddenly panicked and called out, 'Sophie – don't leave the crab orchard – you have no idea what lies beyond it!' The tangled branches trapped the sound and strangled it in shadows. But he thought, perhaps my apprehension is not for her at all, but for myself.

Should he have taken her in his arms, that far-off night, and held her by his side for ever? It was not his style. He was too clever and self-possessed for that kind of thing, even in those days.

'Hey,' the girls used to say to him at the bus stop, 'you're really shy, aren't you?'

'If you can't tell shyness from cleverness and self-possession, you won't get many Certificates between you, nor achieve what you want to in life.'

'What do we want Certificates for? We're quite happy to have fun with our boyfriends, and go out for a good time.'

'You'll be caught and strung on an abacus!'

They just laughed at him and made faces. Filled with self-possessiveness he stopped waiting at that bus stop and began to walk home, growing cleverer and cleverer all the time.

'You think you've got rid of us,' they mocked whenever he met them again. 'But we'll always be waiting for you. When you turn around and find you need to live in the real world, you'll realize that it's our world, and then you'll have to pay our price, whatever it happens to be!'

'Society isn't the world.'

'It's ours – and yours.'

'No – that won't do. There has to be a new kind of education. Society must change, for it's based on relationships without wisdom or love. Without, in other words, fulfilment. If society ever fulfilled what it promises, it would end the striving on which it depends, and thus destroy itself.'

'You don't know us. You don't know anything about us. You just like playing games with words. But don't forget, the names of things change quicker than the things themselves.'

'I believe in truth, and Sophie does too.'

'You say that – but do you really know? If Sophie tells you in the crab orchard she will devote herself to truth, how do you know she doesn't tell us at the bus stop that only a chancer will do for her – with money in his pocket and an open-topped car.'

Debate, if you wish, with the shades of Byron, Shelley and Keats during their last long summer at Coldharbour, Evan thought to himself. Debate with the mysterious stranger said to have joined them there, claiming to be in search of a certain relic. But don't start arguments with girls at bus stops, because they're not educated enough to know when they're wrong.

In any event neither Neill nor the others would agree to intervene in the case of Sophie's marriage, and Evan was too full of self-possessiveness to tell her what was on his mind. The marriage failed, because it turned out that the chancer drank her blood like wine, and eventually she did indeed return to the Stepping Stones to take up her father's old post running the little school there, and renewed her original ideals as a teacher. That was where Neill Fife rang her and said it was her turn to assist with the task they had been given, and she told him the authorities were moving against her. But long before that, Evan, feeling himself abandoned by everyone, had decided to become a Schools Inspector and change his name to Matthew Arnold.

100

'Education?' Byron had exclaimed nearly two hundred years earlier, 'I'll tell you the meaning of education. I've had Jane Austen today – by the devil I have! Three times in an afternoon. In the summer house, then up against a tree, and in the bottom of a skiff out on the ornamental lake. Gave her a good blasted rogering. That's education. Comes across very prim and proper, but believe me, she was damned well gagging for it.'

But fact and fantasy were always very close with Byron. He believed that to tell the truth is to bear false witness to the imagination. He only died a hero because he was pretending to die a hero, and by the time he found himself out it was too late. Shelley, of course, believed the story had been invented to annoy him and that only he had a special relationship with Jane Austen, for she had taught him everything she knew. She was thirteen years older than Byron, who spent his life looking for ways to be outrageous. Shelley asked Fingal Derwent, the mysterious under-gardener whom he had brought back from his Italian trip, whether he had observed any evidence of Byron rogering the great novelist. But Fingal Derwent said that although he was pledged to uphold the truth, sometimes it could be better upheld by refraining from telling it than by letting it out. He did, however, believe that education was the most honourable vocation the world had to offer, and vowed that one day he would tell Shelley how he came by his own.

101

'Education, education, education,' said the Prime Minister. Then, in case anyone had not heard, 'And again, education.'

At the highest level, a meeting of ministers was convened to review changes in the education system and promote liaison with top industrialists to ensure *its* products were correctly specified to manufacture *theirs*. 'The last batch of kids you sent me were flaming useless!' Myles Overton, for one, was on record as saying. But he pledged himself to work with the authorities in creating a personnel resource that would rival that of the most competitive overseas economies.

'But the problem', added the Prime Minister, 'is not the children – it's the teachers.'

They had initiated a system of league tables of schools and mass sackings, but things were not going fast enough for the Prime Minister's liking. 'It gives me no pleasure to admit that little slant-eyed yellow

Japanese kids are still outperforming nice pink British ones in every area. My inspectorate must be even more relentless in rooting out the bad apples from the barrel, and ripping out the dead wood from the crab tree. The policy is zero tolerance. There are still failing schools out there. They're failing their pupils, they're failing their parents, and they're failing the community!'

Educationalists agreed that the fault lay within the teaching profession, and no expense was spared to find and deal with the guilty parties. Clearly, naive idealism from the late sixties until the mid eighties had initiated a culture of failure. The pendulum had swung from subject-based to project-based tuition, and the destructive consequences of this could not be overstated. Under the guise of self-expression and personal fulfilment children had been allowed to smash their abacuses and abandon themselves to areas of study that could not hope to contribute to the industrial base. Perhaps the inspectorate could be overzealous, although there was no truth in stories of teachers mutilated, psychologically damaged or burned at the stake during the dawn raids for which it became notorious. But everyone understood that without education there would be no certificates for people to show potential employers – a state of affairs that few were willing to contemplate.

'Perhaps,' said the minister responsible – who had been given the portfolio of Education when events in Turkmenia and Kara-Kalpak made it inadvisable for him to continue in Foreign Affairs – 'Perhaps selective air strikes against failing schools would be an option, of the kind that have been so effective with North African despots.'

'This is certainly not the time to rule out any course of action, however unpopular,' replied the Prime Minister, 'although it must be emphasized that Education and Foreign Affairs are very different areas of government, and what works in one may be inappropriate for the other. But before we resort to military intervention, I believe there are specific schools we ought to make examples of.'

On this there was unanimous agreement, although the Minister for Culture said that, especially in an education debate, one oughtn't to end a sentence with *of.* And Myles Overton said was it all right to end one with *off*, because if it was, he had a sentence for her, and it only had one other word in it.

'We are agreed then,' said the Prime Minister, banging his personal organizer loudly on the table. 'And for the first example, as the Schools Inspector has recommended, we have the Stepping Stones School, near Coldharbour.' And at this, he and Myles Overton exchanged a glance that could have meant everything, or nothing.

102

The Schools Inspector took the humility of his office seriously, arguing that he was the servant of the servants of education. His only concession to immodesty was that he believed himself to be The Absolute Truth. He refused to take a salary, and lived largely on the hospitality of the schools he visited, which was freely, if nervously, given. When moving about the country, he would travel only by mule, or occasionally all-terrain bicycle. Because his two security guards each had a Land Rover Discovery, however, they made a slow ominous motorcade, and people drew their curtains as they came through the little villages near Coldharbour, and hurriedly pulled their offspring into doorways. The Schools Inspector favoured long black coats and dark glasses, but his security operatives wore tee-shirts saying 'parent power' on the front, although on the back was the name of their corporate sponsor. They gained their information partly through a series of tests carried out at the schools and correlated by a central computer, but mostly through a clandestine network of informants and supergrasses, incentivized by cash payments and personal grudges. Had one of these fingered the Stepping Stones School? Anything is possible. When the Inspector spoke to the minister responsible he had definitely meant to propose that an example be made of any school in the country other than this one. But perhaps the words had not come out as he intended, and he had found himself recommending – no, actually urging – a course of action that would inevitably destroy his childhood haven and the person who once meant so much to him.

The Stepping Stones did not, at first sight, fit the stereotype of a failing school. It was as far from the inner city as a school could possibly be. Its former pupils included high achievers such as bishops, politicians, generals, genetic engineers and social psychologists. The Duchess of Westland was known to take a personal interest in it, and had opened its new language lab. Its low position in the league table was less to do with test results being poor, than that the Head Teacher rarely bothered to send them in. She said she was educating the whole person, and she did not believe it proper to reduce a human being to a row of ticks on a multiple-choice pro-forma.

The Stepping Stones School nestled among beeches, cherry trees and crab orchards with its own beautiful overgrown grounds inside the curve of the river three miles from Coldharbour. Red ivy clambered across its grey stone walls so that when the sun was on it, it seemed to burn like fire. On its site there had been educational establishments at least since Druid times, when little Celtic children learned to honour the Tuatha de Dannaan, use runic symbols based on tree shapes, cut mistletoe with golden sickles, and perform suitably expurgated versions of the ancient matriarchal mysteries.

Was it the distant days spent in that little schoolhouse with its abundant, wooded setting that tied Neill and his companions to each other, to Coldharbour, and to the secrets they shared? Blood is thicker than water, but school custard is thicker than either, and few forget the companions of their formative years. Evan wondered whether those years were the happiest of their lives. They were certainly the most intense, he decided, and intensity is more important than happiness, as it is a state of being, not of feeling.

103

'If one begins with the three Rs – nothing can go wrong!' thought the Schools Inspector, Matthew Arnold, née Evan Hall, who had tried to change his name once again to The Absolute Truth but been refused permission by his employers, who thought it would appear pretentious on press releases. Slowly, he rode along on his bicycle, the Land Rovers rumbling before and behind. 'The three Rs, and a unified curriculum. One must hold to those, even if all else fails. People think modern education is about helping children to reach the truth of things. How shallow their understanding of the task that confronts us! It's about preventing children from reaching the truth of things. When one wishes a boat to sail correctly, does one fill its keel with cork? Of course not.

On the contrary, one uses only the most ponderous lead for that purpose. As Myles Overton puts it, unless the community destroys the individual, the individual will destroy the community. Perhaps people will say, "What can a lowly Schools Inspector do?" Yet although it seems a lack-lustre profession, we hold the line against chaos and main anarchy. It began in the sixties, when education was invaded by radicals, hippies, and fellow-travellers, and the rot has gone deep. It starts with project-based rather than subject-based lessons, but it ends on the barricades, amid the reek of innocent blood. God forgive me, I too was part of that, in my time! But the children are our investment for the future, and the teaching profession is our stockbroker. If one's independent financial adviser greeted one in an Afghan coat with a shoulderbag full of jazz Woodbines, and asked one to give him five high, one would be justifiably concerned!'

In many schools his job was simple. They would deliver up their underperforming members of staff as soon as his two security operatives tapped their nightsticks suggestively against their leather-clad thighs. Such schools wanted no trouble, and one curriculum was pretty much like another. The dyslectic spelling master, the tone-deaf singing mistress, the squeamish biology teacher; it was not hard to see who was letting the side down, and for everybody's sake, the Schools Inspector could not afford to show leniency.

At other schools there was more resistance, and elaborate interrogations were necessary to determine areas of weakness. Electrodes, thumbscrews and red-hot soldering irons have no place in the apparatus of modern democratic government, and often the mere threat of the Schools Inspector's powers was enough to force a confession. If violence was required, it was carried out discreetly, in such a way that the marks were unlikely to show. More often, the Schools Inspector was able to force his victim's hand by producing video footage of them splitting an infinitive or having sex with an underage girl. The Schools Inspector always regretted it when his position obliged him to cause physical pain or death, but a single under-performing school can ruin the lives of thousands, and, whatever his personal feelings, he had to retain a sense of perspective.

In the schools system of that time there was a lively debate between what might be called the educators and the trainers. One can train a

Virginia creeper, but one can only educate a human being. Training has to do with information, or at most knowledge. Education has to do with wisdom, or at least knowledge. Training subjects the individual to the task, education exalts the individual above the task. Training is directed at supplying answers; education confers the ability to formulate questions. An educator is perhaps the highest calling to which a human being can aspire. A trainer is a kind of shoe.

The lively debate took the form that trainers were put in charge, and educators were summarily dismissed, or, when more subtlety was required, the subjects they taught were abolished for being academic, abstract, wishywashy, unfocused and completely useless in the business of life, which was implicitly defined as the life of business. Life was generally assumed to imply working in one of Myles Overton's factories, doing the National Lottery, and acquiring fitted kitchens. If the people could be fitted to the kitchens rather than vice versa, it saved time and money for all concerned. Therefore more esoteric approaches were banned in favour of the Three Rs, electronic engineering, strategic marketing, brand development and other subjects which would have been as unrecognizable to Socrates, Max Planck, Shelley, Byron, and the authors of the *Mabinogion*, as the names of Byron, Shelley, Planck and the rest were to students in the schools where such subjects were taught.

What did that have to do with the under-performance of Stepping Stones School, and why did the Schools Inspector already suspect he would have his work cut out?

Certainly, Sophie Greenwood as Head Teacher could take or leave Socrates, since she resisted a purely epistemological theory of ethics. Again, she inclined to Einstein's view, against Planck, that 'God does not play dice', believing the mathematics of quantum theory to be flawed, perhaps in the treatment of infinity as an integer. But for Byron and Shelley her enthusiasm amounted almost to infatuation. The Schools Inspector also had damning evidence that the school espoused a project-based rather than a subject-based approach – perhaps the most pernicious of all educational heresies. But he was uncertain how he would react to Sophie Greenwood when they met again. Being certifiably insane had done much to insulate him from the pleas and supplications experienced routinely by members of his profession.

But Sophie, the Stepping Stones, and Coldharbour were something else.

104

Sophie Greenwood was naturally compliant and respectful towards authority, and bore no grudge against Evan (Matthew). She scarcely imagined, indeed, the scale of his obsession with her in the old days, for he had been too self-possessed to reveal it. She told Neill Fife that she might therefore have gone along with the Schools Inspector's line, except for a dream that came to her each night at midnight, and which she could not get out of her mind.

In the dream, she saw the shipment of children that had been prepared for Myles Overton. They stood with their polished shoes and their neat certificates, their faces white and nearly transparent, their small bags packed with essentials: a toothbrush, a notebook, an abacus and a shiny apple. Security men carefully arranged them in stainless steel crates, each child given sufficient room so that it touched, but was not forced against, its neighbour.

There were many children, perhaps many thousands of children, but Sophie found herself able to search each separate face as the crates were stacked on to waiting eighteen-wheelers and the marshalling attendants waved one truck at a time out of the parking bays and through the main gates. In the distance were trees, mountains, and the far-off surge of the long sea-shore, but the children would never see any of these things.

For what did Myles Overton need so many children?

For what – and far worse – did Leatherwing need them?

Would Sophie's lost sister Karen be there, when they reached their destination?

It seemed to Sophie in her dream that when she looked into the children's white, transparent faces, she could see that they knew the answer to this question, and that they knew also that only she, Sophie, could help them.

105

When Jane Austen saw Shelley after his brief exile to Italy while the Castlereagh faction contemplated sedition proceedings over *Queen Mab*, she was too well bred to remark on the change in him. This was in 1814 when he was still only twenty-two, so it was a surprise to see the shadows around his eyes. The bantering look she loved was gone, and in its place was something dark and indefinable. As if he had gone too far out, and reached down too deep. When you looked at him sideways he seemed sly, but straight on he seemed only weary and troubled in spirit.

'You have been with Lord Byron,' she accused. 'You went to see him before you came to see me.'

Byron to her meant opium, easy women, and worse. She knew these things as part of the remote, inexplicable world of gentlemen. But Shelley to her was still a child. There had been a special bond between them since their first meeting on his father's estate in Sussex, where, with her own reputation already established, she came secretly to give him lessons.

'Write only what you know,' she said. 'Use a few precisely drawn characters in a familiar setting, and a plain unornamented style.'

It was a lesson he never forgot, for her words trickled through him like a clear stream. 'I am planning', he told her, 'an epic drama around the incarceration of Prometheus, the creation of the world, the betrayal of men by God, and the final conflict between good and evil. But I will try to bear in mind what you say.'

'Have a care', she warned, 'that you do not end up like Lord Byron.'

That was years ago, but now she let reproach hang in her voice, for there was no longer room for ambiguity. Time bayed at their heels. He told her, yes, Byron had left a message at the shipping office, marked urgent. There had been a meeting; some connections Shelley made in Italy were a source of fascination to the Satanic peer. An Irish seafarer had returned with Shelley to Coldharbour itself, and the two poets had offered him the position of under-gardener. Clearly there was more to it than that, but this was a part of Shelley's life he could not share with Jane Austen, or with any woman.

Instead he tried to pretend things were still as they had once been. 'I would be honoured', he said with some of his old gallantry, 'if you would join me for a turn round the ornamental lake in the cutter.'

The wavelets slapped and gurgled, clouds swarmed anxiously from horizon to horizon as if they had forgotten an appointment until the last minute. Water splashed up occasionally, wetting Jane's dress. She looked, though no longer young, still delicate and attractive. Byron said he'd been her lover, but Shelley, if he was honest, thought better of her. Over the years she had come to be far more than his teacher. For although he was by now married to Mary Wollstonecraft's daughter, whom everyone said was the up-and-coming talent, Jane Austen was his mentor, and she meant more to him than he could easily explain. She had held him in her arms once when he was fifteen and, gripped with terrible self-doubt, cried out that he would never succeed in being a major Romantic poet. Now, though not yet forty, she had a few grey hairs, although he was too polite to mention it.

'I had thought your homecoming would be an occasion for rejoicing,' she told him, 'And my sisters were hoping for a ball. But I fear there is something troubling you.'

'You are the only one I can trust,' Shelley said, pushing the reckless curls back from his face.

'Then trust me.'

He scanned round the horizon. 'The wind's getting up. Look. Mares' tails. Cirro-stratus coming in from the west. Better tie your bonnet as we go about.'

Jane watched the broad blue backs of the sailors in front of them, handling the boat. She was glad to be going back, because sailing always made her want to go to the powder room. It was the cold. But at the same time, she wanted to learn more of Shelley's secret.

'I will tell you, but I must compose my mind first.'

'It had to do with your meeting with Byron?'

'It runs deeper than that. Further, and deeper.'

'But there's a connection?'

He looked at her, and she understood why it had been so hard to make out what was in his eyes. It was something she had rarely seen there before. It was uncertainty. 'I need to find something here,' he said, 'before I return to Italy on what may be my last expedition. I promised I would help in a particular matter whose resolution lies here at Coldharbour. For it will take the minds of poets, or children, to fathom out what needs to be done.'

'Something's worrying you. Is it Mary, your wife? Are you having trouble with the ending of "Ozymandias"? Is it something you did, or failed to do, in Italy, which even here can reach out and haunt you?'

But shrewd as Jane's guesses were, he would not tell her more at that time. He begged, however, that she would do something for him, saying there was no-one else he could ask. When she agreed, he made out a list of some essentials, together with the names of certain books and documents such as an antiquarian bookseller might procure. 'They are not for myself,' he said mysteriously. 'But if anything should happen to me, give Byron the titles listed here, or have them placed in the schoolhouse library. For sooner or later, they will be needed. You are the only living person I can trust in this, and there is but little time left.'

Jane took the list. 'I understand,' she said. And suddenly she kissed him, although in those days such a thing would have been considered shockingly Bohemian. Could either of them have believed then, that within a few short years Jane would succumb to a fatal illness, and both Byron and Shelley would die under mysterious circumstances from which foul play could not be entirely ruled out? Or that it would be left to the dedication of a teacher and her little group of fourth-formers to solve the riddle left by their untimely deaths?

106

'Look,' said Evan (for Sophie insisted on calling him Evan and refused to call him Matthew, or The Absolute Truth), 'I'm trying to make things easy for you, because we knew each other in the old days. I can tell you, I'm putting my job on the line. I have enough on this school to close it down tomorrow. I have witnesses that, contrary to express directives from the Department, and indeed the minister himself, you've been pursuing a project-based approach! I could have you fined or even imprisoned. I can make sure that if you're ever again caught so much as house-training a cat, you'll be brought before a judge for practising education without a license so rapidly that on your way out of the courtroom, you'll meet your own bottom coming in.'

'The key is to get Sophie Greenwood, as Head Teacher, to condemn herself out of her own mouth,' the minister responsible had told him. 'Downing Street views this as a test case. Anyone can carpet a few slumland headmasters and drum up a dozen headlines about rejuvenation, inner cities, and parent power. No. Unless we hard hit at Middle England's holy-of-holies, at the heartland of Shelley, Byron, and Jane Austen, the modernization of the education system will always be a charade. This comes right from the top.' He did not say whether he meant the Prime Minister or Myles Overton, but as their views were substantially interchangeable, the distinction was not important.

Three times the Schools Inspector pedalled up the gravelled drive while his assistants respectfully held the wrought iron gates open for him – but how different it seemed now, from long ago! Three times he interviewed Sophie Greenwood in the little room that was her office, always decked with fresh flowers and smelling of apple-wood and chalk. Three times his henchmen stood over her, slapping their batons against their thighs. But although he tried all the tricks he knew, he was unable to elicit a single answer which would betray the lack of orthodoxy he was certain she was guilty of, or, as he put it in a letter to the Minister of Culture, of which he was certain she was guilty.

'You favour a project-based approach – confess!'

'Projects? What projects?'

'I know you have been working on a presentation entitled "The Last Long Summer", and dealing with events surrounding the final sojourn of Byron, Shelley, and other Romantics at Coldharbour Abbey. I have photographs, cheque stubs, and interlibrary loan requests from the archives at Oxford, Yale, and the British Museum. I know your theory is that the poets were harbouring a strange itinerant through whom they obtained a treasure you believe still to be buried somewhere in the house, its grounds, or the school. I know that although you haven't told the children, you believe this is somehow associated with Karen's disappearance and Myles Overton's past attempts to make Coldharbour his own.'

'You seem to know so much, I don't know why you're even bothering to talk to me. It seems you should be the teacher and I the pupil. But then, I always thought that.'

The Schools Inspector coloured: he did not wish the matter to become personal. Once again, he took her through the standard questionnaire, but could not fault her replies.

'What is the purpose of the modern education system?'

'To provide the nation with a human-resource base superior to that of our overseas competitors.'

'What three things, amusingly described as all beginning with R, form the basis of the national curriculum?'

'I think we both know very well.'

'Put in order of importance the following six subjects: business studies, engineering, social studies, brand management, poetry, and philosophy.'

'Phil who?'

She played her part perfectly. Clever, thought the Schools Inspector – but perhaps not clever enough.

107

'Look,' said Sophie, on the phone to Neill, who thought it better if he did not become directly involved, 'the project is nearing completion. I've brought the deadlines forward as much as I dare. But if the children miss even a single clue, everything will be for nothing. We have the papers we need. We've found leads in published poems even their authors didn't know about – for you wouldn't catch us falling into the intentionalist fallacy. Still, Evan Hall knows too much, and I'd bet money that those assistants of his are directly in the pay of Myles Overton and Linden Richmont. You have to think of some way of stalling him.'

'Have you found out whether Byron had Jane Austen in the arboretum or not?'

'I don't think you appreciate quite how serious this is.' She thought again, fleetingly, of the endless string of trucks heading westwards, and the endless lines of pale transparent faces pressing against shiny bars.

108

Byron and Shelley were talking about education and the search for truth, sitting on the bank of the river and idly throwing stones at an old Madeira bottle as it floated past.

'Education', said Shelley, inaccurately lobbing a large flint, 'is about the perfection of the divine in us, and the annihilation of the merely human.'

Byron drew his pistol and let fly at the bottle with a deafening report, though like Shelley he failed to injure it in any way. 'Egad, sir!' he riposted. 'Who is to say which is which? Or even which is best! When I was in Greece I heard a story about Alexander the Great and his tutor Aristotle, the philosopher. The two of them had climbed a small hill behind a town the Emperor's forces had just overrun, to watch the pillaging and rape from a convenient vantage point. "I have conquered India," said Alexander, "Italy, Ireland and Persia. I have conquered Afghanistan and the icy steppes beyond. Tell me one thing in the known world that I have not conquered, and I'll give you a purse of red gold!" "There's one thing you have not conquered and never will, though you think yourself such a smart Alec," replied the wily Stagirite. "You have not conquered your own desire for conquest." Alexander eyed him darkly, "I shall consider giving you a cut in salary for that remark." As I say, Percy, education cannot change who people are, although it can make them better at being themselves.'

Shelley thought about this, and whether it was his own secret obsession that made him say what came next to his lips, or just a piece of banter to wile away the hours, was not clear in any record Sophie Greenwood's students could unearth. 'I know all about your education, sir, and you about mine. It is the education of the privileged class. No surprises there, for my parents own much of Sussex, and yours much of Lincolnshire. But take Fingal Derwent, the under-gardener, who bears such an uncanny resemblance to Seàn "Four Quarts" McHogshead, the celebrated broadside balladeer. For sport, let us ask him about his education, which he's promised so many times to reveal to us.'

'That will be a merry game! We'll send word to Jane Austen, John Keats and your wife Mary to join us, for I'll warrant we'll hear something that will give us not a little amusement.'

But when Fingal Derwent was asked about his education the expression that crossed his face was not of happiness but pain. For he was none other than Finbar Direach in an elaborate disguise, and if there was one thing that caused nearly as much trouble to the world as the matter of Mannannan Mac Llyr Mac Lugh's message, it was Finn's education, which had been fatally bungled, although the fault was not his own.

'It occurred, your worships, like this,' began Finn, when everyone was assembled, and soon he told the poets that he was not what he seemed, but had once been high in the counsels of the Tuatha de Dannaan, and instrumental in many key events in the ancient world.

'This is capital stuff!' exclaimed Byron. 'A heeltap here, ho! A good Madeira! For I sense a tale that will take us well into the evening.'

And he was not wrong.

109

Finn's education, according to Finn, was treated as a serious matter by his parents, and they were determined no expense should be spared in it. Then, as now, people acquired their education in different and unexpected ways. For instance Finn's namesake, Fionn Mac Cummail, came upon a fisherman who had just had the good fortune of catching a magic salmon, to taste the flesh of which was to acquire all the wisdom in the world. The fisherman gave the salmon to Fionn Mac Cummail, instructing him to cook it but to refrain from eating any, which is certainly not something he would have done had he possessed any wisdom in the first place. Inevitably Fionn burnt his finger, licked it, and acquired universal knowledge. Something similar is narrated of Taliesin in the *Mabinogion*, although that version slanders Caryddwen. Odin, in Norwegian folklore, had to exchange his eye for knowledge which was got from well-water, although that was only knowledge of the future, which raises fundamental questions regarding free will. The Jews and Christians cite an apple rather than a salmon, the Greeks a fountain, the Aztecs a chocolate derivative – the list goes on. What these stories have in common is that they appear to be more about ingestion than instruction, and are more appropriate to a good-food guide than a serious account of moral enlightenment.

When the time came for Finn to be educated, therefore, his mother threw a great feast, and let it be known that all teachers then practising were invited to their castle, and that each would be set a test to establish his or her fitness for the task in hand. This was, perhaps, the earliest league table for education. The most successful applicant would be entrusted with the task of educating Finn, and as a reward would receive a single piece of red gold for every subject in which he graduated, and a share in the fruits of Finn's greatest achievement in life, whatever that should prove to be.

Many teachers were enamoured of this proposition, with particular reference to the red gold, for a single piece was more than most of them could expect to earn in seven years. Although equally, Finn's most outstanding feat might be the capture of a city, the seizure of a rich merchant vessel or the procurement of beautiful handmaids in some foreign campaign. Clearly a slice of the action from any of these was better than a slap in the face with a wet fish, unless the fish in question happened to possess the secret of universal wisdom.

'Teachers!' declared Finn's mother when they were all assembled together, shuffling their feet and squinting up at her, or re-arranging the books under their arms. 'Education is the investment we make for the future, and must take precedence over all else. And yet where can two experts be found who agree upon any distinct body of knowledge? The more elevated the alumni of a particular discipline, the more entrenched the differences in their positions. One sometimes wonders whether truth, or reputation, is the real issue! But truly, it is said that one cannot teach anyone something they do not already know, so I have devised a test by means of which a tutor for my son can be selected. My question is this: what is the most valuable lesson a person may learn in life? Answer correctly, and I will willingly entrust my son to your care. But think carefully before you offer the solution to this riddle, for if anyone answers incorrectly, I will order the release of poisonous birds, which will quickly deprive them of health and life.'

When the teachers heard this, many of those who had been hoping to bluff their way through the selection process were taken aback, and began to think again about the whole affair. It was not that they lacked suitable precepts. 'To know oneself,' some of them might have suggested. 'To understand that everything changes, yet everything stays the same. To learn to love others, so one can love oneself. To do as one would be done by. To mind one's own business. To see that everyone gets what they deserve.' These, and many more, were their stock in trade. But when push came to shove – and Finn's mother was well known to have powers over birds of all kinds, and poisonous ones particularly – they realized that their answers might be mistaken for hollow slogans, learnt by rote to cultivate status rather than observed in selfless and altruistic deeds.

'Our ideologies might be seen as cosmetic,' reflected the teachers, 'and our words less substantial even than the breath that articulates them.' Slowly, alone or in small garrulous groups, they drifted away from the rowan tree under which Finn and his mother stood, until only three were left.

'I perceive', said Finn's mother to those who remained, 'there is more substance in you three than this other rabble. But are you sure you want to take on the challenge after what I have said?'

'Education takes precedence over everything,' declared the first pedagogue, who, from his turban and his purple slippers was clearly not native to those parts, 'even life itself. Nor, as I should explain, am I any newcomer to this business. I have travelled the length and breadth of Europe and taught in the court of the Eastern Emperor, the Caliph of Baghdad, among the Shamans of Finland and the icebound North, and in a dozen academies on your own small archipelago. Yet I do not wish to be judged by my record. If you allow me to speak to the boy for just a few moments, I will certainly teach him the most valuable thing in life, and in doing so reveal my qualities as an instructor.'

When this was agreed, he carefully arranged his books, and motioned for silence. 'It goes without saying that I will be able to guide your son ably in the arts of literature, swordsmanship, calculation, and fiddle-playing in both Arabic and Western styles. But it is in moral instruction that I believe the most valuable lessons of life are to be learnt, and I can best illustrate my point by a metaphor.'

This seemed appropriate and as there were no objections, he soon embarked on his narrative.

110

Some years ago, according to Finn's first would-be teacher, the camel, having devoted his life to blasphemy, apostasy, shameful acts and regularly breaking the Sabbath, decided that since age and affliction were upon him and the shameful acts were losing their spice, he would make a pilgrimage to Mecca and square his account with Allah (than whom there is no other God). By a coincidence he had no sooner decided upon this course of action than he happened to meet Ali Nesrudin Naqshband.

Delighted by this good fortune, he asked the holy man how he should set about reaching Mecca. 'Go eastwards across the Great Desert,' was the reply, 'and after one hundred days' journey you will come to two high mountains with a pass between. Climb up this pass, and if you look forward and upon your right hand, you will see the holy city of Mecca nestling in the sand like a grey pearl in a setting of gold.'

Off went the camel, the first teacher continued, but the frog, which had never missed an opportunity to involve itself in rapine, extortion, and activities of the very vilest description, overheard what was said and thought to itself, 'Now I know the way, I too will make the pilgrimage to Mecca. I am sick and tired of being dissolute.'

The frog therefore set out across the desert but the sun dried and chafed its delicate skin, and when it came to climb the high pass between the two mountains it experienced great feelings of debilitation and died. Later that day Kdhir, the Guide, passed by and noticed the little corpse. 'It only goes to show,' he said to his companions, 'that what is good for a camel, is not necessarily good for a frog. It's a pity because if the frog had only asked, I could have given it to understand that the stream in which it lived runs for a hundred leagues, right down into the centre of Mecca itself. We would have sent the camel that way, but he cannot swim.'

'Thus', concluded the pedagogue, re-emphasizing the main point of the story, 'the most important lesson in life is to realize that what is right for a frog is not necessary right for a camel, and vice versa.'

Finn's mother thought for a moment. 'That is a good lesson,' she replied. 'But I do not think it is the most valuable thing one can learn. If, for example, one was neither a frog nor a camel, it would be of little practical use.'

The pedagogue bowed his head, and turning without a word, walked away from them in his purple slippers. But as he did so, Finn's mother opened her hands and a flock of tiny poisonous birds rose from her outstretched fingers and settled around the teacher's face and neck, and soon he sank dying on the cold indifferent earth.

The second tutor was clearly oriental rather than Mesopotamian in character, and might well have benefited from the same quality of far-eastern tuition which would so incense the Prime Minister when, far in the future, he sent the Schools Inspector on his destructive mission.

'One can only teach a person what they already know,' said the oriental sage, shaking a bamboo rattle-stick for emphasis. 'Eternal truth is best expressed by temporal fiction, just as eternal order often appears as temporal chaos. Yet the clarity of language is subverted because historical factors have created three mutually exclusive ways of describing the world, and their distinctness is seldom understood. Thus the greatest enemy of truth is not falsehood – it is other, incompatible, truths.'

But when they asked him to amplify the point by analogy, since they could not understand a word he said, he was only too pleased to do so.

111

Lao Tsu, according to the second pedagogue, one day came unexpectedly across the Tao when it was resting on top of a snow clad peak. It was winter, and the bamboos were stiffened with frost, but, moving so subtly that the crust of the snow did not even crack beneath his bare feet, he crept up and leapt upon the Tao, subduing it with all his strength until it at last ceased to struggle.

'Let me go,' boomed the Tao, 'for I am the Tao!'

'That's as may be,' declared Lao Tsu doggedly. 'But before I let you go, give me something to take back to the people, for their lives are short and full of misery and self-recrimination.'

The Tao said, 'I will give you something, since you are so resolute. But what the people make of it is up to them.'

With that the Tao turned itself into an eagle and flew away, but as the flurry of snow it had raised settled again, Lao Tsu saw that there were at his feet three volumes, the first bound in gold, the second in tortoiseshell, and the third in leather.

The gold cover read as follows: 'I am the book of knowledge according to the way the soul perceives – carry me to the sages, the Brahmans, and the mendicant monks.'

Seeing this, Lao Tsu bowed to the book, and said: 'I will do so.'

The tortoiseshell cover read: 'I am the book of knowledge according to the way the mind perceives – carry me to the law-makers, the scholars, and the psychoanalytic counsellors.'

Lao Tsu bowed to this book also and said: 'I will do so.'

The leather cover read: 'I am the book of knowledge according to the way the brain perceives: carry me to the engineers, the men of empirical science, and the behavioural psychologists.'

As before Lao Tsu bowed, and said solemnly that he would do it. 'For it is fitting,' he added, 'that I've been given the instruction manual for the universe, properly divided into theological, moral and empirical descriptions, so people can clearly see the different ways of looking at reality. This will throw light on the way things are, and put into sharp relief the apparent contradictions and paradoxes with which human beings so often blind and oppress one another. For a true paradox has value because it will send consciousness off in a dimension perpendicular to the line of the two opposing arguments, much as an orange pip flies out when you squeeze it between finger and thumb. But the world is full of false paradoxes which have no philosophical worth, and a great deal of nonsense is talked wherever one goes.'

So he called his three most trustworthy disciples and gave them one book each. 'Take them, oh disciples, to a reputable printer well versed in the mysteries of his trade, and with a working knowledge of both direct and offset technologies, in so far as these have developed in our culture. Have him run off seventy million copies of each, and distribute them among the classes of people for whom they are ordained.'

'We will do so,' said the disciples, bowing, although for all they knew it might be a question of large numbers of monks painstakingly copying out the folios.

'Oh, potential employers,' the oriental pedagogue lamented to Finn and his mother, 'human beings are subject to pride and cupidity – to some extent these characteristics dwell in all of us! No sooner had the disciples got out of Lao Tsu's sight than they fell to arguing and then to physical violence, each one contending that he should have been given the exclusive trust of carrying out the errand with all three volumes. When the fight was over and the three disciples slumped maimed and exhausted in the churned-up snow, they were appalled to perceive that, in the fray, the three books had got torn apart and their leaves were scattered over an area of forty acres.'

'But doubtless', Finn's mother guessed, 'that was not the end of the matter.'

'You're right,' said the pedagogue, but sadly he was obliged to reveal that things would have turned out better if it had been. For, he said, the disciples were at once seized with contrition, but remorse affected the soundness of their judgement.

'Alas,' said the first disciple, 'I believe we are not entirely innocent in this case, and we are bound to receive harsh words if we return and tell Lao Tsu how things have turned out.'

The second disciple said, 'You are right, for although what has taken place is undoubtedly due to destiny, there will be those who would level the accusing finger toward us. I suggest therefore that we collect all the pages and bind them together just as before, and no-one will ever know the difference.'

This course of action was agreed upon, but as the disciples were wholly unable to read they made a number of errors in reassembling the books, and indeed, nowhere did two pages appear beside each other in the correct order, or even from the same volume. Obliviously, the presses rolled, and confusion was unleashed on the unsuspecting world. Doubt clutched at the hearts of the priests, whose science suddenly appeared to be a mass of ambiguities. Contention was found among lawmakers – they could not agree on a single text. Inaccuracy dogged the behavioural psychologists, unknowingly saddled with a hotchpotch of terms drawn from irreconcilable fields of discourse.

Lao Tsu heard of this when meditating in a distant place, and scarcely had the news reached him than his lips pinched together in anger. 'This affair does not redound to the credit of my disciples, and I shall speak to them harshly in due course. But first I must go and sort the muddle out before the whole world becomes like a drinking den in which people's minds resemble those of small children and their legs cannot support them.'

He rose in haste but this proved his undoing, for his gait had lost its accustomed deliberation and subtlety and before he had taken a dozen steps he tripped over a bamboo stump and precipitated his head against a rocky outcrop, bursting his brain and ending his tenure in a world where he had commanded such respect and veneration.

They took and buried Lao Tsu, but in their grief they failed to notice his final message to mankind, scratched into the very rock that gave him so fatal and unexpected a blow. It was therefore only discovered when St Brendan the Navigator happened upon the spot many years later while searching for America.

It read:

> The Tao that can be written down is not the eternal Tao, but nevertheless it was a bad day's work in the matter of the three books, and confusion will be the inevitable result. Bury me now by the stream of my beloved Yangtze, near the great Bodhi tree, so that when its blossoms fall they will cover my grave like February snow. For there I shall await the day when whatever has fallen will rise, whatever is muddled will be put in order, and whatever is shattered will be made whole. This will be done when six sisters recover the last fragment of the Magic Wok of Kwan–Yin, the Chinese goddess of fertility, but the secret of achieving this is . . . '

Sadly, at that point the message tailed off, indicating that Lao Tsu's spirit was finally dislodged from its organic residence, and gone somewhere, or nowhere, depending what frame of discourse one chose to speak within.

'If only Lao Tsu had continued just a little longer!' exclaimed the oriental teacher. 'But he died, as he lived, an enigma, for everybody knows the Bodhi tree bears no blossom, and is never found in the vicinity of the Yangtze.'

'That is a good lesson,' said Finn's mother considering it carefully. 'But I do not know whether it is the most valuable lesson one can learn in life. For instance, the disciples, if they could not read, might easily have taken the folios to somebody who could, and saved a great deal of suffering.'

'With hindsight that is true, your majesty,' returned the tutor, 'but they did not think of it at the time.'

'Had your lesson been that one should take hindsight into account before one begins anything, I would have been tempted to accord you the honour of my son's education. But as things are, although I regret to do it—'

And no sooner had the teacher walked seven paces away from where she sat, than the little poisonous birds once more flew up out of her hands, and soon the second teacher was prostrate alongside the first, his face stretched in a ghastly rictus of death.

112

When the poisonous birds had finished off the second teacher, Finn and his mother half-expected the third to decline the challenge, since red gold is one thing, but being destroyed by poisonous birds is quite another. However, the third teacher turned to them calmly, and throwing aside the dark cowl that had hitherto been an impediment to recognition or identification, stepped forward as a beautiful, slender girl with apple blossom in her auburn hair and eyes dancing like sunlight on flowing water.

'I may be young,' she said, 'but there is no known correlation between wisdom and age. Indeed, because the opposite of wisdom is not ignorance but self-deception, the young have an advantage in that their minds have not been so greatly distorted by compromise and pragmatism. True wisdom is true freedom, but before you unleash the poisonous birds, I'm not offering that as the most valuable lesson a person can learn. However, if I may take the young student for the space of a single hour, since my approach is more project-based than subject-based, I believe I may be able to satisfy the criterion you have laid down.'

She held out to Finn a hand that was as light and soft as swan's down, and Finn was not at all loath to take it. 'Hold on to my robes,' she cried, and as he clasped her they immediately rose up into the clean air above the castle, so that the crowd of disconsolate failed – and two dead – teachers was nothing but a cluster of dots far below them. When Finn perceived they were going to the moon, he felt within himself that here, indeed, was a teacher worthy of his great destiny. Partly because of this, partly from the vertiginous height, and partly because the sense of her warm body near his was a source of considerable gratification to him, he clung ever closer to her silky robes and the rippling form beneath.

'Look,' she said, using two old Celtic words that have since passed out of the language, 'I know you're worried about falling, but could you stop rubbing your **** against my ****?'

'Sorry.'

Because the moon was closer in those days they did not experience the technical difficulties reaching and surviving on it that bedevilled later expeditions. This is not, however, to detract from the young girl's achievement, and when they arrived the landscape was bleak and rugged enough in all conscience, and the air was very thin as if on the top of a large mountain, and nothing grew there but lavender and aconites.

'Are you certain', asked Finn, 'that you know what you're doing?'

'Oh, I know what I'm doing,' said the young girl, and the words fell from her like blossoms from a crab tree in a May breeze. 'But let me take you to our castle. You'll be safe enough there.'

'When you say *our*, as opposed to *my* . . . ' began Finn.

'Don't worry – for very soon, you'll know everything!'

Sure enough, it was not very long before they came to a gaunt obsidian fastness set into the shoulder of a particularly forbidding alp. Many were the moondogs that barked when Finn and his companion arrived, and many were the wonders he saw in the approaches and the outer courtyards – although, strangely, when asked about them later he could never remember precisely what they were, which often happens to people who have been to the moon.

Yet if Finn could never remember what was outside the castle, he could never forget what was inside it – and with good reason. Does truth appear in a pedant's gown, or in an oread's gauze? This is perhaps a valid question, but the girl whose subterfuge had so cunningly persuaded Finn to fly with her to the moon and put himself entirely in her power, turned out not to be all she seemed. For when it was too late for Finn to do anything useful about it, she did not hesitate to reveal that she was Caryddwen's beautiful but wicked sister, Bloeddwen, that she was in league with Leatherwing, and that in bringing Finn to his present whereabouts, she had not had his best interests at heart. 'For this', she said, 'is Leatherwing's castle, and although it's not yet time for him to reveal himself, his power is everywhere.'

Sure enough, in the room where they now stood there was a large black throne, as if for a king. On its left hand was a rather smaller one on which Bloeddwen seated herself with every appearance of smugness and complacency, giving a little smirk in Finn's direction. 'I will speak for Leatherwing – since he does not choose to appear in person. Don't worry about the throne on his right-hand side, for its occupant has not yet learnt of its existence, much less consented to sit in it. But these things are only a matter of time, and time is of no consequence to someone in Leatherwing's position. The day will come when he will take her to him, and she will be his second consort, although before that happens it is also foretold that the vessel of Leatherwing will race the vessel of Neill Fife three times round the island of Scarba for the last piece of her dowry.'

'You've lost me,' said Finn, to whom the name Neill Fife naturally meant nothing. He wondered whether he could make it to the door before she caught him, and if he could, how he could get down from the moon without sustaining injury, or worse.

'Perhaps you're wondering about this castle, which I can also reveal is a fully operational poison factory,' Bloeddwen told Finn. 'The Tuatha de Dannaan did not approve of Leatherwing's methods, but the measures they took were as always inadequate. Perhaps they thought, when they imprisoned him on the moon, that they had heard the last of him! Yet to someone who thinks positively there is no such thing as a setback. Working skilfully with the limited materials at his disposal he managed to make a tiny harrow out of tin and lapis lazuli. Harnessing a broken-backed shrew and a stag-beetle to this crude device, he was after a thousand years able to plough sufficient of the inhospitable soil to raise a crop of lavender and aconite flowers, and these he used to lure young children in country lanes, who provided the labour needed for the construction of this fortress and the smooth running of the poison factory. For this reason aconites have always been called moonflowers and to pick them is considered bad luck.'

'This is all very well,' Finn put in, 'but you were supposed to be telling me the most valuable lesson in life.'

The place oppressed him. He saw long rooms filled with shelving where the children's minds were taken out and stored in jars while their bodies performed menial tasks at Leatherwing's or Bloeddwen's bidding. He saw prison cells prepared for individuals who had not yet even been born. He saw a chair next to Leatherwing's for a bride who would run free and unsuspecting in Coldharbour countless years in the future, only to be caught in a net of shadows and taken beyond the reach of those who loved her, until a final contest should decide once and for all the outcome of her fate.

This was the opposite of everything Caryddwen's refuge at the south western extremity of the archipelago had been. No wind blew, and no bird allowed its voice to be heard. No rain would ever fall, and no sea would ever run. Only the low lonely rumble of the moon plodding round and round its parent planet like a bullock ankle-chained to a post. Finn did not think the bowels of the earth could yield a place so dreary and dank, nor the cradle of the ocean one so dark and oppressed as that fastness in the thin air of the moon, and more than ever he wanted to return home.

'Unfortunately,' Bloeddwen said, anticipating his putting this request into words, 'things are not that simple.' She confided that Leatherwing did not rule out letting Finn return home but gave him to understand that his parents would never see him again, nor he them, unless they agreed to supply Leatherwing with a certain number of well educated young children each year, which Leatherwing would use for his own purposes.

Finn argued strenuously against this idea, and even banged the table and demanded to see Leatherwing himself – which was courageous. But Leatherwing knew that the time had not come for him and Finn to confront each other. In the meantime, he had work to do, for the output of the factory was paramount, and it was his intention to poison the minds of more than a few people in positions of power and influence. In due course, therefore, a letter was sent back to Finn's now distraught mother, spelling out Leatherwing's terms, and indicating that if she was unable to acquiesce to them speedily, small pieces of Finn would be dispatched to her one at a time, in the hope that these would facilitate the decision-making process.

'For', said the letter, 'the most important lesson a young man can learn in life is neither truth nor goodness, but never to trust anyone but himself, and never to trust even himself where scantily dressed young girls who offer to fly him to the moon are concerned – for it's a hundred to one they're up to something.'

When Finn told this to Byron and Shelley they were naturally eager to learn by what ingenious ruse he managed to extricate himself from the fix he was in, avoiding death, injury and imprisonment for himself while preventing the suffering of countless generations of innocent children, snatched from the arms of their parents and teachers and brought to a barren place that offered them nothing but toil, torment, and premature age.

'It's not without shame that I look back on the episode,' confessed Finn, 'since it was competitiveness and pride that got me into that predicament and much bad luck came of it. But the only ingenuity my family displayed was to decide it was better on the whole to pay the terrible ransom of children that my captor demanded. It pains me to say that the same ransom has been paid from that day to this, and is being paid still, even as we speak. Legend has it that the situation can only be redeemed when Caryddwen's cauldron has been re-assembled and matters in the world once more put right – but that will not be easy.'

'I don't know', said Shelley knitting his brow, 'but that this isn't a metaphor for modern education.'

'Everything is a metaphor for something else. But by the same token, everything is real,' said John Keats – his only contribution.

They were silent, thinking of children robbed of their childhood. Each reflecting, perhaps, that he had himself been robbed, and that the experience is nearly universal. But none of them realized there was another consequence of Finn's education, which would be important in the distant future. Finn's mother, though bitter at what she saw as the girl's deceit, was forced to concede she was right about the most important lesson Finn could learn in life. Therefore, instead of releasing the poisonous birds she gave her a certain amount of gold, and pledged she should receive her portion from Finn's most singular achievement. Delighted with the bargain, Bloeddwen vowed that whatever it was would be a birth-gift to her eldest daughter, hoping it would help her make her way in life. However Finn's most significant achievement turned out to be the destruction of Caryddwen's cauldron, and although Bloeddwen received one of the fragments as her due, she believed herself hard done by. Moreover as a result of Finn, during the long flight up to the moon, insistently rubbing that part of his body for which the Celtic name has now past out of the language against the corresponding part of hers, and what with the thinness and diaphanousness of her clothing, she conceived a child, which in her anger she set adrift in a small basket upon the bosom of the ocean. But the reader will have already guessed this.

113

For Sophie, the documents dealing with Finn's education served only to emphasize how crucial it is that impressionable young minds receive the correct guidance, although she could not tell how much was Finn's own narrative and how much came from the inventive minds of the two poets. There was evidence, in any case, that, in the period following Finn's narrative, Shelley was preoccupied and spent more time than ever closeted with Lord Byron and Finn himself, smoking opium and talking about Celtic mysteries.

One day Jane Austen came to him when he was walking alone in the crab orchard, determined to say what was on her mind. 'We have known each other too long for any pretence,' she told him. 'I cannot stand by and see you suffer. You're being used, sir, in an attempt to find what had far better remain hidden. I did not wish to do it, but I have informed the authorities about Lord Byron. I know that they are planning to move against him.'

Shelley hid his face in his hands to conceal his emotion, for he knew this could spoil everything.

'I ask for no thanks,' she continued, 'but I have helped you all I can, and I only did what I felt was right. The documents you asked for are in a safe place, together with a brief account of the events of the last few weeks. Tomorrow, a carriage and four is to be sent for me from Dorking, where I shall visit my sick aunt and afterwards join the Bennets and the Knightleys, who plan a picnic upon Box Hill. My world is not your world, and our acquaintance must forever remain a secret, but even if this is the last time we meet, I will always wish you well from the very depths of my heart.'

His impulse at this was to throw himself at her feet like a lover in a

German play, but he thought she admired restraint and self-possession above all things. 'You must do as you wish, madam,' he told her finally, and bowed. 'Here is my hand upon it.'

But after she had gone the crab orchard felt somehow emptier, and he had a sudden impulse to call her name.

114

Although the papers Sophie's class unearthed in the school library seemed comprehensive, there was still something missing, just as there was something Byron and Shelley themselves had missed, although Sophie was certain the truth must be staring them all in the face. It did not help that Evan Hall was still convinced that project-based techniques were being used in the school, even though the curriculum expressly forbade them.

'I am doing what I can for you,' he told Sophie. 'I am holding the line against the authorities, but they demand results. My report is almost ready, and we both know I can hold nothing back.'

He could not understand why she was so unreasonable. If she co-operated, he could still save her, and with time and re-training, there was no reason why she should not be again a productive member of the teaching profession. She had no need to make everything so personal. More than once his frustration brought him close to losing control.

'You were always my friend – and now I need your friendship again,' she told him.

He gripped her arm, fighting the impulse to throw himself at her feet like a character from the Australian soaps on Myles Overton's leisure channel. He yearned to tell her that if she would abandon everything he would do the same, and they could make a new life together somewhere where their faces were unknown, and the issues that separated them irrelevant. But he could not form the words, and she seemed to him as dispassionate as she always had.

'Believe me,' he told her, 'there is more at stake than you realize.'

'No,' she sighed, 'there is more at stake than *you* realize.'

'Well, if that's the way you want it—'

'I don't want anything but a quiet life in my own little school, at the bend in the river. But I have a responsibility to the children.'

He lost his temper. 'Well – you're teaching them nonsense – and dangerous nonsense. I know you've taught them about Byron's Circle.'

'I don't know what you are talking about.'

115

'Tonight, everything will be revealed.'

Shelley's eyes were wild and his hair flailed in the west wind as he spoke to Byron and the little group of poets, editors, libertarians and voluptuaries who, after the picnic at Box Hill was over, had made their way up to the amphitheatre by Coldharbour's old oak grove because it was rumoured there was to be an evening of poetry – or worse.

'Tonight we will venture all, and if we fail, that will be the end of it. But for God's sake don't ever let Jane Austen find out.'

'God', said Byron, 'is nowhere in it.' Although Byron had the reputation for being thoroughly bad and constantly summoning up the Devil, he was only attracted to evil because good was insufficiently exciting. When the two offered equal stimulation, he had no preference at all. He also made little attempt to see things from other people's point of view. Had he known how seriously Shelley took their little dialogues, he would have been appalled. Life, thought Byron, is serious enough, without my adding to it. Shelley's problem was that he was an atheist who could not help believing in God. His other problem was that he did not want to face growing old. Byron saw that, and even raised a rueful smile on his friend's face.

'Whatever you're looking for, it's unlikely to have the ability to turn age back to youth like Medea's cauldron in the classics, or Caryddwen's cauldron in the romances of Iolo Morganwyg, which everyone says are forgeries.'

'Perhaps you're right and that is what I'm seeking – the chance that life is circular rather than linear, and contains the possibility of its own renewal. Look at me. People say how young I am, but the years already feed on my heart like wasps on an apple. What they devour is not flesh and blood, which are unimportant, but ideas and ideals. Where has the world gone since Wordsworth wrote about youth and revolution? Nowadays the dream of freedom has turned into rote learning, political economy, and corn laws. Yet one night in Italy I was considering this in despair, a bottle of Madeira and a pistol my only companions, when the one we know as Fingal Derwent came to me and revealed that there might be another way, and that part of its secret lay close to Coldharbour, although he refused to be more explicit.'

'Have a care, Percy, have a care. There's more to your fellow there than meets the eye – even if the stories he tells are far-fetched. These devils are tricky blighters, and it's easy to bite off more than you can chew.'

'This is not about the Devil, or even God. I merely long for a time when people were more innocent, and the issues were simpler. My purpose is to find the secret which might secure freedom for countless generations as yet unborn; the truth that flows from the mysteries of an ancient culture, which were simply the education of their day, stamped out by authoritarianism and dogma.'

Byron thought about this, drawing on his pipe and chewing arrowroot. He knew how Shelley felt. Freedom was everything – or if not freedom then truth. More and more he wanted to go to Greece and die gloriously in the defence of everything he imagined he believed in. Yet his belief in cynicism was even stronger, and he was determined to mock what inwardly he most treasured.

'You're confusing simplicity with simple-mindedness, and innocence with self-deception.'

'I confuse nothing. Even before I left home, I knew that Nature and the old ways breathed through my blood. I felt always in touch with Nature, and her strength ran through me like oil through a wick. When I wrote *Queen Mab* I burned with the impossibility of doubt – for though an atheist I knew I had touched the infinite soul of God – and I was able to explain right and wrong in terms the plain man would understand.'

'Well now, but how did you know it wasn't the infinite soul of the Devil? For isn't Queen Mab a corruption of Queen Maeve of Skye, the most evil witch that ever lived? And aren't these "mysteries" just another form of sensuous excess?' Byron challenged. He said it like a joke, but both of them knew he had a cloven foot and slept with his half-sister, and the vulgar believed him to be the Devil himself, which he encouraged, playing to the gallery whenever he could and spitting out balls of pitch which by a trick burst into flame as they flew.

'The Devil has no soul,' said Shelley, who wanted to see where the conversation would go. 'That is why he needs other people's, and burns them up like a wick that is not dipped in oil. That is why the Devil doesn't really exist. Only people exist, and God is made to exist by poetry, because poetry makes the human spirit divine.'

'You don't need to be the Devil to enjoy dipping your wick from time to time,' countered Byron. 'And that's as divine as the human spirit, as you call it, normally aspires to become. As for poetry – pah! Let's not give ourselves airs! Personally, I have no time for it – cheap conjuring tricks with words—'

' You're decrying it because you know it's the only thing you truly value. What about *Childe Harold*—?' began Shelley.

'Graffiti on a boghouse wall,' said Byron.

'*The Bride of Abydos*?'

'A mad dog's footprints in wet cement.'

'*Lara*—?'

'The track made by a snail climbing up the window of a mortuary.'

'*The Skylark*—'

'One of yours, damn it! No, if you ask what George Gordon Noel Byron's poetry is, I say it's the damp patch on a whore's seat when she's watched a whipping in a stage-play.'

'You deliberately under-rate yourself. Everyone admires your skill with words.'

'I use words to conceal how futile my thoughts are, as do all poets. The truth is, we have no idea about the truth. We spread snares of words in the hope it might blunder by and be unable to escape. But half the time we can't even tell if it has or not. There was a new creature discovered by Linnaeus called the Squid or Nautilus, which I believe is a monster of much the same kind as the Kraken. This creature when frightened or confused emits an immense quantity of ink amidst which it conceals itself from sight. Now there is your true poet, revealed, or rather concealed, as he really is.'

'Keats asserts that truth is beauty – what do you make of that?'

'The man's a milksop, and takes too much opium, as Coleridge does.

Truth may have something to do with beauty, but language has little to do with either. Language is the brown ring round the side of the tub after truth has had a bath, and poetry is the hair in the plughole.'

'You do not, then, concede any value at all to the ethical and aesthetic endeavours of human beings?'

'Tell me why good is better than evil, and I will tell you whether I concede, or not.'

'I shall consider your remarks, but I think you're cultivating this cynicism to conceal your passion for everything that is fine and valuable in the world, and I think you will help me find what I'm looking for.'

'Well, I may help you, and I may hinder you, but whatever people say of me – it would fill volumes – it will fill volumes – I have never been accused of refusing assistance to a friend. Fill the glasses, and bring ladies of the night, since to do the thing properly, some orgiastic mysteries will be needed, over which I shall myself be pleased to officiate. When all is done, get me my cane, or if that is not around, any hazel wand will answer as well. For I will draw a circle in the ground at the centre of this once sacred grove, and whoever walks into it, we will question as best we can. Assuredly they will be compelled to tell the truth – or if they won't, then damn it, they will have to fight me.'

116

In the best traditions of project work, 'Shelley and Byron's Last Long Summer At Coldharbour' was a communal effort, but Sophie kept to herself most of the material about the night Byron drew his circle in the grove by the amphitheatre, and scored it with lime and saltpetre. While there was no question of human sacrifice or anything untoward, orgiastic mysteries of matriarchal sects are always on the spicy side, and copious amounts of sexual activity and fighting made it, in Sophie's opinion, unsuitable for a class of fourth-formers. The fourth-formers agreed, for they all came from good homes. 'We will learn more about that sort of thing when we grow up,' they said.

'In the presentation on Parent's Day we'll use the big black veil from the shed where the beekeeping equipment is kept, and you, Amanda, can step forward and say, "We draw a veil over the proceedings of that night, except to confirm that Lord Byron did as he had promised to do, but with the drink, the opium, and the lateness of the hour there was widespread confusion. It appeared many of those present had come for the wrong reasons, and did not care about helping to find what was missing, repair what was broken, and reverse the misfortunes that began when Queen Maeve of Skye, last of the great orgiastic matriarchs of Britain, abducted Mannannan Mac Llyr Mac Lugh.'"

In this way Sophie summed up what she could gather from her sources, but as elsewhere in the project, records were tantalizingly garbled and imprecise, even when supplemented by interpretations from Byron's notebooks and published poems. At times, in the dark reaches of the night, Sophie questioned the reliability of her methods, and the value of the information she was able to extrapolate. Perhaps the whole affair had never happened. Even the evidence of Byron's and Shelley's whereabouts was equivocal. Other sources put them in Italy, Switzerland, or West Penwith. Jane Austen was certainly at Coldharbour and informed the authorities of queer goings-on there, but she may only have visited for a picnic in the grounds or a sail on the lake. It was impossible to gauge to what extent Shelley or Byron themselves might have exaggerated or fabricated what evidence existed, as the apocryphal story about rogering Jane Austen showed.

Yet, as Sophie and Neill Fife agreed, was not the entire thrust of the Romantic movement that ideas are as real as the minds by which they are produced? Certainly Byron's and Shelley's fantasies live on, long after their actions and experiences have ceased to have any relevance. If Sophie's fourth-formers traced the historic grindstone that Neill and the others were seeking, the value of their efforts would be beyond doubt. If not, much else in the unsettled edifice of the sisters' lives might tumble and fall, as the walls of Coldharbour Abbey had already tumbled and fallen since the days when the great poets walked beneath them.

117

The morning after the orgiastic mysteries Byron came to Shelley and cried that he, Byron, had fought with God and won. 'But you, my friend, look as if you fought with the Devil, and lost.'

At first Shelley took his friend's claim simply to be high spirits. He himself was in a blur of pain, and the last thing he needed was Byron's self-aggrandizement. His head ached, he needed a drink and his shirt was covered in blood from some sort of conflict. He was in a large, chilly room and he could hear two servant girls going about the business of cleaning up after a copious celebration of which Shelley had no recollection whatsoever.

'Bring the cloth and the bucket, Maisie!' Shelley heard. 'There's a pool of bodily fluids two inches deep over here.'

Although an atheist and for all he knew, since the previous night was a complete blank, a devil-worshipper too, he was shocked by this, as he had always regarded women with reverence and respect.

'Must have had balls like a walrus,' one of the girls remarked, cleaning up.

'Here,' said the other girl after a few minutes silence, 'can I ask you something?'

'Ask away!'

'Do you think good is better than evil, or vice versa?'

'Go on!' laughed the first girl. 'As if that was for the likes of us to worry about. Pass the pail back here. If we can't see our faces in this floor, you-know-who will give us the whipping of our lives.'

'Last night I went with him – I mean, Lord Byron,' the second girl persisted. 'This morning Gregory from the farm asked to marry me. Sometimes I feel like I'm two different people, one good, and one bad.'

'Feelings pass. Folk must take their pleasures where they can find them. Now – where's the soap?'

Then Shelley knew that only with education comes the fear which strips away innocence, and until a person finds out how to fear, she need not worry about Heaven or Hell, because neither will have anything to do with her. She might as well concentrate on cleaning things off the floor. 'The masses', said Shelley, 'must always be in leading-strings.' But in the meantime there was Byron to contend with, because he was obviously cock-a-hoop about something. 'Give me a drink!' Shelley called out, leaning up on his elbow. 'What happened? Where's Fingal Derwent? Did anyone walk into the circle? Did we find what we were seeking?'

'Hang what we were seeking. Didn't I tell you? I fought with God,' repeated the Satanic peer, 'and won!'

Unlike Shelley, Byron did not seem at all affected by the fact that he had spent all night fighting and trying to conjure up imps and had personally had intimate relations with five women, a black man and a monkey. Since the other poet lacked the strength to stop him, he commenced to give full details of his unusual duel.

'God is dead,' asserted Byron. 'Or at least, badly injured. I can conceal the truth no longer. I met him walking near the circle early this morning, and mistook him in the half-light for Ephraim Goldstar, the money lender, whom I owe something more than a pittance, if all be known, and so was glad of the chance to make a reckoning. I said: "Tell me what I need to know, or answer with your sword!" "You shall have your answer soon enough – tho' it may stick in your craw!" he replies, and puts his hand on his hilt.'

'He certainly sounds a force to be reckoned with,' said Shelley, who knew Byron was anti-semitic, although he would have expected him to make an exception where God was concerned.

Byron, in any case, was always ready to acknowledge a worthy opponent. 'We fought', he continued, 'until the fog had cleared and the sun was high in the air, and then I said, "Hold up, there, for I can see you are no Jew, but a gentleman born despite your rabbinical appearance. For there never was a Jew any good with swords, or horses, or women, except conceivably in the matter of pawning them, but of that we shall not talk. I conceive I have mistaken you, sir, and therefore offer you this opportunity to withdraw, with honour even on both sides."'

'Honour, indeed, is everything in these affairs,' said Shelley, although duelling was not his own usual style.

'Well, it was a fair offer,' said Byron, 'and to be honest not entirely disinterested. For I am out of condition these days and the fellow's fencing master evidently knew what he was at. Furthermore he was a damned big broad villain despite his white church-robes. But he, for his part, refuses my suit for peace, and when I saw how it was to be, I made a good effort and broke under his guard and touched him very deeply in the side, and to all appearances hit an old wound, for he cries out terribly that he is undone, I have made an end of him, &c., &c. "But", he says, "it serves you right that from not asking civilly you will never know the secret your friend Shelley is trying to find out, if you live to be a hundred."'

'But did He tell you anything ?' Shelley asked, his eagerness impossible to conceal.

'I was determined to get to the bottom of things, so I pressed him hard about the matter. But God just laughed, and repeated that I would never know it from him, but he would allow that, true to form, you were trying to save the world from the consequences of an accident perpetrated by a fool, by which I infer he meant this Fingal Derwent of yours.'

'The question', said Shelley, 'is about a treasure or an heirloom some say is to be found hereabouts, and will one day play its part in the final struggle of good against ill—'

'That is precisely what I told him,' Byron replied, 'but he remained intransigent, though he added this had been an ill day for himself, but might still prove a good one for me. "If you wish to know why," said he, "you must meet me tonight at sunset, beside the watchtower on the end of the escarpment, since although I will not answer your question, to the extent that you have bettered me in this bout, I am bound to give you a reward. Let me make no further secret of it – I am sworn that if any man could defeat me in swordplay, he should have his choice of the Three Historic Blades of Britain, which were long ago confided to my keeping. But now – I must pay attention to my wound, for it is not impossible that it will be fatal. Farewell, and I hope you have no occasion to regret what you have done this day."'

Shelley listened to this story carefully. Although used to Byron's exaggeration, he wondered whether some important truth lay behind it. When you were with Byron, it was easy to believe life was bigger than God, and if life grew that large, there would be no need of God at all. But Shelley grieved for the past, when in his innocence he had stood foursquare behind the precept that God is bigger than life, although as an atheist he used different words. Then, he would have laughed at the idea that God might acknowledge Byron to be the better man.

Now, he was sure of nothing. Uncertain even how to reply, he tried to confine himself to generalities while he collected his thoughts. It was important to know what bearing, if any, all this had on the relic Fingal Derwent had told him they must recover, but would not say how, or from whom.

'Your tale is a noble one, Byron,' he said, choosing his words carefully. 'And maybe in time it will shed a little of its opacity. But it'll take more than spitting fireballs and drawing circles in the moss with your swordstick to convince me of your allegiance to the Dark One, no matter what happened last night, and even if you did have a contretemps with God. For one thing, I believe you and Fingal Derwent rescued me from whoever I was fighting and indeed risked your lives to save mine, although I shall never be able to prove it. For another, I believe a poet's soul belongs to truth, and truth belongs to the divine whether in God or man. Besides – there's something else. White robes are two-a-penny. How do you know it was God at all?'

'He made no secret of the fact. If I'm honest, He told me Himself, bold as you please. After we discussed the arrangement with the swords, I offered Him my hand to shake on the matter. I revealed that I was none other than Lord Byron, the Satanic peer, and He said, "I know a trick worth two of that – I am none other than God!"'

'Gog,' said a diffident voice at his elbow, 'if you will pardon me for saying so, sir. Not God, but Gog, saving your reverence.' Fingal Derwent, who had apparently heard all that was necessary to know what the conversation was about, stood by with the air of someone who can explain things better than they have been explained until now. 'Gog,' he repeated, 'if you please – he's my own first cousin, although he's always after getting into scrapes, and you cannot trust him worth a damn.'

A whole section in Sophie Greenwood's class project deals with Gog, the British hero allegedly defeated by Brutus, who landed on the archipelago after escaping from the carnage of the Trojan war, ably described by Homer, Virgil and many other authorities. As in Byron's description, Gog was certainly large. Dimensions are given as three feet between his brows, three yards across his shoulders, and the sword he carried was nine feet long. Animal skins were more his line than clerical robes, but fashions change. His statue and that of his brother Magog can be seen in London's Guildhall, although they are reproductions because the originals were destroyed during the recent war with Germany. In the project work a photograph of these statues, taken by Elizabeth Thomas (14) when she went up to town with her father, is neatly Sellotaped into the relevant page.

'Damn you for an impertinent whippersnapper!' Byron said, but curiosity prevented him from ignoring what Finn Derwent had to say.

'As for being damned, sir,' Finn told him equably, 'after some of the things I've been through that would be like a rest-cure at Bath, with Jane Austen—'

'Keep her out of this – if you are a gentleman,' Byron commanded.

'A blessed aristocrat, if it comes to that,' Finn said. For although he had fallen on hard times and like Shelley seemed not to have done well in the fighting the previous night, it was still true the blood of the Tuatha de Dannaan ran in him, and he had reminded better men than Byron of it in his time whether in contests of marksmanship, music, or wrestling. 'Well,' he continued, 'perhaps I do look a mite down at the heel. But as you will have gathered from the story of my education, I have knocked about the world quite a bit in my time, and since I am fully empowered to tell people what they have found out already, I will let you know a little more about the way things stand. For mark my words, sir, this Gog, he's a sharp one.'

'He has *got* three antiquarian swords, hasn't he?' Shelley asked anxiously.

'Oh, he has them – he cannot lie – at least, not in so many words. But look out for foul play when he comes to hand one over, because these are much out of the usual run of weapons. Ocris, the first, was the sword with which the celebrated Irish chieftain Cuchulain fought the sea – for nothing else could defeat him. Yet some take that tale as an allegory for his efforts at raising flood defences after my own misjudgement with the performance at the bothy. The second is Lan, the sword with which Llyr – Mannannan's father, about whom Shakespeare wrote the play – slew a sea monster that was about to eat the island of Iona, which in gratitude took the form of the woman he afterwards married. The third is Excalibur, the weapon with which Arthur Mac Uther, the sixth-century Cornish chieftain, made such a name for himself against barbarians, brigands, and ultimately his own half-brother.'

'Damn me, but these are famous swords, if their provenance can be established,' Byron admitted, although still irked by the revelation that he had not out-fenced God.

'Provenance or no provenance, if you will be guided by me you will leave them, all three, for there is a far greater treasure, and one whose value is as far raised above that of the three swords, as the value of life is above that of death.'

Shelley turned pale – for he was already beginning to understand.

'Be guided by me,' repeated Finn, 'for you know that I have been searching here for pieces of the ancient cauldron of Caryddwen, referred to in the *Mabinogion*. Yet what you have stumbled upon may be as valuable, if the search for the final fragment goes as I suspect it may. Therefore, go up to meet my cousin Gog near the watchtower as agreed, affecting a careless and unsuspicious demeanour. But take this buff jerkin I am giving you and carry it loosely in your left hand – for if he is true to form he has some treachery in mind. When he swings at you, throw the jerkin over his head and shout, "There is no Gog!" and no harm will come to you.

'When he sees his attempt on your life has failed, he will become fawning and obsequious, and, rolling out a great grindstone, he will offer to sharpen the Three Historic Blades of Britain up for you, so that you can try which one of them suits you best. But mark this – you must display the utmost interest and admiration for the swords, but never for a moment take your eyes off the grindstone he uses to give them their edge. For just as the greatness of the pupil is so often a mere reflection of the greatness of the teacher, so the keenness of the Three Historic Blades is derived purely from the virtues of this grinding-wheel, which gives an edge that can never fail.'

'I'm beginning to get the picture,' Byron interrupted.

'That is good,' continued Finn, 'because when you feel the time is right you must approach the grindstone with the words, "Though these swords are sharp and bright / I'll take the grindstone if that's all right!" To be truthful, the verse is my own poor effort, so you may feel you can improve upon it. But do not fail to throw your weight upon the grindstone and set it rolling down the hill towards the river, and take off after it at the best pace you can manage, throwing down the buff jerkin so that it entangles the giant's feet and wins you the precious seconds you need.'

'Apart from the doggerel,' Byron put in quickly, 'I believe I am with you.'

'But remember,' said Finn, 'you must neither stop nor look back until the grindstone has tumbled itself safely into the shallows of the river, where you can recover it later, and you yourself are safe across the stepping stones and back here at Coldharbour.'

It all turned out very much as Finn said. Gog did indeed take a swing at Byron when the peer came within the arc of his sword-arm, but this was averted by the buff jerkin. The blades, when produced, took Byron's breath away. But as directed he concentrated on the grindstone, and even that was, in its way, impressive. Large and crudely shaped, it had a colourful history and indeed had been the very stone Arthur's sword Excalibur was originally stuck in. Had Arthur upon separating the two had the sense to throw away the sword and keep the stone, the history of these islands might have been entirely different.

Be that as it may, as soon as the opportunity presented itself, Byron gave the grindstone a prodigious shove so that it jumped out of its trunnion and bowled merrily down the hill. He flung the buff jerkin where Gog slipped and tripped upon it, giving Byron the vital seconds he needed. Down the hill he ran, with Gog after him, and at last made it across the stepping stones in the nick of time, Gog being, like all his kind, unable to cross running water – which often assists ordinary people in their dealings with them.

But the race was still a hard one, and coming to the middle of the stream, where the stepping stones were widest apart, the Satanic Peer risked one fearful glance over his shoulder. At once, he stumbled and nearly lost his footing, twisting his left ankle under him. Ever after that his limp, which he already had as a result of the club foot, was exaggerated in character and some say the infection from this injury eventually reached his heart and resulted in his death in the remote commando camp near Thessalonica.

118

Although Evan Hall believed himself to be The Absolute Truth, his assurance continued to be shaken by Sophie Greenwood's obduracy, and her seeming conviction that *she* was in the right. 'What is needed', he said to himself, 'is hard evidence. Unless I miss my guess, the curriculum is being departed from, and now I know how to prove it. I've tried my best with Sophie, and even put my job on the line for her sake. But that's over. Tonight will pay for all.'

After waiting for nightfall he gave his two assistants the evening off, because what needed to be done, he had to do alone. Keeping close under the hedgerows to avoid detection, he made his way down a well remembered route and negotiated a well travelled river crossing, so that soon the old school building loomed above him. For a moment he experienced a vestige of the austere authority the place exerted over him as a child, but then he remembered that now all authority was his own, and he felt glad. After tonight, his report would be in the hands of the Cabinet Office. The timetables would be re-written, and the Head Teacher replaced – how could he be so stupid as to have thought they could reach an understanding? The crab orchard would be bulldozed to make way for a new computer facility with internet links and corporate sponsorship.

Without progress, thought Evan Hall, one could not move forward.

He ducked through the hibiscus bushes, sneaked down the side passage and slid a ruler along the edge of the toilet window to release the old-fashioned catch – a well tried trick when you were late for Assembly and didn't want to be spotted coming through the main doors next to the Head's study. Although the manoeuvre was less easy than it had been in short trousers, he was quickly inside and, breathing heavily, made his way up to the library. The key was where it had always been, hidden behind the Sheridan adjacent to the door. In moments Evan Hall was where he needed to be, but his eyes widened. Even he had never dreamed they would go so far, and penetrate so deep.

No attempt had been made to conceal what was going on. Playing the beam of his torch round the room, Evan Hall could see the whole of the *Last Long Summer* project. Chronological presentation sheets with visual material were arranged round all four walls. Photocopies and original documents were meticulously laid out on the work surfaces, with extensive annotation and cross-referencing paperclipped in place. At the end of the room stood two state-of-the-art micro-computers for processing data, logging, scanning and imaging. Evidently the work was still not quite complete, for the last of the displays was still blank and a whiteboard was covered from top to bottom with notes, speculative comments and untidy sketch diagrams, some of which had been hastily hatched through. And across the whole of this was scrawled an enormous question mark.

To procure the damning photographic evidence he needed was the work of moments, and yet Evan was unable to prevent himself from lingering over the material, appalled and yet somehow fascinated by the boldness of vision and yet painstaking attention to detail it revealed. It was no secret that Shelley, Byron, and other literary figures took a tenancy at Coldharbour for that last long summer they spent together on British soil. But the strange significance of that time for their writings, their own lives and deaths, and the culture of their age was previously unguessed at. 'Who would have thought', Evan Hall found himself musing, 'that Byron had Jane Austen in the arboretum?'

Like a hunter who momentarily admires the beauty of the very creature he is about to destroy, Evan paused for a few seconds. But the mood would not have lasted long had not his eye been caught by something else in the Jane Austen section. The guiding principle of the *Last Long Summer* project was as much to show material as to comment upon it, and among many rare documents discovered by Sophie's children, one of them appeared to be in the distinctive handwriting of the author of Pride and Prejudice herself. As Evan scanned the text, he knew at once that the story about Byron was false, but the truth was more outrageous than he could ever have imagined. And as he read, it seemed to him that his whole life swam before his eyes, and for a moment he no longer knew who he was.

119

'Until J*** was threatened with its loss,' wrote Jane Austen in a manuscript clearly not intended for publication, 'she had never known how much of her happiness depended on being first with Mr S*** in interest and affection. Satisfied it was so, and feeling it her due, she had enjoyed it without reflection, and only in the dread of its loss found out how inexpressibly important it had been.'

As Evan Hall read this tortured combination of autobiography and fantasy, the novelist's tragic personal life gradually became clear. While secret, her relationship with Shelley had clearly been the guiding principle of her existence. Although as a novelist she confined herself to romantic themes, her first love was the study of truth in all its forms, and she may indeed have collaborated in William Godwin's *Reflections on Education* but concealed the fact so as not to prejudice her chances of making a good match. This love of truth she shared with Shelley (surely Mr S*** in the manuscript) from their first meetings, when he was a callow adolescent and she already a celebrity. But she never admitted either her passion for abstract thought or her tenderness toward Shelley himself, because she delighted in affecting indifference to what she most truly valued. Furthermore, although he was always kind to her, she thought him without any symptom of particular regard, but always correct and self-possessed. Threatened, therefore, by her own burgeoning love and the gulf imposed by their age difference, she treated him coldly, and one day in a nearby crab orchard said farewell, determined to go to Bath and make a new life for herself.

There, the manuscript suggested, while in poor spirits following that parting, she was captivated by the easy charm and plausible words of a man who later turned out to be a chancer, a wastrel and a rake. In contrast with similar situations in her published work, the manuscript spoke of a secret marriage with this individual, which however was soon made untenable by the defects of his character and the fact that he turned out already to have a wife in Portsmouth. Compromised and full of bitter regrets, J*** returned to Coldharbour resolving never to trust the male sex again. Instead, she would throw herself into her work and devote her life to guiding others, so that through perceptions of truth about human relationships they could find the happiness she herself would never know.

The narrative could have ended there, but an epilogue, seemingly penned much later, referred to one final visit. J*** intended to declare herself at last, even though she was nearly forty and the object of her affections was by now married to the author of F***kenstein. Yet when she arrived she found her former companion much changed, sullen, and drawn by his friendship with Lord B*** into a bizarre obsession she could neither comprehend nor share. In a fit of pique, J*** denounced Lord B*** to the authorities for participating in orgiastic mysteries, intending to leave the place for ever on the morning Mail. Yet before she went she met Mr S*** one final time in the crab orchard to tell him what she had done, and that she had acted only in his own best interests. Mr S*** was preoccupied and self-possessed. Although she thought at one moment he might fall on his knees and pour out his feelings in a spontaneous overflow of powerful emotion, he remained composed, and wished her adieu with a sad formality. When she left his side, according to the manuscript, she felt a terrible emptiness, but suddenly, as the night-jar stilled its erratic song, she heard him calling out her name. Her hand flew to her cheek as she blushed like a young girl and half-turned to see him reaching out for her. And as they sank into the long grass, the evening dew covered them as if in a bridal bed.

Small wonder, thought Evan, that Sophie struggled to find an acceptable way of editing this material in a presentation by fourth-formers. Nothing in Jane Austen's published work prepared the reader for her description of that single night of passion between a young man and an older woman whose love was outlawed by the conventions of their day. Its consummate sensuality made Anaïs Ninn read like James Herriott. Perhaps, thought Evan, it was the first and last time the celebrated author wrote from her heart, even though that heart was broken by dreams of what could never be.

The episode ended, as all accounts of the meetings at Coldharbour do, with J*** travelling by carriage to Dorking, where the Bennets and the Knightleys awaited her. The draft as a whole, Evan thought, was elegant yet unremarkable. Most of the best bits had been used in *Emma* or *Pride and Prejudice*. But to him, it had a special meaning, and as he read his heart rushed back to the summer's evening so long ago, when Sophie first walked out of his life, and when, unlike Mr S***, he was too proud to call her back.

'At last,' he breathed, 'I know what I never knew, and can understand what goes through a woman's mind when she leaves a man in a crab orchard.' And it seemed to him that every decision he had ever made was incorrect.

120

'I can't hold the line any longer,' Sophie told Neill and Triona on the telephone. 'Evan Hall knows everything, and besides, there are rumours the authorities may resort to extreme measures. There is no grindstone. If there were, and Byron or Shelley had to hide it before their flight to Italy, they would have left some clue, however well disguised, and my children would have found it. The whole thing is a disaster, and my only hope is to destroy the project work at once, and face the music as best I can.'

'It's a decision only you can make,' she heard Neill's voice say, sounding as old and rough as the grindstone itself. 'And yet . . . '

121

'Miss?' said Melinda Wright, the smallest girl in the project class, as they went over the available material for the final time.

She was shy and self-possessed. Boys did not interest her. She had only ever wanted to be like her teacher, whom she loved with a tiny inchoate love that could not express itself. Many teachers would not even have noticed she was there, but Sophie took a special interest in her, as she did in all her pupils. How could she countenance such a grave, delicate little girl being loaded into a cage and shipped off to Myles Overton?

'Miss, I think I've thought of something.'

'Descartes tells us', Sophie said without any trace of irony, for she prided herself she could make a lesson out of anything, 'that if we think we have a thought, it is self-evidently true that we do. From that premise, he deduced that he existed and was in fact René Descartes, although, as the idea originally came from Thomas Aquinas, a Druid philosopher would contend Descartes had conclusively proved he was St Thomas, yet see no contradiction, believing that one life is not all.

That is the advantage of project work. A single line of reasoning can open up entire worlds, and—'

'Miss,' said the little girl, torn between her wrapt enjoyment of these much loved accents and the fact that Sophie was totally missing the point, 'you said we have all the information, and we still can't work out the answer. But you said Neill Fife said the answer would be there – if only we learned how to recognize it.'

'That's why some say you can only teach people what they already know. Teaching is the process of leading them to recognize that they know it.'

'The gap in the middle of the stepping stones isn't any wider than the rest.'

'Pardon?'

'I come across them every morning. All the gaps are the same. But in the text, Byron's injury comes from turning as he leapt across the gap between the two middle stones, which was wider than the other gaps. The story can't be right. Unless—'

When the realization came, it came to them all together. It was like the feeling some people experience at the culmination of sexual activity, but infinitely more sustained and powerful.

'You mean . . . ' Sophie began.

What better way to hide something – for who would think of looking where they can already see? It was hardly even necessary for Sophie to check that the central stepping stone was shaped from material different from the others. Later, she told little Melinda Wright that one day she would be her successor as Head Teacher, but in the meantime she was to keep a low profile and not say anything to anyone. Sophie told her that times were troubled, but they would get better. In the meantime, she had a message for Neill and her elder sister Triona, for the project work was complete – if only Evan Hall, and his report, did not ruin everything.

122

'Evan Hall, and his report, can save everything,' was the word in the Cabinet Office. 'We know he's already got what he needs. There's clear evidence that the children have not been working to the curriculum. Yet he hasn't called in, and we're beginning to fear for his safety.'

'Or perhaps', said the Prime Minister softly, 'for the soundness of his judgement.'

'Downing Street is uneasy about Evan Hall,' said the departmental officials. 'We always thought him to be a sound man, but his report is a long time coming, and there's talk of personal involvement. Nothing must be left to chance.'

'Don't worry,' was the reply, 'We have our own people on it. We anticipated something like this might happen. Of the two assistants, one is loyal to ourselves, and the place of the other has been taken by a trusted lieutenant of Myles Overton. They should be arriving at the school any time now.'

123

When the children who had been asked to watch the roads returned breathlessly to tell Sophie there were assistants approaching in an unmarked car, it was no more than she had expected. The library had been tampered with the previous night, and valuable material on Jane Austen was missing.

'All right, everybody. You know what you have to do!'

'Yes, Miss Greenwood,' chorused the children.

'The paraffin is in the tool-shed, and the garden braziers are round the back of the compost heap. Don't forget, all the material must be collected, every last little bit, or it will be the end for us. It must seem as if this project never existed, however sad we may feel about destroying what we have all worked so hard to create.'

'Yes, Miss Greenwood.'

'I need to leave you for a few minutes and deal with our new guests, for when I've finished with them I don't think they will give us too much trouble. After that, I shall light the fire myself, although I think it will break my heart.'

Not without misgivings, she fled from the building, ducked between the hibiscus bushes, and doubled back through the crab orchard to put into operation her plan for the two assistants, since what happened to them would be no more than they deserved. After they had been dealt with, she returned by the same inconspicuous route, and collected a small package she had prepared earlier. Moving silently towards the river, she could soon hear the prattle of water as it swirled around the steadfast stones. As she set foot on the first of them her heart was beating quickly. But as she set foot on the second, her blood seemed to freeze. From the opposite bank a familiar figure in a long coat and dark glasses had started crossing towards her.

'It looks, then, as if you're no different from a thousand other teachers!' called Evan Hall as soon as he was within earshot.

'I don't know what you're talking about.'

'Your policy is evidently one of *Do as I say, but not as I do*, is it not? Or am I mistaken that, after telling the children to gather all the project work to be burnt in the crab orchard, you yourself have copied it on to a zip drive which you intend to hide in a secret location?'

Sophie instinctively gripped her little package tighter, and then, with another thought, looked down at it, and then at the turbulent stream. If she could not save the project, at least the authorities would not have it, nor this terrible, changed Evan Hall, who had once meant so much to her.

'Why bother,' he said, following her eyes, 'for I have everything here, in any case.'

And from under his coat he produced a large black portfolio embossed with lions, unicorns, and other emblems of authority, on which the words Official Report were clearly legible.

'This', said Evan Hall, 'is the end of the line.'

With that, he stepped on to the next stone, looking Sophie straight in the eyes for the first time in his life. Then, suddenly, he took one last look at the report he had so painstakingly compiled, and with a magnificent gesture hurled it away from him into the boiling current, where it was immediately sucked down to the depths and never set eyes on again.

'You mean . . . ?' breathed Sophie.

'Yes . . . '

But the words they wanted to say were stilted and stiff from remaining so long unspoken, and as at the end of a Jane Austen novel, they were scarcely able to express the soaring emotions that both of them felt.

So instead they rushed towards each other with all the abandon their precarious footing would allow, and standing together on the massy rock that laid the edge on the most famous blades in Britain, they swayed back and forth in a dangerous embrace.

124

Later, back in the schoolhouse, they talked far into the night, since they had a great deal of catching up to do. Large parts of their lives seemed to have been lived by someone else. They needed to get their bearings. But they chuckled together when Evan asked what happened to the two assistant school inspectors who had betrayed him to the authorities. For Sophie's final errand, when she had visited the crab orchard before their fateful meeting at the river, had not been to the assistants' benefit.

'I got the idea from the project,' she told Evan. 'Finn's mother and the tiny poisonous birds . . . .'

It was certain her presence of mind bought the vital minutes which ensured the authorities could never succeed in fingering the little school at the bend in the river, even if it had espoused the very worst type of project-based education. For Sophie dreamed one night that in the centuries after Finn received his unfortunate education, the tiny poisonous birds over which his mother exerted such fatal control were condemned by the Tuatha de Dannaan to be called *bees*, as a punishment for the harm they had done. It was required of them that their sole motive must be to produce sweet honey in an attempt to atone for past misdeeds. But when the treacherous educational assistants arrived at Sophie's school the bees in the crab orchard did little atoning, for she took the lids off their hives and ruthlessly sent them against the intruders, and neither of the assistants was safe against their rage.

'But I'm sure', Evan Hall chuckled, 'you were never intending to set the bees on *me*.'

'I'm sure I wasn't!' she said, and her eyes spoke volumes.

He looked at her as he had never looked at anyone else in his life, and decided that his choice was made. 'I will change my name', he told her, 'to The Affectionate Companion and Partner.'

'I don't think changing your name will be necessary,' she said. 'For soon, my belief in you will restore you to what you used to be. The greatest lesson in life is that what people are called is less important than what they are. And to me, you are everything.'

As soon as she said these words the last remnant of the madness that overcame him when he found out she was marrying the chancer fell away, and he was his old self once more. But even though the magic grindstone had been found, and two more people had found themselves in the process, there was still much work to be done.

VIII

The Restitution

125

'And so . . . ' Sophie read, as Dawn's two little daughters happily closed their eyes and images became dreams, 'the sisters took the Infallible Grindstone back to the Hundred Sons of Genghis Khan, who gave them the Impenetrable Shield to take back to Martyn McMartyn formerly of the Silver Fingers, who gave them the Bottomless Pitcher to take back to General Jihad, who gave them the Chain of Command to take back to the Clay Man to exchange for the secret of the whereabouts of the last lost fragment of Caryddwen's cauldron, so they could restore the ancient heritage of the British archipelago and save the world from the machinations of Myles Overton and their eldest sister from the oppressions of Leatherwing.'

Perhaps, in the uncritical minds of the two little girls, things really were that simple. Perhaps in their uncritical minds they were really being read to from the *Mabinogion*, the ancient mythic cycle which embodies the aspirations and moral precepts of the lost Celtic commonwealth. How could they know that this deliberately sparing narrative was in fact from Neill Fife's own latest work *How the Hourglass Was Broken*, which the sisters saw at its galley-proof stage?

Yet to those who did know, the whole matter raised serious questions. Did Neill Fife really have something to say, or was his latest offering merely an elaborate way of disguising the poverty of his imagination? His style was consciously ambiguous and evasive. At every turn, his readers were left guessing. Why did the title allude to an hourglass, if the narrative dealt primarily with a cauldron? When he referred to shields or grindstones with unusual properties, was he implying those properties existed in the real world, or merely drawing on his personal brand of psycho-symbolic post-modernism to suggest the narrative dealt not with objects, but states of mind?

Neill himself would have replied that, to the ancient Druids, an object *was* a state of mind. 'Fine,' a critic might say, 'then we would cordially recommend any ancient Druids amongst our readers to purchase Dr Fife's book, but the rest of us will be better off with the latest Iain Banks, Hunter Steele, or (*subs to fill!*). Let Neill Fife try explaining to his publisher that the resulting remaindered copies are not objects, but states of mind.' But then again, if Neill Fife's account of events was inaccurate, what were the true facts? The debate would not be laid to rest in a hurry. Even the sisters themselves were perplexed by it, and they should have known better than anyone. Perhaps they were, by now, just weary. At the end of the day, they said, the truest test of any literary undertaking might be its effectiveness in putting to sleep two bolshy six-year-olds. And from that point of view, Neill's manuscript performed an exemplary job.

'I don't think', his publisher told him, 'it will ever replace the *Mabinogion* as a standard text of the Celtic heritage. On the other hand, it may not need to. If the market is defined by *Mabinogion* sales of say 20,000 copies of the popularized paperback version at the equivalent of £5.99 in the UK and North America, a penetration of only 20% would yield an annual gross revenue of £24,000 which after discount and production costs could give £10,000 in the first year. And if, as you say, there is interest from an independent production company to use it as the basis for a six-part series on urban myths for Myles Overton's Leisure Channel—'

'Nothing's settled yet,' Neill put in hastily.

'Nothing ever is, with independent production companies. But still, if we can get an endorsement from the Heritage Commission, plus personal appearances and lecture tours—'

'It wasn't written for the money,' said Neill.

'Nothing ever is,' replied the publisher.

126

When the summer migrants had fled from the woods of Coldharbour, and the winter migrants had yet to arrive, the Heritage Commission announced the completion of plans for a lasting monument, although, they said, negotiations were being concluded for certain exhibits still in foreign hands.

'Restitution', said a spokesperson for the Heritage Commission, 'before restoration.'

But although no details could be released and evidently there was more at stake than just money, it was clear that the Heritage Commission would do what had to be done. In the past, after events at the Centre for Alternative Healing and the disclosure of its relationship with Strategic Marketing Plc, the Heritage Commission had been called a toothless watchdog guarding a broken door. Now they were taking things seriously.

Neill Fife was interviewed on the BBC World Service to see whether he, as an eminent psychologist, really believed that a time of symbolic change was at hand, and whether the so-called shift in attitudes was purely an effect of media hype. 'Change', he said evasively, 'is the only consistent aspect of the human condition. Why, there are rumours that the World Service itself is selling a majority interest to Myles Overton's Leisure Channel – and some re-structuring will be inevitable.'

'But do you believe the world is about to become a more spiritual place?'

'In my latest book, *How the Hourglass Was Broken*, I argue that too many people perceive only what they can measure, and measure only what they can perceive. It is not my place to defend the mythic legacy of these islands, or express an opinion on the marvellous artefacts upon whose recovery it has recently become fashionable to speculate. You must talk to the Heritage Commission about that. But I agree that certain features of our cultural landscape need to be restored to their proper place and perspective if we are to be saved from moral desolation, or, as you might put it, the psychological equivalent of being taken over by Myles Overton's Leisure Channel.'

Blame for allowing these remarks to be broadcast fell squarely on the independent production company, for it was a sensitive area, and unfortunately there had been a breakdown in communications. But the news items supporting the interview told their own story. Correspondents from Central Asia spoke of an uneasy cessation of hostilities. At home the inner cities were quiet but expectant, as if their dreams had not quite been laid to rest. In his desert fastness, a mournful despot sat beside a dry canal, dreaming he could satisfy his people's desires. For he had forgotten that the role of a leader is not to satisfy desire, but harness it. Myles Overton had always known this, and one of the other things he knew was that the sisters were excavating the river-bed near Coldharbour Abbey, though he could not see how doing so would serve their purposes. But he made it understood that as he had been let down so often, Tom Baleworker was to take charge of the day-to-day running. There could be no more pussy-footing around, and he needed someone he could rely on, who was not a drongo.

Tom Baleworker said nothing, for events were playing into his hands.

Linden Richmont, if she suspected anything, was also silent. Her faith in her uncle was shaken but not shattered. She knew Tom Baleworker saw marriage to herself as part of his plan, and Dave Doom would never leave her alone even for twenty seconds and kept brushing against her front as if by accident. But deep down it grieved her that each was more obnoxious than the other, and she had never been able to find a man with whom she could fully share herself. Before the cold hands of time closed around her heart, she wished for a house near the mill stream at Godalming, a husband with a lawnmower, and a telephone number Myles Overton could not ring. 'I didn't ask for this life,' she thought. Although equally, she had not said no to it, when it was offered.

Meanwhile the four remaining sisters and their friends spoke together, and there was no doubt as to what should be done. At last, everything was ready. Under cover of darkness, the Infallible Grindstone was exhumed from its watery grave. Triona met Finbar Direach at a secret rendezvous, and thought he looked at least a thousand years younger. 'You have done well,' he said, 'and although I cannot accompany you to the Aral Sea, you may borrow my bubble car.'

Neill's Isuzu would have been a better choice than Finn's Isetta but it seemed impolite to refuse, and the grindstone was duly loaded in the back, for Triona planned to make the trip only with her sister Chantal, feeling that two women travelling alone in a bubble car with a large rock would attract less attention.

'We will use the back roads,' she said, 'and move mainly by night.'

'Supplies won't be a problem,' Chantal added, 'for I have many friends along the way. If they're not dead, or in the hands of the authorities.'

'I only hope the Hundred Sons of Genghis Khan will keep their word.'

'To them, honour is a way of life. Besides, the name of Chantal Greenwood still means something.'

'Yes – it means trouble. It always has. But never mind all that. We need Thermos flasks, maps, and mosquito coils. We will take the ferry from Newhaven at midnight, and from there we'll be on our own.'

127

Everything turned out as Triona had predicted, and within a fortnight they were back beside the silent sea. Without hesitating, Chantal blew a single note on the horn Ivana had given her to summon the ancient dory which would transport them to the uncharted island.

'You came!' said Ivana, as the friends embraced at the door of the same low building while shadows lurked all around. 'You kept your word.'

'It remains only for your hundred sons to keep theirs,' Chantal replied.

At this, what they had taken for shadows emerged more plainly, and they suddenly saw that the hundred sons of Genghis Khan were holding out their two hundred hands. 'Give us the grindstone first, and we will give you the shield!'

'What about *you* giving *us* the shield, and then we'll give you the grindstone?'

There was a tense moment, but despite their warlike appearance, the hearts of the hundred sons of Genghis Khan were true, and the question was resolved without bloodshed or loss of face. But when the sisters received the shield and offered the grindstone, a strange expression came over the faces of the hundred sons of Genghis Khan. 'Put it over there,' they said, 'for we need to talk.'

By this reluctance, Triona knew, as Finbar Direach had warned her, that the whisperings of Leatherwing had reached the ears of the hundred warlords. Clearly they feared that by taking the grindstone now, they might be playing into his hands. For it was not impossible the sisters would need it to use against him in the trials to come. 'Maybe it would be better to wait', they told Triona, 'until the last lost fragment of Caryddwen's cauldron is brought back to Coldharbour. For legend has it that the cauldron must be reassembled before the night of the three-thousandth anniversary of the Tuatha de Dannaan fleeing west from the banks of Aral, which were their original abode, and founding a new dynasty beside the shores of a new and still greater ocean. We have given you the Impenetrable Shield, but to show you the warlords of the steppes are as true as any in foreign lands, you may also keep the grindstone until your task is complete. Meanwhile, we will defend our mother and our heritage by the unity of our hearts alone, together with a certain consignment of equipment that Chantal and Damien Lewis have managed to divert into our possession.'

'Time and again', Triona said, 'the *Mabinogion* is shown to be too parochial, taking too little account of events beyond our own little archipelago. But now, as two sisters to a hundred brothers, we salute you. As you wish, we shall put the Infallible Grindstone back in our bubble car, together with the Impenetrable Shield, and carry it back to the safe-keeping of Coldharbour, so that the possibility of Leatherwing or his allies taking possession of it is eliminated.'

When this was confirmed, they embraced the hundred brothers and Ivana with ill-concealed emotion, for they knew how vulnerable this gesture would leave them, and therefore how deeply in their hearts sprang the hope of a new epoch.

128

When Chantal and Triona returned to England with the shield and the grindstone, the others marvelled at the wisdom and generosity of the human spirit. Nor did they marvel any less when Martyn McMartyn – once they were led back into his buried crypt by Jenny Greenteeth, who was now the only one who knew the way – showed himself to be almost equally open-handed. 'My years of care are at an end,' he told them, although in reality he had eyes only for Dawn, 'and you have brought back what was stolen from me. But I too have heard the whisper that, by taking what you offer, I might be playing into Leatherwing's hands. With the passing years I have lost everything, even my fingers, and all I have left to remind me who I am is the blue robe of a Celtic chieftain. But rather than take the Impenetrable Shield from you while Leatherwing is still at large, I will instead commend it, like the grindstone, to the safe-keeping of Coldharbour. If, as a result, dreams brim over from the well I have guarded so long, I will tear my robe in two pieces, and with the larger piece I will mop the dreams up, so no harm is done.'

Tears blinded their eyes when they understood what he was saying, but they were no more blinded than when they spoke to General Jihad amid the distant dunes of his solitary retreat, for as soon as he saw they had kept faith and brought him the Bottomless Pitcher, he too replied with a gesture of supreme self-sacrifice. 'They say a pitcher is worth a thousand words,' exclaimed Jihad. 'Why then can I find no language to express my admiration for what you have achieved? Or the kinship which, through Nuala, I feel for all the sisters? Why can I not tell you how much, for her sake, I wish to help you succeed, and win back the sister who is still lost, and will be lost for ever unless the cauldron of Caryddwen can be restored? But take the Chain of Command, and take back also the pitcher that is never full and never empty. I now know that a ruler must win his people's affection not by ancient relics or esoteric power, but by the honesty of his conduct, the openness of his policies, and the love of his heart. These principles I will honour as long as I live, and perhaps hold democratic elections next spring. But meanwhile, my blessings on your own sacred quest. The Islamic tradition recognizes no calendar but that which starts with the birth of the Prophet (peace be upon him). Nevertheless peace, and indeed wisdom, are the same in all cultures, and I can only pray you succeed in the task you have set yourselves, before the date you view as so important.'

129

Well satisfied with these arrangements, the sisters returned to Coldharbour, although – apart from the Chain of Command – Triona had the relics temporarily placed in the British Museum. For, she said, no-one would ever look for them there. This done, they contacted Tom Baleworker and arranged a secret rendezvous in a sacred grove. They brought along the chain with trepidation, for they realized he was not beyond some form of treachery.

'I'll face him alone,' said Triona, 'since I've a score to settle with him for Peter Goodlunch's death, and if he turns nasty, I know how to handle myself.'

'You may be right,' said Oswald Hawthorne. 'But I should be the one to face him, since there's unfinished business between us. I may be only an accountant, but this is one account that must be settled, once and for all.'

Triona might have argued further, but Finbar Direach came to her when she was between sleeping and waking, and told her that although Tom Baleworker was capable of most things, his peculiar nature was that he could not break his word, so if he said he would tell them the whereabouts of the last fragment, he was bound to do so. 'But', said Finn, 'as I told Oswald Hawthorne when I was disguised as an auditor, the great thing with clay men is never to give way to them, but to stamp one's foot, strike one's chest three times, and say, "Here I stand!" For that they cannot abide.'

It was therefore Oswald who led the way when they reached the appointed place, at the appointed time.

Tom Baleworker recognized him immediately.

'What news has the little bean-counter for the Chief Executive?' he asked mockingly.

'No news,' said Oswald formally. 'Except that we did what we said we would do, and returned as we promised.'

When Tom Baleworker heard this, he dropped all pretence at levity. 'Give me the Chain of Command!' he snapped. 'Give it to me now!' There was an unpleasant gleam in his eye, but they had no alternative. Besides, there was always an unpleasant gleam in his eye.

'Remember,' they said, as they handed it over, 'you promised to tell us who has the last lost fragment, and where they are.'

'Maybe I did, and maybe I didn't. But it's true I cannot break my word.' With that, he abruptly slipped the Chain of Command around his neck, and they saw too late that he was up to no good, because they knew only too well its wearer could not be disobeyed. 'Now,' said Tom Baleworker, 'I order you to put your fingers in your ears!'

Despite themselves they were obliged to comply, so although he gave full details of who had the last lost fragment of Caryddwen's cauldron, in what form they were keeping it, and where they were presently to be found, none of the companions could hear a single word, and they were left no wiser than before except as to the advisability of placing any trust whatever in a clay man.

'I hope', he said, after ordering them by sign language to take their fingers out again, 'you'll recognize I have fulfilled my part of the bargain! Now I must bid you farewell, for I have work to do. But don't worry! I'll come for you in due course, when I have dealt with Myles Overton, made my own pact with Leatherwing, finished Dave Doom, and claimed Linden Richmont for my bride. For from now on, I'm going to be the most successful clay man in the world!' To emphasize his point, he took off the Chain of Command and swung it to and fro in an arc of triumph.

Oswald Hawthorne was a diffident individual who would rather suffer a painful and lingering death than send back an undercooked burger. Yet he suddenly became filled with what he assumed to be anger, although he had never experienced it before. He stamped his foot, and thumped his chest with a clenched fist, and shouted, 'Well, that's as may be, but as I told you before, if you want to harm Triona or her sisters, you'll have to get past me first. Here I stand, and you can do your worst!'

At first, the Clay Man looked as if he might be going to laugh, but then the fury slowly gathered in his face, as the thunderheads gather above Coldharbour before a summer squall. He turned red, and then horribly pale. Great drops of sweat stood like studs on his forehead. 'Now you've done it!' he shouted. 'Nobody thumps their chest at me! If people thump their chest at me they soon learn that I thump my chest at them. And harder!' To prove this, he thumped his own chest with a sound like the summer thunder at its height, and everyone took two steps backwards.

'Everybody thumps their chest at me,' Oswald admitted, 'and they don't even stop to think about my feelings. Ever since I can remember, people have been abusing me, pushing me around, or pulling me out of my treehouse. But in each person's life, there comes a time when they have to make a stand.' And to the horror of those looking on, he deliberately thumped his chest at Tom Baleworker again with a sound like a little kettle drum struck with a cracked stick.

In all his waking life Tom Baleworker had never encountered such impudence, particularly not from an insignificant little bean-counter, and without pausing to draw breath he thumped his mighty thorax again making a sound like the boom of an approaching avalanche.

Oswald, however, felt a curious sense of detachment, as if his feet were a hundred miles from his head. He looked Tom Baleworker in the eye, and suddenly fear was only a word to him. He struck his chest again with all the strength he could muster.

When Tom Baleworker raised his fist for the third time, silence filled the clearing. Everyone thought things would end badly for Oswald and regretted all the times they had teased him and called him an oick. Tom Baleworker set his legs slightly apart like great stone shores, and driven mad by temerity, thumped his chest again. But this time he was as surprised as anyone. For he struck his ribcage with such vehemence and force that his heart shot up through his oesophagus and popped right out of his mouth like a muffin out of a toaster. And Oswald, with commendable presence of mind, dived forward and caught it like a fielder in the slips.

When Oswald saw Tom Baleworker's heart was small, improperly secured in his chest, and made of green onyx, he knew he had him at a considerable disadvantage. He saw he had only to let the heart fall and shatter on the stony ground, and it would infallibly put paid to the Clay Man, although, as with everything, there would be a cost.

'Smash it on the ground!' Chantal cried. 'Put paid to him!'

But although taken aback by the loss of his heart, Tom Baleworker still had one more trick up his sleeve and he rapidly seized hold of Triona, who was so surprised that her years of training in T'ai Chi deserted her and she completely forgot how to do the Position of the Striking Crane. 'Now', he told Oswald, 'you've got my heart in your hand – but I have yours! Shall we talk a deal?'

'Take no notice of him!' said Triona, for although the T'ai Chi had gone, her bravery and sense of purpose were as strong as ever. 'Say you'll only do a deal if he tells you the whereabouts of the last lost fragment and lets us know where Karen went. Tell him if he does that, we'll try to ensure he gets a fair trial, and that's our final word.'

'Don't tell him anything,' repeated Chantal. 'Smash his heart on the ground before he harms Triona!'

'Take no notice of her!' cried Triona. 'If you do, we'll never find the last fragment, Karen will be nothing but a memory, the world will be claimed by Leatherwing, and everything lost. Destroy the green onyx heart and you destroy our only hope.'

But Chantal had already lost two sisters and was reluctant for it to become a habit. 'Let go!' she cried again. 'Let the Clay Man's heart shatter, and take the consequences.'

'Hold on!' shouted Triona bravely. 'Whatever happens to me, the important thing is to save the universe.'

'Give me back my heart', menaced the Clay Man, 'or it will be the worse for all of you!'

Oswald wished Neill Fife could be there to tell him what to do, but Neill had an important interview on the BBC World Service to promote his book and clarify the situation about the memorial the Heritage Commission were planning, and the future development of popular culture. His only advice to Oswald had been that change is the one consistent aspect of the human condition, and that people perceive only what they can measure, yet can only measure what they perceive. 'I'm on my own,' Oswald reflected. 'But then, perhaps everyone is on their own.' It came to him that only through recognition of one's distinctness could self-determination be achieved. 'At last', he exclaimed, 'I understand what the fish in the auditor's story meant! Love is a state of being, not a state of feeling, and the only way to hold on to something, is to let it go.'

'Can I say this is a bad time to start acting on vague generalizations made by a talking fish?' Triona gurgled, for by this time the Clay Man had his hands round her neck.

'Yet it's still true', Oswald hesitated, 'that I'm holding the key to the last fragment – and that may be the key to everything.'

'Hold on!' he heard Triona shout.

'Let go!' Chantal's voice countered.

Perhaps he would have stood there for a thousand years, a frozen figure in the frieze of history, as their words flew in and out of his ears like owls through a ruined keep. But then he looked at Triona again, and as the Clay Man's grip tightened he thought of the single night she had given him, and nothing else, not even the fate of the universe, seemed important. 'Don't worry', he shouted to Triona, 'I'll save you!'

He held the green onyx heart over his head and dashed it against the stony ground, where it exploded into a cloud of dust which quickly dissipated in the draughty air. Nor did the Clay Man outlive it, since the moment it was gone there was a single unearthly sound and he crumbled and collapsed. Later, the official explanation referred simply to heart failure but there is no doubt it was fudged. For after the green onyx heart was shattered, the three sisters and Oswald could see nothing to indicate Tom Baleworker had ever been there except a small pile of sandy loam and a mysterious antique chain, lying on a Savile Row suit with a picture of Tracey Dunn in its top pocket.

130

'But who', asked Sophie when she arrived on the scene with Evan Hall, 'is Tracey Dunn?'

Oswald could not answer, because he held Triona in his arms, and although the price may have been the destruction of the world, he was sure he had done the right thing. 'I love you,' he told her, 'and I want to spend my life with you.'

But the moment he said this he knew it was untrue. Oswald had dreamed he would show Triona who he really was, and by destroying the Clay Man fulfil both their needs by winning her love forever. But when he finally managed to let go of the green onyx heart and everything it represented, he also let go of his love for her. He saw, indeed, that what he had considered to be love for her was only an excuse for not loving himself. And from both the love and the excuse, he was finally free. 'Love and freedom are one,' he exclaimed, 'so the love that seeks to bind another is clearly nothing more than self-deception. A state of feeling, but not a state of being. Besides, when I come to think of it, you're not really my type.'

'You're not really mine,' she said, thinking, unaccountably, of Neill Fife. 'But I'll always love you, nevertheless.'

It was then that Oswald realized some words say more than they mean, and just when you think something is sorted out, someone will always chip in with a remark that completely fails to stack up. Well, in the last analysis, he was on his own, and he liked it that way. Or if he did not, he would have to get a life. In the words of an old Celtic proverb the mysterious auditor once told him, there's an old shoe to fit every old foot.

'And if I get bored with collecting tin openers – I can always go fishing.'

'You'll find another Triona,' she said to him, 'just as I'll find another Oswald. If the authors of the *Mabinogion* are correct, history just rolls over and over the same interactions like an old dog in an aniseed patch. But who's Tracey Dunn? And where's Neill Fife? I'm very grateful to you for saving my life – but we may have lost everything, and that must give us cause for concern.'

131

'And so,' Dawn read to the two little girls, 'Oswald Hawthorne put paid to the Clay Man, but at the same time, seemingly put paid to their chances of finding the last lost fragment of Caryddwen's cauldron, and rescuing Karen.' She told them how Oswald began to reproach himself for this, for no matter what his success in life, he was always willing to see himself as a failure. He said he was no better than Finbar Direach, and although he had killed the Clay Man, the day would come when due to his action, all men would be made of clay.

For, he said, he thought he had heard the sound that accompanied the Clay Man's demise once before, the night Karen disappeared. And increasingly it seemed to him it was not a cry of despair at all, but a laugh. Worse still, it was the laugh of Leatherwing.

But Triona said, 'You did what you had to do, and humanity cannot be destroyed by an act of humanity. We'll get Neill Fife, because he'll know what to do.'

IX

The Corryvrecken

132

When Triona and her sisters learnt the full story, they were very willing to explain to Neill what he ought to have done the night Tracey Dunn came to offer him her ring – which now seemed somehow connected with the last lost fragment – even though at the time he had contemptuously refused, believing it to be a listening device. But hindsight is a wonderful thing. They would have felt very differently if, through naivety and lack of vigilance, he had welcomed a spy for Myles Overton into their midst. To be honest, Neill had nothing to reproach himself with. He acted as he thought proper. Besides, it is a fundamental tenet of positive thinking that one does not dwell on the mistakes of the past, and it would be more polite if other people didn't dwell on them either. Neill was a successful, highly motivated professional. He was married to a supermodel, although they were now separated and his eyes sometimes met those of Triona and veered off as if to say, 'Yes, but on the other hand, life is too complicated.' He also had three beautiful children with a combined reading age of fifty-one. He was respected in the academic world and held important consultancies with blue-chip companies. He was invited on to *Any Questions* and other reputable programmes where audiences were spellbound by his ready wit, the clarity of his thought, and his essential humanity.

'If there is a contemporary Renaissance Man,' people said, 'if there's one person in these islands further from the abyss than any other – then that man is Neill Fife.' Even his association with Chantal Greenwood and his continuing friendship with Damien Lewis and Oswald Hawthorne were seen in a positive light. The former added colour. The latter was thought of as commendable loyalty, even if unwisely bestowed. People said, 'For our money, Neill Fife has it all. He's clever, but he's a good bloke, and you can trust him. Not like that Myles Overton – slippery bastard – did you hear him on *Any Questions* the other day? I'd count my fingers after shaking hands with him. I'd get bloody Price Waterhouse in to do an audit on them!'

'Something's troubling you,' Oswald said to Neill, as the two sat silently by the quiet drift of the river, throwing stones at a passing bottle.

'No, nothing worth mentioning,' Neill told him, making another throw with a great affectation of insouciance.

'Yet,' said Oswald, 'there's a far-off expression in your eyes. You affect insouciance, but your concentration is suffering. For instance, that wasn't a stone you just threw at the bottle, it was your mobile phone. I'm your friend, and you can't hide your feelings from me. Either you're unhappy with the monthly standing charges, or you're preoccupied by some problem . . . '

'When you look at the stars in the sky and the measureless immensity of perceptible space, you realize just how small the problems of human beings are,' Neill replied.

'On the other hand,' Oswald said, 'when you look at neutrons, photons, quarks, and other sub-atomic particles, you realize they're pretty big after all.'

'Although people think I have it all,' said Neill, 'sometimes I think I have nothing. Sometimes I think I'm just scraping the toast of life, like everybody else.'

'That certainly goes for me. After what happened with the Clay Man, I was sure Triona would be mine. But,' Oswald went on, noticing how Neill avoided his eyes at the mention of Triona, 'after making that terrible sacrifice, which may well result in the universe being destroyed, I found my yearning for her just disappeared. My love must have been a state of feeling after all, and not a state of being, and by putting love above all else, I gained, not love, but freedom from love.'

'That's an astute analysis. It could have come from my latest book.'

'It did. Dawn lent me the proofs when the kids got bored having the narrative extracts read to them.'

'Well, you can't teach a person anything they don't already know.'

'Still, this business about the last lost fragment. As far as that goes, no-one knows anything at all.' Yet unlike the sisters Oswald had sufficient delicacy not to say what a pity it was Neill seemed to have already held the tiniest fragment in his hand yet failed to appreciate what he had, which might still spell disaster for everything. Now the trail had gone cold. The authorities, if they knew anything, would not reveal it. As early as Peter Goodlunch's suicide, Neill, as a psychologist, was questioning the official line. Using his connections he was able to interview the police inspector heading the enquiry, and what he had been told, after a few jars, was startlingly similar to what he had eventually got out of the old, retired police inspector he once tracked down to ask about Karen's case.

'The truth will never come out,' both policemen had made clear, 'because it is not wanted to come out. Let's put it this way – we was tipped the wink from upstairs. Can't say it clearer than that. *We was tipped the wink from upstairs.*' But precisely what kind of wink they were tipped Neill could never ascertain, other than that it involved the conspiratorial closure of one eye.

If Neill could do nothing about what happened to Karen he thought he could at least prevent a cover-up following the demise of Peter Goodlunch. Unfortunately, when Tracey sought him out, he mistook her for an agent of Myles Overton and gave her short shrift. A scientist by training, he nevertheless failed to consider that the world is made up of tiny particles, many of them too small to measure. Also, he was at fault in failing to recall his fourth-form marine biology. Tracey's mother, when she claimed her share of Finbar Direach's most far-reaching achievement, was given the very smallest fragment out of spite. It was a tiny speck almost impossible to see. But cunningly she took the speck down to the bottom of the sea and fed it to a friendly oyster, which in due course formed a beautiful pearl around it.

'This', she told her new-born daughter, 'will be your only heirloom, and the white spindrift will be your Christening gown.' So saying, she placed the baby in a wicker basket and set her floating on the deep, to encounter whatever fate lay in store for her. But although it drifted for a thousand years, the infant was at length suckled by friendly seals, and survived to be washed ashore on the Isle of Orkney, where all marvelled at the beautiful baby girl with what appeared to be a pearl in her navel. The incident was celebrated in its time, although some perplexity was created by ill-informed reporters who thought the Old Man of Hoy to be an individual rather than a geological formation. In any case, as was thought best, the child was taken in by a poor fisherman and his wife who brought her up as their own. In time, there was friction with her adopted parents because they would not take her seriously. Taking with her the few possessions she could call her own, she travelled south in an attempt to find out who she was, and took a job as Peter Goodlunch's secretary.

But Neill Fife did not know this the night Tracey turned away from Coldharbour feeling as if her heart would break, and she herself was confused as to her origins and those of the pearl, believing at the time that her true father was the Old Man of Hoy. Since the only friends she could hope for had rejected her offering and failed to take her seriously, she knew she was on her own. But perhaps, she said to herself, everybody is ultimately on their own. There was nothing for it but to lie low until things had settled down a little. Then, perhaps, she could make for her parents' cottage in the remote north. Hoping, despite harsh words exchanged on parting, they would forgive her and take her in.

'Or,' she thought, 'I could take the easy way out – as Peter did.'

Tracey was nevertheless more resourceful and tenacious than anyone suspected. She went for the lying-low and making-for-Orkney option, so nothing was heard of her for a considerable time, either by Neill, who began to suspect early on that he had made a fundamental error, or by Linden Richmont and Dave Doom. The Clay Man knew, but it suited the Clay Man to do nothing, and before this could change, he was put paid to by Oswald Hawthorne. When Tracey's apartment was searched and her friends questioned, the only picture to emerge was of a lonely, introverted girl who had fallen out with her parents, got a crush on her boss, and finally disappeared off the face of the world.

'She was unimportant,' Linden told her uncle. 'She need not be taken seriously.' She thought when she visited Myles Overton with this information: he looks older these days, and spends more time in his underground crypt with the iron door which nobody's allowed to open. Perhaps he has some terrible secret, or the business is underperforming his expectations. Perhaps the Far Eastern deal is on the rocks, or the banks are calling in their marker. If he'd only talk to me, I could help. But those days are gone – perhaps forever.

As for Tracey, she stayed in a women's refuge in Oxford, and then took temporary work for a few months on a farm in Burton Hastings, near Nuneaton. Travelling mainly by night, she made her way northwards toward Carlisle, lovely Kirkcowan, and the Rinns of Galloway. Surmising correctly that Myles Overton and the authorities would be watching the movements of commercial shipping, she made for the fishing harbour at Portpatrick in the hope that a friendly long-liner would agree to take her northwards past Cape Wrath, and back to the lonely shores she had for nineteen years been accustomed to calling home.

'My line is long,' said the long-liner, a small, wiry individual somewhat resembling Seamus 'Eight Pints' McGallon, 'but my dreams are beyond control. I will help you on this occasion – for there may be more between us than you suspect.' By this she surmised that, though a long-liner, he clung secretly to a non-linear vision and was one of those who believe that one life is not all and whose loyalty is still to the Tuatha de Dannaan, whether they know it or not. He would not, however, reveal to Tracey the nature of the dreams which so oppressed him, although, he said, he had been the victim of many misfortunes and errors of judgement, and even now it was not certain his mistakes could be rectified. Yet while making ready for the voyage his eyes filled unaccountably with tears and he related a conversation he claimed to have overheard when his boat hove alongside a remote outcrop where the Great Silkie of Sule Skerry was yarning with his best friend the Old Man of Hoy, as they lobbed stones at passing pieces of flotsam.

'Life is an endless seaway,' the Old Man of Hoy intoned, 'breaking on a shelterless shore. But nothing mortal lives for ever. You have kept the child a thousand years, and in all that time she has grown no older. She should be given the chance to live a normal life, among her own kind.'

'But I love her as if she were my own.'

'That's not the point. You have to consider her interests.'

'If she is brought ashore she might encounter misfortune, or fall into bad company.'

'Sometimes we must love someone enough to let them go, even if we do not know where, or with whom.'

'Well, if it has to be, it has to be.'

'I will bring her ashore myself,' said the Old Man of Hoy, 'and leave her above the high water mark, where she is sure to be found by a poor fisherman.'

'Is there any other kind?' said the Great Silkie of Sule Skerry, and threw a bitter stone, missing one of the pieces of flotsam only by a whisker. He whispered to the infant, 'This is the hardest thing I ever did in my life. But I hope one day, little one, that we will meet again, and if you need me, do not forget to call . . . '

Although Tracey did not understand this story, she could hardly doubt that some meaning was concealed beneath it, and she had much to think about when the little boat set sail on the morning tide. Neill, by this time, was not far behind. He had put the word out on certain specialized newsgroups, and mobilized his contacts in universities, hospitals, and women's refuges to trace her whereabouts. By the time he heard about the fishing boat in Portpatrick it was too late to go himself, but he engaged two young assistants to work, as the old stories put it, for meat and fee, and they believed that, if they acted at once, then the job could be done.

'At all costs,' counselled Neill over the telephone, 'take it easy, and maintain a low profile. Do nothing that could cause alarm. This is a young, frightened girl. She may behave unpredictably. The situation must be handled with the utmost restraint and discretion.'

'A nod is as good as a wink to a blind bat,' said the two young assistants to one another. 'Neill Fife can depend on us. We'll hire powerful jetskis on the Isle of Jura and head them off as they pass through the Corryvrecken.'

Perhaps in another context this would have been a good plan. Unfortunately when two masked figures on screaming wet-bikes slammed towards her through the overfalls in one of Scotland's most hazardous stretches of water, Tracey feared the worst.

'We're here to help you!' yelled the taller of the two assistants as he brought his craft alongside the wallowing MFV. 'Throw us a rope!'

'Back off!' Tracey shouted. 'I'm warning you.'

'We work for Neill Fife!'

But Tracey, though no psychologist, could tell when trickery was afoot. The fact that they looked and behaved exactly as she would have expected two hoodlums in the employ of Dave Doom to behave convinced her she was the victim of an elaborate double bluff. Her enemies obviously intended her to think that Dave Doom would never be so stupid as to send people who looked exactly like what they were, and thus expected her to conclude that the two wet-bike buccaneers were in Neill Fife's employ after all.

'Clever,' she said to herself. 'But not clever enough. Well – this is the end of the line. But if it's about my pearl, since Neill Fife didn't want it, I can at least make sure it never falls into the hands of Dave Doom or Myles Overton.' And with a single movement she slipped it from her finger and hurled it into the waters of the Corryvrecken, which run both cold and deep.

133

'So the trouble is,' Neill told Oswald, as they sat by the water throwing stones, 'things have gone from bad to worse. The three thousandth anniversary of the Tuatha de Dannaan first setting foot on British soil will soon be here. Through no fault of my own, the fragment I once held in my hand is forever beyond reach. My only consolation is, there's still a chance Finbar Direach is an impostor, Caryddwen's cauldron a practical joke by Karen who was never abducted at all, the Night Caller, Jenny Greenteeth and the guardian spirit of the Aral Sea are but unhealthy fantasies, and the actions of all of us a hollow attempt at self-dramatization to give meaning to otherwise empty lives.'

This was hurtful to Oswald because it tended to belittle his own achievement with the Clay Man. But he understood that beside Neill's feelings his own were of small consequence. The more positive a person's mental attitude, the more positive their sense of unfairness and injustice and being let down when things go wrong. 'Well,' he said,

'I dare say you're right. And if you are, not even a thousand years of arguing would be enough to make you wrong.'

'I'm sure I'm right. And even if I'm not, it doesn't change anything. As Lao Tsu memorably said, when there's nothing to be done, the superior man does nothing. Even if some course of action presented itself, I'd be up against Myles Overton and all the resources he can bring to bear. As I see it, play for time, keep a low profile, and see how things develop. There's no sense in rushing into anything that will afterwards give cause for regret.'

'If that's what you think,' said Oswald, 'I'll back you up with the others, as I always have.' He absent-mindedly flung a large jagged stone at the bottle, which to their surprise burst into several pieces and sank out of sight, leaving a sheet of white paper with blue writing floating on the surface.

'It's probably nothing,' said Neill.

'Let's leave it,' said Oswald.

When they got it ashore, not without becoming covered from head to foot in mud and duckweed, they found a few well chosen words were scrawled across it, on whose meaning they scarcely needed to speculate. The first word that Neill Fife read curled his lip up like a peach leaf with fire blight and he laughed long and high, but the second word that he read caused a tear to obscure his vision, for its message was as follows.

> Beware the ostrich of procrastination, that hides its head in the sands of time! It is only on the darkest night that one may observe the most distant star, and only when you believe all is lost, that the smallest fragment may be found. A person may think their efforts have been bungled, but nothing happens that is not meant to happen. Look for what is lost, if necessary, in the abyss itself! For human nature is deeply ambiguous, and prone to hide from that which it pretends to seek, and flee from that which it claims to pursue. In these final days, the only way out is through, and there's no turning back – for any of us!

'I've never met Finbar Direach,' said Neill with some bitterness, as he picked a tadpole out of his ear, 'but you can rely on him never to convey his messages simply, if a way can be found to make things complicated. There's no need for him to be so dramatic – I already knew what I had to do.'

'I'll come with you,' said Oswald. 'I'm only an accountant, but I'm your friend, and I proved myself with Tom Baleworker, who turned out to be a clay man.'

'You proved yourself – but what about me? Oh, everyone assumes I've got nothing to prove. But Finbar Direach is right. I've always fled from what I pretended to pursue, and hidden from what I pretended to be in search of. You look surprised. Can't you see that with a wife, three beautiful children and a high-flying career, my worst nightmare was that Karen would one day return? That love would destroy everything I've built?'

'I'm finding this hard to follow. I thought you—'

'Human beings, Oswald, are not simple, but they are not so complicated either. Perhaps, deep down, I *wanted* the young assistants to frighten Tracey Dunn with jetbikes. Perhaps it was even myself who suggested that approach. But whatever I have done in the past must be atoned for. This time it's down to me. I will go to the Corryvrecken, whatever the cost. I must go alone, as you were alone when you faced the Clay Man. If I don't return, tell my wife and children that they were in my thoughts, at the last. I leave you my mandolin, and any tin-openers you find in the kitchen drawers you may take for your own. Most of all, I leave you with my unfinished task, for what we've undertaken is larger than any single person. If I fall, you must take up where I left off, and lead the others to success.'

'You'd be better off asking Chantal, or Damien, or . . . '

Neill smiled wanly. 'Which of us is the psychologist?'

But psychologist or not, at that moment Neill looked to his friend like a man who has stared into the abyss – and who lives in fear of what he has seen.

134

'I know I said I'd go to the Corryvrecken,' said Neill Fife to himself, when Oswald had gone. 'On the other hand it can't be wrong at least to speak to Myles Overton, before I assume the worst. It is always best to try reason and negotiation rather than confront a situation head-on. Direct action often serves simply to make the attitudes of both sides more entrenched. Whereas the skilled mediator can find room for compromise even between the most irreconcilable positions.'

He did not tell the others where he was going. He would not expect them to understand. But he gave it considerable thought, and decided that although it might appear like a bid to dodge his obligations, this was something he must, in all fairness, attempt. Neill's reputation as a thinker resulted from him having a great deal of practice at thinking. Neill thought all the time. Because if he stopped thinking even for a moment, he thought of Karen. And that made thinking unbearable.

'Neill Fife,' he told the receptionist at the entrance to the famous glass tower, 'to see Myles Overton. I don't have an appointment, but I shall not take up much of his time.'

The receptionist on the main board spoke to a secondary receptionist, who spoke to a secretary, who spoke to a personal assistant. 'There's someone for you in reception, Mr Overton. He says his name is Neill Fife.'

'You can tell that poncy bastard to ponce himself straight back where he came from. Bloody nerve. Wait. On second thoughts, why not give ourselves a laugh? But keep the bastard waiting a while.'

An hour later, Neill was given a security pass. His name was handwritten on it and he had to fix it to his lapel with a safety pin like the price tag on a supermarket turkey. A smart assistant came down in the glass lift to collect him. Her mouth said, 'Welcome to the Myles Overton Group, Dr Fife. Please come with me,' but her eyes said, *You must be out of your famous mind.*

Myles Overton's office had been the subject of many articles in design magazines, constructed as it was out of whorls of exquisitely extruded glass. 'You won't find any bloody angles,' was Myles Overton's little joke – for he prided himself on being down to earth and straightforward, although in fact he was more devious than a hatful of eels.

'Mr Overton,' said Neill, extending his hand.

'Doctor Fife,' nodded the entrepreneur, indicating that a handshake would not be necessary. A peculiarity of his Australian accent made 'doctor' sound like 'dog-turd'.

'I came here', said Neill with a breath, 'so we could both put our cards on the table. I don't believe either of us wants a confrontation. We both have too much to lose. As for this childish business of a Celtic artefact that allegedly . . . '

Myles Overton gave him a look as if to say, *What artefact, what cards, and what table?* 'Do I have interests in antiques? Call me a flaming dipshit – I didn't know. I don't get involved with day-to-day stuff. More with acquisitions and long-term planning, right?'

Neill had worked for him indirectly in the past, and they had been consultants to the same government committees, although they had never met. But Neill knew he had the reputation of being hands-on. 'We both know what's been going down,' he said.

'I don't know Jack Shit, mate. Suppose you tell me?'

'Dave Doom was at the Stepping Stones School disguised as one of the assistants, and before that at the Live Show, and even Strategic Marketing.'

'Tell Dave Doom to come up,' Myles Overton said into a machine on his desk. And when Dave Doom did, 'Were you at that school and those other places, you drongo?'

'I don't know what Dr Fife's on about,' said Dave Doom sounding like a bad actor reading from a worse script. 'I was home in bed, watching television.'

'Dave has not been too chipper,' Myles Overton said. 'Got pecked by a poisonous bird.'

'There are no poisonous birds.'

'You've never been to bloody Oz, mate. Everything's poisonous there.'

'Also, Linden Richmont was at the Centre for Alternative Healing, of which you own an undisclosed percentage. And she got to Nuala Greenwood in prison.'

'Tell Linden Richmont to come up,' Myles Overton said into the machine. 'Politely!' But Linden had bags under her eyes and fidgeted with the ends of her hair. She said she had worked hard to succeed in the alternative-healing business, and her position at the Centre owed nothing to her uncle's stake in it. She said that Nuala had been her friend, and there wasn't a law about people visiting their friends in prison.

'Well, I'm bloody well glad we cleared that up,' Myles Overton said sarcastically. 'Or maybe there's something else my people can help you with?'

'Tracey Dunn. When she left Strategic Marketing, you had her followed.'

'Linden?' Myles Overton asked.

'Strategic Marketing is not part of the group – just a sole supplier.' Linden said mechanically.

Myles Overton beamed at her as though his point was proved. Linden added that she didn't think there was a law against trying to trace employees who suddenly absconded, possibly with sensitive documents or information. Besides, there was reason to be concerned about Tracey Dunn. According to her personnel file she was emotional and prone to delusions. Strategic Marketing only kept her on because Peter Goodlunch had a soft spot for her. A psychologist, Linden was sure, would understand, she told Neill. And just for an instant, their eyes met.

'I still say she was followed,' Neill said, looking at Myles Overton, not Linden.

'You can bet on it, Doctor Fife, that when I have some bastard followed, they bloody well stay followed.' He exchanged glances with Dave Doom at this point, and Dave Doom for all his robust appearance changed colour like a frightened squid.

'Look,' said Neill, 'nobody likes confrontations. As you say, pieces of some old relic are of no interest to you. Even *we* only started down that track because of the Karen Greenwood case. Maybe we could work something out.'

'I like confrontations,' said Myles Overton. 'I hate working things out.'

'There are things', Neil ventured, 'that, if the authorities knew about them, they would—'

Myles Overton's shriek of mirth sounded like a Japanese 4X4 driving over a dingo. 'Don't bother bringing those dipshits into it,' he sniggered. 'They know which side their bread's buttered on. But if you want to talk turkey, that's something else again. My guess is you came to cut a deal, and nobody knows you're here, right? Mates wouldn't approve, is my guess. But then, it isn't the first time you cut a deal, is it? Like

Launceston, in the summer of '84? Or am I getting my bloody facts mixed up?'

Neill started, for Myles Overton seemed to know more than should have been possible. There were, as Neill had told his wife, the super-model, aspects of his life he did not talk about. The events surrounding Karen's disappearance for example. Or why Oswald Hawthorne collected tin-openers. 'But whatever you do,' he told her, 'never mention Launceston, or the summer of '84. That way lies madness, or worse.'

The truth was, after Karen's disappearance, Neill threw himself into his work. Even at an early age he knew he must become an expert on the human mind and motivation. Many were the white rats that gasped out their meagre existence in the service of Neill Fife's quest for knowledge – or success. Many were the cats that had things stuck in their heads. By the summer of '84 Neill had gone further than anyone before him, and penetrated deeper into the mysteries of consciousness. Yet still the final breakthrough proved elusive. He ate only Mars bars and dill-pickle sandwiches and lived the life of a recluse. But one day the Head of Department made his way down to the laboratories where Neill was working, in the lowest levels where few had occasion to go. He was fascinated, yet finally appalled, by what he saw.

'You've gone too far,' he told Neill, looking at the rows of specimen jars, the strange apparatus, and the unusual chemicals, 'and penetrated too deep. You leave me no alternative. This matter must be raised with the Senate – and perhaps with the funding authority itself.'

That night Neill walked the streets of Launceston. He took drink after drink, first in the saloons and then in the public bars. His mind was in a whirl. Everything he had worked for could be swept away by pettiness and folly – and that was a possibility Neill was not prepared to contemplate. 'He leaves me no alternative,' he confided to a shadowy figure who happened to join him on the park bench where he at last slumped down, exhausted and weak with emotion and alcohol.

'Bosses, eh?' said the shadowy figure, for all the world like an ordinary Saturday-night drunk. 'They're all the same. Who needs them? Don't talk to me about bosses!'

'I give him a scientific breakthrough. He gives me Sunday-school ethics. To Hell with him! He's a small-minded bastard. He can't accept that the over-riding purpose of science is to improve the human condition, and if sacrifices have to be made, so be it.'

'Your work. Sounds pretty important,' slurred the drunk, exuding a cloud of admiration and vaporized White Horse.

'Through it, I am convinced consciousness can at last prevail over circumstance, and the gap between intention and action can finally be closed, so that *akrasia* becomes no more than a Greek word. There are just a few more experiments to do, and the cats are already on order.'

'But your man is kicking up about it?' the drunk guessed.

'Aspects of my work might be considered controversial. I could be brought before the ethics committee.'

'Perhaps I might be of assistance,' said the drunk, his voice changing subtly. 'For nobody is quite what they seem, and it's never too late to cut a deal.'

'I'll drink to that,' Neill said.

'Mine', said the drunk, 'is a double.'

It had all been many years ago. A person can easily make a mistake in his recollections of a night when he became blind drunk and ultimately passed out on a park bench. There is nothing unusual, Neill had thought many times, about meeting itinerants on park benches, and no reason to think they are more than they seem. Still less to connect them with the half-forgotten legend of Leatherwing, which itself may have been distorted through immemorial re-telling, or have no basis in fact at all. Again, what happened to the Head of Department could easily have been accidental.

'I've always said', insinuated Myles Overton, 'that success is bought at a price.'

'I don't know what you're talking about,' said Neill, with a sense that he was losing the initiative.

'Only that you once had a bit of a falling out with your boss. But I heard it sorted itself quite nicely. Poor bastard got ill, I heard, and his job went to you, and you got the funding you were so bloody desperate for. All in the bloody past, anyway, eh? Like your Karen Greenwood. Let bloody sleeping dogs lie, right?'

But Neill was already unable to recall quite why he had come here, and besides, he was becoming oppressed by the idea of something darkly familiar moving many storeys below them. Something that made a confrontation with Myles Overton seem like an audience with the late Mother Teresa of Calcutta. 'I think we've both made some useful points,' he said to Myles Overton edgily. 'Perhaps now we understand each other a little better – which was the main purpose of my calling on you. But you're a busy man, and a busy man has many demands on his time.'

Myles Overton inclined his head. Dave Doom and Linden Richmont inclined theirs, although in Linden's case, Neill thought she again looked at him meaningfully. She looked like someone who needed someone to talk to. Someone who was realizing they had gone further than they ever wished to go. But Linden Richmont's problems were Myles Overton's affair, and perhaps it was best to leave Myles Overton to his own affairs, and not enquire into them too deeply. Meanwhile, Neill thought, I have no alternative. I must go to the Corryvrecken, and face whatever is waiting to face me.

'He's scared,' Myles Overton said when Neill had gone.

'I agree with you,' said Dave Doom, swallowing.

'He's just feeling alone,' said Linden Richmont.

'I wonder,' Neill asked the receptionist before he handed back his security tag, 'could I use your toilet?' She indicated where, with one hand. The request was not unfamiliar.

135

Karen's and Triona's parents always felt Neill, of all the kids, could be trusted. They were not overkeen on any of their daughters' friends. They had their little conceits, such as Karen's mother claiming to be from the oldest family in Britain, but it was their nightmare that Triona or Karen might meet someone with a hidden agenda, and the worst might happen. Besides Karen, although full of fierce energy, was delicate. She had chest infections and asthma, so she had to carry a tube which she squirted into her mouth. They did not like her being out at night. Her father did not like Damien and Oswald, who wore their hormones on their sleeves and could never contain themselves. Evan was too quiet and obsessive, but Neill was respectful and decorous – to be honest, all the parents liked Neill.

'He's more mature than the others – he thinks things through,' said

Karen's mother, although really she liked Neill because he would talk to her about long-dead Celtic enchantresses.

'Certainly more than Damien – bloody little show-off,' said her father, who liked the intelligent way Neill could discuss abstruse legal distinctions.

'Certainly more than Evan Hall – there's something very funny about that one,' agreed her mother, even though she herself was funnier than Evan would ever be.

'Mind you, he's still a radical. He still talks about world peace, a united Ireland, and animal rights.' As a successful lawyer, Karen's father could not be expected to be in sympathy with Neill's political views. 'On the other hand they're like that at his age. At least he's a realist, and believes in change from the inside.'

Although her father never knew it, Karen, like Chantal, did not believe in change from the inside. She believed that a pig might go into a hamburger factory with the idea of provoking change from the inside, but that the pig would do well to be circumspect. Neill thought that open resistance was futile – one would be discredited and made an object of derision. Sophie thought the important thing was education, which compounded truth with humanity; truth, she said, was like potassium, too reactive to survive in an uncompounded form. Dawn at first felt the key was women; that men had screwed things up – in many cases, also screwed women up – and some other gender ought to be given a chance. Later she thought the key was children. Like Chantal she went where Neill could not follow, and they fell out for many years. What nobody knew, because of Neill's easy manner, was how much Karen really meant to him.

'Neill Fife could be good for Karen – in the long term,' said her parents. Even during the most outrageous teenage escapades, they clung to that. But when their worst nightmares were realized, they clung to nothing, not even Triona, nor Coldharbour itself. Karen's mother ceased even to cling to life, but spoke to her daughters out of a rowan tree, and then was heard no more. Karen's father received the offer of a high-salaried post in Melbourne. The name of Myles Overton was not mentioned although this was the city in which the entrepreneur founded his original business. Soon he too was seen no more. Triona wrote a letter on the 28th of each month, saying that she still thought of him.

But it was increasingly difficult to do so. His letters back were hollow and stilted, as if he wanted to forget he had ever lived.

136

The police thought that Oswald was the last person to see Karen, but there was another person. At that time Neill possessed a motorbike. It was only a BSA Bantam 175, but he maintained it himself and he and Karen used to ride it out as far as Lulworth Cove in the West, or up to London if the weather held. People may laugh at this, but without the Bantam 175, would the Honda Benley have appeared in the form it did? Yet in a narrative concerned primarily with moral instruction, it is pointless to debate the merits of two under-powered and now out-dated motor cycles. In any case Neill, like Oswald, saw an unmarked car, although he did not get a good look at the dark figure Oswald said held Karen in the rear seat, because he was already on his way to fetch the Bantam 175.

The car was neither a Volvo nor a Ford nor any type recognizable to Neill yet it lacked neither power nor handling. Once he cut through the country lanes to make contact, he needed all his concentration to stay with it and yet keep out of sight. The driver took the winding roads at speed, swinging well over to the right on left-hand bends and intermittently losing the rear wheels. Neill leaned the Bantam into the same curves and held his place. But as the roads opened out – two small roundabouts and then the dual carriageway – the advantage was lost. 'You need a BMW for this type of job,' he thought. They would have lost him as they passed Oakhills, but they stopped for fuel at the petrol station at the start of the Ridge Way. Neill pulled the Bantam off the road as far from the overhead lights as he could. Beyond the trees, unsuspecting villages stretched out along the dark countryside. But the petrol station was its own isolated world. He watched as one figure, indistinct, remained with Karen in the back seat while the other two purchased essentials at the kiosk. He could get close enough to hear them talk. But it was clear they were only assistants and had been fed some kind of a line. They seemed convinced they were working for the authorities and Karen suffered from a rare disease which, if details of it leaked out, would cause unnecessary panic and despair. They spoke as if the girl had accompanied them on a voluntary basis, for they could not guess what hold their companion had over her.

'She needs to be taken to a secure facility, where she can do no harm to herself or others,' the assistants said.

'It's ultimately for her own protection. She knows that as well as anybody.'

'She's got some disorder of the mind – a rare imbalance of the belief system. It makes her think the Tuatha de Dannaan are only sleeping, and the fate of the world is in the balance. Worse, the authorities say it can be spread from person to person by genetically altered midges and bed bugs, perhaps released by an unfriendly power. Without proper containment, there's every chance of an epidemic.'

'If word got out, no flying insect could count itself safe. There'd be a national outcry. No – the authorities are acting for the best. When we took this business on, we knew the risks. But at least what we're doing is in the public interest.'

'I don't like the look of that bloke over there in the motorbike helmet, though. If you ask me, he's up to something. Shall we bash his head in with a piece of flint, or just floor the throttle and lose him at the next roundabout?'

'Better ask the guv'nor. This is his show, not ours.'

They spoke, Neill thought, as though acting in good faith, but the plea of official sanction has masked far greater crimes. He could equally well believe all three of them were sharing an elaborate fantasy built around their compulsion to kidnap and perhaps murder a sixteen-year-old girl. In all probability they themselves had been bitten by genetically altered mosquitoes and contracted a mind disorder. Or, they were hired by someone who had. But he was distracted from further speculation because the third conspirator, who he thought was guarding Karen in the car, suddenly came round from behind and struck him violently on the side of the head with a solid object. Out of sight of the kiosk, he was dragged into the trees behind the forecourt, and left as if to die from blood loss, hypothermia and skull breakage.

'It's for his own good,' the assistants said. 'Or at least the good of the community, which is the same thing.'

He who struck the blow was silent, but Neill was afterwards saved in a peculiar way. Damien, always a Jack-the-Lad, had got one of the sisters whose name need not be mentioned to go to bed with him by means of colourful stories about old Celtic heroes and countless top-ups of hogweed ale. He chiefly did this to offend Chantal and show he was a person without a conscience. But on the stroke of midnight the sister suddenly sat bolt upright and said, 'Where's Neill?'

Damien, still sleeping, answered in a voice not his own, 'Karen has vanished on the night of her sixteenth birthday, and things will never be the same again. But Neill is dying at the end of a rainbow. We must go to him, for he needs our help.'

Neill's life was saved by his BSA Bantam. Now that the manufacturer is defunct, libel laws cannot prevent the observation that they all had extremely leaky crankcases because the two parts of the casting were joined vertically rather than horizontally, as in Japanese equivalents. Consequently, everyone who knew Neill was familiar with the rainbow-coloured oil signature the BSA Bantam confided to the surface of whatever road it travelled along. Following this trail, it was no trouble to find the now deserted petrol station, and Neill was quickly placed in the recovery position to make sure his airway was clear. But when he woke up in a bandage, there was something important about Karen and the grey car that he could never quite remember. Was he the last to see her alive? And exactly what did he see? It was thought best to leave Neill's part in the affair out of the statements made to the police, as it would only confuse them.

'If I get another bike,' said Neill, 'it will be a Honda Benley.' In fact the next bike he bought was a BMW, which he never rode. Like other successful forty-year-olds, he thought that when he laid his money down he was buying back his youth. But he forgot that his youth was a draughty Bantam with a leaking crank-case. This great purring machine was a kind of illusion. He never rode it at all, but when the time came to go north and try to salvage something out of the ruins of his quest for the last fragment, he suddenly felt a sense of occasion. He climbed into custom leathers and astride the shiny German tourer like an iron-age chieftain taking battledress and pony.

'I will meet you at St Elmo's Cove on the night of the sixth,' he told Tracey Dunn by mobile telephone when he finally managed to get hold of her after the two jet-skiers convinced her of their credentials.

He had to hold the receiver away from his ear when they exchanged explanations, and she let him know what she thought about his handling of the situation. 'Life is a rimless wheel,' he told her, 'rolling down a traceless track. So far, my achievements have been the opposite of what I intended, but I can only do what I can.' Soon Coldharbour was a dot on the horizon, and Neill knew that if and when he saw it again he would not have grown any younger.

137

When Neill reached St Elmo's Cove there was spray in the air, the fishing fleet had remained in harbour and Tracey Dunn was waiting for him by the old breakwater, the fresh breeze in her hair and accusation in her eyes.

'Haven't you done enough damage?'

'I've done my best,' he said with unusual humility.

'You could do better by just staying out of it. Anyway, my pearl is lost, and that's that. Linden Richmont's been here, but I told her the truth, because what's the use? I gave a present to my boss, he gave it back, it got thrown into the Corryvrecken. These things happen every day. She seemed all right. She said she knew what I must think of her, but she wanted me to know she would help if she could.'

'It's a trick. Linden Richmont is loyal to Myles Overton.'

'Well – at least two people think she is – you and Myles Overton. If you ask me, he didn't know she was here. But what's my opinion worth?' She looked at him, brimming with misery. The time since Peter Goodlunch collided with a row of Wimpview houses had weighed heavily upon her. Her cheeks were hollow and her clothes had not been ironed. She kept looking over her shoulder as if expecting Dave Doom to be there. Neill wondered if he ought to put his arms around her. But that moment was gone. They went for a coffee at the quayside café, and he told her that he intended to brave the Corryvrecken, and do the best he could.

He would have said more, but they were approached by a poor fisherman and his little daughter who had been washed ashore in a basket only recently and whom the fisherman and his wife had decided to bring up as their own, as commonly happens in remote seafaring communities. 'I'm pleased to meet you,' Neill said when they had introduced themselves. 'We're strangers here. I need help with some recovery work offshore. I need to speak with the owners of your most powerful trawlers. For engines, they will need four-hundred-horsepower Caterpillars, and they must be equipped with underwater scanning devices, sonar, cable drags and unmanned submersibles. Perhaps even this will not be enough, for I scarcely need to tell you the reputation of the Corryvrecken.'

'Maybe we can help you, and maybe we cannot,' said the fisherman, although at the mention of the Corryvrecken, he shuffled uneasily from foot to foot. 'But first we must welcome and entertain you in the proper manner. For you need not think your coming here went unobserved. The other villagers have asked me to receive you as honoured guests. Tonight, you must know, is the eve of the day when, according to the old stories, St Patrick embarked from this very spot when he went to invade Ireland. That, indeed, is why our village is called St Elmo's Cove. For we hold that St Elmo was St Patrick's original name, and that he altered it so as to sound more Irish. Be that as it may, I am to extend the time-honoured welcome to a stranger at this season, and challenge you to the traditional curragh race. For it is in this way we celebrate the abiding harmony and goodwill between different peoples of the Celts in Ireland, as a result of the saint's historic voyage and his meeting with your namesake Niall Mor, High King of Erin at that time and ancestor to the proud O'Neills so prominent in the island's history. Choose which villager you wish to compete against, and your boat and equipment will be prepared for you by sunrise. But tonight we must feast, and re-tell the old legends.'

Realizing that their best means of gaining acceptance was to comply with this unusual tradition, Neill and Tracey sipped the local potheen by firelight. And as the flames made shadows dance among them, as if they sat amid the joyful capering of the Tuatha de Dannaan themselves, the most accomplished storytellers in the village were quick to let them have details of what passed between St Patrick and Niall Mor, for they had not encountered this narrative before in any intelligible form.

St Patrick (revealed the accomplished storytellers) was a Welshman, who hated pride and greed, and said wealth lies not in what you have, but in what you do not need. The sword that hung by his side was long as the steering-oar of a curragh, and the book he held in his hand was thicker than the mattress in a Glasgow brothel. It was from St Elmo's Cove that his armies embarked, and a great dun stone was erected to commemorate the occasion, and it was upon the headlands of Wexford, Cobh and Kinsale that the watchfires were lighted in order to communicate to the Irish and their chieftain Niall Mor, who was reputedly high in the counsels of the Tuatha de Dannaan, that a threat had been raised up against the security of their eastern seaboard.

Fierce were the armies that faced each other across the glens of Killarney that day (explained the accomplished storytellers) and fierce would have been the battle that was fought. However, Niall Mor was in essence a peaceful individual, despite the many deaths for which he was responsible. 'On this fine day,' he said, 'when the sun is standing high in the sky, and the grass is lying low in the meadows, it seems a pity for so many to die and be killed, when the issue between us might be resolved so much more simply.'

'I'll be needing to know what you have in mind,' said St Patrick warily. 'For I'm not about to fall for any of your Irish tricks.'

'Only this,' replied Niall Mor. 'That we take stout curraghs of the traditional design, and each choosing our six ablest boatmen, we race three times round the Isle of Blasket, and through the treacherous Blasket Sound, as the appointed course will show. To the winner goes the soul of Ireland for all eternity, but as for the loser . . . '

'I begin', answered St Patrick, 'to get the picture.'

Accordingly, two boats were prepared for the contest. Fresh thole pins were fitted to take the strain of the oarwork, the ribs of ash and elm were doubled fore and aft, the leather hides that bound them oiled with linseed and lard, and the boltropes winched in until they hummed like harpstrings. Finally, the great rowan branch of the Tuatha de Dannaan was reared up as a figurehead in Niall Mor's boat, while St Patrick opted for an equally substantial cruciform structure.

Fierce was the curragh racing that took place on that day, and avid the competition between two equally matched crews! The oars bent like rushes as powerful backs strained upon them, and the sails bellied like bagpipes in the vigorous wind. However, as they neared the end of the third circuit and entered the notorious waters of Blasket Sound, the honours were close to equal, and the game could go either way.

'Lighten the boats!' the cry went up, and there is no doubt every moveable item was thrown into the sea at that point, and some of the rowers were so caught up in the spirit of the event that they plucked the rings from their fingers and the very teeth from their jaws to help reduce weight. But the boats still ran bow by bow, with great bones in their mouths as they surged up the narrow channel of the Sound. Finally Niall Mor, in a fury of competitiveness, threw caution to the winds and tore out of the bows the heavy rowan branch which they had to invoke the protection of the Tuatha de Dannaan, and flung it into the boiling tide with a shout of defiance.

Immediately, the lighter curragh began to draw ahead, and St Patrick, raging with frustration, quickly laid hands on his own figurehead with the intention of lightening his boat in the same way. Alas, it was a fragment of the True Cross, made of cedar wood, and it would not budge. When Niall Mor noticed he had won, he prepared himself to cut St Patrick's head off, as their bargain allowed him to do. But with Niall, everything was pride. He had not really the heart to decapitate someone who had run him such a hard-fought race, for he felt St Patrick had suffered enough by being beaten, and cutting off his head would only add to his troubles.

'Go in peace,' said Niall Mor. 'For there is room in Ireland for both of us, and our two armies, and although I won, you might say I threw overboard my principles to do so, whereas you stood by yours, even though it meant defeat.' But St Patrick secretly knew that he tried to throw the cross overboard, but could not get it loose from the structural woodwork, and in his heart he felt compromised and deprived of the moral high ground.

When Neill and Tracey heard this stirring tale of competition and forbearance, they were glad to be part of its continuing tradition by racing round the Isle of Scarba, which was more convenient for St Elmo's Cove than Blasket, although also about ten times more hazardous. It was therefore quickly concluded that the race would take place the following sunrise. Because it was their privilege to choose their adversary they looked around the little circle of villagers, but soon saw that there was one who held himself somewhat back from the firelight, and mingled his dark form amongst the encircling shadows.

'In such seamanlike company, what could be harder than to choose a worthy opponent for tomorrow?' said Neill, raising his tankard of potheen in a ceremonious way. 'Some of you are so mightily muscled in chest and arm that we're afraid of suffering a defeat of such ignominy it would be impossible to bear. Yet those of you who are older and less physically powerful seem wily in the ways of the sea. Doubtless you know secret channels and swatchways, rips and eddies that can be taken advantage of only by consummate local knowledge. Nevertheless a choice must be made, for otherwise dishonour would fall on all. Therefore we choose as our rival the person to whom I offer this cup of potheen. May the best crew win! But more than that – may we row a fierce and creditable race that will do honour both to the participants and the spectators.'

When they heard this generous speech the villagers applauded unrestrainedly, clashing their tankards together with a loud convivial sound. But when they saw Neill had selected Black Jack McTavish, some of them muttered seriously to each other. They were too polite, and had too great a sense of occasion, to make dispute of the matter. Yet they knew what they knew. 'He has a bad reputation among us', they said to each other, 'for stand-offishness and ill temper. It's said he killed a man in his youth, and kept bad company. Well, maybe those days are over, and when all is said and done, if he is the choice, he is the choice. Let's have another drink, and then we'll up and prepare the boats.'

138

For those who have not seen it on the Myles Overton Leisure Channel, the art of racing boats at sea is governed by a few simple rules which require a competitor to sail as close to his or her rival as possible, and then – giving a great shout of *Starboard!* – crash into them. Starboard, like port, is a specialist term employed in the maritime environment and under most circumstances the two words can be used interchangeably. Of course none of this needed explaining to Neill, who had been no stranger to the sport in the years when he was seen at major events with supermodels and the tabloids dubbed him the Playboy Professor. It also didn't need explaining to Black Jack McTavish, who was oblivious to rules of any kind. Besides, curragh racing is not like yacht racing, and curragh racing through the Sound of Scarba and the Corryvrecken is like no other sport ever devised by man, and should only be undertaken when certain death is the desired outcome.

'Do you mind telling me what you're doing?' Neill asked Tracey when she tried to get into the boat.

'I'm coming with you, of course.'

'In case you hadn't noticed, it's blowing half a gale from the South-west, there are no lifejackets and I'm about to race a fifteen-foot cockle-shell through the Corryvrecken against a psychotic Scotsman. At the risk of being brutal, this is no place for any lovesick secretary.'

But Tracey was tired of not being taken seriously, and spoke as forcibly as he had ever heard her, the Orcadian accent coming through now she was close to home:

'Lovesick? I like that fine – I really do! Coming from someone who made a pass at someone just because we were put up in a double room last night. Coming from the person who got us into this mess in the first place. Maybe you've forgotten I was bred and born in the Northern Isles, and was handling small boats in the tide-rips of the Pentland Firth when your idea of adventure was a raft race across the ornamental lake at Coldharbour.'

But when they saw the villagers were all looking at them, they realized this was no time for a quarrel. Neill was also aware he needed all the help he could get. Their opponent, who was spitting on his fingers and flexing his oars in a peculiarly baleful and menacing manner, was evidently not going to be a pushover. And unless they made a decent fist of the affair, it was unlikely they would receive the help they needed from the simple fishermen of the village.

Furthermore, the Corryvrecken is not a place to be trifled with. For example, Fionn Mac Cummail had once for a wager anchored three nights in its stream – but his boldness cost him dear. The first night he had used a chain of purest silver, but this snapped as the ebb reached its greatest spate, and his boat was swept nearly to disaster. The second night a chain of pure gold was employed, but this gave way when the flood reached the height of its flow, and again the destruction of the vessel and the annihilation of its owner were narrowly avoided.

The third night, as might be guessed, rope woven from the hair of a virgin was employed. But nothing is what it seems, and Fionn Mac Cummail was deceived about the love life of the person he had the hair from. Some say a marriage and the fate of a kingdom turned on this matter – but it is a long story and adequately dealt with by the *Mabinogion* or similar books. The rope parted, suffice it to say, compromising the safety of Fionn's craft to the extent that he was lucky to make it out of the wreckage and scramble ashore through the cavernous inlet that is, to this day, known as Fingal's cave.

Perhaps catastrophe was inevitable even had the supplier of the rope's raw material been more prudent. Yet Neill Fife once pointed out that in former times contraception was less well understood and the loss of virginity was frequently associated with pregnancy, which reduced metabolic calcium, creating brittleness in nails, teeth, and hair. Perhaps, Neill argued in his seminal paper, dietary supplements could be used in future attempts on the Corryvrecken. 'But count me out!' Writing those words ten years ago, how could he have known that one day, with a secretary from a strategic marketing company by his side, he would have to confront his greatest fear?

'Ready?' came a great shout, breaking into the reverie of anyone who had been considering the history and reputation of the Corryvrecken.

'Ready!' confirmed the oarsman in the black curragh, and the two oarspeople in the white curragh.

And at once the race was started in the traditional manner, by slapping a huge halibut on the surface of the water to make a report like a gun going off.

Fierce indeed was the curragh racing that took place on that day! Well matched the two crews turned out to be, taking into account that Black Jack McTavish was on his own and both Neill and Tracey had at least some skills with a small boat. Nevertheless the tides are wild in the Corryvrecken, and if one breaking sea slopped a hatful of water over the weather bow, then a hundred did so, and they were not small hats either.

Despite all their efforts, by the third circuit of the island the two crews were still level-pegging. As the little craft dipped and tumbled through the Sound for the last time with great bones in their mouths, the cry of 'Lighten the boats!' went up from all sides. At this, Neill realized that the race had reached a crucial point. He laid hands on their figurehead, which comprised the beautifully sculpted skull and antlers of a fallow deer brought from Coldharbour on the offchance they might be challenged to a curragh race or anything similar, and hurled it into the boiling tide.

Everybody expected Black Jack McTavish to follow suit and throw everything movable over the side of his own boat – even to rip out the thwarts, as well as the great rowan branch he was using as a figurehead. Instead, a strange thing happened, as he rapidly changed into a *gruaghre*, which is a species of eighteen-foot-tall ogre largely confined to the highlands of Scotland, and broke the mainmast with his knee. Then he snatched up the rowan branch, and rather than cast it into the sea brought it down promiscuously on Neill, Tracey, and their boat, damaging their skulls and staving in the bottom of the frail craft so that it sank deep into the fretful waters, never to rise again.

All this happened in the space of a few moments and afterwards Black Jack McTavish denied having turned into a *gruaghre* and the police believed him. But that was of no help to Neill and Tracey, who thought their last moments had come.

139

There is a river at the bottom of the sea, though few have traced its mysterious course, nor steered between its vast and overarching banks. When they had been stove in by a *gruaghre*, Neill and Tracey felt it was all over for them, and who can blame them if they experienced a kind of relief?

As they sank beneath the boisterous swell, the ocean closed about them as cold and close as a hangman's hood. Water pouring into their lungs was initially a source of great oppression, but as time went on this became easier to put up with, as most things do. Weighed down by their heavy equipment, they sank through changing layers of green colourless light, and then through changing layers of darkness. They clung to each other's clothes and bodies as they travelled downwards.

In his confusion Neill may have breathed 'Karen' or Tracey 'Peter', although there was nothing erotic about the love they felt.

Dying together, they thought, brings people closer than living together.

When they reached the bottom of the ocean they found themselves on the banks of the aforementioned large river. It was still not easy to breathe, but because the water in those parts is oxygen-rich from the mineral upwellings of the deep ocean, and because they had a positive attitude, they managed to get by. Perhaps, indeed, Neill's pioneering work at Launceston had finally paid off, and they had found a way of making consciousness prevail over circumstance as, according to Neill, it is always able to do. But at the time he was more inclined to think their sensations were the result of being hit on the head by the *gruaghre*. He surmised they were experiencing the final chaotic flickerings of a disconnected brain stem, but they might as well make the best of things while they could.

Being underwater, it was impossible to make a fire or employ any easy means of getting dry, although they found their stove-in boat nearby and managed to patch it up with some waste material. Neill said it would be best to set off down-river and deal with problems as they presented themselves. They launched the boat from a small sandy cove, balancing it uneasily with their oars as it twisted in the current.

Before long they were progressing cautiously through the headwaters. The banks, with their great burgeonings of kelp and laminaria and sea lettuce or *ulva lactuca*, began to draw further apart. Simultaneously the visibility cleared, and they saw unsuspected islands in the river that was at the bottom of the sea, each with its own distinctive pattern of hollows and hills, and occasional signs of habitation.

'Perhaps', said Tracey, 'there are people here, and they'll be able to help us.'

140

Yet as they approached the first island slantwise across the powerful current, it appeared the boot might be on the other foot. The islanders could already be heard crying out for help themselves, and tearing at their clothes in a distraught fashion. 'Help us!' they could be heard to cry, when Tracey and Neill were close enough for words to be distinguished. 'For our princess is becoming invisible, and we don't know what to do.'

Using all the skill at his disposal, Neill guided the little curragh up a shallow inlet and twisted the painter around a convenient outcrop. Blue flowers grew on the island and small flightless bats hopped in and out of the vegetation. To all appearances it was an earthly paradise, and yet a terrible sadness gripped its inhabitants. 'Our princess', they explained, 'is the creature we love most in the world. Imagine our consternation that we're becoming unable to see her! Yet she's to be married tomorrow night, and everyone will be there. Something must be done, but we fear all avenues have been explored!'

Indeed, it seemed no-one could account for the girl's lack of opacity, nor discover who was to blame for it. Her father, banging his forehead to show how solid it was, said: 'There's never been any invisibility on my side of the family.' Her mother only sighed, and looked into the distance.

When Neill had ruled out the more obvious explanations for this problem, such as all the people simultaneously going blind, he asked to be brought into the presence of the princess. They were soon introduced to a beautiful but melancholy girl who seemed blurred around the edges, and through whose body a keen eye could unquestionably discern details of what was behind her. Behind her, and indeed in front, and on either side, were piles of offerings and gifts brought by the islanders, either because of her coming wedding, her affliction, or just through the simple love they bore her in their hearts.

'The happiness of our princess', explained the people, 'is the most priceless thing we own. Giving her our possessions simply enhances their value by increasing the happiness she experiences.'

Neill thought that the princess did not look very happy at all, and was getting less happy and less visible by the minute. An idea occurred to him. 'You!' he said. 'And you, and you! Fetch valuable commodities! Pearls, lapis lazuli and ambergris, as quickly as you can.' Sure enough, when these were presented to Neill and he presented them in turn to the princess, Tracey was amazed to see that she immediately became less visible even than before, whereas the pearls, lapis lazuli and ambergris became more definite and distinct in proportion.

'It's clear', Neill explained, 'that the gifts you're giving your princess are usurping her visibility, and detracting from the identity that should rightfully be hers. In exalting her as an icon, you're diminishing her as a human being, and that's the meaning of what's happened. Everyone should beware of giving gifts to those they love, lest the same thing occurs!'

Instead of being grateful for this analysis, the islanders appeared inconsolable. 'If we stop giving her gifts, our princess would stop loving us, and how could we go on?'

'The trouble is', said Neill, 'you've come to value yourselves only by the value of your gifts, and believe others value you in the same way. It's a hard one to solve – but perhaps there's a way. There is one thing which can help you – for it came from Caryddwen's cauldron – and which restores all things, even a person's lost self-esteem. Unfortunately it was thrown into the Corryvrecken due to a misunderstanding. To a casual observer it would seem like a small ring with a pearl in it, but appearances can be deceptive, as I know to my cost. If you direct us to it, I'll certainly come back and do what I can for the girl who's becoming invisible.'

The princess looked at him with a wan smile, but the islanders thought this was a fair offer. They said they were not themselves aware of anything fitting the description. But, they said, the people on the next island were nearer the mouth of the river, and it was highly possible that they would have news of it.

'This information is more valuable than you know,' Neill told them. 'If it leads to what we seek, you will hear from me before sunset.' With that, he and Tracey pulled out into the stream, leaving the people wailing and groaning behind them, but a little less than before, because hope heals all.

141

As they drew near to the second island they could again see a large crowd gathered on the foreshore. Once again, although the flower-fringed coastline with its tumbling rocks and shady rills was the quintessence of scenic beauty, they were able to make out a terrible wailing and crying.

'Help us,' wailed the people of the second island as soon as the curragh came within hailing distance. 'For our princess has chocolate ears!'

These islanders, Neill and Tracey learnt as soon as they came ashore, had prayed fervently that their princess would be born normal. When the child was found to have chocolate ears, they became aware their supplications had been fruitless. The girl grew up with an overwhelming sense of having something to protect. Intelligent and desirable, she found her relationships dominated by the idea that even her closest friend might one day turn against her. All were regarded with suspicion, especially those who betrayed evidence of a sweet tooth.

'From the first, I felt alone,' she told Neill, when the people brought him before her to see what could be done. 'Nobody else seemed to have the same problem. Or they were better at concealing it. There were boys of course – some even seemed fascinated by my peculiarity. But this just reinforced the feelings of isolation. I became incapable of accepting that anyone could like me, or dislike me, for any other reason than my ears. But for those I thought attracted to me because of my oddity, I could feel only contempt. I know having chocolate ears does not rule out marriage and a normal life, but in practice this knowledge carries no conviction. I've become everything I hate. I resent people who believe that my condition sets me apart from others, yet no-one holds that belief more strongly than I do myself.'

'I'll do what I can,' said Neill cautiously. 'But you'll have already tried conventional treatments.'

The islanders confirmed that other experts had been brought in, travelling from as far away as California. Some took the view that the girl's mother had undergone some kind of trauma during pregnancy. While interesting, this provided no obvious solution. Apparently there were new drugs which might offer hope for people with chocolate ears, but it would be years before they were available commercially. The experts told her parents she was a very interesting case and to let them know if things got any worse.

'What, you mean if her hair turns to candyfloss?' enquired her father scornfully.

Not old enough to realize that having chocolate ears isn't funny, her friends tittered at this, and the princess ran from the room with tears scalding her face. Even the experts, although outwardly sympathetic and professional, would sometimes smirk when they thought she wasn't looking. She came to hate them worst of all because, as she saw it, her suffering was their living. Also she found their discussions irrelevant and unhelpful in the extreme.

'Do we not all, in a sense, have chocolate ears?' the psychotherapist would say to the neurologist.

'I believe not.'

Then the psychotherapist would get sulky. 'Well, I can't go into this any further until I have all the facts in front of me.' But what facts, he never explained. In the end the two of them teamed up and wrote a learned paper which they published in a learned magazine. They speculated as to whether the aetiology was primarily environmental or genetic. They called it Kornblutt Kleinstein's Syndrome, after themselves. They did not name it after the princess, even though she was the one who had it. Later they got bored and decided to follow up the case of a South American mother whose breasts, it was said, produced Coca Cola. They stopped visiting, leaving the princess to pick up the pieces of her life as best she could.

By the time Neill and Tracey arrived on the scene, there seemed little hope. Even though she had found a man who was right for her, she had lost the ability to return affection and become inward-looking and self-obsessed. 'You must help us,' said the people of the island. 'Tomorrow is her wedding day, and if a cure cannot be found, all will be lost!'

'I'm no specialist,' replied Neill. 'Also, your island lacks equipment that a modern psychiatric facility would regard as essential. The one thing that might prove effective was thrown into the Corryvrecken as a result of ill judgement and misplaced suspicion, for which I am myself partly to blame. If you can help us to find it, I'll try to do what I can.'

'That's all we can ask for,' said the islanders. 'We may have heard of what you describe, and we may not. But if you ask directions on the next island, which is nearer the mouth of the river, we're certain they'll be able to help you.'

'Thank you,' said Neill and Tracey. 'If we find what we're looking for, we'll certainly return and cure the girl with chocolate ears.'

142

With a single movement of their oars, they launched the little boat back into the current, and continued on their way. Yet with the next island as with the previous two, they were soon struck by the lugubrious carryings-on they heard emanating from the wave-lapped shore. As they drew closer they saw the islanders were tearing at their hair and breaking their possessions in grief.

'Help us!' they cried, as Neill and Tracey approached. 'For our princess has no wings!'

Sure enough, when the people led Neill and Tracey in front of the princess, they could see she was sitting naked on a rock, her knees drawn up level with her chin, her whole body freely exposed to the scrutiny of islanders and guests alike. And it was clear to all that she had no wings.

'How long has this been going on?' asked Neill, trying to avert his eyes. But it was clear that the islanders had somehow compelled their princess to behave in such an outrageous way, on such an outrageous rock. The pressure their love imposed upon her was too great, and their disappointment about the wings was too hard to bear.

At first, Neill and Tracey learnt, all had been well between the princess and the people. Her dresses were talked about with wonder, yet at charitable events she said the most normal things to the most normal people. 'In that', said everyone, 'lies her greatness.'

'It's nothing,' replied the princess, her tears flowing like meltwater. 'If I can teach people's hearts to love – my life will be complete.'

Then, slowly, they began to suspect something was wrong. Before long they hired agents to keep her under observation twenty-four hours a day, to open her correspondence and go through the contents of her waste-paper basket. They were certain she was holding out on them. 'She's got some secret, which she's either afraid or ashamed to share with us. Such behaviour, in a princess, can neither be excused nor condoned.' Imagine their dismay when, only days before she was due to be married, they learnt she had no wings. They had no alternative but to insist she went and sat on a rock, in the manner described.

When the islanders called on Neill to help them, he was a little perplexed. 'I've never come across a case like this one before. It could be that, rather than a psychologist, you require an aeronautical engineer. However, if anything can help you, one thing might, but it was thrown into the Corryvrecken to save it from jet-skiers. If you can shed any light on its whereabouts, I'll try to use its powers to best advantage.'

'If you mean the small ring with the pearl, we've heard rumours, though nothing too definite. Sometimes it seems everyone's looking for something, and if they haven't thrown it into the Corryvrecken, they've thrown it away somewhere else, and thrown their lives away with it. But because you promised to help us with the wings we'll tell you what we can. Go onwards down the river, avoiding the smaller islands and sandbars, until the banks are no longer visible on either side. There, in the open water, you may find something, or something may find you. For remember, the answer lies in the abyss, as perhaps you've known all along.'

143

'They're rambling,' Neill said when they left the third island. 'The people down here live too much through their princesses. Small wonder things go wrong. In psychology we learn that people should stand on their own two feet.'

'Outside psychology we often learn that too. But who's that on all those other islands?'

Drifting down the river that runs through the ocean's great sump, they found that it broadened into a prodigious estuary or firth, dotted with small outcrops of rock, islets and overgrown reefs from one blurred horizon to the other. As they were swept past the smaller islands, they saw no more wailing people lamenting problems with princesses. Instead, on each little bight of land there seemed to be a single person, and all were reaching out their hands to Tracey and Neill, as if in mute appeal for them to stay, or to take the occupant of the island wherever they were going.

Although the features were indistinct it was clear that those on the rocks and skerries resembled people they knew or had known, except that they appeared to be young children in colourful children's clothes, their hair combed into old-fashioned styles. There was Triona dressed to the nines for her ninth birthday party. Chantal, her face masked with mud, as she had been the day she piled up the local fox hunt on an improvised barricade, making regional news. Oswald, earnest, quiet, pretending he had shirked his homework like the others but secretly doing it on the bus. Nuala and her olive-skinned sweetheart. A chubby-faced urchin resembled Myles Overton, doing deals for fag-ends in the gutters of an unfeeling city. Linden Richmont, waiting for news of her lost parents. Evan Hall taking himself too seriously, while Sophie Greenwood waited for him in the crab orchard making daisy chains. Damien Lewis refusing to take anything seriously. Dave Doom, no time for anything because he did two paper rounds.

'Look!' said Tracey.

On a long thin ridge of rock a little Peter Goodlunch played with a plastic Porsche, but he too reached out his hand, imploringly, as they were carried past.

'Look!' said Neill.

Together, on a misty outcrop, a little boy and a little girl held hands and looked towards the curragh with longing eyes, but the eyes were those of Neill himself, and Tracey beside him, although in their childhood days they had never known each other, nor even suspected one another's existence.

What children had been carried here, to this lonely place? They were not the children who had been carried by the eighteen-wheelers, whom Sophie had mentioned to Neill when she asked him about her dream. These children wore their ordinary clothes, and had no bags or apples. 'They're the past that we betrayed by growing older,' breathed Tracey in sudden understanding. 'They're everything of ourselves that was lost in the ocean of time, because time is an ocean in which all things are lost.'

But Neill had lost Karen, and he had lived with loss for too long. He could not tear his eyes from the islands and their little inhabitants, and as each one passed, his heart seemed to break. Then, on a final twilit islet, he saw a girl with raven hair, but her head was in her hands, and something dark prevented her from raising her eyes. When Neill knew that it was Karen he caught up the anchor from the bows of the curragh and threw it overboard, expecting any minute for the boat to round up into the current as the line came taut. But after a while, when nothing had happened, he looked over his shoulder and saw the anchor floating along in their wake like an inflatable toy. Inspecting it more closely, Neill was appalled to discover that due to a design fault it had been made of cedar wood and was unsuitable for its purpose. He tried to shove it under with a boathook but to no avail, and soon they had been swept past the islands.

And the lost children with their plaintive voices were only a memory.

144

After this, Neill fell into despondency, and would not talk or lift a finger to aid the progress of the boat, despite all Tracey could say to cheer him up. 'This is my doing,' he said. 'Whatever happens to me now, it's no more than I deserve for my mistake over the ring and a thousand worse things of which the past accuses me. I saw everything in the eyes of the children on the rocks and skerries, though their words were indistinct. "You think we were drowned in time," they seemed to be saying, "but you drowned us in arrogance and cupidity, and with us, you drowned your own innocence."'

'What's gone is gone,' said Tracey. 'Our only chance is to follow the southern shore of the estuary in the hope that it rises to the level of the ocean surface, so that we can make it back to St Elmo's Cove and safety.'

'That will never happen,' said Neill, 'even if the laws of topology and fluid tectonics permitted it. I'm weighed down by guilt, and you're weighed down by me. I've always known I would one day be drawn into the abyss. But now I realize it is an abyss of my own making, and that every action I took to rise in the world made the abyss a little deeper.'

145

As if to lend emphasis to his words, looking up to windward they saw a dark ship bearing down upon them. To Neill's stricken eyes, there seemed nobody at the helm but his old Head of Department from Launceston, who had fallen suddenly ill in the summer of '84 with depression and anxiety-induced disorders, and had been unable to work again, and died. Further, it seemed to have no crew but a tremendous number of white rats mutilated in various ways or psychologically damaged from being made to go through mazes and receiving electric shocks, and cats with loose scalps. They managed the old ship handily enough, scrambling among the lower stays and hauling in the stunsails to bring their vessel up alongside the curragh. But one could see they had many wires trailing from them and were in considerable discomfort.

When Neill's eyes met those of his former Head of Department no words were needed, for each knew what was in the mind of the other. 'It's been a long time,' Neill said, trying to put things on some kind of footing.

'An eternity,' replied the former Head of Department.

'I thought you might be here.'

'I waited for you. There was no hurry – I knew you'd be along sooner or later.'

'What happened . . . I can explain. It wasn't what you thought.'

'You planned it in every detail. You knew my health was already delicate. You slept on a park bench in the cold, and picked up a genetically altered flu virus from a transient. You deliberately breathed on me – it was enough . . . '

'There were no witnesses. My breathing on you could have been an innocent act.'

'We both know you were at a crossroads that night, and you met a dark man, who gave you directions. We both know you cut a deal. Before, you were just another obsessive researcher, frustrated and starved of funds. But you were promised success, fame, and a wife who was a supermodel. It's the same old story, and it has the same ending.'

'I fell asleep on the park bench and had a bad dream. Nothing was ever proved. Besides, it was about Karen, everything was about Karen. Through my work, I thought I could get closer to where she had gone.'

'Perhaps you have. Every deal has its price, and I'm here to collect the debt.' But increasingly the helmsman of the dark ship did not look like Neill's old Head of Department at all, but like the park bench transient. Nor was even this transient what he seemed, because he came increasingly to resemble a nightmarish figure Triona had described to Neill from her dreams, except Neill needed no description, for he had dreams of his own.

'Leatherwing . . . ' Tracey said, mouthing the word.

'What would you know about—?'

'I know nothing – except what Peter Goodlunch said the night he told me his deepest fear, and why he could no longer go on working for Myles Overton.' But there was no time to go into detail because the helmsman of the dark ship at once grew outrageously tall and broke the mainmast with his knee. Suddenly they both knew that he and his crew of abused laboratory animals had come here with only one purpose, and that was to stave in Neill's and Tracey's boat, so they would be plunged into the final abyss, from which there is no return.

146

It's a bit much, Tracey caught herself thinking, after being so catastrophically stove in and sunk to the bottom of the ocean, to be sunk once again to the bottom of the river at the bottom of the ocean – and on the same day. Even in the *Mabinogion* such bad luck is rarely encountered. She thought this would be the last thought she ever had. But strangely another thought came to her as if from far off. She seemed to recollect a tiny child, pitching in a daubed wicker basket upon the ocean's broad and boisterous swell two decades ago – or a thousand years. Across that gulf of time, and through the immense gulf of water, she seemed to hear articulate speech, whose tone and intonation reached deep into her being. Whether it was the voice of the father she never knew, or the repenting mother whose only action was to put a pearl in her navel and launch her towards an uncertain and watery fate – she could never afterwards recall.

Nonetheless the words were clear enough – for they said, 'Tracey, the seals! Call the seals!' Then, although she did not feel her lips move or think even the thought of those kindly creatures who protected her when she was most vulnerable, the sea was full of whiskery faces. And as her lungs were ready to burst and anoxia or heart failure would certainly have set in, the seals' circling motion buoyed her up in a whirlpool. Neill, however, was thrown clear of this maelstrom, and she saw him sinking away and down, ready to be claimed by the abyss, as the dark ship hovered above him.

'Neill Fife!' As she called him he seemed a great distance away. But although people did not take Tracey seriously, she had her own kind of loyalty. Besides, she instinctively knew it would do her reputation no good if too many of the men in her life died violent and premature deaths.

'Leave me!' Neill's voice came back. 'There's nothing you can do – I brought it on myself.'

'I won't!' She cried, and dived after him, with the seals still weaving around her, until she caught him by the heel, and could allow the upwelling water to take them both. Moments later they were thrown bodily out into the waves, and borne with flippery speed through the tide-rips and up towards the beaches of Jura, nearly two miles from where the boat had originally sunk.

How they met there with the Great Silkie of Sule Skerry, and what reunion occurred between the huge gentle creature and the young woman he had last seen when she was a tiny golden-haired child, is recounted in a hundred different versions, and none of them loses in the telling. The moral of this story is that if one is brought up by seals, it is always worth calling out to them if one finds oneself drowning at the bottom of the river at the bottom of the sea. But also, while they are at it, it is worth asking them to recover anything one might have dropped in the Corryvrecken.

'You have already done so much,' Tracey said. 'But would it be possible?'

The Great Silkie of Sule Skerry smiled a whiskery smile, and quickly dived into the nethermost depths and amongst the clams and lobster shells, locating the trinket with very little strife.

But as he swam through the secret places of the ocean, near where the river runs along the bottom of the sea, he took the little ring and touched the princess who was becoming invisible, and she immediately presented a more opaque aspect to the eye. He touched the princess who had chocolate ears and she was miraculously cured, and the princess who had no wings suddenly found her subjects had lost their obsession in this respect, and indeed, fell to telling each other how ridiculous they had been for even expecting them. Therefore the people of those islands were very happy and praised the name of Neill Fife, whom they thought had sent a magic seal to alleviate their plight. But Neill and Tracey were even happier, when they saw that what was lost had been returned.

'I've always said', said Neill, 'that only by throwing oneself into the abyss can one escape from it.' But later he denied everything. 'What we saw and heard today', he told Tracey, 'was the result of residual brainstem activity, and can only have been caused by the blows on the head we had at the hands of the *gruaghre* and our subsequent immersion. A dream, take it from me, and a hallucination. No more.'

Tracey was a little hurt by this, since it tended to belittle her achievement in fishing him out of the depths by one heel. Besides, she reminded him, he had not thrown himself into the abyss but had been knocked into it by an eighteen-foot-high ex-Head of Department, and it was Tracey who had to throw herself in to get him out. Also, the brainstem-and-dream theory did not hold water. 'How could we both have dreamed the same thing?'

'We were both hit by the same piece of rowan branch,' replied Neill.

'And yet – nobody can deny that we have the fragment of Caryddwen's cauldron.'

'Nobody would want to,' replied Neill. 'Unless, perhaps, he were Myles Overton. Or Dave Doom.'

147

Far away, in a glass tower built to resemble the high pinnacles of Cader Idris, a sound was made that was between a roar and a shriek. The employees, toadies and hangers-on felt each individual hair on their body stand perpendicularly on end, like soldiers on parade before an unusually brutal and sadistic commander.

'How was I to know', lamented Dave Doom, 'that her stepfather was the Great Silkie of Sule Skerry? I thought he was the Old Man of Hoy.'

'You're flaming paid to know!' roared Myles Overton. 'You'll be telling me next you don't know her real father is Finbar Direach, who pulled the flaming wool over your bloody eyes by disguising himself as a long-liner. Strewth! Give me strength! Get the Hell out!'

'Am I fired?'

'You should be so bloody lucky! Get!'

X

The Dance of Leatherwing

148

When reaching the point in a story when the main characters have outwitted their adversaries and achieved their principle objectives, someone might legitimately ask, thumbing the folios, why are there so many pages still left? Surely if it's just a matter of people realizing that they have always loved each other, and getting married, it should be possible to knock it off in a couple of thousand words? Unhappily, the answer is simple. It is exactly at the point when success is within people's hands, that failure is most likely to trip their feet.

It was nearing the three-thousandth anniversary of the Tuatha de Dannaan arriving in Britain. A date to commemorate throughout the world, although like many pagan festivals, effectively hi-jacked by a later culture. Yet the date had special significance for Triona since as a Heritage Commissioner it was her responsibility to prepare a lasting monument. Only she, and perhaps Finbar Direach, knew what she had in mind, or guessed the scale and significance of her plan. Meanwhile they were on the eve of an even greater day. The last lost fragment was to be brought home to Coldharbour, and the delicate process of re-assembling Caryddwen's cauldron could begin.

'But before we pursue that arduous task,' declared Finbar Direach, when Triona met him in secret beside the ruined wishing well as the evening masked the sky with clouds, and night-frets swirled around causing him to vanish and re-appear with dream-like unpredictability, 'I will organize a great feast – for it's no more than we all deserve!' Finn confided only in Triona, but, he said, if she would give him the fragment now, he would put it with the others he already had, and that night would show himself to her companions as he really was, arrayed as befitted one who had been high in the counsels of the Tuatha de Dannaan.

'Wouldn't it be better to fix the cauldron first, and have the party afterwards?'

'That's the trouble with today's modernizing regimen,' declared Finn. 'There's no sense of occasion any more. No. We will have a feast. And it will be a feast such as will stand in the memory of those present for the rest of their waking lives, and even when they are dead they will still dream of it, so mauve and yellow flowers push up out of their graves. There will be bagpipes, and mandolins, and bodhrans, and instruments which still, today, do not even have names. The mead and the potheen will flow in unstinting quantities, nor will there be any dearth of hogweed ale. People will come in their most splendid clothes. They will wear the fine purple and the good red silk, some in designer labels and others in honest home-made garments, with accessories and ornaments to suit. But why am I telling you this, when I could be preparing the very preparations of it? Have your companions assemble by the old amphitheatre tonight at midnight, with such guests as they think proper to bring. For the person who does not get drunk and fall about in a gregarious manner tonight, will be considered less of a man (or woman) for omitting to do so.'

Triona was still sceptical. 'I'm only trying to say that for every day that passes, we have one day less. Karen, if we're to believe all we hear, remains fettered in the dungeon of Leatherwing. Linden Richmont and Dave Doom will already have told Myles Overton how things stand, and he'll know he needs to raise his game. We need to be on the look-out for some sleight of hand. I'm only trying to say there's much to do, and little time to do it.'

'The joyful heart is a salmon that leaps the weir-gates of time, and it's certain we'll carry all before us. But the matters you speak of are for tomorrow. Tonight belongs to the cittern, the pipes, the stout tankard, and the tall glass.'

'I see that like your namesake Fionn Mac Cummail you're one of those who can never let slip the opportunity for a celebration. But there's the question of food and drink. Besides, there aren't enough of us.'

'As for the food and drink, that will not be a problem. As to the company, it would be a pity indeed if we cannot make an adequate throng. In the old days, at the gatherings of the Tuatha de Dannaan, a thousand was not considered too many. Leave it to me! I was not known in some circles as the Magic Fiddler for nothing! I give my word, which can never be broken, that you'll not be disappointed.'

149

'Finn wants to have a party,' Triona told the others grudgingly, 'to thank you for what you've done. I warn you – he can be quite volatile. He's going to take care of the booze, and the invites, and nothing I can say will stop him. I think we should play along with it, but be careful not to overdo things. And look out for signs of treachery.'

Oswald did not like parties. He clearly recalled it was during a party in the amphitheatre at Coldharbour that Karen had fallen out so disastrously with Neill during a discussion about the meaning of life. And, after shrieking at him that he was incapable of making a commitment, she had rushed into the night never to be seen again except by Oswald and several times at a distance by Neill himself, in an unmarked car with a stranger. Another party at Coldharbour would surely stir up too many unhappy memories. Besides, he did not feel Finbar Direach – if he was what he seemed to be – could entirely be trusted. And if he was not what he seemed to be, then Triona couldn't. Even though it was painful for Oswald to think such a thing about the woman he had for a long time thought he loved.

'It could be dangerous,' he argued. 'Although we have the last fragment we're in a vulnerable position. Any one of us could've been followed here. Myles Overton could still make his move – and if any piece of the cauldron were stolen or damaged at this stage . . . '

'I said that to Finn,' replied Triona, 'and he said the cauldron and its components can't be stolen or damaged, they can only be given as an act of free will, which, under the circumstances, we're hardly likely to do. Still – it'll do no harm to stay on our guard.'

'Finn this, and Finn that,' said Oswald, with no charity at all in his voice for Triona's mentor. 'No good will come of it.'

'If you know something the rest of us don't – you'd better tell me,' said Triona.

'I don't know what I know. I just think Finn's up to something. We've got him the fragment – but how do we know he's who he says he is? I've seen him somewhere before. I've seen him when he was disguised as an auditor, but I've seen him somewhere before that. There's something fishy about him, with all his salmons and weir-gates.'

Triona looked at him narrowly, and said she hadn't mentioned salmon or weir-gates, which made her think Oswald himself had been up to no good. 'When I was talking to him this morning, you followed me, and hid in the bougainvillea!'

Oswald looked at his feet.

'Well,' she said, 'that settles it. You can damn well go and hide up your own bottom, because I'm off to help collect wood for the fire. We're having the party, and anyone who doesn't want to go can suit themselves.'

But the others did want to go to a party, and started capering about and clapping each other's palms in enthusiasm, and singing songs about parties, drink, and mandolin-playing. Perhaps, after being shot up in Turkmenia or dragged along the sump of the Corryvrecken, they deserved a break after all. Besides, it would remind them of the old days. What? Could any of them have forgotten?

150

Could Oswald have forgotten? He tried to remember exactly what happened at the last party they held at Coldharbour when Neill and Karen had such a terrible row, although this had been concealed from the police, for fear Neill would become the object of suspicion, particularly as he was found in a remote place and had obviously been in a struggle.

Women, and perhaps men, sometimes enjoy being the recipients of declarations of love, reflected Oswald. That was the cause of all the trouble. It is useless to point out that declarations of love do not mean anything. It is useless to observe that in saying one loves someone, one is simply making a statement about the condition of one's own endocrine system. People fond of receiving declarations of love are not thinking in terms of endocrine systems. They are thinking in terms of pledges or commitments. They are thinking of the past, of the future, and of two hearts hand-in-hand, leaping the weir-gates of time. Together, say the people who are fond of receiving declarations, we can conquer the world, and use the great whirling galaxies as frisbees in our games together. Love annihilates work, for what is done out of love is done willingly, and work is not an action but a state of mind based on the subjugation of one will to another. Love annihilates pain, for one's own suffering is of no consequence. Love annihilates age, because it cannot count.

That's a load of crap, say the people who prefer to resist fatuous figures of speech. It comes from soap-operas on Myles Overton's Leisure Channel, Hollywood epics, and cultural constructs dating back to the romances of Chrétien de Troyes in the fourteenth century, who made such a pig's ear of re-working the *Mabinogion* that for centuries people believed Britain was conquered after the siege of Troy by Brutus, who overcame a giant called Gog.

'If you can't make a commitment to me – it's over between us!' Karen had shouted.

But Neill was young and inexperienced. He was certain that if she could only follow his arguments she would agree with him, and so he tried to explain them again. 'All I need is a little time,' he said.

When people want declarations of love it is better not to be a prig, thought Oswald. If they required a critique of cultural semiotics or metalinguistic philosophy, they would have asked to borrow a copy of *Ones and Zeros* by Sadie Plant, *Mythologies* by Roland Barthes or simply Plato's *Symposium*. Karen believed the world would be destroyed by indifference, so what she was asking of Neill meant very much to her. But Neill believed the world would be destroyed by nonsense, and could not give her what she asked. She ran screaming into the night, and later Oswald, who did not like parties, was out on his own, walking back by the main road and breathing the night sky, when he saw her far off, being hustled into a long grey car by a male Caucasian of indeterminate age and appearance. He returned to Coldharbour assuming it was someone she knew, and told Neill. Neill started up his small motorbike, and by taking the country lanes he closed with the grey car on the by-pass, since it had turned right and crossed the river by the Bailey bridge – which at that time was a slow route, although improvements were made when these roads became feeders for the M25. But others said Neill and Oswald colluded in the grey car story, for, they said, Oswald always backed Neill up. They said it was more likely that Karen, after a blazing row with her lover of the kind that only two emotional sixteen-year-olds can have (but Neill denied being emotional) had been heard to threaten to strip naked and throw herself over the weir. Most likely, they said, she took the easy way out.

'But she didn't, though,' Oswald whispered to himself, thinking of the car with the number plate he could never quite remember, and the individual he had seen Karen with.

151

Myles Overton paced in his high tower, thoughts choking his mind like bindweed. A self-made man, he mused, can never relax. If he loosens his grip even for a moment, he knows how easily he can be unmade. The previous night he called his accountants together and asked how much money he had. There aren't enough of us to count it all, the accountants had said. 'Hire more accountants!' he told them. But later he fell into a fretful sleep and dreamed all the accountants were bailiffs in disguise, and when they had finished counting the money they would take it away. He awoke to find the City was jittery, and there was a message from his merchant bankers saying they would like to discuss the situation.

'When there's a bloody situation,' he faxed back, 'we'll bloody discuss it. Now get off my case!'

This all started, he thought, with Neill Fife, Triona Greenwood, and the Heritage Commission project for a lasting monument. But deep inside he knew it had started long before. Myles Overton had not always been in a position to buy and sell the futures of individuals and indeed entire nations with the stroke of a pen. When young he attempted little and achieved less. He represented himself as a self-made man but when he emigrated from Poland to Australia in the 1950s, he came from a well-to-do family and smuggled out many valuables. Biographies say he was associated with the Polish wartime resistance as a child hero. By his own account the years of Nazi occupation were spent 'in unceasing struggle against the evils of communism'. This was fine as far as it went, but although occupying German forces were accused of many things, communism was never among them. Granted, Myles Overton (then Mile Oveitsky) was young, and one flag looks a lot like another. But the rumour he belonged not to the Polish Resistance but to the Hitler Youth died hard.

After he landed in Australia, he spent several years as a courier, augmenting his income by copying the documents entrusted to him and selling them to his clients' competitors. This employment eventually brought him into contact with his compatriot Otto Bronski, Chairman of the Universal Trading Corporation, which had interests in print, leisure goods and what was later termed marketing, although then it was called buying low and selling high. Bronski wore brogues with the stitches scuffed out and a black suit made the day the Archduke Francis Ferdinand was assassinated at Sarajevo. The dandruff on his shoulders resembled snow on the branches of a rowan tree. He cared for nothing, for he knew whatever you care for eventually betrays you, either because it is not what you think it is, or because you are not who you think you are. But he had a daughter he wished to see settled, although her frocks were crumpled and she had the physiognomy of a bandicoot. 'When you care for something,' he told Myles Overton cynically, 'not only does it betray you, but you betray yourself. Therefore I am going to give you half my business, and my daughter's hand in marriage.'

Yet after the old man's death Myles Overton discovered his bride owned the other half of the business and had a stubborn streak. Walking through midnight streets when the Southern Cross was low in the sky, he struck his forehead in frustration. But on a park bench, it was rumoured that a shadowy figure came to him, proposing a shady deal. 'You may find my terms a little strange,' the shadowy figure said. 'But so long as you refrain from asking unnecessary questions and seeking unnecessary answers, we will get along fine. I've been playing a long game, and now it is nearly ended, there are some details with which you can be of help.'

When Myles Overton heard it would be necessary for him to become the richest man in the world, he readily agreed not to ask questions, and soon his wife was no longer a problem, and his name began to be mentioned in the highest financial circles. 'But for this harmless bee in his bonnet about heritage issues in the British Isles,' people said, 'he has the best business mind around.'

In the end, however, the best business mind might not be good enough. The day the final fragment came home to Coldharbour, the market-makers were running scared, and the long-awaited correction seemed imminent. Dark clouds piled over the western horizon, and even Myles Overton's football club allowed itself to be trounced four goals to nil by non-league giant-killers.

The authorities spoke of a sea-change in attitudes, the increasing importance of a pre-industrial legacy in the nation's consciousness, and shifts in public opinion in tune with the coming epoch. 'I don't give a shit about heritage issues in the British Isles!' Myles Overton shouted when he phoned them to look for support. 'There's something going on – and I want to know what!'

'Suppose you tell us,' said the authorities smoothly, and he thought he detected a subtle alteration in their demeanour.

The city analysts were more guarded, for they knew that when Myles Overton was on the ropes he was at his most dangerous. From their point of view, the issues were simple. Myles Overton's businesses were highly geared and some would say, over-extended, owing their credibility to the force of his personality. Yet it looked to them as if the group had exposed itself needlessly on a number of issues, and that there was a sustained campaign against it. For instance, an incident at the Centre for Alternative Healing cost Myles Overton grant revenue and the prospect of expanding a promising franchise. Industrial-relations problems at Strategic Marketing plc raised serious questions. The company lost a vital contract for the Heritage Commission's lasting monument, which was now slated to go ahead without involvement from the private sector. Again, the group was involved in controversies about privatization in the penal system, the distinction between armaments and leisure products, over-zealous lobbying activities, and abusing the relationship between industry and education.

The analysts took no moral stance; rather the reverse. But some women called Greenwood kept popping up in the background research. Everybody knew about the disappearance of the eldest sister, Karen, when Myles Overton was negotiating to buy Coldharbour Abbey. It was eventually taken over by the Heritage Commission and the entrepreneur instead commissioned an architectural carbuncle on an industrial estate in Wales. Everybody knew Karen's sister, the eccentric but popular Heritage Commissioner who was always being invited for interviews on *Woman's Hour*, had taken a stand against Myles Overton's expanding interests. The bottom line was: if Myles Overton was using his businesses to further some private agenda and, worst still, being unsuccessful at it, there was going to be a crisis of confidence.

'Put all that down in the reports,' said the analysts to their assistants, 'and circulate them through the normal channels. But don't you dare mention anything about cauldrons, magic seals, or General Jihad, or you'll be fired without references. Oh, and mark all the Myles Overton holdings down from 'accumulate' to 'neutral'. That way he'll be forced to buy his own stock to maintain prices, and the institutions will make some of their money back.'

As always, they were on the side of the institutions, and Myles Overton, despite his bold words, was still seen as an outsider.

152

'I shall prepare a great feast,' Finbar Direach told Triona, 'and no-one will lose face by it. My own honour, and the honour of my people, depends on doing everything correctly. It will not be the largest feast in the history of these islands, because everyone knows which feast that was. But it may well be among the most memorable!'

'So long as you keep your promise to help me reach my sister and fulfil the deadline for a lasting monument. Or I'll certainly lose face, to say nothing of my job.'

'Nothing could be easier,' Finbar Direach exclaimed. 'Why – it's as good as done!' And he began to gather what was necessary and make arrangements to improvise what could not be gathered, all the while humming an old song about the Tuatha de Dannaan coming to the islands.

When the Tuatha de Dannaan first came to the archipelago, sang Finn, the people wanted no trouble. They collected the most precious objects they had, which had been formed when the world was young. A chain whose wearer could not be disobeyed was the first, and the second was a shield nothing could penetrate. A pitcher that was never full and never empty was the third, and the fourth was a grindstone whose blades nothing could resist.

'These gifts are good,' declared the Tuatha de Dannaan. 'But we know of something better.' Shamefacedly the people brought their most valuable possession, many hundreds of them struggling beneath its vast bulk.

'That', said the Tuatha de Dannaan, when they saw the cauldron, 'is more like it.'

They knew that the cauldron had been formed before the universe was even created, and that it had contained a strange fermentation of dreams from which, when condensed due to the activities of a magic beaver, all life had sprung. But others said the cauldron was the life itself, and its walls comprehended the entirety of human existence, and people only perceived themselves as removed from it because they were removed from their true selves.

Whichever account was accurate, the Tuatha de Dannaan gave the cauldron to Caryddwen, the most trusted of their number, and ordered the preparation of a great feast. An entire forest was cut down to provide logs and kindling for the fire, and even now the area thereabouts remains destitute of trees and is called Salisbury Plain. In the centre of the cleared area they built a vast cooking hearth of granite pillars and cross-members to support the cauldron above the flames. When it was lifted in place the Tuatha de Dannaan made a portentous brew to celebrate their coming to the archipelago and got drunk, recited poetry and fell down in the traditional way. Caryddwen later had the cauldron moved to the south western peninsula, but (Finn sang) the great stone pillars of the cooking hearth stand to this day, although their purpose and origins have been widely misinterpreted.

The local people were a little disgusted by these excesses, but they counted themselves lucky not to have suffered any physical damage, and since the Tuatha de Dannaan had expressed an intention to go to Ireland, everyone thought it best to keep their head down for the time being. Only Queen Maeve of Skye nursed revenge in her heart. When much later the opportunity arose, she was quick to imprison Mannannan Mac Llyr Mac Lugh, and attempt to force from him the lesser secret of the well of dreams which he had by then concealed in a Druidical mist, and the greater secret of the recipe Caryddwen had begun brewing in the cauldron with the help of her assistant Little Gwion, and which represented the symbolic birth and rebirth of the archipelago.

'That's a good song,' Triona said, when the narrative had finished. 'But what does it mean?'

'It doesn't have a meaning – it's a song,' Finn replied.

'It refers to someone keeping someone prisoner in order to discover their secret. But I can hardly listen to it without thinking of my sister Karen, held against her will by Leatherwing.'

'Perhaps,' Finn said mysteriously, 'you should think also of your sister Nuala, who said that what most imprisons people is their need to make prisoners of others.'

'But Nuala was set free.'

'Exactly.'

153

High in his tower, Myles Overton knew as much as anyone about imprisonment. Yet there were some questions he had promised long ago he would never ask, and although he was sometimes mad, not asking those questions kept him sane. He called for Linden Richmont and said, 'I don't hold you here against your will, do I?'

She shook her head.

'Then it must be someone else.' He shook his head too, as if dreams were cobwebs one could shake free from.

'Your businesses. Haven't they been doing well?' she asked, fearing the worst. But until recently they *had* been doing well. All except for the business with the Greenwood sisters, and the fact that he was supposed to use the resources of his commercial empire to frustrate their efforts.

Efforts to do what? To restore a cauldron. But what then? According to sources that Myles Overton was not at liberty to reveal (but who would dare impose boundaries on Myles Overton's liberty?) the cauldron could destabilize the markets and affect the linearity of human history. Human history, Myles Overton thought, could go hang. But the markets were something else. They soared when Stephen Hawking came out against a recurrent universe, thereby endorsing the Gothic model of cause and effect. Now they were behaving as if some other factor were weighing in on the side of cyclicity and the chaotic notion that everything causes and is caused by everything else.

Like most leading businessmen, Myles Overton employed a cosmologist to help interpret the impact of universal forces on the world's equity markets, but when Linden brought him in, the man was ambiguous and unhelpful. He kept looking at the door as if about to make a dash for it, or dismally picking his nose as if he thought he might uncover hitherto unsuspected deposits of cold dark matter. 'I don't make the future,' he squirmed. 'I only measure it.'

'Pull yourself together and stop bleating. Tell me what's going to happen!'

Again and again the cosmologist ran the numbers. 'It's close. Too close to call . . . '

He did not say: it depends on whether the wellspring of dreams is closed up by the Impenetrable Shield. He did not say: it depends on the hundred sons of Genghis Khan, and the sharpness of their swords, for some say the world only turns so that the stars can bathe themselves in the Aral Sea. He knew certain ancient artefacts and above all Caryddwen's cauldron itself were fundamental to the structure of the cosmos. But he was, perhaps, afraid to speak his mind. In Neill Fife's latest book there was a well authenticated account of two cats laying hold of an eminent physicist and shutting him in a box with a phial of cyanide and a particle generator. The universe was fighting back. Perhaps the Druids were right after all, and objects were merely states of mind.

'How can I, who have always defined by measuring, measure what is not defined?' he asked finally.

But that was one of the very questions to which Myles Overton had promised not to seek an answer, so he found himself no further forward than before. 'I see', he told Linden, 'that cosmologists are just a load of bloody drongos and dipshits, like the rest of the pack. In the end, there's only you and me. And someone else. But that's my problem – or my opportunity! Come here. Come closer. We've had harsh words, but I see now everything's been the fault of that wanker Dave Doom. You've been loyal to me, as you always were. But I may soon be fighting my biggest fight. I've got enemies, Linden, and my gut tells me the bastards are gaining the upper hand. I'm going to release you from your obligations, and give you money. Get clear of this place, and keep your head down until you hear I've won. I know a few more tricks, but it's better you're not around to see them.'

Even then, Myles Overton meant to rely only on the tried and trusted methods by which he had single-handedly built his empire. His tricks were a matter of covert relationships, misinformation, blackmail, and bluster. He did not contemplate the alternative course, but Linden contemplated it. She knew there were secrets he had sworn never to enquire into, and she understood the issues that confronted him. She well knew the story of how Caryddwen's cauldron had been broken and the Tuatha de Dannaan dispersed through the most inaccessible mountains and islands. Perhaps as a direct result, the land was held for four centuries by a Mediterranean empire, and then tribes from the East came in long ships, and the unity of the Celtic commonwealth was lost.

Yet the idea that Myles Overton was involved in re-enacting that loss came to Linden only gradually. The historical sequence of events is common knowledge. Mannannan Mac Llyr Mac Lugh finally freed himself from Queen Maeve of Skye, although he suffered a dislocated jaw as a result of the beard escapade and had to lie low. She, in her rage, formed an ill-starred alliance with Leatherwing. While she disguised herself as the Gothic princess Rowena and seduced Vortigern, then King of Britain, Leatherwing billeted Rowena's compatriots Henghist and Horsa at Coldharbour Abbey on the pretext that their help was needed against Queen Maeve's own Picts. In the months that followed, Henghist and Horsa betrayed Vortigern's hospitality and established a bridgehead for invasion. They pillaged the countryside and brought deadly diseases such as German measles, to which the Celts had no natural immunity. Ultimately they hunted down the British leaders and put paid to Queen Maeve of Skye into the bargain, so that the real Rowena, until then held hostage, could be rescued by Vortigern for the final futile flowering of their love.

Some say they captured Caryddwen too, although more likely the name was used by one of her descendants. The rest is well known, except that the invaders, even with Leatherwing's guidance, were never able to stamp out efforts to rebuild the heritage of the Tuatha de Dannaan and search for the cauldron of Caryddwen. Linden surmised from her conversations with Nuala that Leatherwing had originally meant to billet Myles Overton at Coldharbour, as he had once billeted Henghist and Horsa. Evidently he saw Myles Overton as the new invader, a spearhead of the new Gothicism. When the sale was blocked by the Greenwood sisters and Heritage Commission, the country was scoured for an alternative headquarters, since it was not easy to find one with an underground crypt suitable for accommodating a shadowy figure. At length the glass tower was constructed over a site which itself had some historical significance. Linden knew the plans as well as anyone. She knew there was a locked door in the basement, and she thought she knew what lay behind it.

'If I act,' she said to herself, 'it won't be any disloyalty. It will be in his own best interests.'

After she left him, she took the lifts and the stairs below the lifts. Here, the glass was painted with a special emulsion which no light could penetrate. The only illumination followed Linden down the winding stairway, and when she opened the door at the foot of the stairs, a single shaft of sun cut across the antechamber and revealed the door beyond. But against that door it revealed also the sleeping form of Dave Doom, who once did two paper rounds, holding his post to the last, with a golden key on a chain round his neck.

'He's a bloody idiot,' said Myles Overton. 'But he wouldn't let me down, if he could help it.'

Nobody knew better than Linden Richmont that Dave Doom had his price, but nobody was more reluctant to pay it. 'I'll come back,' she whispered, 'when he's sleeping more soundly.' But before she closed the door, something seemed to flit past her up the beam of light she had allowed to enter. It might, she told herself, have been a moth or a Maybug, but deep inside she knew that both were out of season.

154

'It's funny,' Sophie Greenwood told Evan Hall, 'after all we've been through, the idea of Finbar Direach and the last lost fragment of Caryddwen's cauldron is still hard to grasp. But this morning, waking up felt like being re-born.'

Evan said that was to be expected, if the old stories were true. The restoration of Caryddwen's cauldron would change everything. There would be no Absolute Truth, he told her with a wry smile. Old certainties required looking at anew. Perhaps they would split apart, and from the ambiguity would thrust up a determined new seedling, one day to become a spreading tree. Sophie and Evan looked out of the window to see sunlight melting the early frost on the rowan branches, and berries of yew and holly standing out like rubies in the crisp light.

Beyond the branches they noticed Damien and Chantal arguing fitfully about whether the bardic prose of Iolo Morganwyg was better than the harp music of Turloch O'Carolan.

'Music', said Chantal, 'is necessarily inferior to poetry, because by its nature it can't have a moral dimension.'

'Don't talk to me about moral dimensions,' Damien said. 'Don't give me that I'm-a-Greenwood-sister-and-off-to-save-the-world business. Didn't music ever inspire great actions?'

But Chantal said she would not listen to anyone who talked about music and great actions while wearing a Primal Scream tee-shirt, and Damien said it was lucky the dispossessed of the world didn't know their greatest champion was an intellectual snob, to which Chantal said Fidel Castro himself was a great devotee of the classics, to which Damien said, whose classics, and who's to say Primal Scream are not classics? 'And who', he added, 'is Fidel Castro, anyway?'

'Oh,' said Chantal, 'you probably wouldn't know, since he's not in the network charts.' They strolled beside the drifting stream, paying scant attention to their surroundings. But as they passed between the lock gates and the weir they had an uncanny feeling that someone was nearby, and noticed a stranger had joined and was walking between them, so close she could have put an arm around the waist of each.

'Until today the winter seemed here to stay,' Chantal observed, finding the silence too much to bear. 'But now it feels totally different.

Look! There's a water ouzel – a dipper. There's a bank vole, and a damsel fly! The weather's mild for the time of year . . . '

Damien said, 'Don't I know you from somewhere? Hey, I'm Damien and I bet you recognize Chantal Greenwood. It's amazing, isn't it?'

Chantal raised her eyebrows. He still got a kick out of being with her, she realized, but it wasn't necessary to be so obvious. Particularly with a stranger. Particularly with a stranger, who – and Chantal looked at her closely, assessing the possibility that it might be Linden Richmont in disguise – might not be as much a stranger as she seemed.

The stranger, however, said nothing.

'Take no notice of him,' Chantal said. 'We're just Chantal and Damien, but our names and what we do are unimportant. Probably neither of us will be doing it from now on, anyway,' she stopped, realizing she might already have said too much. There is no telling what identity a stranger might conceal.

'The important thing is that we have each other,' Damien added. 'But the more important thing is that we realize what's important. Although she finds it hard to stop bickering.'

The lady smiled, but did not speak. Her face was composed and her demeanour friendly yet strangely remote. There were crow's feet round her dew-bright eyes but that only accentuated her beauty, giving it depth and urgency. She wore Jaeger, as is appropriate during winter in a rural setting, her make-up was by L'Oréal, with accessories by Dior. But she radiated an elegance all her own, artless and without affectation. Damien and Chantal thought their surroundings flowed into her, creating the impression of something vital and charged. Or that her personality flowed into the woods and water, as Ivana's had flowed into and out of the Aral Sea. Everything seemed heightened, as if just ready to come to the boil and start bubbling out all manner of extravagances which were normally condensed and contained. She was a compelling woman, in other words, although she did not seem to speak.

Damien said, 'We walked together beside this river in childhood but we didn't know how much we knew. Then we went our different ways. Who betrayed whom is in the past, and doesn't matter.'

'Although,' added Chantal, 'it wasn't me.'

'Anyway,' said Damien, 'a person has to achieve their desire, before they can discover what their desire really is.'

'We're certainly not going to bore you with our relationship,' Chantal assured her. 'But until you've hauled someone into a moving helicopter amid a hail of bullets in some foreign trouble-spot, you don't really know them, nor they you.'

'I hauled her,' Damien put in. 'She didn't haul me, Chantal Greenwood or not.'

'Because at the time I was risking my life to comfort an old friend.'

'To be honest, we argue all the time,' Damien said. 'We don't agree about politics or the way to brew hogweed ale. But the day a person considers their life complete, is the day they no longer need to live it. All we can say is we have each other, and that's good enough for both. And when harsh words break out, as is bound to happen, we remember the battle of Kara-Kalpak, and our commitment to each other comes back ten times as strong.'

But the elegant lady smiled, and did not reply, although she was still close enough to put her arms round their waists had she wanted to. When they reached the grassy lip of the weir, she turned and nodded to them, as though thanking them for their company, and they watched her walk across the verges and back on to the path beyond, which led into the trees and away across the escarpment.

'It's funny,' said Chantal. 'It was Karen who said that when two people are in harmony with each other, they're in harmony with everything. Karen seemed to see what the rest of us missed, although I admit I turned the colour of houmous the night she predicted you and I would end up together. Now she's gone, and in spite of what Triona says, I don't think we'll see her again. But she still feels close, and sometimes it's as though she's been beside us all the time, giving us the strength to carry on.'

They looked again at the strange lady, now receding into the distance, and Chantal called out in surprise, 'Look – she has golden feet!'

Sure enough with every step she took, whether on grass, amongst the leaf litter or across the hard asphalt of the towpath, she left little yellow footprints made of celandines.

155

'Well,' said the authorities, 'everything seems quiet enough in the Myles Overton camp. Perhaps he's not such a bruiser after all. After today's falls in the market, you'd expect to hear from him. Then again, everyone knows he's got a special relationship at the very highest level. He might still pull something out of the bag.'

'Well, we must keep the minister informed.'

'Something is afoot,' said the minister. 'The joint chiefs must be kept informed, and likewise the Head of the Special Section. It's not yet time to make a move, but the word is, something big may be going down.'

Linden Richmont knew what was being said. But trained in public relations as she was, she also knew when not to comment. What could she say? That the most robust, down-to-earth and pragmatic businessman of all time was pacing an upper room, blaming the crisis on speculation as to the possibility of a non-linear universe? Linden had her own reputation to consider, as well as her loyalty to her uncle. Once again, she thought of the door she had nearly attempted to open, the recumbent Dave Doom, and the key.

'Whoever is behind that door,' she said to herself, 'whoever or *whatever* is behind that door – their time has come.' But when she descended the stairs and stood in the shaft of light her courage failed. She looked again at the sleeping form of Dave Doom and thought of the feelings he had for her, and what he would ask her to do if she asked for the key. For he had, indeed, asked her to do it only a few days ago, and Linden said she would rather do it with a dead wart hog.

As before she said to herself, 'I'll come back later, when the time is right.'

But again it was as if her intentions had reached ahead of her actions, for the door trembled as though it were not shut so tightly as before. Again there was a sense of weightless movement, and something seemed to hang briefly in the shaft of light as it passed Linden by, although it was like no kind of bird or bat that she had ever heard of.

156

Oswald fell asleep in the afternoon, but woke to find the sun had pierced the curtains like a dirk. Yet that was not what woke him. For he heard a knock on the door, as of someone asking to be given entry.

This time there was no difficulty in recognizing Karen. She still had a kind of otherworldliness, as though if you tried to touch her, she would vanish again. But Oswald remembered she was always like that. Far from wearing Jaeger, as she had been when Damien and Chantal failed to see what was in front of their eyes, she was dressed only in the finest Versace, with accessories by Ralph Lauren. Her dress was short, but shiny black boots reached right up to her thighs, perhaps in an attempt to contain the growth of celandines, although a few of these flowers protruded shyly from the top of the boots like golden stars in a shiny leather sky.

'Hello, Oswald,' she said, and her voice was like the wind in a rowan tree.

'Aren't you coming in?' he asked, immediately at a loss for words.

She looked awkward. 'I have to be careful. Why don't you carry me across the threshold? That way, if anyone knocks, you will be able to tell them truthfully that I never set foot inside your door.'

Oswald did not have the heart to say he had no problem with telling lies anyway so it would not make much difference. He was surprised how light she was under the heavy coat. She would not eat or drink, but said she had only a little time, for she had been released only by an intention, not an action. It was essential, she said, that he must listen carefully.

'I don't want to listen carefully. I want to get Neill, and the others. Where have you been? Why didn't you phone?'

'The time's not right for me to meet the others yet – there's still danger.'

'Then why have you come to me?'

'Sometimes people are closest to people they're less close to. Too much intimacy prevents people getting near each other. Besides, I know the part you played in this affair, and the Clay Man. I'm proud of you.'

'I still don't understand. I'm just an accountant. Besides, as you said, I've played my part already.'

'You only have to understand this. At all costs, my sister must shun the red-haired queen, and likewise Finbar Direach must shun the beggar at the gate.'

'That doesn't make sense.'

'I daren't make it any plainer. Listening ears are everywhere, and even those one trusts most can betray the game by a single ill-considered act. Now – I must leave. Time pursues me like a wolf-pack in full cry.'

'Stay with us!'

She looked startled. 'It's nearly evening. I may already be too late!'

157

Twenty years previously there was a party at Coldharbour, the huge fire of beech logs throwing vast shadows that leapt and danced against the surrounding trees, the tumbling walls and the wishing well. That was Karen's party. It was Karen's last party, and what occurred there changed the lives of everyone present – for ever. Now, on the anniversary of that event, the fire was re-kindled, and the blackened walls of the old abbey echoed with the sounds of music and mirth once more. For that, everyone said, was how Karen would have wanted it.

But this party was Finbar Direach's.

Why was the evidence from those at the previous party so confused and contradictory? Why did accounts of the more recent one conflict with each other in the barest essentials, and even where they agreed, relate events which were uniformly far-fetched, bizarre, and paradoxical? The answer is one word in the arcane dialects of the Cymri and the Picts, but two in contemporary speech. The words are: hogweed ale. Anyone who doubts the claims made for it is welcome to send in to the publishers of this volume for the recipe, with the sole caveat that if the proportions given are departed from even by a single drop, certain death will be the inevitable result, and indeed is a not uncommon outcome even when the brew is prepared correctly.

As a result of the hogweed ale, then, many of the details given here are suspect, and what took place may well be the exact opposite of what is described. Nevertheless, some attempt must be made to correlate the many rumours that arose from the evening's work, and the best place to start is the initial appearance of Finbar Direach himself, who made himself known to the companions before the serious drinking began, and whose presence is to that extent credible.

'Peace to you,' Finn told them, stretching out his hands and using a Celtic phrase. 'And peace to all in your household. I have waited long for this day to come!'

Even those of them who lacked a sense of occasion could not help admitting that Finn looked, as Rufus Stone put it, the dog's bollocks. Clad in the full regalia of a Gaelic chieftain, he received each guest in turn, and each saw in him what they most wished to see in themselves. To Triona he was the Finn she knew of old, but to Neill he was a philosopher king in scholarly robes, although his face resembled Neill's old Head of Department at Launceston. To Dawn he was a calm, parental figure such as one might expect to find in a remote woodland gully preaching to the wild birds; a man, yet in touch with his feminine side. To Chantal he was a fierce warlord comparable with Genghis Khan, and to Damien he was a cool dude who understood that a man has to do what he must. Nuala greeted him like a close friend, for she was now a guest of the Tuatha de Dannaan themselves in the dreamy region where they had their being. Finn had arranged her presence with some difficulty, and she was on a white horse from which she was forbidden to descend since if her feet touched soil other than that of Tir N'an Og no good would come of it, as indeed happened to Oisin some years before.

But when he came to Tracey, neither spoke for a long moment. The Tuatha de Dannaan had allowed Finn neither marriage nor intimate contact with the female gender during his long years of wandering, so the chance encounter while being abducted to the moon was his only experiment in paternity. Tracey, for her part, longed for someone who would take her seriously, and since hearing that the Old Man of Hoy was nothing but a legend, she craved the stability of a normal family environment.

'Three thousand years is a long time,' Finn said, at length, softly.

'We have a lot of catching up to do.'

He touched her brow with the tips of his fingers, as if to ensure she was real. 'We will talk,' he said. 'We will talk late into the night, and still be talking as the morning fills the sky. I will tell you the old stories, and the legends of our people. But from now on we must live ordinary lives, and learn how to grow old. We will get to know each other, and go on a camping holiday in Wales, as fathers and daughters should.' She nodded, and among the onlookers more than one felt their eyes heavy with tears.

Oswald alone seemed unaffected by this reunion. If anything, he felt his existing resentment towards Finbar Direach was sharpened as if by a magic grindstone, for only an hour ago Tracey was telling him she had no-one, and he had said, 'Well, I am someone, although I am only an accountant. If I met the right person, they could share my house with the beige curtains, my cat, and my tin-opener collection, because I now know the thing with Triona was just a form of self-deception.'

He felt upstaged, and he could not admire the stature and status of the chieftain who stood proudly amongst them, and still kept muttering about being sure he had seen Finn somewhere before. But there was no dwelling on the matter, because it was time for the last lost fragment of the cauldron of Caryddwen to be placed in the circle Neill had made what seemed like a thousand years before. And for their pledge to be fulfilled.

'Place it there quickly,' urged Finn, 'before the guests arrive!'

It was Tracey Dunn who stepped into the centre of the circle with her heirloom and laid it down with simple dignity. It seemed for a moment incongruously small, considering all that had been necessary for its recovery. But Finn said that one of the properties of Caryddwen's cauldron was that every part of it contained the whole, and as Tracey stepped back, they had the impression that the music of pipes, citterns and mandolins came out of the air and inside Neill's circle rose up a host of further fragments, lifting themselves out of the soil from their secret hiding place in the foundations of Coldharbour Abbey, where brave human spirits who assisted Finn in his task had concealed them over the aeons. The pile of fragments was circular, and it seemed to cover an acre of ground in perfect symmetry, so each piece lay next to the ones from which it had broken away when the ocean's resistless torrent shattered the cauldron and washed it through the land. At this sight, and the music, and the grave expression of Finn himself, the companions took another drink, but their eyes were again blurred with tears.

Once the ceremony was complete and the vast vision of fragments had sprung up like a huge incongruous fairy ring in the grounds of Coldharbour, the party progressed and its keynotes were drunkenness, self-congratulation and good humour. As Finn had promised, the wild animals of the woods did indeed attend and Finn, by a peculiar gift he had, created in them the semblance of great kings and queens, although their ears remained the same. This was, indeed, one of the tricks for which Finn was famous before he blotted his copybook with the Tuatha de Dannaan. Whenever a social gathering had insufficient guests or too many had fallen down drunk, Finn would always make new ones out of animals, and so successfully that people often approached the host and congratulated him on the company. 'But,' they would say, 'we don't understand why you saved the best guests until last.'

The human participants, although initially confused, were delighted. It could have been elaborate fancy dress, but Neill was asked to dance by a beautiful queen who had doe ears as well as doe eyes, and Chantal by a grumpy and tenacious old monarch with badger ears. Damien pressed his attentions on a lively princess whose ears suggested a vole, a dormouse, or a squirrel. There were hedgehog kings, stoat and weasel lords in the purest ermine, bishops with the ears of owls, counts and countesses who only hours before had been bounding about the hedgerows in the shape of rabbits or hares. There was hardly a guest but betrayed some evidence of royal blood and was skilled in table manners and the arts of dance, flirtation, maintaining lofty discourse about abstract issues, and drinking hogweed ale.

Finn made a passable band out of small songbirds and grasshoppers, while acorns and chestnuts raided from the winter stores of squirrels were skilfully turned into canapés and a finger-buffet of quality unmatched even by the big London hotels. As was traditional, each guest was required to sing, recite, or please the other party-goers in some way. But Finn laughingly said that on this occasion there would be no prizes for the most accomplished performance except the admiration and applause it elicited, and no penalty for the least successful but the turning down of thumbs and throwing of comestibles.

He himself was on form, as befits someone who has had little to celebrate for several millennia. He played the fiddle, sang numerous songs, and caused considerable amusement and laughter by recounting the incident of the message from Mannannan Mac Llyr Mac Lugh and the way he, Finn, had brought death, disease and suffering into the world as well as flooding large tracts of land. He told the story entertainingly with many jokes at his own expense. He did the voices too, but was careful not to sing the specific song that caused all the trouble, for few people make the same mistake twice, even when they are drunk.

It was an evening of the utmost conviviality. Despite that, or because of it, Triona felt a kind of sadness. After all, this had all been done for Karen, the fragment had been recovered for Karen, but now everyone seemed to have what they wanted, and amid the merriment Karen herself was forgotten. For the moment there was nobody with whom Triona could share this thought. She avoided Neill because he was trying to get off with some tart with deer ears. Frankly, even if he kept shooting glances at Triona as if to say, 'I'm only chasing her because you're avoiding me,' Triona knew that men like to have their cake and eat it. She was also avoiding Oswald because she noticed he had noticed she was thinking of Karen and not enjoying herself, and she did not want to give him the chance to say he had told her so.

Unfortunately, Oswald noticed this avoidance but not the reason for it, so he felt offended in his turn and muttered under his breath, 'Well, I had something very important to tell you, but if you can't share your secrets with me, I don't see why I should share mine with you.' He refilled his glass and went to look for Tracey Dunn to let her know again that he took her seriously even if no-one else did, but that if people are suddenly told by a complete stranger in a gold kilt that he is their long lost father who conceived them by rubbing against an enchantress during a trip to the moon, they should take it with a pinch of salt. Triona wandered a little apart from the main group to be alone with her thoughts and the wind sighing in the trees.

'It's good to be out of the crowd,' a voice said behind her, making her jump.

'Who are you?'

The newcomer, who did not wish to enter the full glow of the firelight, was a slender, fine-boned and exceedingly handsome woman whose robes were trimmed with white fur and whose fiery red hair was topped by a golden crown and two beautiful pointed ears. 'Can't you guess?' she said. 'I'm the Fox Queen. But enough about me! You look tired and sad in all this conviviality. Yet I sense that, without you, what they're celebrating would never have been achieved. Perhaps they're forgetting that. Perhaps they owe you a debt that has not yet been paid, and you look on this frivolity as premature. You feel you've been used, possibly by people who don't even have your best interests at heart. But there! I'm prying too hard. You must slap my wrist for a nosy old queen. You must tell me nothing at all, and not even open your lips. But give me your arm so we can walk together in silence, and listen to the sighing of the wind in the trees.'

So Triona walked in silence with the Fox Queen, thinking that no-one had understood her so well since the day she was born, but after a while she didn't mind if she did talk to her new companion about this and that. After a little longer, and a drink of hogweed ale, there was no help for it but to bury her head in her new friend's breast with a flood of tears, and pour out the whole truth about her first meeting with Finn, how she had been beguiled into getting everyone to find things in exchange for the return of her sister, how, suddenly, when the task was completed, no-one wanted to know about Karen any more, how Oswald had gone off in a huff, and she felt, frankly, she had no other friend in the world but the Fox Queen, who in the morning would turn back to an ordinary fox and be lost to Triona in her turn.

'There, there,' said the Fox Queen, stroking Triona's head soothingly. 'I understand, I understand. But the morning is many miles away. If I can help you, I will. If I can answer any question for you, I will try to do so.'

'You'll never know the answer to the question that's in my heart,' replied Triona.

'Yet sometimes it helps to share one's problems, even if they are difficult to solve.'

'The question is this: where is my sister Karen, and how can I get her back?'

'The answer is this: beneath Myles Overton's glass tower there's a subterranean crypt giving on to a tiny chamber hewn out of solid rock, where in former times the enchantress Morrigan is said to have imprisoned Merddyn Gwyllt – whom the *Mabinogion* calls Merlin, mentor to the legendary King Arthur. There Karen lies, and with her is the one they call Leatherwing, but an iron door one hand's-breadth thick guards the place. The only key is kept by Myles Overton's trusted lieutenant Dave Doom, who would no sooner part with it than he would with his own internal organs.'

'The matter, then, is hopeless. Besides, once Leatherwing knows we've found what we were looking for, my sister's life will be worth nothing in his rage.'

'You're right to be concerned,' replied the Fox Queen. 'But what if I take you to the glass tower, and we look for a solution?'

'The glass tower is two hundred miles west of here. Even with clear roads, it would take all night.'

But the Fox Queen's eyes gleamed. 'I will turn into a great red she-fox that can race over standing corn or flowing water, and even run along the clouds in the sky on autumn days when they come low enough. Take a sip of that good ale you're carrying, and climb on my back. For I promise that no sooner will you feel your feet leave the ground than you'll alight at the glass tower, and no word of a lie.'

Feeling events were escaping her control, yet now beyond caring, Triona did as she was asked. Sure enough, it seemed only seconds and a rushing of wind before she climbed off the she-fox's back, and it was transformed once more into a stately queen with a crown and pointed ears, and the mighty silhouette of Myles Overton's world headquarters stood between them and the moon. When she saw it, Triona was once more downcast after the brief elation of the ride.

'No-one could get in there – and get out alive.'

'Linden Richmont could.'

Triona started, and suddenly tried to give the Fox Queen a hard look, although it was tricky to focus with any exactitude. Evidently her new friend knew more than she let on. Evidently too, she had come prepared, for from underneath her priceless garments she produced an auburn wig and a distinctive ring. When she had put them on Triona and made some adjustments to her make-up and clothes, she produced a hand mirror. What Triona saw made her gasp, for the resemblance was uncanny.

'But how will I get the key from Dave Doom?'

'You already know how you will get the key from Dave Doom. Haven't you dreamed long enough of what you had to do tonight? Haven't you avoided amorous entanglements for exactly this reason?

Unless, of course, the affection you have for your sister is insufficient to make you undertake the matter?'

'I understand what you're saying,' Triona replied, but she took a stiff draught of hogweed ale nevertheless. 'I understand. Except if you're hinting that but for this I'd have set my cap for Neill Fife, I must say you've got a lot of gall. Frankly, Neill Fife means nothing to me whether his wife is estranged or not. He's too full of himself. This Renaissance-Man stuff is over-rated. Having said that, you seem to know more about my business than is altogether healthy, considering you're only a fox got up for a party. But whatever needs to be done must be done, even if under ordinary circumstances ten thousand pounds wouldn't make a person do it. Dave Doom has lusted after Linden Richmont for years – that's common knowledge – and tonight he'll get what he desires. But so will I!'

158

Dave Doom was a narrow-minded sociopath who lacked anything resembling imagination, and who undeviatingly followed Myles Overton's orders. People confused this with stupidity. In fact Dave Doom was of above-average intelligence, but luckily he was stupid where women were concerned. Many men, if they asked a woman to sleep with them and were told she would rather sleep with a wart hog that died four weeks ago of tertiary syphilis, would become suspicious if someone closely resembling the same woman seemed eager to leap between their sheets before the metaphorical wart hog had lain in its grave a further seven days.

Dave Doom, however, had no understanding of women. He had read in a book that they were an alien race which invaded the earth three thousand years ago, landing on the British archipelago in an immense starship shaped like a cauldron, and that this had been the symbol of their power for many years before being shattered into fragments which, if they were ever reassembled, would release them from the subjugation they had since experienced. 'Women,' he used to say, 'have big breasts, and are not like men. Communication with them is impossible, because they say one thing one minute, and another the next. They can never go easy. If you ask me they're only good for one thing, and most of them aren't even very good for that. But that Linden Richmont. *Phwoar!* You don't get many of those to the kilo.'

Because Dave Doom could not look at the whole person, but only at the breasts, Triona's little deception worked perfectly, and even her ill-concealed expression of loathing was misinterpreted as ill-concealed passion. She was lucky to find him working late in his office, because although Myles Overton had told him not to move from the iron door in the crypt, he had also told him to finish up some important paperwork. Dave Doom had once done two newspaper rounds, but even he could not be in two places at once. But when Linden Richmont apparently appeared at his door, he soon concluded that she was gagging for it.

'I've been reconsidering what I said about the wart hog. Perhaps I was a little hasty,' Triona said, using a line suggested by the Fox Queen.

'*Phwoar!*' said Dave Doom, and without wasting any more time, suggested that she could lie across the filing cabinet and if she gave him a moment he would hang his underpants over the surveillance camera. Myles Overton had left for the night, and all the other video surveillance tapes came to Dave Doom anyway, so nobody would ever know.

Perhaps a veil should be drawn over the sacrifice made that night in the struggle for a Celtic-as-against-a-Gothic future by Triona Greenwood, who loved her sister even more than she loathed Dave Doom. Perhaps a veil should not be drawn over it, but the offensive words should be put in asterisks, which readers can fill in at their leisure, drawing on their personal knowledge of human anatomy. The *Mabinogion* has no asterisks, but then the *Mabinogion* fails to address the essentially visceral quality of the human condition, preferring to stick to white deer and salmon-weirs.

The bed on which the union of Dave Doom and the false Linden Richmont was consummated was a filing cabinet with hard corners and a cold top, and she had to lean over it in an undignified way while he fondled her ****, before sticking his enormous **** in and flolloping backwards and forwards for two and a half minutes and then disgorging millions of thankfully never to be realized potential half-Dave-Dooms into an industrial strength prophylactic which the Fox Queen coincidentally had had about her person.

'Now,' Triona said, when he had recovered his breath and she her knickers, 'what about the key – as you promised?'

He looked at her cunningly, 'Not unless you let me **** in your ****.'

She did that as well, twenty minutes later which was the time it took for his **** to get **** again.

'Now – give me the ***.'

'The what?'

'The key.'

But he was already asleep after his efforts, slumped across the filing cabinet where she had been earlier, and exuding terrible contented breaths that smelled like a dead wart hog. Good, thought Triona, although her **** hurt. She never expected him to give her the key in the first place – if that had been her plan she would certainly not have waited until now, because she knew men experience a change of perspective at the point of sexual completion. All Triona needed, however, was to follow his eyes when she mentioned keys, for he made a covert sidelong glance, and that was enough. Also she needed the surveillance camera to have underpants put on it, under circumstances where the security guards on the main screens would simply leer knowingly at each other and say, 'That Linden Richmont. *Phwoar!*' and make gestures by putting their left palms on the joints of their right arms and flexing them upwards with clenched fists as if to say, 'You don't get many of those to the pound!'

Sure enough, when Triona followed Dave Doom's covert glance she found the key in its secret hiding place underneath a pile of copies of *Rampant* magazine. Clutching it, she made for the service lifts and hit the buttons for the lowest level, and then descended the stairs to where the Fox Queen was waiting, a cunning smile spread across her fine features.

'Hurry!' she told Triona, 'For we must get back before we're missed. The steel door is down these steps and across the underground cavern, but there's no time to lose. Put the golden key in the iron lock and turn it three times. But remember, you must on no account open the door from the outside! Your sister is not alone, and although she will hear the key turn and immediately know what has happened, she must choose her own moment.'

'May we not wait for her?' Triona asked when she had done as the Fox Queen said, although the key felt like electricity between her fingers.

'We may not – for I don't advise meeting your sister during the hours of darkness. She has been long with Leatherwing, and may have changed in unexpected ways. But wait until she comes to you tomorrow, in daylight and of her own accord, and whatever has happened to her, with time and the loving affection which only a sister can give, she will be restored to her old self again.'

'At least let me peep through the keyhole and look at her!'

But at this, the Fox Queen grew irritated and impatient. 'You're not ready – and neither is she. And even now the effects of Finn's transformation are starting to wear off, and my own time is limited. Take a good drink from that bottle you are carrying. Now – wait while I turn into a great red she-fox, and climb on to my back, and even before you feel your feet leave the ground, we'll be in Coldharbour once more.'

'Karen!' called Triona, but her voice was swallowed up by its own echoes, 'Oh, Karen . . . ' It was like a dream.

Then she was among her friends again, and there were hundreds of kings and queens in every direction, all with animal ears, and there was Oswald, but there was no fox, and she ached all over.

'I feel like I just shagged Dave Doom,' she said to herself confusedly. 'God, I need a drink!'

159

But Linden Richmont, from whose office Dave Doom's was clearly visible, had also been working late but had fallen asleep over a pile of papers. As her mind struggled amid turbulent dreams, she was astonished to have an out-of-body experience in which she thought she woke up and observed herself entering Dave Doom's office at midnight and offering him everything.

'Perhaps,' she thought, 'I subconsciously desired him all these years!' She sensed that things were coming to a head, and it would soon be time to face the choice she had been postponing for so long – perhaps for her whole life. Nobody can criticize someone for the love they bear the only real father they have ever known, but there comes a time in everyone's life when they need to make a stand, or be forever fallen.

'I've always had my doubts about what's right and what's wrong,' thought Linden. 'What if my mind is trying to tell me something? What if it's trying to say to me, Linden, you're letting yourself get fucked over by everyone – even Dave bloody Doom.'

But she narrated the experience to no-one, and felt somehow compromised by it.

160

Nobody who has ever attended a wild party will need details of what occurred in the grounds of Coldharbour Abbey that fateful night. The band played, glasses were refilled, old stories were told, new songs were sung. Some couples danced openly, and others retired together into the bougainvillea, perhaps to discuss philosophy or acquaint each other with interesting observations about the legends of the *Mabinogion*.

At the height of the festivities, however, a message was brought to Finn that there was a poor beggar outside asking for alms, and Finn commanded that he should be brought forward. Sure enough, when the wretch approached, he had all the hallmarks of a hapless itinerant. His clothes were ragged and offensive to the human nose, his skin was inflamed with boils and whitlows, his manner self-deprecating and servile.

'Be heard!' commanded Finn magnanimously, 'And speak without fear of punishment or rebuff! For tonight of all nights must be dedicated to munificence and open-handedness. For thousands of years I have searched, and now, with the help of my companions here, I have found what was lost, and am in a position to restore what was broken.'

'Excuse me,' put in Oswald, who could not help recollecting what he needed to say to Finn, although his feelings of resentment had prevented him from mentioning it before.

'Later!' Finn told him imperiously. 'For although this is only an itinerant beggar, of humble origins and covered in dirt and excrement, I have invited him to speak, and my word can never be rescinded.'

'But wait!' began Oswald. In a sudden panic, he rushed forward, but whatever he was going to say next could never be heard by any human ear, for he tripped over a set of bagpipes and knocked himself unconscious on a root, which henceforth became known as the root of all evil, as no-one could have anticipated the consequences of its being where it was.

'Too much hogweed ale,' declared Finn indulgently, signalling some nearby kings and queens to make sure Oswald was all right. 'But now, Sir Beggar, we have waited long enough to hear from you, and I would be glad to know what you have to say.'

'You're very kind', replied the poor beggar, 'in offering to let me address the company – and perhaps even I, a poor beggar, might be able to spin a tale or two for the amusement of your guests, or give voice to some melancholy lay, or unravel some abstruse mystery that has puzzled scientists and philosophers for many decades. But the truth is, times are hard, and it's few who can indulge themselves with the finer things in life. What with the modernizers and pragmatists who currently frame thinking on social issues, and the National Lottery as well, it's hard to bum up the price of a cup of tea, let alone a warm bed for the night.'

'Our hearts go out to you,' said Finn. 'But you'll not find the present company so mean-minded. Far from it! For I give my oath – which cannot be rescinded – that you have only to ask, and whatever is in my power to give you, will be yours.'

But as soon as these words were out of his mouth he would gladly have swallowed them again, even if they had been engraved on fragments of the cauldron itself. For to everyone's surprise the beggar stood up straighter and taller than before, and lost some of his servility. Finn, although he had an indefinable presence, was definitely on the short side. In contrast, the newcomer reared up far beyond average stature, and assuming a proud demeanour, threw off his ragged garments to reveal the fine purple and the good red silk, although his face was still hooded and there was a sinister aspect to him. By this they soon realized what in their hearts they had known since the moment they saw him. For they understood this was Leatherwing, Finn's ancient adversary, and that things were taking a turn for the worse.

'Why then,' cried Leatherwing, realizing everybody's worst fears,

'Since you offer me anything that is in your power to give, I claim the fragments of the lost cauldron of Caryddwen!'

What Finn said cannot be translated directly from the ancient Celtic, although it was clearly an expression of considerable frustration.

'Don't give it to him!'

But Finn could not break his word, unlike the modernizers who are in positions of power today, and all any of them could do was watch as he agreed with Leatherwing that the fragments of Caryddwen's cauldron would be handed over to him the following morning and loaded on to heavy vehicles, which would carry them westwards to an undisclosed destination.

'For today', cried Leatherwing, 'I was set free! But tomorrow – I will fulfil my destiny.' But when they asked him what all this was about being set free, Leatherwing gave his answer in the form of a terrible dance, in which he danced all the detail of the terrible life he had lived, and struck fear into every heart.

First, he danced the journey of the Tuatha de Dannaan out of the East from the bords of the Aral Sea, through Europe and across from Brittany to the Western Archipelago where they made their home. He danced their great deeds of love and war, and the birth of the children they had among themselves, and those that resulted from liaisons with the indigenous inhabitants of the archipelago. He danced the birth of two brothers, one a frivolous character, an idler and a dilettante, the other an introverted and studious individual who loved only books and wisdom and dedicated himself to the improvement of mankind. He danced the favouritism of the parents for the frivolous brother, his marriage to a great princess of the Tuatha de Dannaan, and the spurning of the studious brother, who was excluded from the wedding ceremony and became the butt of cruel jokes and unkind humour because he did not like parties and preferred a good book.

He danced the birth of a young son to the princess, and the bungled attempt to select a tutor which led to the boy's abduction by an agent of his own uncle, whose rejection had turned loneliness into malice which could only be assuaged by a fearful ransom of children. He danced an overwhelming natural catastrophe, the punishment of Mannannan Mac Llyr Mac Lugh's messenger by the Tuatha de Dannaan, and their cynical use of the same uncle to compound the punishment and foil its remission.

And he danced the sudden prospect of a world in which one life was not all, and the destruction of this prospect by a last-minute reversal cunningly engineered by the alienated uncle himself – Leatherwing.

'So you see,' he explained, when he could dance no more but sank down with sweat streaming out from under his cowl, 'I was once high in the counsels of the Tuatha de Dannaan, but I loved a daughter of Mannannan Mac Llyr Mac Lugh, though she would have none of me and preferred my brother, Finbar Direach's father. Full of jealousy and vindictiveness, I challenged Mannannan Mac Llyr Mac Lugh and his clan on the field of battle, and was able to draw around me many malcontents. The battle raged back and forth for nine weeks without stopping, and only at the greatest price was the victory procured, and myself banished from the palaces of the Tuatha de Dannaan and imprisoned on the moon. Nor could even that cheerless billet hold me forever, for once I had secured a plentiful supply of children it was a simple matter to weave their hair into a rope long enough to reach down to an unsuspecting world.

'That I subverted Finbar Direach's education to acquire these children is well known. But that was not the limit of my malice. Having the accomplishment of shape-shifting like many of my kind, I hit upon the plan of turning myself into a rustic bothy upon a remote hillside, and when a company of poets and balladeers sheltered there for the night, I contrived without their knowledge to position myself in Finn's path as he travelled southwards with a message for Caryddwen. The rest you know. It will hardly be a revelation that I cut a deal with Myles Overton to acquire suitable lodgings, and exploited the mismanagement of the well of dreams to exert influence where the reality of my situation would have precluded it. But all these triumphs were nothing compared with what I have achieved this very day. For the Fox Queen was in the pay of nobody but myself when she sought out Triona Greenwood and, affecting sympathy, carried her to her sister's prison and arranged the deception of Dave Doom, the theft of the key, and the unlocking of the door to the dungeon.'

But Oswald had recovered consciousness in time to realize that his tardiness in delivering Karen's message was likely to have unfortunate consequences.

'Yet why would you collude in Karen's release,' he asked bravely, although he was getting an uneasy feeling about the whole affair, 'when you were the one who imprisoned her in the first place?'

'You haven't guessed, Oswald Hawthorne. Yet you've always known deep inside that the figure beside her in the unmarked car that night was neither Leatherwing nor Dave Doom, nor even Myles Overton. It was in fact Finbar Direach.'

Oswald's stomach turned over like a duvet in a tumble-drier, but he could not deny this was so. In fact, the more he thought about it, the more he thought the registration of the unmarked car, which perplexed his mind for half a lifetime, was a characteristically ostentatious one, and that it was the letters FIN 1 that had so long eluded his memory.

Leatherwing saw Oswald's realization in his face, and laughed a mocking laugh. 'You've finally recognized, then, it was Finbar Direach who took Karen away, and struck Neill Fife on the head so violently he forgot the vital clue – that since Karen made no move to escape when left in the car by all three strangers, she cannot have been there against her will. But the reason Finbar Direach took her is obvious. She was the only living being powerful enough to confine *me*. You haven't guessed that she is none other than Caryddwen herself, even though her own sisters did not know it. Her behaviour, the tensions between her and Neill, her efforts to penetrate Myles Overton's organization – all these were linked to her plan to contain my ambitions until the last fragment was found. Even her appearance at a notorious nightclub, where our perverse seduction of one another began, was a move in the dangerous power-game she was playing with me. Did you never learn that the jailer is imprisoned by his need to confine his victim? Karen was incarcerated by the necessity to incarcerate me. Every night, when my powers were strongest, she lay on top of me so I could not move. Every day, when she might otherwise have been able to steal forth and contact her friends and family, I lay on top of her. By this means each of us limited the other's strength, and although I was able to contact Myles Overton and perhaps she too had her secret forays, neither could exert their full potential. Had she not done what she did, you may be sure that you would have met with little success in the tasks you undertook, because you would have had far more to contend with than one greedy entrepreneur, his prig of a niece, and an idiot like Dave Doom.'

'You mean', began Triona, 'Karen is Caryddwen, and when I turned the golden key in the iron lock . . . '

'You turned victory into defeat. For after Neill Fife recovered the fragment from the Corryvrecken and my bid to destroy him in a curragh race misfired, it looked as though I could not prevent Karen from fully regaining her identity as Caryddwen, and my intention to install her beside me on my shadowy throne would be for ever frustrated. Then you yourself performed the only action that could release me in time to prevent the cauldron being re-assembled, the Tuatha de Dannaan being re-awakened, and the future of the archipelago being redeemed.'

Their faces, watching him, reflected the moonlight as if they had been chalk. They stared at him at first with a terrible fascination and fear, but then they stared at him because they were too ashamed to look at each other. Suddenly Neill cried out and snatched a brand from the fire and ran at the tall figure which confronted them, but when he reached the spot where Leatherwing had stood, there was no-one there, and no sound but the wind moving the branches and the muffled hiss and crackle as the embers settled again.

And when, a moment later, Karen appeared and confirmed that her true identity was Caryddwen, everybody said, 'You've come too late.'

XI

The White Doe

161

'This was to be a time of symbolic healing. But now, I shudder to think . . . '

Neill's words hung heavy in the air like the downland dew, slow to disperse as the sunshine rallies its forces amid ominous folds of cumulostratus. Listlessly he tossed a small stone into the river, but it sank without trace.

'I shudder as well,' said Oswald. 'Yet to seek a confrontation now would be to court disaster.'

'Our choices are limited,' Triona said. 'Suppose the pieces of the cauldron are destroyed, or taken away from the archipelago . . . '

Neill shook his head. 'Destruction is not an option. A fragment is a fragment, and breaking it into smaller fragments is what we scientists call a quantitative rather than a qualitative change. No, the problem, as Finbar Direach says, will arise if they're taken from these wave-kissed shores. For then the sleeping remnant of the Tuatha de Dannaan will fall ever deeper into the sombre and irreversible sleep of death, and Leatherwing will enslave the future for ever.'

'You don't need to spell it out,' said Chantal. 'But give me a hand-picked force of half a dozen die-hards with the latest equipment, and—'

'It's useless. We can't take the cauldron back by force. It's too large and well guarded. It'd be like trying to steal Croydon. Besides, we know to our cost the fragments can never change ownership unless given with goodwill.'

'I've already contacted the Heritage Commission,' said Triona. 'They may be able to bring some pressure to bear. National heirloom, and so forth.'

'Yet, sadly, the Heritage Commission is a toothless watchdog, that guards a broken door.'

'Well what do you suggest? Stand outside Myles Overton's offices shouting, "New cauldrons for old"?'

This sparked off another long but unhelpful conversation about why it would have been a really good idea for Finn not to have put himself in a position where he had to hand over their hard-earned prize to Leatherwing. They did not know how Myles Overton and Leatherwing would get the greatest archaeological discovery since the Egyptian pyramids clear of the country without provoking a national outcry and adverse comments on the *Today* programme. But they knew their opponents were clever people, whose cleverness was honed by an implacable malevolence.

162

After the fateful feast at Coldharbour, the loss of the fateful fragments of Caryddwen's cauldron, and the realization that Triona Greenwood's self-sacrifice, far from releasing Karen from the captivity of Leatherwing, had released Leatherwing from the captivity of Karen, things were looking bad. Karen herself, when she saw she had arrived too late, made little ceremony of the reunion but immediately drew aside with Triona and Finbar Direach to see what could be done. She told the others, even Neill, she would greet them properly when the time was right. They may have been upset by this casual treatment but they knew the score, since, if she was who she claimed to be, she would certainly die once the cauldron was taken abroad. They understood there was no time for niceties, and little for anything else.

There was little, besides, to stop Leatherwing from unleashing the full implacability of his malevolence on an unsuspecting world. Even so, everything seemed outwardly normal. A number of supermodels including Neill Fife's estranged wife had got together to do a Christmas song for world peace which had topped the network charts. The government was perceived to have education and foreign affairs under control, and the nation was intrigued and flattered because the President of the United States was coming to see the Prime Minister for an important summit to see if they could think of any small nations they could cultivate moral indignation towards and drop bombs on.

This was called an historic summit, although the *Today* programme suggested it was contrived as a distraction from the impoverishment of the domestic policies of both leaders. But everyone thought, since the world was on the eve of a new epoch, it was a time of symbolic healing. It was fitting, they thought, that the leaders of the world's two greatest nations should meet to re-affirm their mutual friendship and shake hands with the very supermodels who had so touched the hearts of common people.

Although the *Mabinogion* has been criticized for its preoccupation with chieftains setting off on hunting expeditions and encountering white deer which lure them into uncanny adventures, it makes no sense to deny such themes have their place. It is all a question of how the narrative is handled. Above all, pains ought to be taken not to insult the intelligence of readers who may have paid good money for the volume they have in their hands – or possibly borrowed it from a friend and forgotten to return it, causing unspoken resentment and risking permanent damage to the relationship. If one could give one message to the authors of the *Mabinogion*, it would perhaps be: lighten up! Anyway, suffice to say that affairs of state took up the first day of the visit, but the following morning the Prime Minister invited the President and an elite party of guests to his country estate for a hunting expedition. This was eagerly accepted, although as protocol demanded it was preceded by an exchange of gifts, and at this point Myles Overton seized his chance.

The Prime Minister had not been Prime Minister for long, in those days, and he was extremely anxious to consolidate his position by ingratiating himself with the President of the United States, so it was most important he gave a suitably ingratiating gift. He was aware the President secretly wanted Tower Bridge (or London Bridge, as he called it). He knew too there would be a public outcry if he handed this over, and it would be hard for people living in Bermondsey to get to work. So Myles Overton's suggestion, when it came, was a godsend.

'I'm a simple bloody market trader, trying to make a buck. I've had my problems lately, but frankly: what goes around, comes around. What do I bloody know about pressies for Presidents? Except the ones that come in bloody brown envelopes. But if there's one thing the Yanks go for, it's history, because they've got bugger-all of their own. And if you're talking history I've got the bloody dingo's bollocks. Christ, I've got his entire wedding tackle! I can let the whole shitload go for far less than market value if it's overseas by the last day of the old year, because the Heritage bastards are already on my bloody back and otherwise there's going to be Hell to pay.'

'I get the picture,' said the Prime Minister. 'We've worked together often enough to know that a nod is as good as a wink. But tell me what you have in mind, since towards an American President, one cannot be too ingratiating.'

'The lost flaming cauldron of Caryddwen,' replied Myles Overton impressively. 'Which, granted, is a bit pranged up, but take any half-decent archaeologist and a supply of rapid-setting epoxy—'

'The lost *what?*'

When everything had been explained to the Prime Minister – for the British do not know the history of their own islands – an agreement was reached. The two men shook hands with many promises of patronage and New Year's honours for Myles Overton, as it was easy to see that the President would be happy with this arrangement.

'I would prefer London Bridge,' said the President, meaning Tower Bridge, when the significance of the gift was explained to him. 'But thinking about the Irish-American vote—'

'Trust me,' said the Prime Minister. 'This is a good present. This is a great present. You wait till you hear the outcry when they find out another national heirloom is going overseas.'

So the Prime Minister went on the *Today* programme announcing the move, and reassuring people that Tower Bridge was safe in the hands of the present government. The President accepted the offering on behalf of the American people, for, having had the fragments examined by leading experts, it was clear there should be no problem in reassembling the structure, which was surprisingly well preserved. Because of its immensity the President thought they could make it into an all-seater football stadium as a tribute to the special relationship that had always existed between the two super-powers. Bringing the dead to life and reviving the Tuatha de Dannaan were not mentioned, because Myles Overton had warned this would not work too well on the other side of the Atlantic.

'The lost cauldron of Caryddwen', declared the President in his acceptance speech, 'was one of the seven wonders of the ancient world, along with the Colossus of Rhodes, and the Hanging Gardens of Babylon, the Chain of Command, and many others my speechwriters can't remember the names of. I can honestly say there is no gift I would exchange for it – unless it was World Peace!'

The last line was the work of clever speechwriters, as the original draft read 'unless it was London Bridge'. But that is why top speechwriters count their salaries in six figures. At the press conference afterwards the whole thing was well received, apart from a few smart-Alec questions.

'Although it's now academic,' said the interviewer from the *Today* programme, 'do you feel it's correct for another piece of Britain's heritage to be going abroad like this?'

'I don't see it that way,' replied the President. 'To me, the cauldron is coming home. The American people deserve a break. You've no idea the crap I sometimes get on state visits. Spears and elephant skins, and so on. It was a bad business over London Bridge a few years back when we accidentally bought the wrong one, and the Irish-American vote is shaky now their homeland faces the threat of perpetual peace. Yet many of my fellow Americans take pride in their Celtic roots and would be thrilled to have Caryddwen's cauldron brought to Manhattan to be re-reassembled as a football stadium. I myself am a supporter of the Cincinnati Porcupines.'

At this the Prime Minister made a polite sound, although privately he though that Cincinnati Porcupines was a most peculiar name for a football club. But then, what Americans call football is a most peculiar activity. It was, to sum up, a great diplomatic and personal success, and everyone was happy except the *Today* programme, who continued trying to be clever and kept banging on about 'the real issues', birthrights, pottage, and so forth. Also a few old friends and sisters who had spent their formative years in the shadow of Coldharbour were even more unhappy, since for them the last play had been played, and they themselves were the losers by it.

163

As the dawn mist lifted above the rolling forests, no-one could doubt that there would be memorable and successful hunting the day after the memorable and successful summit. As well as the President and the Prime Minister and their many hangers-on, toadies, and sycophants, the nation's most beautiful women and most powerful men were invited to join the hunt and bring friendship and fortune to the day's activities. Myles Overton was there on a gigantic grey horse whose nostrils billowed great gusts of steam into the windless air. He showed no signs of stress from recent reverses in the markets, and the word was that his companies were bouncing back big-time, and his football club was buying a Brazilian striker. Next to him on a bay gelding was his niece Linden Richmont, who, everyone knew, was being groomed for the top job even if she did not suspect it herself. Apparently relaxed in her saddle was Triona Greenwood, ex-wife of the late marketing guru Peter Goodlunch and representing the Heritage Commission. Little did anyone guess her role and that of her sisters in the provenance of the Prime Minister's gift, still less that beneath her impeccable cool, her proud heart was crushed by the loss of the cauldron and the disarray of Coldharbour.

Neill Fife concealed his discomfort less adeptly, but the Prime Minister would not hear of him absenting himself. He was a considerable figure in his own right and well liked by party intellectuals, but as husband of one of the supermodels he was doubly welcome. The supermodels themselves, on identical black mares with accessories and tack specially designed by Yves St Laurent, flirted impeccably with the camera lenses, although a few people asked where Vanilla Kohn was.

Dave Doom, in his official capacity as head of security, bestrode an irascible crap-coloured horse which kept walking sideways and eating leaves and dribbling a kind of green dribble. The horse caused him enormous anxiety. It had tried to kick him before he got on and he was fairly sure it was waiting to kick him when he got off, but protocol forbade him to use a four-wheel drive. He mumbled tersely into a small radio from time to time, as security people do, but there was no reason to suspect foul play. The President had brought many individuals in helicopters and dark glasses, although they were as discreet as the occasion permitted. The weather held – and the omens were propitious. The horses were restive, the beaters prepared, the dogs strained at the leash and the hunt professionals were satisfied that all was as it should be.

'Move 'em out!' exclaimed the President, and with much blowing of bugles and similar instruments the chase was under way.

164

At first, things went according to plan. In order to eliminate any unwanted element of chance, the quarry animals had been rounded up the previous evening and electronically tagged. The tags contained small transmitters which were tracked by satellite and could be monitored by hand-held receivers carried by the hunt professionals. Thus the animal designated to be killed by the President, the one for the Prime Minister, and so on down, could be accurately pinpointed. Kills were ranked by status; a five-point stag for a national leader, a yearling buck for a bishop, a hedgehog for a press officer, and so on. Intercept positions were calculated by computer and relayed to camera teams and sharpshooters in helicopter gunships in case one of the celebrities missed and thus risked spoiling an important photo-opportunity. Further security teams patrolled the perimeters. Although field sports are a time-honoured tradition and the *Mabinogion* hardly speaks of anything else, certain ill-informed and malicious killjoys, largely ignorant of the countryside they claim to defend, would not hesitate to sensationalize the occasion for their own purposes.

As the day wore on, however, the hounds were surprisingly unsuccessful in starting a scent, despite all that satellite technology could do. Then, suddenly, a beautiful snow-white doe leapt from a thicket almost under the hooves of the President's horse, the pack gave tongue like a single beast, and the hunt surged wildly forward across rough ground and smooth, over streams and through tangled brushwood. For many miles the pursuit continued, until, breathing heavily, the two heads of state found themselves separated from the rest in a part of the woods the Prime Minister had never seen before.

As they bent low over their pommels and thrust through ever denser undergrowth, their cheeks were slashed by thorns and low branches, but they scarcely noticed the pain. Their breath came in short excited gasps. Always the white doe led them onward. Yet the President had sworn an oath by the American constitution which no President dares break, that the white doe would be his. And the Prime Minister had sworn that no distance would be too far, nor any forest too deep, if it afforded an opportunity of ingratiating himself with the President. Then, just when they thought they could go no further, the trees opened out to reveal a clearing, and a sight met their eyes that they would never forget if they lived to be a thousand years old.

165

'That the true heirs of Druid antiquity are still at large is difficult to affirm,' Neill told Triona in soft ambiguous accents, staring at the tips of his fingers in an attempt to appear unconcerned. 'Yet it would be mean-spirited to deny some do indeed persist, lurking in the dark hidden places of our woodlands where no-one ventures, or if they do, they swiftly forget what they see.'

Triona drew her horse under the shade of a spreading beech as the sounds of the hunt receded into the distance, and looked at him expectantly.

'Not everyone's life is their living,' he elaborated. 'And not everyone's living is their life. It's this that causes despair and enmity among us. Yet peace is a flower that blooms neither on hill nor heathland, but burgeons in the thinking heart and emancipates us from chaos. In the legend of Caryddwen's cauldron, there is a lesson for us all.'

'You need to be more specific. I know you're trying to tell me something – but I haven't the foggiest idea what you're talking about,' she replied – although perhaps she too was saying less than she could have done.

'Once I said we were among those who hide from what they pretend to seek, and flee from what they claim to pursue. But now I think we've gone beyond all that. I said we were not strong enough to change the world but too strong to be changed by it. But what happens today may finally change us, for better or for worse. True, we're invited here with a group of people who see themselves as movers and shakers. But you and I know they are only moved and shaken by Myles Overton, and he by Leatherwing. I've done what I can. After so long I was upset that Karen had only harsh words for me, and didn't appreciate the difficulties we were under, or how nearly we succeeded.'

'She said you can never resist over-playing your hand, and you wasted six months by blowing it with Tracey Dunn,' Triona reminded him. 'But you should've heard what she said about Finbar Direach!' She added this by way of consolation, for she secretly knew she had given Karen a version of events that did not necessarily paint Neill in a favourable light. Perhaps she was angry with Neill for some reason only a woman would understand, although surely the prospect of his resuming his old relationship with Karen should make her happy for them both.

'Time is a river, and life a millwheel,' reflected Neill. 'Or perhaps the other way round. It's all the same. That's why I've accepted this last invitation, and accompanied my estranged wife into a world of people as estranged from themselves as they are from their companions, and deceived by the very illusion they create to deceive others. Perhaps I'll get close enough to Myles Overton to trip his horse and finish the job with a heavy stone so it looks like an accident. Perhaps I'm still deluding myself with meaningless fantasies. But I wish just once I could see Karen again to let her know that whatever I've done, I did for her, and whatever I failed to do, I would have done for her if I hadn't encountered bad luck and been let down by other people.'

Having made these remarks he patted his horse's neck with the resigned self-assurance of a person who knows they have spoken no more than the truth, and although it was still early, took a sip from a silver hip flask containing the remnants of last night's hogweed ale.

'Events have taken an unfortunate turn,' Triona agreed. 'It seems our enemies have all the winning cards, to say nothing of the freehold on the casino. Yet we can't allow ourselves the luxury of self-pity. If there's a final throw to be made, we must make it today, and here. Talking of which – where are the Prime Minister and the President?

And where's the white doe? Stay here with the toadies and hangers-on and keep an eye on Myles Overton, Linden Richmont and Dave Doom! Something's afoot, and as sure as Karen is my sister, even if she's turned out to be Caryddwen, I'm off to see what it is. For there's no time like the present, even though the past used to be like it, and the future will probably also turn out pretty similar to it in due course. But that, perhaps, is what we have most to fear.'

'I think you're right,' said Neill. 'But our fears will prove well founded, unless you know anyone who can transform themselves into Tower Bridge and offer themselves as an alternative gift to the President.'

She looked at him strangely but declined to answer, for, she noted, time was a swift flowing torrent, and many an unwary individual had been broken on its weir.

166

Where the downland meets the forest, foliage breaks on the rough turf like a tree-green ocean on a grass-green shore. A river ran there long ago, but in time its course became overgrown by thorns and elders. The river flowed for countless millennia, rounding the curve below the escarpment before dipping through the woodlands, overhanging boughs carving eddies and streaks in the current, and woodland birds such as tree creepers and nuthatches mingling with bitterns, herons and water ouzels above its dark and resistless waters; but that was then, and this was now.

'The job', Caryddwen told Little Gwion all those years ago, before the river changed its course, 'is to shut up and stir.'

Llew Llau Gyffes, eyes like embers, urged the magic curragh of Naimhe against the morning ebb of the Tamar. Gog and Magog faced the outlander from their fastness at the ridge of Pin Hill to the North and West of Loughborough. Rowena and Vortigern, emancipated too late from the duplicity of Queen Maeve, embraced hopelessly beneath a mountain ash. Caryddwen's cauldron, broad as a dewpond, dispersed dreamlike miasmas across a misty dawn.

'The history and culture of these intemperate islands', pleaded Little

Gwion, 'have always been of compelling interest for me. So when I heard you had a position, I thought—'

'*I* think,' corrected Caryddwen. 'You stir. That's the way it has to be.'

'I can see there is a certain amount of stirring associated with the job,' Little Gwion acknowledged, looking at the long copper spoon which she was waving to illustrate her point. The cauldron was, however, so large that the only way to stir it effectively was to sail round and round in a small boat, dragging the spoon behind and tacking through the prevailing wind. Before Caryddwen, Little Gwion believed, it had belonged to Bran, although people were clearly mistaken if they said Bran's brother Evnissyen smashed it to fragments to subvert the insurrection of the Irish King Matholwych. The reason it got smashed to fragments was still in the future. When Little Gwion came to Caryddwen it was long before the catastrophic incident which turned huge tracts of land over to fishes and spider crabs as a result of Finbar Direach's betrayal of the trust placed in him by Mannannan Mac Llyr Mac Lugh. Long, indeed, before the latter was made prisoner of Queen Maeve of Skye and charged Finn with a message for Caryddwen that, had she ever received it, might have changed all subsequent history.

'This cauldron', said Caryddwen, 'not to put too fine a point upon it, contains nothing less than a re-creation of the original recipe of the Dagda, and is filled with the undreamt dreams of the people of these islands, and without it they would lose touch with unreality and become estranged from their essential selves. It's called Caryddwen's Rescue Remedy – capable of curing a thousand illnesses and also of restoring death to life and prose to poetry, if the old stories are to be believed. But some have another name for it, although at the present stage of your apprenticeship, you are not permitted to know what that name is, because, from your point of view, all that's important is to shut up and stir.'

'How long do I have to stir before I am given, so to speak, the bottom line on all this?'

Caryddwen looked at him with an unhurried look. 'For these things, it's necessary to be patient. Although I seem a beautiful young woman, I am myself more than a thousand years old, and the rigours of my employment have made me a martyr to housemaid's elbow. It was this that obliged me to advertize for an apprentice to take on the more menial aspects of my charge.'

'You have other duties?'

'My task, you must understand, is to send my messengers on their wet and windward way right across this land to the northern reaches of Cape Wrath and the islands beyond, and along the sunwashed coves of the South. Whenever a word of wisdom falls uncomprehended between the lips of the speaker and the ears of the hearer, these messengers snatch it up and add it to the contents of my urn.'

'There's nothing worse than when you say something clever, and people don't get it,' agreed Little Gwion. 'You daren't say it again, in case they think you're trying too hard.'

'I'm empowered to catch up the dreams that are dreamt without the dreamer's knowledge in the moment between sleep and waking, and to collect the aphorisms uttered by individuals advanced in their cups, which their companions are too intoxicated to appreciate and which they can't for the life of them remember the following morning. For it's always been accepted that even though the vessel might be broken and its custodian lost, if the recipe itself can be retained, our people might some day have the chance to become once more what, in reality, they have always been.'

Little Gwion was impressed by her words, although he initially made the classic mistake of inexperienced job applicants, and led with his weaknesses rather than his strengths. 'The truth is I've never done this kind of thing before. My arms are weak and my sight so blurred and imperfect that I can't distinguish a sloe-tree from a shoe-tree at five paces. On the other hand I can relate to people at all levels, I'm a good team player and very willing to learn. What I would like to know is how soon I can become, like you, a noviciate of that ultimate wisdom which all instinctively crave, even though most spend their entire lives evading it.'

'It's important to start at the bottom in any job. Nevertheless I'm not by nature an authoritarian or restrictive person. If your stirring shows promise, after the first thousand years I will let you change direction.'

There was not much encouragement in this concession. Still, even in those days Little Gwion was aware that however broad and rich in prospects the world proved to be, those for which his own abilities and experience equipped him were woefully few. Nor could he conceal, even from himself, his ambition to serve as an acolyte at the altar of truth, even if this meant a sacrifice in terms of material recompense. Yet the job Caryddwen offered clearly lacked both intrinsic and extrinsic benefits.

'And yet,' she told him, 'it is not without the prospects of promotion, for you may one day become one of the messengers who travel the country seeking out and distilling poems, songs, aphorisms of all kinds, scientific theories and metaphysical paradoxes, wherever they may be found. Messengers like Finbar Direach, for instance, whose name means 'Finn the Reliable'. But if you wish ever to be like him, you must first prove yourself by remaining in this clearing and stirring the mixture.'

'At least it doesn't sound too hard,' said Little Gwion.

'Ah, but don't think the enemies of our enterprise will leave you unmolested. On the contrary, they will come upon you in many guises, and instigate many ruses and stratagems to distract you. After a certain length of time, for instance, a monstrous blowfly will come rampaging over the eastern horizon and feed upon your lymph with relentless jaws, but you must neither desist nor deviate from your task, not even to swat it away with your hands.'

'A fly', said Little Gwion, 'is only a fly. Even if it's a big one.'

'Well,' said Caryddwen, 'perhaps that's nothing, but in due course a terrible noise will arise and a fiery wind will come, igniting the air around you until your very clothes burst into flame. And even then you must remain steadfast in the discharge of your responsibilities and not remove even a finger from the handle of the spoon to assuage the blistering heat.'

'At least', said Little Gwion, 'I won't have to worry about getting an all-over tan.'

'But even that's not the worst,' Caryddwen said. 'Because some time after that, enchanted music of harps and mandolins will fall upon your ear and – this is the greatest threat of all – a white doe will dance into the clearing and become a woman of uncanny and sensual beauty. As a result of having just changed from a white doe, she will lack clothing and her appearance might be too much for someone who's been alone in the forest for many centuries.'

'I can imagine the scene,' said Little Gwion, trying not to look as if he was enjoying doing so.

'Then let your watchwords be, *Shut up and stir!* For this, and the bizarre events to which it will be a prelude, must not be allowed to distract you. The way you conduct yourself at this time will pay for all. If you fail to act correctly, the consequences will bring disaster and devastation into lives as yet unlived, in realms and epochs as yet undreamed of.'

'I hear what you're saying.'

'Well, don't let anything I've mentioned put you off. To tell the truth, there were few applicants and you're the only one to have turned up for interview. What if I give you five hundred years' trial and we'll see how we go?'

When she put it like that, it was difficult to argue with her. But it was with mixed feelings that Little Gwion established his position in the midst of Caryddwen's clearing, stoked the fire of hazel and yew branches, and addressed himself to the task in hand.

Five hundred years can often seem like a long time, and Little Gwion's experience as Caryddwen's apprentice was no exception. Nor did the succeeding centuries and epochs seem any shorter. While Little Gwion stirred the cauldron, empires rose and fell, the cults of Babylon, Nazareth and Mecca bloomed and declined, the forests of Europe were levelled and turned into warships which battened upon each other and vanished into the deep, and the plains of America were leavened into dust by horse tractors, steam tractors and diesel cats, and the absolute deferred to the relative, which in turn provided a more universal absolution.

'There must be more,' said Little Gwion in his youthful foolishness, for in all the years of his employment, Caryddwen did not permit him to grow any older. 'There must be more to existence, to the human mind, and God.' He could never believe, as she seemed to, that the universe is nothing but God's own cauldron into which his apprentices superinduce a slow unending cyclicity, perhaps merely to stop the stars sticking to the sides. Often, during the early days, it occurred to Little Gwion that Caryddwen might be holding out on him, and deliberately concealing from him the wisdom he craved. But he was not without loyalty, and kept stirring anyway, until something should turn up. Although she beat him often, there was a kind of affection between them, but it would perhaps take a psychologist to explain this.

At length Caryddwen announced she had accumulated nearly sufficient ingredients for what she had in mind, but said the work still needed a certain essential, which would necessitate leaving Little Gwion in charge. 'The remedy is nearly ready,' she told him. 'But one constituent is missing, and obtaining it may be more hazardous than anything attempted so far. Yet that must not deter us! If life were a river, it would be as deep as it is long, and though the length of our experience can be measured by clocks, its depth can be measured only by the faith of the human heart, and the peace attainable when that faith is kept against seemingly impossible odds.'

Although she could not resist speaking in riddles, Little Gwion guessed the missing ingredient was nothing less than the White Flower of Aranrhod, and that she intended to send Finbar Direach, her most reliable messenger and also an accomplished fiddler, to play beneath the prison walls of Mannannan Mac Llyr Mac Lugh, who alone knew its whereabouts. 'Without the White Flower of Aranrhod,' Caryddwen confirmed, 'the remedy will never be complete – but naturally, the fewer people who know this, the better.'

Little Gwion easily understood why that should be. Who could forget that upon the untimely death of Bran, the giant King of Britain, from injuries sustained in wars against the Irish, his head was cut off and buried upon White Hill in London, facing eastwards? 'For,' said Bran, 'if you do this, no invasion from that direction will succeed for very long.'

Fewer still would be ignorant that shortly after this burial took place, a blue flower grew out of Bran's right eye, and a white from his left, in a manner marvellous to see. But the flower that grew out of Bran's right eye quickly withered and died, and to avoid the same thing happening to the other flower it was spirited away by an unknown person – but everyone agreed Aranrhod took it and gave it into the keeping of Mannannan Mac Llyr Mac Lugh. Also it was said that because Bran was a celebrated peacemaker, if nectar of the white flower was tasted by his true successor in the hour of the world's greatest need, the cycle of history would be fulfilled and harmony between men restored.

By this Caryddwen knew that if the flower could be found and she could squeeze only three drops of its juice into the remedy she was preparing, her work would be complete. Finbar Direach had an easy way with words and was the ideal person to convince Mannannan Mac Llyr Mac Lugh to part with his secret. But conscious of the need for discretion, Mannannan Mac Llyr Mac Lugh concealed the information in a long and heart-rending lay entitled *The Lament of Mannannan Mac Llyr Mac Lugh on being Incarcerated by Queen Maeve of Skye*, which, since it was so sad that it could not be written down, he considered safe from general publication.

'Make haste across heath and hillside,' he told Finbar Direach. 'And if you come to a river, fall on your face and swim. There is no time to lose. Already Leatherwing is on the trail of the white flower, and while I myself languish in chains, Caryddwen is the only hope.'

But as the days went by, Caryddwen grew more and more anxious, and paced to and fro beside her immense cauldron. 'I worry about Finbar Direach,' she said. 'I fear some terrible misfortune has overtaken him, perhaps at the hands of Leatherwing. There are rumours of floods in the northern lowlands, and the voice of the banshee has been heard on the hill.'

When there was still no news, she made her decision. 'I must go myself, and find out what has happened. Yet I sense great danger, and from this journey I may never return, or, if I do, I may be changed out of all recognition. Don't let that prospect deter you from your task. While I'm away you are in charge of the cauldron and all operations concerning it, of which stirring is, as we have agreed, paramount. Although I can't expect you to be as ingenious and reliable as Finbar Direach, yet you're the only one left, and you must do as best you can. And now, farewell, for the waters are rising, and nobody knows what the future may bring.'

Of the many truthful words Caryddwen spoke, this was arguably the most truthful, because, before she could get to Finn, history intervened, the land became inundated, the cauldron was broken, and of the enchantress herself all trace was lost. Some said her heritage was preserved down the generations in the darkest sister of the oldest family in Britain, and others that she was miraculously changed into a magic doe to wander the land disconsolate. Little Gwion, faithful to the last, escaped eastwards from the flood waters with sufficient of his incomplete mixture to fill an old hopper he procured from an itinerant peddler.

This, however, lacked the properties of the original cauldron and was wholly unable to bring dead things back to life, even though he tried with the corpses of many shrews, hedgehogs and other woodland casualties that came into his hands.

Broken, alienated, yet unable to break faith, Little Gwion completed his first thousand years, and then another thousand. He clung to the hope that one day Caryddwen would return, her remedy would be put to work in the world, and her own cauldron would be restored to ensure that one life was not all. He was visited by huge blowflies and fireballs but despite horrific injuries he did not cease to stir the mixture, although no white doe appeared and transformed itself into a naked woman, which left him strangely disappointed.

As the years passed, the landscape changed. The river beside which Little Gwion had established himself became diverted from its original course, and now powered the mills and engines of estuarine cities. Engines that were used in turn to despoil the forest through which the river once flowed and whose upper regions, by catching and combing the clouds that drifted across the ridge of the Weald, drew down rain that spawned the river in the first place. The people in the cities did not know this, for ignorance was endemic among them. Sooner or later, Little Gwion saw, the clamour of machinery would be audible from this very clearing, and after that, it was only a matter of time. He longed to have Caryddwen there to ask what he should do. Sometimes, indeed, her voice returned to his ears, keen as watercress, and when she said, *Shut up and stir!* the words seemed to take on a new meaning, and a renewed urgency.

'For countless years I've been your apprentice,' Little Gwion complained, as if answering the voice. 'And all that time you never taught me anything except *Shut up and stir!* which, although a valuable lesson, serves only as an *hors-d'oeuvre* of knowledge, stimulating my appetite endlessly for more substantial fare. Once, perhaps, we were lovers. Later we became bound by a force more enduring and powerful than love – a purpose out of which our identities grew like two branches out of the same root. For identity is the name for all non-linear and non-predictive forces in psychology, despite the fact that it has been used in quasi-predictive theories. But enough of that! I'm Little Gwion, not Neill Fife! You've never allowed me to be more than a child, but children are the jury of the future, and their imaginations must be cultivated with care. But teach me one further thing, and I will ask for nothing more!'

'A person can only be taught what he or she already knows,' said the voice in the trees. 'But it may be that I've taught you more than you think. Perhaps my leaving you is a test of that knowledge, and of my faith that the knowledge will stand you in good stead. But if you want to learn one more thing it is this: every person's refuge is their prison, and one must never forget that the mill wheel turns because the river flows, rather than the other way round. But who is the mill wheel and who the river, you may not know until the day of my return. Now – I have said too much already. Bank up the fire with fir cones and almond blossom, pull your cloak around you, and whatever happens – and you may be sure that something will – just shut up and stir – and all may still be well.'

167

The President of the United States had not always been absolute ruler of the most powerful nation in the world. Once he had been a small boy, hiding beneath the covers from invented monsters and strange chimeras of his own imagination. Always the sensitive one, he had seen his brothers become soldiers, film producers and corporate raiders, while he himself lived in a strange fantasy world where he drank from enchanted cauldrons, and fought with *gruaghres*, and chased white does which transformed themselves into beautiful princesses. Shy and academically unpromising at school, he was bullied unmercifully, and once, for not knowing the words of the American national anthem he had stinging nettles rubbed on his testicles so viciously that they swelled up to the size of his head and he had to spend an entire week in hospital, after which the doctors told his mother that he would unfortunately be impotent in adult life.

The President's mother herself was a successful Hollywood actress and supermodel who had married a television tycoon, ironically with a 30% share in Myles Overton's own Leisure Channel. Unable to face the prospect that her favourite son was destined for anything less than greatness, she sent him to a counsellor at the age of fourteen, who recommended deep hypnosis and positive thinking. Both the counsellor and the deep hypnotist found him polite, considerate and good-natured, but they were able to assure his mother that such conditions were nowadays quite treatable and there was every prospect of a complete cure.

They told the boy that people are no more than the sum of the thoughts and beliefs they hold, so whatever one believes oneself to be, one will inevitably become. 'The secret of a successful life is to believe in oneself, to believe in one's aspirations, and to kick shit out of anyone who doesn't,' they explained.

'But what if one is thereby diminished in the opinion of one's friends and acquaintances? I don't want to get thrown in the stinging nettles again,' said the President-to-be.

'The greatest fallacy of modern times is that being pleasant creates popularity, which creates success. Psychologists know that being unpleasant creates success, which creates popularity. This is why vicious, self-serving psychopaths are invariably more popular than decent, kind-hearted altruists.'

When their young client understood this line of thought, he resolved that nothing would stand in his way, and it was time to put the past behind him. After the corporate raider perished in a mysterious boating accident, unexpectedly leaving all his wealth to his younger brother, the President-to-be stood in local and then congressional elections, married a leading supermodel, and soon was tipped for the highest office in the land. Yet as he slept in his lonely bed (since the supermodel was notorious for her affairs and not even the two psychologists could reverse the effects of his childhood accident), did he still dream he followed a white doe through the gaunt and twisted branches of a primeval forest? A clear answer cannot be given, for our dreams are our own, even when all else has been taken from us.

The President had not expected to enjoy his trip to England, for he had a great deal on his mind. At home, Congress was volatile and the news media preoccupied with irrelevant trivia of his past business dealings, his wife's marital irregularities and the circumstances surrounding his elder brother's death. Nobody seemed interested in the solid policy record of the current administration on welfare, tax, and helping the army become homosexual. The British were courteous but curiously unemotional, like

Martians, and unable to say aluminum and toemaydoe. The British Prime Minister would not give him London Bridge, but instead unloaded on him a heap of old prehistoric crap that was covered in dirt and would need an aircraft carrier to get it back to the States so the nerds at Caltec could stick it together and win him the votes of a few maudlin Micks. His dream of Britain – if he ever had one, for it was hard to remember – had been so different. 'But one's dreams', thought the President, 'are the first things they take from one.'

The hunting expedition, however, stirred some distant recollection deep inside him, and the sights and smells of the woodland around the Prime Minister's secret country retreat made his skin tingle and the hairs on the back of his neck stand up. By the time the white doe started from almost under his feet, the President was already feeling as if he was somebody else entirely, and, it seemed, somebody else who swore that they would take the animal's life, or forfeit their own in the attempt. Somebody else with whom he had once been acquainted – friends, even – but had long ceased to communicate with even at Christmas and Thanksgiving. The meaning of all this was confusing and difficult to follow, but no more difficult than the white doe herself, who – if he were honest – took the whole of his concentration and effort.

'Asshole!' exclaimed the President, as Americans do, when a bramble, larger than the rest, swung across his path and laid his face open – but then, all at once, the undergrowth thinned. As he and the Prime Minister entered a clearing the sight that met their eyes was unusual in the extreme. For the white doe was entirely transformed into a beautiful woman, standing naked next to a dwarf who stirred a billycan as large as himself over a fire of fir cones and wild cherry branches.

'Asshole!' said the President. He was at a loss for words. Nothing like this ever happened to Robert de Niro. The scene, indeed, had a dream-like quality and the President was not surprised when he found himself raising his gun.

'Wait!' cried the Prime Minister when he realized that most Americans are more dogmatic than most British, and if they are chasing a deer, a little thing like it turning into a beautiful woman may not divert them from their purpose.

'I'm sorry,' said the President, pronouncing it sawry. 'This is something I have to do.'

The Prime Minister never forgot the calm in the eyes of the strange woman when the gun was levelled, as if she knew nothing could happen unless it was meant to happen, and whatever was meant to happen could not be changed by all the positive thinking in the world. Yet two things intervened to prevent the beautiful woman getting riddled with bullets before anyone had time to blink their eyes. The first was that the President was a very poor shot. Even at West Point he had almost failed to graduate on this account as a result of inadvertently putting a hole through his marksmanship instructor, although he had been saved by family connections, and the marksmanship instructor by transplant surgery. The second was that the saplings on the periphery of the clearing suddenly shook violently and Triona Greenwood galloped into view with a tremendous shout that caused entire tree-trunks to split asunder and even the tiny moles to quake and shudder in their underground fortresses.

'Wait!' shouted Triona.

'Asshole!' shouted the President, pulling the trigger with all his strength. But the bullet sailed off in a direction entirely different from that intended and made a small round opening, not wholly unlike an asshole, near the bottom of the receptacle which the dwarf still stirred on the brushwood fire. Immediately they all heard a hissing sound as what was in the hopper began to make its way down among the embers. Also the surrounding vegetation was set in motion again as several more riders – 'This is getting like the Grand National,' the Prime Minister muttered nervously – were attracted to the spot by the sound of gunfire: Myles Overton, Neill Fife, Dave Doom, Linden Richmont and several toadies and camp followers. For a few moments everyone repeated each other's names in bewildered or excited tones, but none more so than Little Gwion, who had until now been entirely speechless, for in the last thousand years he had nearly given up hope.

'Caryddwen!' he murmured, as if his whole world was in the name.

'Shut up and stir!' she told him, though not unkindly, for when she sniffed the boiling liquid she knew how well he had fulfilled his charge, although there was perhaps a little too much chilli in it and the last ingredient was still missing. 'Keep stirring, Little Gwion, for as I predicted, your greatest test has come. And try to stop the mixture running away – or the day will be lost!'

'Karen!' exclaimed Neill Fife, in the confused accents of someone who has only yesterday been re-united with the childhood sweetheart he believed for two decades was dead or kidnapped, only to see her chased through ten miles of forest in the form of a white doe and re-appear as a legendary enchantress thought to have drowned when the nation's lowlands were submerged by the floods which overwhelmed its land bridges to Europe and the Western Isles.

Perhaps Neill, more than anyone, felt the full force of the events of the last few days. Of what they had achieved, and what they had so tragically lost. Yet to see Karen like this was almost the last straw. Words failed him, and good manners too. He added, 'Who's the midget?'

'There's no time to explain!' she told him. 'For things are coming together. Or falling apart! I need your flask!'

Neill saw that lengthy enquiry into the reasons would be inappropriate. Besides, he knew his silver hip flask contained the remnants of last night's hogweed ale, and he realized at once that the white flower of Aranrhod must be the hogweed itself, which was no longer as rare as it used to be. Sure enough when he threw it to her, she shook three drops into Little Gwion's hopper.

'Karen!' cried Triona. 'What the hell's going on?'

She would have answered, but despite Little Gwion's efforts liquid was continuing to drain from the hopper like the blood from the wounded heart of a hero, and the President, taking advantage of the momentary confusion, was taking aim again, egged on by Myles Overton and Dave Doom.

'Go for it, Pres! Splatter the bitch!'

'No!' shouted Neill Fife in his turn. His voice reached the President as though it came from a thousand miles away, but it brought a renewed sense of ambiguity and hesitation.

The President felt that as a young boy he had already lived this scene many times, yet not always as the same person. Always a fierce hunter pursued a white doe through hidden trails and twisted branches. Is it not the fantasy of every red-blooded American male that he hunts down such a dazzling quarry, that she turns into a beautiful naked girl, spreading her arms joyfully to receive the bullet he will discharge into her? Yet sometimes the girl waited in the clearing with her arms spread by golden chains and iron bands, and the President-to-be burst through the trees only to see another, more terrible hunter level his weapon, and to hear a cry for assistance break from the victim's lips. Nor was it lost on the President that this hunter sometimes had the face of Myles Overton, although his glowering height, clawed fingers and baleful eyes suggested something more ancient, and less human. Sometimes the boy who became President dreamed he raised his hand against this fearful opponent, but in his most secret dreams he was neither the hunter nor the rescuer, but the girl herself, stretched out ready for a sacrifice she knew must be made.

'Wait!' shouted Neill Fife again, and several others too, for clearly something was about to be done which could not easily be undone.

'Wait for what?' the President demanded.

'To keep the bargain you made,' cried Neill. 'For you entered into an unbreakable agreement, and I'm here to make sure it's enforced.'

The President, forced partially back into reality, lowered his gun a few degrees and asked Neill whether he were some kind of asshole, or what bargain was he talking about?

'Only this,' said Neill. 'I now know the ancient name for Caryddwen's remedy, the name Caryddwen would never reveal even to Little Gwion, her own assistant, who I assume is this shortarse here. The name, nevertheless, that embodies the whole of the secret teaching of the Tuatha de Dannaan, through which our world may still come to its senses, turn from its path of spiritual desolation, and re-build the lost cauldron and all it stands for. For the name of the remedy is Peace, although the old Celtic expression has a deeper resonance, and the Scots, Welsh, and Irish all put their special inflexions into it. Peace is commonly thought of merely as the absence of war, as harmony between nations and individuals, the beating of swords into ploughshares, and various animals not eating each other, although the implications for world ecology cannot be ignored. Yet while it may be all these things and more, the Tuatha de Dannaan believed it could be made in one's own cooking hearth by mixing certain rare herbs and mushrooms. What matter how it's pronounced, or how it's produced? In your acceptance speech you declared, in what amounted to an unbreakable pledge, that the only thing you'd exchange for the fragments of Caryddwen's cauldron was World Peace. But Caryddwen's remedy is nothing less, so before it all runs out of the hole you shot in Little Gwion's hopper, I charge you to take on the obligation of Bran's true successor, and taste a wiser and more forbearing posterity.'

'Don't do it!' shouted Myles Overton, inwardly planning what he would do to the President's speechwriters. 'You'll blow the whole deal!'

'Do it!' urged Triona, and a kind of radiance stood round her, as befitted someone whose sister was none other than Caryddwen. 'Do it! For once you've tasted the remedy, your name will no longer be Lincoln P Schwarzenegger the Third, but Taliesin – Golden Brow – which although the *Mabinogion* naively equates it with being yellow-haired, should properly be construed as the Enlightened One, the Bringer of Peace.'

The temptation to follow her advice was strong, for the President had never liked being named after a car, and considered his central initial incongruous. Having got his knowledge of Celtic legend from the Penguin translation of the *Mabinogion*, like most people, he rather thought wisdom and not peace was the consequence of tasting Caryddwen's brew. But he was aware there are many inaccuracies in that narrative and he knew language and therefore thought are pyramidal in structure, so that the most elevated concepts are the most convergent in meaning. But before he could reflect fully on this, or even climb off his horse in order to inspect the dwindling ichor more closely, Myles Overton again laid a hand on his arm, playing for time.

'Come on, Mr President! Don't be a flaming drongo! Ask yourself what would happen if peace was allowed to get a stranglehold. Strewth – don't even talk about it! Peace isn't just about having no wars. It's a whole different bastard ball game. It's creeping bloody impotence – a world with its cobblers chopped off. The global economy would go straight down the dunny. We're talking worldwide poverty and bloody billions off the price of shares. Perish the bloody thought, worldwide poverty might even be ended, and the spectre of poverty is the bloody driving force of economic production. Greed and fear drive the whole bloody shooting match, and we bloody tamper with them at our peril, if you'll excuse my French.'

'Impotence', said the President, who had stopped listening after the first few remarks, 'is a medical condition and should not be treated as a metaphor for weakness or ineffectuality.' And dismounting from his horse, he approached Caryddwen, uncertain yet determined – as a schoolboy, surrounded by his friends, approaches the nurse for an inoculation.

The onlookers had by now mostly climbed off their own horses and Dave Doom had been kicked in the head by his and therefore was unable to intervene at Myles Overton's behest. And for the first time in his life, Myles Overton himself seemed to hesitate. Oswald, who had turned up somehow with Chantal, Damien and Sophie, even though it was a top-security event, was asking Triona how she felt about her sister so unexpectedly turning out to be Caryddwen, and Triona was telling him that in a sense everything was everything else, that people were no more than the sum of the thoughts and beliefs they held, so if you believed you were a famous long-dead enchantress, nothing could stand in the way of your becoming one.

The other onlookers sensed they were on the brink of an historic occasion. 'Not only that,' they said, 'but it's all happened without the intervention of any supernatural events other than a deer turning into a woman, and in particular without the sensationalism of a climactic battle between champions of a non-linear against a linear future – that is to say, Finbar Direach against Leatherwing. The writers of the *Mabinogion* have a lot to learn about the way things take place in real life, for while credulity can be much stretched, all stretching has its limits.'

No sooner had they said that, however, than in the most shadowy corner of the clearing the patterns of shade seemed to knit themselves into a dismal dark cloud, and out of it stepped a shape that brought apprehension to every heart. Perceiving it was Leatherwing, the security men turned ashen pale and even their dark glasses grew entirely transparent. Their trigger fingers grew numb, and their knees knocked together like castanets making incongruous little rhythms.

'Enough of this prevarication,' boomed Leatherwing. 'I'm going to kill Little Gwion and empty away the last remnants of the remedy untasted! While I'm at it, I might as well kill the rest of you too. It's not for nothing I'm called the most evil person that ever lived apart from General Jihad, and recent events have indeed revealed him to be the pussycat he always was.'

'Pardon me,' said a voice from the underbrush. 'But I think I'll just stop you killing them.' And suddenly the small form of Finbar Direach, looking more like Seamus 'Eight Pints' McGallon than ever before, faced the large straggling form of Leatherwing and his long veiny arms. Yet the heart within Finn was large, and his commitment unshakeable, even if in the past he had sometimes lost the plot.

'I accept!' cried Leatherwing. 'This is the moment I've been waiting for. I have in my hand two bright broadswords, and you need not think they were acquired cheaply. One is Ocris, the ancient blade with which Cuchulain fought his last battle, challenging the unconquerable sea itself in a mortal feud, and the other is Excalibur, which needs no introduction, and to get them I was forced to slay the giant Gog and go through many other hardships. But now, take your choice, for you shall have the better blade, and I will have the worse, and you shall strike the first blow, as if you were the offended party in this quarrel. But after that I'll make short shrift of you, and when you are dead the world will be at my feet.'

'I choose Ocris – because although Arthur was a great warlord and his sword never failed to complete a stroke, he was defeated at Camlan and it had to be thrown in a pond. As for the other, I've never heard it called by that name and for all I know you made it up. But it looks a nice piece of work, although it wasn't very useful against the sea, as might be expected. Besides, it is fitting I inherit Cuchulain's blade, because it was me who brought the sea upon him in the first place, and by using his sword I might redeem myself, and all history with me.'

'So be it,' said Leatherwing, shaking his blood-red locks. 'But that is very unlikely.'

As the world teetered between war and peace and Caryddwen's remedy slowly drained away despite all Little Gwion could do to put his finger in the hole, hampered as he was by the need to continue stirring, the two contestants each removed their left boot in token of irreconcilable enmity, and faced each other with wary eyes. They circled round and swung the long, serious-looking swords with palpable belligerence. But Leatherwing was treacherous and cunning, and struck Finn first, even though he had said he wouldn't, so that Finn was wounded in the thigh, and disadvantaged, and would probably have been killed there and then had not the blade been rather blunt due to the loss of a grindstone sometime before.

'That'll teach you never to believe what I say, unless I tell you that in the next five minutes you'll be dead, and beyond the reach of any assistance or help.'

Because Leatherwing, before the Tuatha de Dannaan repudiated him, had been Finn's father's brother, the two had often fought mock battles up and down the heathery banks of their native home, and Leatherwing taught Finn everything he knew. Although their styles were different, the frightening energy and swingeing strokes of Leatherwing were matched by the dexterity of Finn's footwork, and the adeptness with which he got his head out of the way whenever the great brown blade swooped down towards his neck. But Leatherwing had the advantage of reach, and of implacable evil, and also had not had a sword stuck in his leg before he was completely ready.

Anyone who has read the celebrated book of *Goddoddin*, Aneurin Gwawdrydd's bloody eye-witness account of the battle of Cattraeth in the fateful year of 610, can form an adequate picture of the slaughter, mutilation and human-rights abuse associated with hand-to-hand combat. At Cattraeth, despite consummate heroism and staggering losses on both sides, it was the modernizers who prevailed. Teuton aggressors drove the Celts westwards, and by establishing a new front from Offa's Dyke up to the Dee estuary in the north, effectively precluded contact between the Cymric tribes of the Lake District, Wales and Cornwall, fragmenting the ancient commonwealth and marginalizing its people. *Goddoddin* numbers the casualties in tens of thousands, and Cattraeth was undoubtedly the most important battle ever fought on British soil, deciding between a Celtic and a Gothic mind-set. Hastings, Bosworth, and Culloden, by contrast, were purely dynastic affairs.

When Finbar Direach and Leatherwing met, the issue of Cattraeth was in effect re-tried, for all present realized that if Leatherwing won, the game would be up, the cauldron would be lost, and all hope with it. But if Finbar Direach won, the modernizers might yet be pushed back, and the immemorial rights of the people allowed to re-assert themselves. 'The trouble is,' Oswald told Triona, who had left Presidents, supermodels and security chiefs to settle beside her old friend and watch the action. 'The trouble is, Leatherwing must lose, but he must lose quickly. For soon the mixture will have drained away, and then it'll be too late to reverse the events that have already been set in motion.'

'Karen'll think of something,' Triona said, with perhaps just a trace of sibling rivalry. 'For she's turned out to be Caryddwen, after all.'

The contestants leapt about the clearing with great unpredictable bounds, turned somersaults, swung from the boughs of overhanging trees, and used many tricks of ancient Celtic martial arts such as handstands and kicks in the goolies. As they fought, the sky darkened and the turf and leafmould were flung about in huge divots, while saplings and full-grown trees were torn up in the struggle and vast areas of woodland reduced to chaff and splinters by their whirling blades. Fully two hours or three it seemed the two heroes fought, until the sweat on their brows ran like meltwater across a salmon-weir or like Little Gwion's jealously tended remedy, which still spluttered into the relentless flame.

Finally, during a lapse in Finn's concentration, Leatherwing with a deceitful kick dislodged his opponent's sword and raised his own in the unmistakable posture of someone about to cut someone else's head off. Before anyone could think or do anything useful, Linden Richmont, who had until then shown no sign of emotion, seemed to come to a decision. She uttered a shrill cry and, tearing herself away from her guardian's side, she rushed forward, seized the hopper with desperate strength and holding it like a shield, launched herself into the path of the descending blade. With a sound like thunder, the sword struck the ancient vessel and shattered it into a thousand pieces, drenching Leatherwing in scalding hot Peace, which raised such fierce blisters and ulcers on his body that he recoiled, tripped over a concealed root (perhaps one of the seven lost roots of the World Tree Yggdrasil) and tumbled backwards on to Finn's blade, which had lodged point upwards in a thorny bush and therefore speedily put paid to him. Yet as Leatherwing died on the bloodstained soil, a shout of triumph died on any lips that opened to utter it. For even Little Gwion's vessel had not been enough to turn Leatherwing's mighty swordstroke aside, and Linden Richmont too was laid low, a fatal stain spreading across her blue corsage.

Everybody moved at once.

Finn and Triona swiftly carried Linden into the shade of a rowan tree, and covered her with a warm cloak. Karen, or Caryddwen, held her head and offered her water, although the wound was too deep and her powers could not prevail over it. Myles Overton cried with horror as he realized what Linden had done, and that she might now be lost to him for ever. With the others, he ran to her and knelt by her side. She too knew they needed to talk. So much was still unsaid between them. Yet something else must be done first.

'Come closer,' she said. But as Myles Overton eagerly bent down she added, 'No, not you. Him. The President of the United States.'

The President, while all this was going on, had been like a man slowly awakening from a dream. He liked a good scrap and had never missed a heavyweight title fight, but he felt in part to blame that this particular matter had not been resolved sooner, and with less animosity.

'If there's anything I can do?'

'You've done enough,' breathed Neill. 'Or too much—'

'It's not my fault,' said the President defensively. 'I have nothing against peace – even though it's no vote-winner. But everything's for nothing, because what little was left of the mixture got spread half across the forest when the hopper burst. Without it there's nothing to exchange for the fragments of Caryddwen's original cauldron, so I can't break my pledge to bring them home, even though I may go down in history as an asshole for my part in this.'

'I'm dying,' said Linden. 'Yet I'd gladly slip from this delicate and beautiful world, if I knew that through my action, its delicacy and beauty could be preserved, and my own memory add to its richness. But delay no longer, and return across the clearing to where the corpse of Leatherwing lies prone amid the trampled growth of dog's mercury and poison ivy. On his neck and breast you'll see the bright blood and the dark, but on his forehead you'll see a thousand beads of sweat still glistening from his recent exertions, and in the midst of them as sharp as a diamond amid fragments of glass, a single remaining drop of the remedy Little Gwion watched over with such diligence, and for which he put his life on hold for several millennia. Touch this drop of moisture with the tip of your little finger, and touch that finger to your lips, and then return, and tell me what transpires.'

As the others watched in silence, or ill-concealed grief, the President crossed the clearing. Although it suddenly seemed like a desert a thousand miles in breadth, he came at last to the corpse of Leatherwing, which seemed like a range of poisonous hills on its furthest edge. Yet among the hills were a thousand pools, each danker and more fetid than the last, until he came to a single clear pool whose glint was as sharp as a knife. But as he leaned to drink, a terrible dread overcame him, and he ran away from it and returned at length whence he came, full of cant and equivocation.

'What did you see?'

'Nothing but the ripples spreading in the pool as I stooped to take my fill.'

'You may be a President, but your words are treacherous and insincere. Return to the corpse of Leatherwing, and do as I asked you!'

But the next time the President crossed the clearing, it seemed like a vast ocean which he was obliged to traverse in an ill-found ship with bad provisions. The corpse of Leatherwing seemed like a treacherous reef on its furthest edge, peopled only by barren weeds and the nests of scavenging birds from which the stink of decay rose to oppress a low and brooding sky. The nests of the scavenging birds numbered a thousand, each one with a clutch of eggs more unsavoury-looking than the last. In one nest, however, the eggs were bright and brilliant blue. But as he stooped to take one, unaccountable loathing filled him, and he threw it down and ran away, never stopping until he was again at Linden's side.

'What did you see?'

'Nothing but the fragments of eggshell that I crushed and threw to the wind after I had drained its contents at a single draft.'

'You may be a President, but your words are empty and devoid or accuracy or truth. Return to the corpse of Leatherwing, and do as I asked you!'

But the next time the President crossed the clearing, it seemed like a foreign country whose inhabitants were dour and xenophobic, and Leatherwing's corpse like a great city on its furthest edge. In the city lived a thousand women, but their faces were grim with nameless torments and tribulations. Each woman walked purposeless, with her gaze fixed a yard in front of her feet and her hands clasped in unanswerable supplication. But one moved among them like an angel, and her clear eyes and floating hair caused the President to stop in his tracks and sink down in front of her, clasping her hands in his own and soaking them with tears. To him, she resembled nothing so much as his own sweet unfaithful wife, on the hot moonlit night they first met during

August on a balcony above the East River, before the vagaries of sex and politics destroyed for ever the purity of their attraction. 'Forgive me!' he said, although it was she who had always been the guilty party. As their lips touched he felt a sudden dread, and self-hatred pierced him like a well sharpened sword. But he went ahead anyway, and felt his identity momentarily dissolve into hers, and through hers into the single immutable identity that is shared by all the diverse people of the world for past, for present, and for future.

'I saw,' he said when he returned, and Linden asked him, 'I saw peace.'

'That's what I thought you'd see,' she said. 'For peace can be found neither on the highest mountain nor in the deepest valley. And though a magic remedy is good, something more is needed, for only in a heart that has conquered jealousy and fear can true peace be discovered, and there it will neither wither nor fade, until the wild deer runs no longer in the quiet forest, nor the salmon on the turbulent weir.' And with these words Linden closed her eyes and sank back in a carpet of celandines, content that her work was done.

'Give her water!' Triona cried. 'And healing herbs!'

But Myles Overton again moved to her side, fearful that his chance to put things right with her had been lost. And when he leaned over her there was no colour in his cheeks, and his words were devoid of their customary colourful epithets. 'In my pride and my greed – what have I done to you?'

Her eyes opened tiredly once more. 'You didn't do it. Leatherwing did it.'

'But I brought Leatherwing into the world.' And sadly he told her how in his youth he had gone further and dealt darker than anyone before. The story about a chance meeting with a shadowy figure was only partially true, he said. Because one stormy night when forked lightning bounced off the edges of the sky and immemorial dreams oozed through into reality, he himself had woken Leatherwing, and made him his slave, obliged to carry out his every whim.

'I must have been out of my head. I wanted to be a world-class player because, I used to say, happiness is a shitload of money.' But, Myles Overton went on, as the years went by, he never stopped to ask himself whether Leatherwing was really subject to his will, or whether he was subject to Leatherwing's. And although he soon had more money than he could shake a stick at, his life was full of emptiness. 'My businesses did well, my name was well known to heads of state and top people the world over. But to be honest they're all drongos. I had everything, yet I had nothing. Then one day I heard about my brother's accident, and you came into my life. A small sad spirit who brought out the care and affection I had always kept hidden, even from myself. I thought, "Linden makes me happy, I'll get her a shitload of money!" I decided nothing less than the whole world would be good enough for you, and to give it to you, I had to get it myself. This led me down the path I followed – not knowing it would end by destroying the very person it was created for.'

'You gave me everything money could buy. I had a Mercedes roadster on my seventeenth birthday. How could I explain that you didn't give me enough?'

When he heard this, Myles Overton looked a thousand years old, and the lines on his face were like cracks in rock, and he bowed his head and cried, the tears falling in great self-recriminating drops. 'Forgive me!'

'I can't forgive you on behalf of the countless people you have wronged, because that would be to wrong them in my turn. But between you and me, there's nothing to forgive. You gave me all you could. Yet before I die – but who can tell whether one life is truly all? – I need to say that since I first saw you until today, you never kissed me or touched even the tips of my fingers, though I've always tried to please you even when it went against my conscience. That's why I secretly called myself Linden the Unloved, and held back from all emotional commitments. But if you will take me in your arms now, and smooth my hair back from my forehead as if I were a young child being put to sleep, it'll pay for all, and I'll die happy.'

For every tear Myles Overton had cried before she started speaking, he cried a hundred when she had finished. As he drew her close to him, he realized that he would give all the money he had ever made, and all the companies he had an undisclosed holding in, to extend her life long enough to say how he really felt. But no sooner had he begun to speak than he saw her eyelids had already closed, and knew that for the first time in a life celebrated for its split-second timing, he was too late.

Triona, coming closer, pulled off her silk jacket and bundled it under Linden's head – not caring whether it cost a thousand pounds. 'I never thought, when we first met in the Centre for Alternative Healing, that it would come to this. Yet even then I knew our destinies were intertwined. I thought I was the self-sacrificing one, but now you've laid down your life to save us all, even though all you had from us was rejection, slander, and offensive language, whether it was merited or not.'

168

Close by the clearing and through the trees, a river flowed. Nobody remembered seeing it when they came through earlier in the day, but it seems preposterous that a waterway which changed its course so many years ago should suddenly be found flowing back in its ancient bed. Yet there was a river, and that was that. Sorrowing, they wrapped Linden's body in silk and broderie anglaise, and strewed it across with sprays of beech, aspen, and weeping willow. They threw bluebell flowers on it, and wood-anemones, and bitter sorrel, and they carried it towards the water with melancholy songs and lamentations.

As they reached the river's edge they saw a barge drifting in towards the bank, though it was unoccupied and no hand guided its tiller. Four companions stretched out to hold the strange boat, and four companions stepped on board, carrying Linden Richmont's body with tenderness and dignity. Those who held the boat were Finbar Direach, Myles Overton, the Prime Minister, and the President of the United States. Those who boarded were Neill Fife, Triona Greenwood and the one they had all known as her sister Karen, and Oswald Hawthorne, who for grief could hardly speak, despite having known little or nothing about Linden Richmont as a person.

When they were aboard, the boat turned in the current and was again carried downstream beneath the green overhanging boughs and past the tumbling banks of birch, bramble and bryony. Broken branches drifting in the current carried with them like outriders in a cortège.

Many hours they travelled down the unhurrying stream without speaking, their hands still holding Linden's body as they had held her when they were carrying her to the boat – as if unwilling to let go.

Linden lay in repose, her mouth gently smiling, as though you could live forever by the very act of dying. Past the walls of Coldharbour and by the Stepping Stones the little craft floated bravely, and Karen sang an old song in a language none of them knew, and all of them understood. In the song, four heroes travelled in a curragh, carrying a fallen comrade to where their enemies would never find her. The song recounted many months of skirmishing and hard living since the peoples of Wales and Cumbria faced the invader in a grim bulwark from Caer leon to Carlisle, then risked and lost all at the battle of Cattraeth when the Marches were overwhelmed and the Cymric heartland laid waste. As the song was composed, Saxon longships with the men and gear that would make the opposing force invincible were already berthed at Anglesey. The council of Druids which maintained lines of power from Ireland across to Byzantium and the Asian steppes was compromised and then destroyed. Merddin Gwyllt was trapped by arts he had himself imparted. He tried to get word to his cousin Caryddwen urging that their hopes were not destroyed but only scattered, yet few believed this, and everyone knew that even if Caryddwen were alive, she no longer had her magic cauldron, and the symbol of the land's integrity was gone.

'If the cauldron is lost, *all* is lost,' the lament went up. 'We will fight and die, but only to find in our deaths a reprieve from witnessing the death of our nation.'

Unexpectedly, then, the refrain changed to a celebration of faithful remnants in the secret places of the land, of the dedication of Little Gwion, the assiduousness of Finbar Direach, the miraculous birth of sisters who played together by a cracked wishing well near a broken-down abbey, a tiny indefatigable group who found what no-one could find, a tyrant king and his beautiful heiress, the gift of Peace, and the final sacrifice of Linden Richmont.

Because, the song continued, lifting itself into a final threnody of sound which seemed to mingle with the river's own voice and the voices of the trees, the rushes and the songbirds past which it flowed, in every end there is a beginning, and one life is not all.

Past the watersmeet and the old mill, the current picked up speed as the banks changed their character; forest gave way to downland meadows and later on samphire and marram grasses as the river became tidal and, instead of twigs and larch cones, crab shells, bladderwrack, and mermaids' purses were borne on its spate. It was a long time before anyone would break the silence that followed Karen's song, for they were afraid their voices would sound like old crows grubbing after earthworms. But there were farewells to be said, and soon the river would flow out into the sea.

169

'Life', began Neill, 'is an endless river, flowing into a bottomless ocean.'

'I see you haven't lost your well known ability to turn a phrase,' replied Karen. 'But you've only scratched the surface of things. There's far more to it than that.'

'How much more?' he asked, more ready to learn from her now than ever in the past.

'Only what is experienced can be real,' replied Karen. 'Since death cannot be experienced, it follows that it cannot be real. Isn't that the central argument of your new book, *How The Hourglass Was Broken*? Yet when you come up against actual events, your theories desert you, and you just want to hide your face in your hands.'

'You still haven't told me how much more there is to it.'

'You already know,' she said. 'Everybody knows. The ancient shamans believed that the key to life is that while many things may be lost, nothing is ever destroyed. For, they said, before history was created by the salmon of life running upon the weir of time, everything that exists was pent in a monstrous cauldron belonging to the Dagda. Nobody needs reminding how, by means of a magic beaver, our forefather Lugh frustrated the Dagda's attempt to create a universe which was wholly unreal. Nor that the day came when through mismanagement and neglect the cauldron was broken. But although in one sense its fragments have been recovered by Finbar Direach, in another they still constitute everything known of today; the planets and the fixed stars, the mountains and the oceans, the rocks and the trees, the wild animals and birds, all the fecundity of life. For the cauldron embodies the cyclicity of the universe and the recurrent nature of events within it, and that is what we've struggled to preserve. In such a universe all cauldrons are one cauldron, and the difference between life and death is merely a difference in organization. Everything lost will be found, as everything broken will be mended, and if it is not, then someone will construct another one equally as good.'

'That would explain why the adherents of the Tuatha de Dannaan didn't mind being annihilated and put to the sword at Cattraeth,' said Triona a little scornfully. For, with Leatherwing dead, it was easy to speak of a non-linear universe as if it had been the only possible outcome.

'They did mind, but there was nothing they could do about it. So they said, "Kill us all you like, but never forget we will return, for nothing is for ever. Or, perhaps, everything is."'

'I still don't understand what all this has to do with turning into a white doe and getting chased by the President of the United States without any clothes on.'

'I don't want Father to hear about the white-doe business. He's bound to think it odd.'

'*I* think it's odd. I think it's *distinctly* odd. It's not the sort of thing I take kindly to any sister of mine doing.'

'You're just jealous because you can't turn into a white doe yourself. Besides, what's all the fuss about? Even Neill will tell you that a fallow deer has 97% of the same genetic material as a human being. It's only a question of how it's organized.'

'I think we both know what I'm talking about. It would have been very nice of certain people, if they knew certain things were going to take place, to have said so to their sisters, instead of leaving them in the dark until the last moment, and then expecting them to go on as if nothing had happened.' And having said this Triona turned her back, hunched her shoulders, and started to whistle a little tune, as though she had not a care in the world.

'Look – you two—' began Neill.

'And don't call us, "you two",' they both said, rounding on him. The thing about world peace, perhaps, is that it takes a little time to start working. But Oswald said, 'Shhh! Think of Linden,' and they knew he was correct. As the river carried her down, the setting sun threw shadows across Linden's composed features. Her hands were folded, and flowers covered her like a priceless garment. A wren sat on her left knee, and a kingfisher on her right, and her feet were wrapped in soft mosses and crimson ivy.

'Goodbye – though I never really knew you,' Triona said to Linden, touching her eyelids.

'Her last words', said Neill to Karen, for she would always be Karen to him, 'were that she died for love. Perhaps if it was good enough for Linden to die for, it's good enough for us to live for.'

Triona gazed off into the distance, as if she were a person who, as well as being totally indifferent to what was being said, suffered from chronic deafness.

'You haven't changed,' Karen told Neill, smoothing down her hair and trailing her hand in the water, making a little line of circular eddies. Her voice made him uneasy. Always, she had been able to run faster than any of them, and steal apples from higher up the tree. Had he loved her at all, or just wanted to put one over on her? Had she loved him, or had all her actions merely been to ensure someone was handy with a flask of hogweed ale when it was needed? When she spoke, she only told him what he was already thinking.

'You wanted success, not love. While I was with you, you loved the person you thought you would become if you succeeded in making me love you. After I'd gone, I was your excuse for not loving anyone else. You concentrated on success, and if you had relationships with magazine editors and supermodels, who will deny you were just using their hearts as stepping stones? Linden's lesson to us was that a person should take love where they find it – for it may be closer than they think.'

Neill looked at her confusedly, and then lifted his head and looked away. For a long moment both he and Triona were therefore scanning the horizon with a great affectation of unconcern, until each peered sidelong at the other and their eyes inadvertently met.

'You mean . . . ' Neill began again – speaking to Karen.

'I don't mean anything. If you thought I meant more than I said, the extra meaning must have come from you, not me.'

Neill looked at Oswald. Oswald looked at Triona, and then looked back at Neill and made a little gesture of spreading his hands, as if to say: things change, as you said yourself in your latest book.

'But I thought—'

'I told you,' said Oswald. 'That was all over the moment I killed the Clay Man. I learned to let go, and it's a lesson I shall never forget. I realized then that I was in love not with Triona, but with my own sense of rejection. That my futile preoccupation had made you, Neill, with the delicacy of a true friend, refrain from expressing your own regard for Triona and instead throw yourself into your work, using the loss of Karen as an excuse to squander your affection on a supermodel with whom you had little in common except a fascination with celebrity.'

'If this is true,' said Triona, again pointedly not looking at Neill, 'we may all have wasted the best years of our lives.'

'Life cannot be wasted,' Karen said. 'It can only be lived.'

'Keep out of this,' said Triona.

'Pardon me for breathing,' Karen said ironically. 'I didn't know there was anything to keep out of.'

'Well then, you don't know everything, do you?' said Triona, and aggressively put her arm round Neill, making the boat rock from side to side and small quantities of water slop over each gunwale. Who could guess whether this was just pique, or the beginnings of something more? Perhaps indeed Neill had been in love with nothing but his own success, as Oswald had been in love with nothing but his own failure. But if Neill was fascinated by celebrity, Triona was on the Heritage Commission, and involved in a vital project for a lasting monument. If he was fascinated by Greenwood sisters, well, one might do as well as another – or better! Karen looked across at Oswald and spread her palms outwards, making about Neill exactly the dismissive gesture Oswald had made about Triona.

Triona saw it, and felt herself free to choose as she pleased. Peter Goodlunch was dead, and many other Peter Goodlunches were gone, with their BMWs and their insouciant charm. Perhaps a person might spend their life seeing Peter Goodlunches, because they knew Neill Fifes would touch something inside them that they weren't sure they could bear to have touched. As Karen said, certain people who had used her disappearance as an excuse for not living their lives, now had no alternative but to face up to their real needs. Had the two of them learned to love, or just got tired of being free? Triona seemed untouchable, but in the dark reaches of the night, perhaps she needed Neill Fife beside her. Neill Fife seemed to have it all, but perhaps all he needed was Triona Greenwood, and the knowledge that she would always be between him and the abyss.

170

The boat floated on, and their thoughts floated with it, although they looked a hundred times into Linden Richmont's face, and speculated a hundred times on what makes people do the things they do. 'Perhaps', Oswald said, 'people are a theatre for each other's actions. Yet some of us must still go on alone.'

'Not', declared Karen, 'if they admit to themselves their true feelings.'

'I don't know what you mean.'

'Let's not start that again. Or have you forgotten what you told me about Tracey Dunn, when I came to you before the feast at Coldharbour.'

'Tracey Dunn is who she is, and I'm who I am. Besides, we talked that evening, and I could see she had no time for me.'

Seeing that he was in danger of falling in love with his own feeling that Tracey Dunn had rejected him, just when he had finally fallen out of love with his feeling that Triona Greenwood had rejected him, they all told Oswald to pull himself together. They said encouragingly what a nice girl Tracey Dunn seemed to be, although she had had a thing about Peter Goodlunch – but, as Triona pointed out, Peter Goodlunch could be very charming. Neill described how Tracey had pulled him out of the depths by his heel, which caused Oswald a twinge of jealousy. They were sure, they said, she and Oswald would be right for each other.

'You shouldn't be afraid of celebrity!' Karen said, and with some insight, since she was technically Tracey's aunt. 'It would be easy to make too much of the fact that she called the seals and was born of a magical people in extraordinary circumstances. To be honest, most women just want to be valued for themselves. If the need is great enough, nearly all of us can turn into a white doe or call the Great Silkie of Sule Skerry to our rescue. But, as Dawn will tell you, we're taught from an early age to underestimate ourselves. Well – that's a matter between you and Tracey, and old friends should not interfere. Still . . . '

'I don't know,' said Oswald confusedly. 'I'm just an accountant, and I don't even have a job.'

But Karen would have none of it. 'You killed the Clay Man, didn't you? You gave up everything for the one person you believed in. You have loyalty, and deep feeling. Everything suggests you shouldn't be an accountant at all, but an estate agent or a theatre critic. Even when the police implicated you in my disappearance and accused you of foul play, you didn't cave in under questioning or deny you were the last person to see me alive, for you were determined to protect Neill, or Triona, or both. I always knew your inner strength, even if certain other people took a long time to see it.'

'You don't know what took me a long time, and what took me a short time,' Triona retorted.

'I'll think about what you've said,' Oswald told her. 'But things aren't easy for me.'

'When one door shuts, another door opens,' Neill said to Karen in his turn. 'But we'll remember your words for ever, even if we don't understand them. It's been a long day, and we're all confused. I don't know whether you're the Karen we knew in times gone by. Your hair, once black, has turned to gold, and your eyes are as bright as fool's fire.'

'Things can't be as they were before,' she replied patiently. 'But that doesn't mean they can't be better. I'll never forget you, and you'll never forget me. We'll always be a part of each other. Now, your friends are waiting on the grassy promontory up ahead. Questions must be answered, and explanations given. As the boat draws in to the bank, you and the others must disembark and do what you can. They won't notice me against the patterns of the sunset reflecting off the water, and Linden and I must make one last journey, to a place where one day we will all meet again in our true colours.'

Sure enough, as the boat drifted onwards they saw that up ahead of them was a crowd of people, including many journalists from the *Sunday Scoop*, Myles Overton's Leisure Channel and the *Today* programme. Four-wheel drives and trailers were drawn up where the green verges sloped down to the water. The Prime Minister was there, and the President of the United States, but they took no precautions against assassination and ran from one person to another, embracing them and laughing like young children. The Prime Minister was less ingratiating than formerly and it was obvious to everyone that the President's impotence had been miraculously cured, although this would lead to some unfortunate events further down the line. Myles Overton himself was there, carrying his sadness with rough dignity, and Dave Doom was beside him, his face creased with tears, for he had been kicked in the head by a horse, had lost the woman he loved in his own unreconstructed way and thought had just accepted him, and had been told he was fired for blubbing. Chantal and Damien were there, Damien punching the air with his fist and saying, 'Well, we got a result!' as though he had done it himself, and Chantal shushing him because she understood the proper way to behave in the presence of the fallen brave.

Rufus Stone was there, and he raised a parting glass to Linden, although he did not know her well. Sophie Greenwood was there, with a letter saying the government was sorry her school got a bad position in the league table, which was the result of a misunderstanding, and no charges would be brought. This was signed by Matthew Arnold – his last action before resigning his post for ever. Little Gwion was there, free at last of having to shut up and stir, and determined to take evening classes or enrol with the Open University. Tracey Dunn was there, for she had received a secret letter from Oswald Hawthorne, but she dared not hope that it meant what it said, and even if it did, she knew it would not be easy to forget Peter Goodlunch, and she would need time. Martyn McMartyn, released like Little Gwion as a changing world made his duties superfluous, accompanied Dawn, whose two beautiful children held hands on which, as a result of what was accomplished that day, a new crop of fingers was already budding forth. The hundred sons of Genghis Khan were there despite difficulties in obtaining visas, but their mother was not, for she had already become one with the Aral Sea, so her presence would obviously have been impractical. Nor was Nuala Greenwood there, but perhaps she was somewhere else, and already holding Linden Richmont in her arms.

On the brow of a nearby hill, a small figure with a bandaged leg stood next to a bubble car. Finbar Direach had lived a long life, and a strange one. Today, he had fought the battle he had perhaps been born for. But now the daughter he never knew seemed to be taking up with an accountant. Jenny Greenteeth, the sister with whom he had just been reunited, had been offered a position by the President of the United States, where the miracle of cosmetic surgery would enable her to mix freely in society. Perhaps Finn would have preferred her to wait for Martyn McMartyn's fingers to grow again fully so that he could attempt to charm back her beauty using the harp of Rhiannon. But it was clear that the new ways were different from the old, and perhaps that was only as it should be. Was Finn himself now a kind of relic, relevant only to a bygone era? He felt strangely alone, watching the colourful throng below him. But what had really changed?

The boat neared this garrulous company at an easy pace, sometimes turning stem for stern in the irregular flow, but all at once there came to their ears a strange eerie sound, like someone playing very badly on the Uillean pipes.

'I'm no expert,' Oswald said. 'But there seems to be an object caught on that salmon weir over there, and from its sorrowful plaint I believe it to be a set of magic bagpipes. If I'm not mistaken they are attempting to play *Carrickfergus* but making a very poor fist of it.'

'I'm no expert either,' replied Neill. 'But what you can hear is the crying of an infant from a wicker basket jammed in the weir-gates.'

Sure enough, when they climbed along the weir, there was a brown-eyed female child, who laughed up at them as they lifted her improvised cradle clear of the flow. Karen, who had watched from the boat, bent down to Linden one last time and whispered a single word in her ear which none of them was close enough to hear. The word, rendered into English from an old Celtic tongue, was 'rebirth'. A marsh warbler trilled in the samphire beds. Karen or Caryddwen took Linden's limp hand and slipped off the third finger a silver ring once given to Linden by Nuala Greenwood, although formerly it belonged to the Queen of Lebanon.

'This', she said to the baby, 'will be your birthright, and your name will be Linden, which means Bright Hope for the Future.' But it was Tracey who took the young child in her arms, remembering her own infancy, and Oswald, after hesitating, took Tracey. After that there was nobody in the boat with the dead except Karen, standing upright and looking out to sea, as the tide took the little craft over the bar and out towards low-lying islands beneath the hinge of the horizon, where once it was thought Mannannan Mac Llyr Mac Lugh ruled from his watery fastness, and his wife Ran or Rhiannon welcomed drowning sailors into her sea-green arms.

171

When the Lord Mayor's show has gone by, it hardly matters whether the fat lady sings or not, for there are few to hear her, and fewer still inclined to listen. In the aftermath of what happened there was no party at Coldharbour. Partly this was because there had been many complaints locally following the previous round of festivities. Partly it was because Neill and his friends, like the Heritage Commission, the minister responsible and the Prime Minister, felt what still needed to be achieved was best carried out away from the glare of publicity, and it would not be in the public interest to create public interest in the events of recent weeks.

If there were awards for cover-ups, the Leatherwing business would have swept the board. Yet, keenly feeling the incongruousness of top civil servants in black ties being presented with little stylized bronze paper shredders and deferentially shaking the hands of minor royalty, the authorities had banned such ceremonies, and the greatest recognition the covering-up profession achieved was to have no recognition at all. Yet one question remained before the whole sorry affair could be laid to rest. It could be summed up in five words.

Where were the lost children?

Although at the end of the Cold War the Special Section had lost its role in international espionage and instead concentrated on drug dealers, subversives and abductions, even at the time these events took place it was a highly secret organization, and a force to be reckoned with both in civilian and military circles. The Head of the Special Section therefore held one of the most responsible positions in the land, and when the dossier on the Leatherwing affair came across his desk, he was aware it was no insignificant matter. Beyond this, he had little actual detail. In accordance with the policy of extreme secrecy maintained at the Special Section, he had never been informed that he was head of that organization or, indeed, anything to do with it. He thought he was the ticket collector at Coldharbour station. The policy of keeping him in the dark had its drawbacks, particularly as far as the reporting structure was concerned, but the minister responsible was adamant, for it was one of his own innovations.

'If the Head of the Special Section is captured, and talks, it could compromise our entire network. No. Far better this way, that everything is dealt with on a strictly need-to-know basis, and that, in all respects, we keep our cards close to our chests.'

The minister was playing a clever game, since nobody else knew who the Head of the Special Section was either. He was the minister's personal appointment, so his identity could be kept completely secure, and he could be isolated from other members of the service who might perhaps have compromised him.

A lesser man might have found the information vacuum created by this policy an impediment. But the Head of the Special Section was a thorough, methodical individual, and although the material to hand was garbled and chaotic, he could see that the events of the last few weeks were of national or indeed international importance, even before he knew what they were.

'The facts, as I see them, are these,' he told his wife at breakfast, wiping marmalade off the pile of press cuttings in front of him. 'A secret installation, perhaps linked to our treaty obligations with the United States, is being assembled on British soil, having been rescued from the hands of a shadowy group of idealists and lunatics led by Chantal Greenwood, who reliable sources confirm is back in the country. Doubtless Arab money is behind this, and one must accept the possibility that the Irish are involved. The authorities, for their own reasons, have chosen to keep things quiet, but in a recent attempt to breach the security of a visiting head of state there was an exchange of hostilities resulting in the death or neutralization of several key individuals. And bringing pressure to bear on Myles Overton's global business empire, whose share price has now been fatally undermined, with consequences for equity markets in London, New York, Hong Kong and Tokyo.'

'It seems', said his wife, 'that without our taking any action, things may have sorted themselves out.'

'That would be true,' said the Head of the Special Section, 'except there was also evidence of a plot to abduct children, perhaps over many generations past. A plot to constrain them, at least figuratively speaking, to a life of toil in which fulfilment and self-determination are mere meaningless words. My task, in conjunction with the Heritage Commission, is to devise a course of action which will finally lay to rest the ghosts of a troubled past – or make them less ghostly by reviving them in the true vigour of their former existence. Although, of course, nothing must be done that could implicate the present government or reveal full details of recent events.'

Fortunately his wife was a sensible woman and used to challenges of this type. She had already begun to suspect that her husband was in some way Head of the Special Section, and she understood the need for discretion. From her own files, the local library, and hacking into some secret government archives via the Internet, she found out what she could and passed him the information in as concise a form as possible.

When the Head of the Special Section opened the secret files and read the first word, his face crinkled up like broccoli and his laughter could be heard echoing up and down the little room. But when he read the second word, his hot tears streamed in every direction.

172

'The flowers of peace bloom neither on the highest mountain nor in the deepest valley,' wrote Neill Fife in his latest book, 'but flourish only in the free and generous heart, and there they can never be betrayed.'

Be that as it may, there was still much to be accomplished after Leatherwing's defeat, and it would be naive to assume that just by giving the President of the United States what may, in essence, have been nothing more than a highly diluted fermentation of hogweed ale, humanity would be changed overnight.

Myles Overton was greatly compromised by the affair, and with Linden gone, he told everyone he had nothing left to live for. But although he had sold his soul to Leatherwing the contract had been quite carefully drafted, and contained an option to re-purchase in the event of insolvency or liquidation of one or both parties. So Myles Overton was re-united with his spiritual essence, although many people thought it was not worth dogdirt anyway. There was talk of prosecution, but it was impossible for him to testify due to a bout of Alzheimer's disease, which did not clear up for many months. He lost his business, but no doubt still had some money salted away. The papers said 'he lost everything' but they meant he was down to his last few yachts and houses in France, and no-one would be surprised a few years down the line when his name re-surfaced in connection with a marketing consultancy, a satellite telephone operation, or cheap flights across the Atlantic.

As for Caryddwen's cauldron, there was now no concealing that it was a discovery of national importance, and the press applauded the efforts of a consortium led by Neill Fife to keep it in British hands, although they played down the deer changing into naked women and the sword fights. Advised by the Head of the Special Section, the Prime Minister decided that in memory of foiling the assassination attempt on himself and the President of the United States just before the anniversary of the arrival of the Tuatha de Dannaan, a huge monument would made from the re-assembled fragments on derelict land to the southeast of London. Nor could any more suitable site be found than the one made available by clearing blast-damaged buildings above the concealed confluence between reality and unreality which Martyn McMartyn had guarded so long. This, it was revealed, accorded with the original but highly confidential plan by Triona Greenwood, whose task was to produce a lasting monument to the epoch. The intention was to make a vast Superbowl and popularize American football and other arena sports, but due to a misunderstanding it was assembled the wrong way up and people thought it looked like the creation of some Gargantuan but slightly insane milliner. Hence it was affectionately called the Millinerian Drome, and became a major landmark.

It is said that when this project was nearly complete the Tuatha de Dannaan woke up and threatened to destroy the world unless a suitable house was provided for them, and that rather than risk confrontation they were introduced to this structure, which they said suited them very well. They divided it into various sections corresponding to their main areas of interest – the soul, war, history, and so forth, and space was left to display the Chain of Command, the Bottomless Pitcher, the Impenetrable Shield, and the Infallible Grindstone, although in the event more interesting exhibits were found, as the organizers did not want to dwell on the past. They did, however, make a vast statue of Mannannan Mac Llyr Mac Lugh and Queen Maeve of Skye which people could walk right through. But one could search the brochures for a hundred years without discovering whether their embrace was intended to symbolize captivity or reconciliation – for, said the creative team, the two things are not so very different. They added that all publicity is good publicity, and in the end everyone agreed it was nearly as entertaining as EuroDisney, although disappointing from a commercial point of view.

When the Drome was finally opened to the public, some people also said all the lost children came walking out of it, even the ones that had been hidden in Leatherwing's poison factories high up on the moon for many thousands of years. But, said such people, this was of course true only in a figurative sense, as education in all its forms can redeem lost and broken minds, and give new hope and generosity of spirit to people of all ages and every culture. In this sense too, those individuals were vindicated who foretold that when Caryddwen's cauldron was reassembled, it would restore the dead to life. Life is nothing but self-awareness, and without education in its broadest and most project-based sense, self-awareness can never be sustained.

But every community has its traditionalists and its modernizers. The Commissioners placed in charge of the Millinerian Drome were no exception, and many of them said things were not like this at all.